"Thanks again for your help tonight."

"My pleasure." Rett's gaze was drawn to the lush lower lip Sin was nibbling on. For the briefest moment, he entertained the possibility of leaning across the console and capturing those pouty lips in a kiss.

But his brain reminded him that kissing Sin was an incredibly bad idea.

She'd either throat punch him or they'd end up back at her place. Neither scenario would be good. Which was why it was probably best if he took his leave. *Now*.

Rett said good night, then climbed into the idling GTO as Sinclair drove off. He sighed and leaned back against the headrest.

He should've let Sin handle this wedding stuff. But he couldn't pass up the chance to work closely with the hazel-eyed firecracker who'd been living rent-free in his brain since their night together. Maybe spending more time with Sinclair would cure him of this persistent attraction to the one woman he should be avoiding.

Yet, as he drove toward Mama Mae's, he was already anticipating seeing Sin again.

ALSO BY REESE RYAN

Second Chance on Cypress Lane

Return to Hummingbird Way

Reese Ryan

FOREVER

New York Boston

Copyright ©2023 by Roxanne Ravenel

Only Home with You copyright 2022 by Jeannie Chin

Cover art and design by Daniela Medina
Cover photographs © Shutterstock
Cover copyright © 2023 by Hachette Book Group, Inc.

Forever
Hachette Book Group
1290 Avenue of the Americas, New York, NY 10104
read-forever.com
twitter.com/readforeverpub

First Edition: April 2023

Forever is an imprint of Grand Central Publishing. The Forever name and logo are trademarks of Hachette Book Group, Inc.

The publisher is not responsible for websites (or their content) that are not owned by the publisher.

The Hachette Speakers Bureau provides a wide range of authors for speaking events. To find out more, go to www.hachettespeakersbureau.com or call (866) 376-6591.

ISBNs: 978-1-5387-3448-3 (mass market); 978-1-5387-3447-6 (ebook)

Printed in the United States of America

OPM

10 9 8 7 6 5 4 3 2 1

*To those brave enough to realize that it's
never too late to carve out your
own path.*

Acknowledgments

Thank you to my family and to my readers for your patience and continued support. A very special thank-you to beta readers Angela Anderson and Stephanie Perkins, for your honest insight, and to author K. Sterling: my friend, cheerleader, and writing companion.

Thank you to readers Regina Elise and Marion Wilson, for coming up with the names of the Beautiful Beginnings Bridal Boutique and the Diamonds & Pearls Jewelry Boutique, respectively.

Thank you to my agent, Pamela Harty, for your guidance, support, and genuine concern. And thank you to Madeleine Colavita and the rest of the Grand Central Forever team, for permitting me the space to write the sexy, small-town story I envisioned for Garrett and Sinclair.

Return to Hummingbird Way

Chapter One

—•—•—•—

Sinclair Buchanan stood at the center of the banquet room at the Holly Grove Island Resort and glanced around, her chin propped on her fist. The frosted sea glass, seashells, and stunning photos of Holly Grove Island Beach, located in the Outer Banks, incorporated in the hotel's decor created the perfect subtle beach vibe. She'd kicked the theme up a notch with streamers, swaths of fabric in coral, soft blue, and a brilliant turquoise, and beach-themed centerpieces for the tables.

The space looked good, but Sinclair needed it to be perfect.

They were celebrating the recent engagement of her two closest friends: Dakota Jones and Dexter Roberts. It'd taken seventeen long years, an inadvertent scandal, the revelation of long-held secrets, and a veritable miracle for the former high school sweethearts to find their way back to each other. But now that they had, Sinclair couldn't be happier.

The momentous occasion required a proper celebration, so Sinclair had insisted on throwing an engagement party for her friends. Dexter's and Dakota's families had been a huge help, especially Dexter's younger sister Emerie. But tonight, she wanted the families to enjoy their evening while she and the resort's staff handled everything. All Sinclair needed to do was ensure that they stuck to her carefully laid-out schedule.

Early arrivals definitely *weren't* on that list.

Still, Sinclair put on her biggest smile—honed during nearly two decades of participating in beauty pageants—and hugged Emerie; Dexter's mother, Ms. Marilyn; Dakota's father, retired police chief Oliver Jones; and his new bride, Lila Gayle, the beloved owner of the town's café.

"What're y'all doing here so early?" Sinclair gently scolded in her sweetest southern belle intonation. She propped one fist on her hip. "The party doesn't begin for another hour."

"Thought you might need a hand with some of the last-minute details," Oliver said.

"We know you said you didn't need any help, sweet-heart, but there must be *something* we can do," Ms. Marilyn added, glancing around.

"Told you." Emerie grinned. "Sinclair Buchanan doesn't leave *anything* to chance."

"No, ma'am, I do not," Sinclair said proudly. She clutched the black, leather-bound planner that contained her entire life: appointments, task and goal lists, and every-thing she needed to remember for tonight's party. "We're all set. So grab a drink from the bar, relax, and enjoy yourselves. I've got everything under control."

Sinclair's phone chimed with a video call from her mother. She excused herself to answer it. Her parents were in DC visiting her older sister Leanne and her husband Michael, who'd just had their third child.

"Hey, Mama." Sinclair smiled. "How are Leanne and the baby?"

"Your sister is a pro at this point." Her mother laughed, raking her fingers through her silvery white hair—a striking contrast to her olive skin, inherited from Sin's Italian grandmother. "And as for your new niece." She flipped her cell phone camera so Sinclair could see the sleeping infant her mother held in her arms. "Isn't she gorgeous?"

"She is," Sinclair acknowledged with a smile. "I can't wait to meet her."

The adorable infant with tight, sleek curls plastered to her little head was even cuter than she'd been the last three times her mother had video called.

"But Dex and Dakota's engagement party is in an hour, so—"

"Right, I forgot." Her mother adjusted the phone so her face filled the screen again, her blue eyes sparkling. "Send Dexter and Dakota my love. And congratulate Oliver again. He must be so very happy that *his* baby girl is finally getting married."

No hints there.

"I will, Mama. Now you have to see what I've done with the space." Sinclair showed her mother the centerpieces she'd painstakingly designed and assembled. Gauzy, turquoise fabric was draped over the centers of the tables and topped with table runners made of twigs. White candles, perched above turquoise pearls floating in water in a glass container, were centered in a goldfish bowl filled with sand and a variety of beautiful seashells.

"That's gorgeous, honey. You have such an eye for design," her mother said. "If you ever get tired of selling real estate, I know you'd do well if you went back into interior design. Especially if you moved somewhere like DC."

"Thanks, Mama, but I happen to love my job," Sinclair said. "Now, let me show you what I've done with—"

"Maybe once your little party is over, you could drive down here to DC and spend a few days with us. Hold this adorable little one yourself. And according to your sister, Michael has some very handsome, very *available* colleagues at his lobbying firm."

And there it was. The only thing left was for her mother to remind her that...

"You're not getting any younger, sweetheart."

Sinclair counted to ten in her head. A coping mechanism she'd developed to deal with the guilt her mother laid on her so masterfully since her mother's heart attack more than a decade ago. It'd been the single most terrifying moment of Sinclair's life. So despite Terri Buchanan's gift for making Sinclair want to scream, she wouldn't risk stressing out her easily excitable mother. Instead, she held her tongue and reminded herself how grateful she was to still have her mom when Dakota had lost hers to cancer six years ago.

It didn't mean she couldn't dish out a little well-deserved sass, though.

"I'm well aware of the status of my geriatric eggs, Mother. Thank you very much." Sinclair turned up her southern twang just a notch. Something that irked her mother—a former English teacher and school principal. "And hard pass on Mikey's lobbyist friends. Leanne tried to fix me up with one of them last time I visited. The man talked about himself, his bank account, his Ferrari, and his house in Barbados the entire time. I couldn't get a word in edgewise."

"You're missing the point, sweetheart," Terri said calmly. "Because all I'm hearing is that he checks off several items on your husband wish list."

"Mother!" Sinclair glanced around the room, thankful Dakota's and Dexter's families were too far away to overhear the conversation. "We agreed *never* to talk about that list."

Her mother had inadvertently seen the list Sinclair had scribbled in the back of her planner a few years ago. She'd written the list after consuming an entire bottle of pink Moscato and listening to a playlist of relationship-gone-wrong country music songs following a particularly devastating breakup. Terri Buchanan had been on a mission to find Sinclair the perfect husband ever since.

Her mother was right. Mr. Ferrari came close to checking off all of the financial components on the checklist. But he lacked the all-important characteristics: kindness, compassion, thoughtfulness, and being both family oriented and involved in the community.

Maybe Sinclair was swinging for the fences, but she wanted what she wanted. She made no apology for that.

Sin held on to the list, drafted during her pink Moscato-tinted breakup haze, because it was a powerful reminder. Trying to tame the quintessential bad boy was an exciting diversion. But never again would she make the mistake of giving her heart to a man who didn't have serious potential as a life partner.

She'd wasted five years of her dating life on a man who would never grow up or settle down. Yet, within a year of their breakup, Teddy did, in fact, settle down with a woman Sinclair had once considered a close friend.

Her ex and former friend were still married and living in Wilmington. Earlier that year, they, too, had welcomed their third child.

Message received.

Sinclair would never waste her time on a man like that again. The kind of guy who was charming and loads of laughs, but never took anything seriously.

"*Agreed* is a strong word." Her mother kissed Sinclair's sleeping niece's forehead. "I think I recall promising to *try* not to mention the list again."

"Terri, leave Sinclair alone." Her father's deep baritone voice made her heart swell. "Let her live her life the way she wants."

Her mother had shifted the screen toward her dad. He smiled at her, his white teeth gleaming against his dark brown skin. His Afro was cut lower and had grown a bit thinner on top.

"Thanks, Daddy." Sinclair smiled.

"We know how busy you must be setting up for the party. So we'll talk to you later. Love you, baby girl."

"Love y'all." Sin blew a kiss before ending the call.

Sinclair sucked in a deep breath and glanced around the room. She was thrilled for Dakota; she really was. But after nearly two decades away from Holly Grove Island, her friend had returned, and they'd quickly renewed their close friendship. Would their relationship become distant after her friend's marriage, the way her and Leanne's relationship had after her sister had gotten married and moved away?

Sin tried not to think about it. Or about the small piece of her that was the tiniest bit envious that her friends had found their happily-ever-after when hers was clearly MIA.

Dexter's and Dakota's families broke into raucous laughter over at the bar. Sin straightened her slumped shoulders and swallowed back the hint of sadness that had crept over her.

Control what you can.

It had been her mother's mantra when Sinclair was on the pageant circuit, where she and Dakota had met as kids. She'd learned the fine art of holding her head high and smiling even when her world was on fire. She could certainly get over a tiny bout of self-pity. Tonight's theme was love and family. She would focus on that and save the pity party for another day.

Sinclair stood tall and broadened her smile. Then she busied herself with something she could control. Ensuring that tonight's party went off without a hitch.

———

"There really is no need for all this fuss. Land sakes, it's just a trifling little cold and a touch of bronchitis," Garrett Davenport's grandmother griped as he handed her another cup of tea with honey and lemon. He laid one of her crocheted throw blankets over her lap. "You're acting like I need to lay out my last will and testament. Spoiler alert: I spent all my money on the younger men I've encountered during my international travels." Annamae Davenport shifted her eyebrows up and down and smirked.

"Seriously, Gram? I'm glad you're enjoying your life, but I don't need to hear about it with that level of detail." Rett shook his head.

"I didn't give you any details." She grinned like the Cheshire Cat, then took a sip of her tea. "I save the good stuff for my girlfriends when we meet up at the senior center."

His grandmother's giggles sent her into another coughing fit. She pulled the blanket up over her chest and settled against the wingback chair a few feet from a small woodstove, which was older than he was. In fact, it might've even been older than his grandmother, who still had smooth, golden-brown skin at the age of eighty-two.

Mama Mae, a barely five-foot sprite, was as strong and independent a woman as he'd ever met. Though never short on opinions and incredibly direct, she was also loving and supportive. Yet, she didn't pull punches. Because, as she often said, "Ain't nobody got time for that."

While he admired her independence, Rett wished his grandmother would let him know when she needed him. Today he'd returned to town for the engagement party of his cousin Dexter, who also happened to be his best friend, and found Mama Mae working in her raised garden bed despite a hacking cough.

He'd insisted that she get in the house, take a hot bath, then get to bed.

She'd insisted that the planting had to be done that day. It was supposed to rain for the next three days, and those tomatoes, cucumbers, lettuce, and pole beans weren't going to plant themselves.

The only way he'd been able to get her to go inside was to promise to plant the three flats of vegetables himself. Once he'd planted everything according to Mama Mae's strict instructions, Rett had taken a long, hot shower to soothe his aching muscles.

He was exhausted, but there was no rest for the weary. He had an engagement party to attend, which had begun a half hour ago.

"You're sure you'll be all right?" He eased into the chair opposite his grandmother. "I can stay, if you need me. Dex and Dakota would understand."

"I'll be fine, but thank you, sweetheart." Mama Mae smiled. "And, Rett, I hope you realize how much I appreciate everything you do for me."

"You know I do." He squeezed her hand. "And you know you mean the world to me."

"You're such a sweetheart." Mama Mae's eyes shone. "A thoughtful, loving man like you shouldn't still be alone."

Rett groaned quietly. "I'm fine with things the way they are."

"Maybe you are now. But what happens when you decide in five or ten years that you want a family, and all your little swimmers done dried up?"

"Gram! *No.*" Rett cringed, mortified. "We are not talking about the viability of my *swimmers*. Ever."

Growing up, he'd been able to talk to his grandmother about nearly anything. But this was a conversation he refused to have even with her.

"Fine. Then you'd better get moving. You're the best man. Don't bode well for you to be showing up late to the engagement party. And don't worry. I'll be fine," she added, with the cluck of her tongue before he could ask if she was sure.

Rett lumbered to his feet. "Can I bring you anything back?"

"Leftovers. Especially cake." She grinned. "With *lots* of icing."

Garrett made his way to his car and settled behind the wheel of the triple black 1969 GTO 400 four-speed that had once belonged to his grandfather. He'd spent the past few years restoring the car, and it was pristine. He turned the key, and the engine roared.

The party would be in full swing by now, but hopefully no one would notice he was a little late. Especially not the self-appointed mistress of ceremony.

Sinclair Buchanan.

Garrett groaned quietly. That name still filled him with equal parts fury and lust.

Did Sinclair still look good enough to eat, as she had when he'd last seen her five years ago?

It didn't matter, because this time he wouldn't give

Sinclair Buchanan a second glance, no matter how fine she looked. An annoying, high-maintenance drama queen like Sinclair Buchanan was bad news. Besides, his pride was still bruised from their last encounter.

One he tried to forget, yet found himself reminiscing over... *often.*

Garrett pulled out of the driveway of his grandmother's house on Hummingbird Way and headed toward the new Holly Grove Island Resort, where Dexter was the director of operations.

Rett wasn't a fan of long-term commitment. He'd seldom seen it work out in his family. Still, he was happy for Dex and Dakota. Dex was a loyal friend who'd always had his back. So Rett was glad to see his cousin get his much-deserved happy ending.

Garrett found a spot in the parking lot, then headed inside, following the balloons and signage to the banquet room. He opened the door and quietly slipped inside, but he was immediately hailed by Nick Washington.

So much for an inconspicuous entrance.

"What's up, Rett?" Nick gestured to a nearby seat. "You should sit with us."

Nick was a few years younger than Rett, but he'd gotten to know him because Nick was friends with Dexter, whom he worked for at the resort. He was also Dexter's younger sister Emerie's best friend. Rett liked Nick, but he didn't buy the whole thing about him and Em just being friends. But as long as Em was happy with the arrangement, he'd keep his opinions to himself.

The volume of Nick's voice, the looseness of his limbs, and that damn goofy grin indicated he'd made his fair share of trips to the open bar. Rett planned to head there himself. He could use a stiff drink before he saw...

"Garrett Davenport, how very nice of you to *finally* show up." Sinclair sashayed toward him, clutching a clear clipboard decorated with a colorful floral design.

Sinclair assessed him with disdain, flecks of green and gold dancing in those large hazel eyes he'd been mesmerized by from the first moment he'd laid eyes on them in high school. She pursed her glossy pink lips, her nostrils flaring, and planted a fist on one curvy hip.

The bossy little she-devil was infuriating, attitudish, and fucking *gorgeous*. And she damn well knew it.

Her floral, sleeveless dress showed off her toned arms and sculpted shoulders—a feature he'd never noticed on a woman before, let alone been attracted to. The hem of the flirty little skirt grazed her midthigh, accentuating her tawny brown skin, a shade that landed smack between her father's dark brown skin and her mother's olive skin tone.

Sinclair flipped her hair, a deep, rich brown highlighted with ribbons of honey blond, over one shoulder and ran her manicured nails through the waterfall of shoulder-length waves. Her gaze bored into him, and if looks could kill, he'd be lying on the floor stone cold.

"You do realize you're an hour late to your own best friend's engagement party." She leaned into him, speaking in a harsh whisper that only he could hear. "You sure you gon' be able to show up for the wedding on time?"

Her nasally voice reminded him of Whitley Gilbert's from *A Different World*. And just a few minutes into the conversation, she'd already intimated that he was an unreliable slacker. Rett clenched his jaw. Yet, as annoyed as he was, he couldn't help noticing how hot Sin looked tonight.

"Sorry I'm late," Rett finally managed. He shoved his hands, balled into fists, into his pockets. "Something came up."

Sinclair's gaze dropped to the placket in front of his zipper momentarily. Her eyes widened and her cheeks and forehead flushed. She quickly returned her attention to the clipboard.

Maybe he wasn't the only one who couldn't forget their previous encounter.

"It's always some excuse with you, Rett." Sinclair wrapped her arms around the clipboard, clutching it to her chest. Her eyes didn't quite meet his.

Was she clutching the clipboard because he made her nervous? Or was she shielding her body's reaction after shamelessly ogling him two minutes into their conversation?

It didn't matter. Because Sinclair Buchanan was as irritating now as she'd been when they'd been forced to hang out together while Dexter and Dakota had dated in high school. She seemed to hate him on sight back then. But he hadn't helped matters when he'd tried to talk his cousin out of getting serious with Sin's best friend.

When Dex had suddenly ended things with Dakota the Christmas after he'd left for college, Sinclair had confronted Rett outside his grandmother's house. She'd been as mad as a hornet and had cussed him out six ways to Sunday—sure he'd been behind the breakup.

He hadn't been. But he hadn't bothered telling her so. Besides, as distraught as she'd been, he'd doubted Sinclair would've believed a single word he'd said.

Since Dexter and Dakota's reconciliation, Sinclair must surely have learned the truth: he had nothing to do with Dexter and Dakota's breakup back then. In fact, he'd been as shocked by it as anyone. But evidently, it didn't matter, because Sinclair clearly still wasn't a fan. Though she certainly had been that night in his hotel room, given the enthusiasm with which she'd called his name and the marks she'd left on his back.

"It's not an excuse, Sin. I planned to be here on time, but I was sidetracked by—"

"Didn't think you were going to make it." Dexter approached, holding Dakota's hand.

The two of them looked ridiculously happy, and Rett felt a slight twinge of envy.

"And miss your engagement party?" Rett slapped palms and clasped hands with Dex. "No way, cuz. Been waiting half my life to see you finally tie the knot with this beautiful lady." He turned toward his cousin's soon-to-be better half. "Congrats, Dakota."

"Thank you, Rett." Dakota's grin lit her brown eyes. She gave him a big hug. "And for the record, I knew you'd be here tonight. It was these two who were sweating it." She gestured toward Dex and Sinclair, then glanced around the room. "Mama Mae didn't come with you?"

"She's sick and didn't much appreciate me fussing over her," Rett said.

"But you did anyway." Dakota smiled. "The relationship you two have is adorable."

"'Cause Mama Mae is the only woman who can get him to behave," Sinclair muttered as she scanned her clipboard. When they all turned to look at her, Sin looked up and shrugged. "What? You know it's true."

"Be nice, Sin." Dakota pointed a finger at her best friend. "You promised you two would get along."

"Fine." She flashed Rett a dead-eyed smile and turned up the Whitley Gilbert singsong southern belle voice. "We are so very glad that you could join us this evening, Garrett. I was just about to ask the staff to take the food away. So please make yourself a plate." She batted her long, thick eyelashes. "In fact, why don't I escort you to the buffet?"

Dexter and Dakota snickered, and Rett couldn't help chuckling to himself.

That was as warm a greeting as he could expect from the former beauty queen, who now employed that same charm in her job as one of the island's top real estate agents. Evidently, she reserved that charm for people *not* named Rett Davenport.

Sinclair turned and walked toward the buffet, indicating that he should come with. He did, captivated by the subtle sway of her hips as he followed in the wake of her soft, delicate scent. All of it taking him back to that night they'd shared in Raleigh five years ago.

Yes, he'd been an immature jerk to Sinclair in high school. She clearly still held a grudge and had no intentions of letting him forget it. Despite the night they'd shared.

Fine. Because he wasn't here for Sinclair. He was here for Dexter and Dakota. For them, he'd tolerate Ms. Thing. But that didn't mean he couldn't have a little fun with her.

Chapter Two

— • • • —

Sinclair set her clipboard on the buffet and picked up a plate and a set of silverware. She thrust both toward Garrett as he stared at her blankly. "You didn't think I was going to make your plate for you, too, did you?"

Rett shifted his dark gaze from hers and accepted the items. He turned toward the buffet. "What's on the menu?"

Sinclair waved a hand toward the row of warming trays. "Stuffed mushrooms, deviled eggs, a mouth-watering lasagna, spicy, delicious meatballs, and shrimp kebabs. On the dessert table, there's champagne punch, mini berry tartlets, chocolate mousse, and, of course, Dakota's favorite— lemon meringue pie."

When Sinclair returned her attention to Garrett, his dark eyes were filled with heat and longing. A shudder rippled down her spine. She shifted her gaze from his and swallowed hard, her mouth suddenly dry.

Why did those mischievous dark eyes and full, smirking lips get her every single time? Rett was tall and handsome. His smooth dark brown skin looked flawless. His low-cut hair, neat lineup, and freshly trimmed beard looked like he'd just stepped out of a barber's chair. The navy blazer and navy pants he wore hung on his large frame like they were made for it. His white shirt hugged his broad chest. And he smelled like soap.

Sinclair clutched her trusty clipboard like a shield, protecting her from the sizzling heat of Garrett Davenport's stare. His hungry look turned her insides to molten lava. And the moment Garrett had raked his eyes over her, she'd regretted wearing a dress made of such thin, gauzy material and skipping the padded bra.

"I'll give you time to eat. Then maybe we can get back on schedule. I put *a lot* of effort into planning the perfect night for Dakota and Dexter. You've completely ruined my agenda."

"Sorry about that, Sin." Rett sounded sincere. He set his plate down and shoved his hands in his pockets again. This time, she willed her eyes not to drop to where the fabric stretched across the front of his pants, offering a hint of what lay beneath.

At least, she'd learned from her earlier mistake.

Who knew that her big-headed nemesis would turn out to be so heartbreakingly handsome, thick-thighed, and luscious-looking? It honestly wasn't fair.

The way Rett had teased and tormented her in high school, she would've expected him to have scales, grown horns and a tail, and be wielding a pitchfork.

"The delay couldn't be helped. But you've done an amazing job tonight. Everything looks terrific, and everyone seems happy. Maybe you could just re—"

"Don't you *dare* tell me to relax, Garrett Davenport." Sinclair shook a finger at him.

A man telling her to *relax* was one of her ultimate pet peeves. As if she were a hysterical "little lady" who needed some big, strong man to come along and handle everything for her.

No thanks.

She could handle just about any situation herself just fine. Sin just needed the ridiculously handsome and annoyingly smug Garrett Davenport to do the bare minimum as the best man. Why couldn't he have the decency to be on time for the party she'd spent the past few weeks planning?

Because he was selfish, self-centered, and never took *anything* seriously. That's why. Why would she expect anything more?

One moment, she was dreamily taking him in. The next, he'd open his mouth and say something that would inevitably take her out of the fantasy of Garrett Davenport and bring her back to the reality of him.

"All I'm saying is you seem stressed. You put so much pressure on yourself to make things perfect." Garrett glanced around the room. "From where I'm standing, you've done just that, so cut yourself some slack."

That was surprisingly nice of him to say.

"Thank you." Sinclair frowned warily. Given their antagonistic history, where she'd given as good as she'd gotten, she felt more comfortable when they were at odds than when Rett was being complimentary. Kind words coming from those sensual lips felt like a Trojan horse meant to catch her off guard. "But I should check on the guests and get ready for the next activity."

He lightly grasped her wrist and leaned in close. His clean, crisp scent triggered memories of that night in Raleigh that she regretted immensely, yet frequently fantasized about.

A mischievous grin lit his dark eyes. "You look gorgeous, Sin. And you smell incredible."

Sin's breath hitched, and her wrist tingled beneath Rett's touch. He'd whispered those words in her ear five years ago when he'd brashly suggested that he could help her work out the stress she was feeling prior to their big real estate test.

She'd elbowed him in the gut and told Rett Davenport exactly where he could stick his offer. But later that night, after a couple of drinks to build her courage, Sinclair had shown up at Rett's hotel room and taken him up on the offer.

And it had been amazing.

No way. No how. Just . . . no. Don't you dare think about it.

Sin thanked him for the compliment, then pulled free of his grip and walked away.

Hooking up with Rett again would be a disaster—no matter how amazing the man happened to be in bed.

An hour in the sack and you'll never get your self-respect back.

She could still hear her grandmother's save-yourself-for-marriage speech in her head.

Sinclair loved her grandmother, but she didn't share her views. Women should be empowered to make their own choices. And yet, when it came to Garrett Davenport, maybe her grandmother had been spot-on.

———

Rett's eyes followed Sinclair as she hurried away from him, as if that luscious, curvy ass of hers were on fire. Despite the hell she'd given him for being late, there was obviously still something brewing quietly between them.

He could feel it, and it was evident she could, too. The dilation of her pupils. The way her breathing became shallow. The pretty flush across the bridge of her adorable nose and cheeks. Then there was his personal favorite: the way those nipples, which he remembered with precise detail—had poked through the thin fabric of her dress.

Sinclair was gorgeous. And she smelled as enticing as she had that night. Like hibiscus flowers and coconut, mixed with a healthy dose of sunshine and the salt water of the beach. In a word, Sinclair had smelled like *home*.

The heat in her eyes when she'd glared at him was unmistakable. He imagined she'd seen the same in his.

Garrett loaded food onto his plate. He'd hardly eaten all day, and working in the garden had made him ravenous.

He glanced over at Sin and couldn't help remembering the softness of her bare skin and the taste of her warm mouth. How she'd whispered, then screamed, his name. Rett shut his eyes against the shudder of pleasure that rolled down his spine. He groaned quietly.

Food wasn't the only thing he was ravenous for tonight.

His night with Sin had been incredible. The connection they'd shared was one he'd begun to think himself incapable of. It wasn't just physical: two people having a little fun. It felt…deeply meaningful, in a way he couldn't quite explain and still didn't fully understand. Despite all of the reasons why he knew they should never hook up again, Rett needed to know if the depth of their connection that night had been an anomaly.

He wasn't looking to settle down. After spending the past several years in Charlotte, he was a top producer for his real estate brokerage. But a friend had asked him to consider relocating to Charleston to join his team there. He'd grown restless in Charlotte, and Evan's offer seemed like an exciting opportunity in a fun, vibrant city. So he wasn't looking to get into a long-term relationship that would keep him there on Holly Grove Island.

Besides, Sinclair Buchanan was a spoiled beauty queen. He didn't do high-maintenance, and he didn't do drama. So he should be glad Sin had slunk away while he'd gone to the bathroom that night. That she hadn't even bothered to say good night. What had happened between them was a one-time thing. Just like any other one-night stand.

Only it wasn't just another hookup. It was Sinclair. The girl he'd spent his teenage years fantasizing about. The girl who'd considered herself far too good for someone like him. And maybe she'd been right.

She'd made it clear she wanted nothing more to do with him and begged him to stay quiet about their little tryst. Just as she'd implored him not to tell anyone about their heated argument that had turned into a make-out session when they were teens.

"Sweetheart, you made it." The voice of his mother, Ellen Ramos, startled him from his daze.

"Hey, Ma." Rett leaned down, allowing his mother, who was nearly a foot shorter than his height of six three, to wrap her arms around his neck and kiss his cheek.

His mother, who was approaching sixty, was gorgeous. Her skin was supple and glowing, and there were only a few fine lines beneath her eyes. She'd traded the bob she'd worn most of her life for a smart pixie cut, and she'd allowed her hair to go all gray. It was a good look on her. The color gleamed against her dark brown skin.

"I'm glad you made it, Rett. Your mamá was worried you wouldn't make it." Hector Ramos, his stepfather, slipped an arm around his mother's waist and pulled her closer.

The man was husky and stout. He stood about half a foot taller than his mother. She leaned her head against Hector's shoulder. The two of them had been married for nearly twenty-five years and they were still very much in love.

It had made him sick to his eleven-year-old stomach to see them so happy together when Hector had shown up in their lives. He'd been missing his dad and was still angry that his mother had ended their marriage.

When Hector and his mother had eloped, his dreams of his parents reuniting had been crushed. The following year, when he was thirteen, his father had been killed in a motorcycle crash. Rett had been devastated, and he'd blamed his mother. Because if his father had still been with them, she would never have allowed him to get that motorcycle, and he would've still been alive.

He'd been awful to Hector and to his mother. And eventually, he'd asked to move in with Mama Mae—his paternal grandmother. It'd broken his mother's heart, but at his grandmother's behest, his mother agreed to let him go live with her.

He realized now he'd been an ass. It wasn't his mother or Hector's fault that his father's bad choices had finally caught up with him. But mending his relationship with his mother and stepfather was still a work in progress. And he wasn't close to his younger sister, Isabel, who was now twenty-two.

"I stopped by and checked on Mama Mae before I came here. Ended up planting her entire spring garden." Rett kept piling food on his plate.

His mother laughed. Something she hadn't done much when his parents were together. "Sounds like Mama Mae. She's all right though, right?"

"Got a nasty cold." Garrett grabbed another plate. He was starving.

"Still eating folks out of house and home, huh, son?" Hector chuckled.

Fifteen years ago, Rett would've taken offense to Hector's use of the word *son*.

You're not my father, and you never will be.

Words he'd hurled at the man more times than he could count. Over the years, he'd gone from being Hector to *his mother's husband* to his *stepfather*. Rett could still remember the first time he'd introduced Hector to someone as his stepfather ten years ago. The man had grinned, his eyes filled with tears, and he'd bear-hugged Rett.

Which, of course, made him feel like the shitty stepson he'd always been. Hector had started calling him *son* soon afterward. It'd bothered Rett back then, but he'd let it slide. It was the least he could do for the man who'd finally made his mom happy. And over time, Hector's use of the word stung far less.

Garrett patted his stomach. "Didn't get a chance to eat earlier. Let's just say I'm making up for it."

Hector saw Chief Jones and made his way over to speak to him, leaving Rett alone with his mother.

"Looks like you've run out of hands," his mom noted. "Why don't I make your dessert plate for you?"

"Thanks." Rett picked up the plate he'd made earlier. He was juggling both plates and his silverware. He glanced around the room. "Where's Izzy?"

"She had to work today, but she'll be here as soon as she can."

"Good." He followed his mother as she put his favorites on the plate, not bothering to ask what he did or didn't want.

"Speaking of *good*...I saw you talking to Sinclair." She grinned. "You two seemed to be involved in an intense conversation. But intense in a good way." She set down the plate, grabbed a glass, and ladled champagne punch into it.

He ignored his mother's insinuation. "She was riding me about being late."

"Sounds like Sinclair." His mom laughed. "The woman knows exactly what she wants and *when* she wants it." She glanced over to where Sin was deep in conversation with Dakota and Dexter. There was a hint of admiration in his mother's dark eyes. "I'm glad Sinclair insisted on throwing this party. I've never seen my nephew happier than he is right now. A love like that *should* be celebrated." She turned toward Rett, holding his dessert plate, his glass, and a few napkins. "Hopefully, it'll be your turn soon." Her gaze drifted back toward Sinclair, whose melodious laughter he could hear all the way from the other side of the room.

"What? No. Mom…seriously. Sinclair? Believe me, I'm not the beauty queen's type. I think she's looking for a man who owns an island and a fleet of yachts or some shit like that."

"*Language*, Garrett Aurelius Davenport." His mother elbowed his ribs without spilling a single crumb from his dessert plate.

"Ow!" His mother's pointy elbows were deadly. "But we both know it's true."

"Maybe." His mother shot another glance at Sinclair and sighed wistfully, like she was window-shopping for a future daughter-in-law. "Or maybe she only *thinks* that's what she wants. I would never have expected that Hector would be my soul mate, but he is. And I've never been happier. Now that the two of you get along so well, it's taken the content-ment in our relationship to a whole 'nother level."

Translation: Your selfish behavior as a teenager ruined our happiness.

He felt badly about that. Still. Not missing his monthly dinner date with her and Hector since he'd been back in North Carolina was his penance for robbing them of some of their marital bliss back then.

"Where are you sitting?" his mother asked.

He glanced over to where his friends were seated, then back at his mother. There was a hint of hopefulness in her eyes.

"Got room for me at your table?"

His mother's eyes lit up with excitement. "Always, baby."

Her heartfelt words warmed his chest and reminded him how grateful he was that they had mended old wounds.

Rett followed his mother to her table to eat with her, Hector, and Izzy, whenever she arrived. But when he glanced over to where Dex and Dakota stood, his eyes met Sinclair's.

Sin quickly dropped her gaze and studied her clipboard before turning and walking away, nearly crashing into a server.

Rett chuckled. His mother's words about Hector being her unexpected soul mate replayed in his head.

Me and Sinclair as a couple?

Never. Gonna. Happen.

Chapter Three

Sinclair was exhausted but thrilled the night had gone so well. No thanks to Dexter's best man. Garrett had waltzed in late, hadn't sat at the designated wedding party table, and had been walking around the place like he was Holly Grove Island's favorite prodigal son.

Rett was charming and gregarious. And it appeared that all had been forgiven for his past sins as a moody teen who'd acted out after his mother's remarriage and the death of his father. Sin was happy Rett had shed his reputation as the town troublemaker. She honestly wished she could let go of their ugly past, too. But she couldn't forget how he'd teased her about her deep, Eastern Carolina accent and called her a pampered princess or Little Miss Perfect.

He'd ridiculed her for taking her roles on the beauty pageant circuit, the cheerleading squad, and as class president so seriously. Things that were important to her. That made her who she was. And yes, she'd teased Rett pretty savagely and said some awful things to him, too. But when he'd said she was like an empty candy shell—sweet and beautiful on the outside but without a heart or a soul—those words had hurt more than anything anyone had ever said to her.

Sinclair had pretended she couldn't possibly care less about his teasing. But Rett's words had pierced the wall she'd carefully constructed around her heart. She was angry with herself for still caring what Rett Davenport thought of her, but even now his words stung whenever she recalled them.

Sin sighed. She and Rett were both here to celebrate Dex and Dakota's love story—two decades in the making. That was all that mattered. She needed to let go of the resentment she was harboring toward Rett and the fiery attraction that filled her body with heat whenever their eyes met.

Dexter and Dakota stood over in the corner, deep in conversation, his arms looped around her waist as she glanced up at him. For a quick, painful moment, Sinclair envied the kind of love her friends had. The kind of love that had eluded her.

Her mother and sister had accused her of being too picky since her failed, long-term relationship with Teddy.

Maybe she was.

She wanted the magic and chemistry of love and attraction, but wouldn't settle for a man who didn't fit into her grand plan of one day running a real estate agency with her name on the sign. And she certainly couldn't abide a man who lived aimlessly with no plan of his own. Rett Davenport fit squarely in that final bucket.

The man had done a plethora of jobs, lived in several states, and from what she'd heard, been through countless women. He was the kind of man who could write his life plan on a quarterly calendar because he never thought beyond that.

Sin enjoyed having fun as much as the next woman. But she had a plan for her life and career. Rett Davenport didn't fit into either.

Still, she couldn't keep her eyes off the man. He was too handsome for his own good, and he practically oozed charm.

Sin glanced over at Rett as he made his way toward one of the servers—a gorgeous, voluptuous brunette who could easily be a pinup model. Rett cornered the woman and flashed his megawatt grin.

The woman tossed her hair over one shoulder and giggled at something Rett said. Sinclair tightened her grip on the clipboard, her blood boiling. The server was being paid to take care of the guests. Not to cuddle up to Rett. He handed the woman a piece of paper and she nodded, a wide smile spreading across her face. Then she turned and walked away.

Sinclair rolled her eyes. Rett Davenport would never change. Not that it mattered to her. If the man wanted to continue being a pathetic skirt chaser well into his thirties, so be it.

"Sinclair, we need to chat," Dakota said as she and Dexter approached, both of them smiling. "Could you meet us in the conference room down the hall?"

"Sure thing, hon. I'll be there in ten." Sin's mind buzzed. What was so urgent?

Sinclair searched the crowd for Dexter's sister, Emerie.

"Em, sweetie, would you be a doll and keep an eye on things for me for maybe a half hour? I've gotta take a quick meeting," Sin said.

"You're putting me in charge?" Em grinned, accepting the clipboard Sin handed her. The younger woman propped her chin on her fist and rolled her eyes upward. "Hmm...should I bring in male strippers or should we do body shots?"

"Emerie Roberts, don't you dare..." Sin frowned when Em went into a fit of laughter.

"I'm just messing with you, Sin." Em draped an arm

over her shoulder. "You've done an amazing job tonight. You can trust me to keep the party on track. We'll save the male dancers for the bachelorette party." She winked.

Now that was a plan Sin could get behind.

Sin retrieved her planner and headed for the conference room, where Dexter sat with his arm looped around Dakota, seated beside him.

"So what's this..." Sin froze. A knot tightened in her gut and a lump formed in her throat.

Garrett was seated across from Dakota and Dexter, and the three of them were staring at her. Sin cleared her throat and slid into a chair across from the couple, leaving an open space between her and Garrett. She tried to ignore the uneasy feeling that slid over her the moment she realized Rett was included in their little impromptu meeting.

"What's going on, you two? Is everything all right?" she asked.

"Everything is fine, Sin," Dexter assured her. "But there's been a change of plans."

"What kind of change? Did you decide to go with the beach ceremony after all?" Sinclair glanced between Dakota and Dexter.

"Dex just learned of a cancellation here at the resort, so we've secured the earlier date," Dakota said.

They'd have a little less time to work with. No problem.

Sinclair opened her planner and pulled out her expensive fountain pen. "How far up are we moving the wedding? Next spring instead of next summer?"

"We booked a date seven weeks from today."

"I can work with seven months. A fall wedding would be lovely." Sinclair turned her calendar to November.

"I'm pretty sure Dakota just said seven *weeks*, Sin," Rett said.

Her attention snapped to his. Then she turned to her friends. "You're getting married in seven *weeks*?"

"Yes, but don't panic. We're going to scale our plans back. Keep things basic." Dakota leaned into Dexter. "I don't need a big, lavish wedding. We just want to get married surrounded by the people we love."

It was touching that Dexter and Dakota were focused on what was important. But Sinclair had helped Dakota plan her wedding. She knew *exactly* what her friend wanted, and it certainly wasn't "basic."

What had prompted this change of heart?

"That's really sweet," Sin said carefully. "But what about all of the plans we made for your dream wedding?"

There was a flash of sadness on her friend's face. A micro expression gone so quickly Sinclair almost missed it.

Dakota *did* want the elaborate cake and custom bridal gowns. None of which were an option in seven weeks.

"Like I said, none of that is really important." Dakota's expression faltered a bit.

Dexter seemed to sense Dakota's sadness, too. He kissed her temple and whispered something in her ear. She offered a forced smile and nodded in response.

Sinclair stood, her arms folded. She stared between them. "Okay, you two. What's *really* going on?"

Dakota and Dexter looked at each other, then laughed. Dakota nodded again.

"We're pregnant." A huge grin split Dexter's face.

"Oh my God, that's amazing." Sinclair pressed her fingers to her lips. Her eyes stung with tears of joy for her friends. "I'm ecstatic for you. But why didn't you just say so?"

"It's still really early." Dakota placed a protective hand over her belly. "I'll be thirty-five when the baby is born, so this is considered a high-risk pregnancy. We wanted to wait until I'm in my second trimester before we got everyone's hopes up."

Sin understood her friends' hesitance. Still, she was a little hurt that they hadn't shared their happy news with her sooner.

"And you'd like to be married before the baby arrives," Garrett said. "No problem. We'll do whatever it takes to make this wedding happen in seven weeks."

"*We?*" Sinclair raised a brow. The man hadn't lifted a finger to make this engagement party happen. All he'd done was float in when it suited him and eaten his weight in appetizers. Now, suddenly *we* were going to make sure this wedding happened in a month and a half?

Yeah. Sure, sporty.

"I'd better get on the plans for your bachelor party." Garrett rubbed his bearded chin.

He hadn't had the beard when they were in Raleigh, and Sin wondered how it would feel.

She cringed, angry with herself for entertaining the thought—even for a moment.

Stay focused, girl. Stay focused.

"With the abbreviated timeline, we'd prefer not to have separate bachelor and bachelorette parties," Dexter said.

"No bachelor party?" Garrett looked heartbroken. "Honestly, it's no big deal. I could plan it in a day or two."

"I know," Dex said. "But even before we learned about the baby, we'd been thinking it would be nice to do a joint bachelor and bachelorette party. Something family-friendly the entire town could attend."

Family-friendly? Now Sin was heartbroken. So much for the penis-shaped cookies she'd planned to bake.

"Are you two sure about this? Because I agree with

Rett." *Now there's something you don't hear every day*. "I know you have a shortened timeline, but we could plan your bachelor and bachelorette parties pretty quickly."

"I realize you're both disappointed," Dakota said. "But we're counting on you to work together on this." Her best friend's eyes pleaded as she glanced between Sinclair and Garrett.

"Of course." Sinclair slumped into her seat.

"Whatever you want," Garrett promised. "We'll make it happen."

"Thank you, Rett." Dakota sounded relieved. "Now, I *really* have to pee. Dexter will bring you up to speed with the new wedding date. Excuse me."

Garrett's phone buzzed. He pulled it from inside his suit jacket and looked at the screen.

Sinclair couldn't help looking at it, too. The name *Nat* and the smiling face of a gorgeous younger woman filled the screen. Sin felt a twinge of something. *Jealousy* maybe?

No, that would be ridiculous. She had no claim on Rett Davenport. What she felt was annoyance. Couldn't the man ever stay on task?

"I need to take this call." Garrett followed Dakota out of the conference room, closing the door behind him.

Dexter tapped his fingers on the table. "Sin, I'm sorry we didn't tell you about the baby earlier, but—"

"It's okay, but there's something else I'd like to talk to you about."

"Okay. Shoot."

"You know Dakota isn't being straight with you about not wanting any of the frills she'd planned for her wedding, right?"

Dexter sighed heavily and rubbed his chin. "Yeah, I caught that just now, too. Kind of took me by surprise because it was Kota's idea to move the wedding up rather than wait until after the baby is born. She seemed completely on board with the idea then."

"I think it just dawned on her what she's giving up," Sin said. "But maybe she doesn't have to."

"What do you mean?"

"I mean I'll do whatever it takes to give my friend some version of her dream wedding." A plan was forming in Sin's head. It would require a little ingenuity and a whole lot of hustle, but with some help, she could make this happen.

"You're a good friend, Sin. I appreciate what you're offering, but Dakota and I couldn't possibly ask you to take this on."

"You didn't ask, I'm offering. In fact, I insist. And I'm sure your mom and sister and Ms. Lila would be happy to help."

"Count me in, too." Garrett slid into his seat. "Whatever you need, I've got you."

"I can handle this." Sin shot Rett a look of irritation. "Besides, after tonight, you'll be back in Charlotte."

"Actually, I thought I'd stay in town for a bit," Garrett said. "That'd give us plenty of time to game-plan this wedding."

"That means a lot to us," Dexter said. "But are you sure you two will be able to—"

"We'll be fine. Right, Sin?" Garrett glanced over at her.

"Of course." Sin sat taller and forced a smile. "Now, let's get down to details."

Sin jotted down notes and formulated a plan in her head. She'd ensure that her best friend had her dream wedding, even if it meant partnering up with *The Devil* Davenport to make it happen.

Chapter Four

· · · · ·

Rett was dead on his feet and could think of nothing he wanted more than to go back to Mama Mae's place and crash in his old bedroom.

It was late, and just about everyone had left, including Dexter and Dakota.

His aunt Marilyn and cousin Emerie had planned to stay and help wrap up, but he'd insisted they go home. Like it or not, he and Sinclair were a team now. So he'd help Sinclair finish up anything the staff wasn't handling.

"I've got it, Rett. You should go now," Sinclair said as he approached. "Your new friend is probably getting off soon."

"My new friend?"

What the hell is Sinclair talking about?

"Here's everything you asked for." Melissa, the server he'd spoken to earlier, approached. She handed him a large bag, packed with leftovers. "I piled on the icing for your grandmother and added a little something extra for you." She winked.

"Thank you, Melissa." Rett flashed a grateful smile. In his business, it was important to remember names. He reached into his pocket and slipped her a twenty. "My grandmother is gonna love you for this."

A seductive smile slid across the woman's mouth, and she sank her teeth into her full lower lip. She raked her fingers through her glossy hair, flipping it over her shoulder. Then she gave him an adorable little wave. "Well, good night."

"Good night, Melissa." Rett curbed his smile. Polite, but not inviting. Under any other circumstance, this woman would be his type. But tonight, he was too exhausted to flirt with anyone.

After a long, awkward pause, Melissa walked away.

When he turned around, Sinclair stared at him, blinking. "What . . . you thought I—"

"I saw you talking to her earlier," Sin said. "I assumed—"

"Have you been watching me all night?" He raised a brow, amused.

"I happened to see you cornering the poor girl. I had to make sure nothing . . . untoward was going on. Doesn't constitute—"

"Stalking?" he offered.

"*Me*? Stalking you? In your dreams, Rett Davenport." Sin folded her arms, clearly insulted. "I do *not* stalk people."

Her outrage was amusing bordering on adorable. But he managed to keep a straight face.

"Hmm." Rett's gaze lingered on Sinclair, taking in the way the light danced off the flecks of gold and green in her hazel eyes, her sensuous lips, and the curve of her throat. Tracing all of the places his lips had once been. He sighed quietly, hating that he couldn't seem to stop reliving the night they'd spent together. "I'll keep that in mind."

Sin narrowed her gaze at him, then gathered her leather planner under one arm. She slipped her designer bag on the opposite shoulder, then balanced an overflowing box on her hip.

"Let me grab that." Rett had to practically wrestle the box from her.

Sin muttered her thanks, then stooped to pull out several boxes stowed beneath a table.

"You were going to carry all of this to your car yourself rather than asking for help?"

Rett admired an independent woman; he really did. But this woman was stubborn and defiant just for the hell of it. He would've thought that the beauty queen would've gotten a kick out of having him schlep around her crap. But no, not Sinclair I'll-do-it-my-damn-self Buchanan.

"There were no luggage carts, so—"

"I'll find one." Rett put a hand on the soft, smooth skin of Sin's bare shoulder, halting her progress toward the door. He set the box on the table. "Just give me a minute, all right?"

She offered a reluctant nod and sat on the edge of the table.

Rett retrieved a luggage cart from a guest who'd just returned it to the lobby. He rolled it into the ballroom. "We got lucky."

"Fantastic." Sinclair hung her bag on a hook. "Now that I have this, I can handle the rest myself." She squatted to load one of the boxes onto the cart.

Rett stooped beside her, trying his best not to concentrate on how amazing Sinclair smelled. "I *want* to help, Sin."

"Thanks, Rett." Sin flashed a hint of a smile.

Is the ice princess thawing a little?

He must've done *something* right. But it was too early to celebrate.

They loaded everything onto the cart. Then he pushed it toward the automatic glass doors, with Sin trailing behind him.

"Where's your car?" he asked once they'd exited the glass doors into the chilly night air.

"My SUV is over there."

The salty sea breeze coming off the Atlantic Ocean swirled, whipping Sin's hair across her face and billowing her dress. She wrapped her arms around herself and bowed her head, shielding her face from the wind.

The early spring temperature had dropped considerably in the Outer Banks since the sun had set, and the air was cold and crisp. The wind knifed through the fabric of his pants and jacket, chilling him.

Sinclair shivered in her thin, sleeveless dress. Her nose and cheeks had turned an angry shade of red.

"Where's your jacket?" Garrett scolded.

"In the SUV." She rubbed her arms, pebbled with chill bumps. "I'll be fine, I—"

He removed his suit jacket and draped it over her shoulders, pulling it closed.

"Thank you." Sin looked stunned by his act of chivalry. Her tone had softened. "But I'm the one who didn't bring my jacket in. You shouldn't suffer because of my poor judgment."

"You wouldn't let me buy you lunch or dinner in Raleigh." Garrett stepped closer, shielding her body from the wind at his back. "But what if, just this once, you let me be the gentleman, huh?"

Rett's eyes were drawn to the movement of the muscles of Sin's throat as she swallowed. Heat radiated in his chest, and time seemed to slow. As the cold winds swirled around them, the warmth between them seemed to grow.

"Then maybe you'd like to pull up the Lexus so we can load it." Sin held out her keys, her breath visible in the chilly air.

Garrett raised an eyebrow, his arms folded. "You trust me to drive your car?"

"SUV," she corrected. "And it's like ten feet. If you can't manage that, I'mma need to call the DMV and suggest they consider revoking your license."

"Point made." Garrett accepted the keys. "Still, I'm counting this as a win."

"Do whatever makes you happy." Sin pulled the jacket around her tightly. "But it's freezing out here, so would you mind doing it just a teensy bit faster?"

"Yes, ma'am. You should wait inside where it's warmer."

To his surprise, Sinclair didn't object. She hurried inside and stood beneath the heat vent.

Garrett jogged over to the black Lexus SUV and hopped inside. He pulled up to the main entrance. Then he loaded the boxes in the rear hatch, as Sin requested.

"The leather seats are warm now," Rett said.

Sinclair approached the vehicle and pulled his jacket around her. The innocuous motion triggered something in his chest. He helped Sin into the SUV.

"Your jacket." Sin started to remove the garment.

Rett held up a hand. "We'll be seeing a lot of each other the next few weeks. I'll get it next time."

"Thank you." Sin settled his jacket on her shoulders again. "Are you staying at your mom's?"

"No. I'm headed back to Mama Mae's. I noticed a few projects at the house that could use some attention." He shoved his hands into his pockets, trying not to shiver despite the frigid wind slicing through him.

"Your grandmother lives in a prime area. If she puts

some money into the place, I could get her top dollar for it," Sin said.

"As could I. Real estate agent too, remember." He jabbed a thumb to his chest.

"I'm sure you know *your* territory well." Her eyes danced with amusement. "But around here, I'm the queen. I've even been dabbling in design whenever my clients require renovations. I throw it in as an extra service, but it nets a bigger payday for both of us so . . . win-win."

Sin opened her planner and handed him a business card. "Let Mama Mae know I'd be happy to come by and look at the place, if she ever considers selling it."

He studied the fancy, embossed gold script lettering against the black card that was so very Sinclair. He shoved it into his pocket.

"Good to know," Rett said. "In the meantime, I'll probably stay through the week. So maybe we can meet in a couple of days to game-plan the wedding and this joint bachelor/bachelorette event." He grimaced.

Sin broke into laughter. "I'm not thrilled about this coed party either. I had some raunchy games and pastries in mind. Definitely *not* family-friendly."

Rett chuckled, too. But the image of the beauty queen handing out dick-shaped éclairs sent him to a place it was best they didn't go. Rett tried to clear his head of the memories running rampant through his mind.

He didn't speak. Hell, he could hardly breathe thinking of that night. Sin seemed to mistake his silence for unwillingness.

"I realize wedding planning isn't your thing. And since we're no longer doing a traditional bachelor party, why don't you just let me take care of the wedding planning and the prewedding party? If we need to consult, we can do a video conference."

"This isn't a question of your capability, Sin. I *want* to be involved. And I'm not taking no for an answer."

Did he want to play amateur wedding planner with the beauty queen? Hell no. But this was the bare minimum he could do to repay Dexter for *always* having his back and for being the voice of reason during those times when Rett's life had gone to a dark place.

He was in this thing, and Sinclair would just have to deal with it. It was seven weeks. They'd survive.

Sinclair sighed quietly. "Where'd you park?"

"Out back." He pointed in the distance.

"Get in. I'll take you to your car."

Garrett trotted around the black SUV and climbed inside. He directed her to where the GTO was parked. She pulled beside it.

"*That* is a beautiful car. But those older cars take a while to heat up. I'll wait while it does, if you want." Sin shrugged.

"Thanks." Rett tried not to sound shocked by her offer. He hopped out and started his car, the engine roaring to life. Then he got back inside Sin's Lexus.

There were a few moments of awkward silence before Sin finally turned to him, half of her face lit by the overhead lighting in the parking lot. "If you're still in town on Wednesday, we could meet for lunch. One p.m. at Lila's Café?"

He rubbed his freezing hands together and nodded. "I'll meet you there at one."

"And don't be late." Sin raised a brow.

"No, ma'am." Rett couldn't help smiling. Maybe working together for the next few weeks wouldn't be as bad as he feared. And while he didn't expect that they'd suddenly become best friends, he at least hoped they could be cordial.

After all, their best friends were getting married and having a kid. They'd be seeing a lot more of each other.

"Thanks again for your help tonight," Sin said.

"My pleasure." His gaze was drawn to the lush lower lip Sin was nibbling on. For the briefest moment, he entertained the possibility of leaning across the console and capturing those pouty lips in a kiss.

But his brain reminded him that kissing Sin was an incredibly bad idea.

She'd either throat punch him or they'd end up back at her place. Neither scenario would be good. Which was why it was probably best if he took his leave. *Now.*

"Let me know you got home all right," he said.

"I'll be fine."

"Then indulge me. Otherwise, I'll be worried. And if I have to come over there in my pajamas to check on you, just know I'm gonna be pissed." Rett was only half joking.

"Fine. I'll call you. Good night."

Rett said good night, then climbed into the idling GTO as Sinclair drove off. He sighed and leaned back against the headrest.

He should've let Sin handle this wedding stuff. But he couldn't pass up the chance to work closely with the hazel-eyed firecracker who'd been living rent-free in his brain since their night together. Maybe spending more time with Sinclair would cure him of this persistent attraction to the one woman he should be avoiding.

Yet, as he drove toward Mama Mae's, he was already anticipating seeing Sin again.

Chapter Five

—◦—●—◦—

Sinclair checked the time on her phone again as the couple she'd already shown five houses to this week bickered over whether or not the home with a shared pool would suffice.

She'd already played referee for this couple on three other "debates" today. Quite frankly, she was losing interest in this sale. Not that she hadn't navigated the muddy waters with indecisive couples with wildly different tastes before. But today her patience was running thin.

She and Rett were meeting at Lila's Café in less than an hour, and the Murphys hadn't even made it inside the house. After she'd lambasted Rett about being late to the engagement party, she could hardly arrive late to their first planning meeting.

Time to play referee again.

Sin put on her broadest smile. "Why don't we tour the house first? If you both hate it, we can move on. Or perhaps you'll find it's worth the shared pool situation."

The man's taut jaw softened, as did the woman's shoulders. He smiled at his wife, and she responded in kind. The man took his wife's hand and they followed Sin into the house.

After giving the Murphys a tour of the spacious first floor, Sin sent them to explore the upper level for themselves. She was banking on them being floored by the view of the ocean from the primary bedroom upstairs.

She picked up her phone and pulled up Garrett's contact. His smiling face appeared beside his name, and there was a subtle fluttering in her belly. Sinclair sank her teeth into her lower lip and tucked her hair behind one ear.

Sin could still hear Garrett's sultry voice when she'd called to let him know she'd gotten home safely. The gravelly, half-asleep sound of his already deep voice sent waves of want down her spine. She found herself wondering whether Garrett slept naked. Something she hadn't hung around long enough to discover during their imprudent tryst five years ago.

Honestly, she felt badly about slinking out of Rett's room while he was in the bathroom without so much as a *Thank you, sir. You completely rocked my world*. She'd often berated herself for succumbing to curiosity and sleeping with Rett. But she was honestly more ashamed of how she'd bounced afterward without saying goodbye.

She'd panicked, suddenly feeling vulnerable about having put herself in such a compromising position with Rett—the boy who'd teased her in high school. So she'd gotten dressed and fled the scene of the "crime" as quickly as she could, hoping they'd both just forget the incident and never speak of it again.

She'd been kinder to the plumber who'd fixed her clogged drain than she had to the man who could run a clinic on how to lay the pipe. Sin closed her eyes briefly in response to an involuntary shudder. Garrett Davenport was *amazing* in bed. The man could teach a master class on how to please a woman. *Repeatedly*.

Sinclair drew in a deep breath, then released it. If she was this worked up just thinking about Garrett's voice, perhaps calling him wasn't the best move. She'd text instead.

Caught up with indecisive clients. Might be a little late. See you at Lila's Café as soon as I can get there. Sorry.

She slipped the phone back into her skirt pocket, determined not to stare at the screen, awaiting those three little dots that indicated he was typing his response. She wasn't fifteen and Rett wasn't her boyfriend. They had mutual friends and one ill-advised sexual encounter. And it had been sex—*just sex*—and nothing more.

Still, when she heard the alert that she'd received a text message, she snatched the phone from her pocket and read it.

No rush. Whenever you get there is fine. It'll give me a chance to catch up with Ms. Lila. But thanks for the heads-up.

A slight wave of disappointment ran through her and she wasn't sure why. What had she expected him to say? That he'd be awaiting her arrival with bated breath?

Seriously, girl. Pull it together.

Maybe it was her best friend's impending wedding and unexpected good news that had made her regard Rett more warmly than she normally would. Or maybe it was because Garrett Davenport had shown up at that engagement party looking like a tall glass of sweet tea on the hottest day of summer, and a sister was *parched*.

Her dating life was a tumbleweed-littered ghost town in the desert. Thankfully, her career and her best friend's return to the island had kept her too busy to dwell on the fact that her lady bits were turning to dust.

"Oh my God!"

Mrs. Murphy's squeal of pleasure brought Sin back to the present. They'd obviously just seen the view.

Sinclair smiled. This house might be the one after all. Thankfully, she was better at finding the perfect home for her clients than she was at finding the perfect match for herself.

———

Rett opened the glass door with LILA'S CAFÉ written on it and stepped inside the diner where he'd spent so much of his time as a kid. The aromas of buttermilk fried chicken, chicken-fried steak, creamy mashed potatoes, and mouth-watering gravy practically wrapped themselves around him, inviting him to sit for a spell.

"Garrett! I was hoping you'd stop by." Lila Gayle wiped her hands on a towel tucked in the waist of her apron. "We barely had a chance to say hello at the party."

She greeted him with the same welcoming grin and warm hug that had made him feel at home there as a teenager. A godsend when he'd been struggling after his mother's remarriage and the death of his dad.

Ms. Lila had taken pity on him and eventually given him a job there as a busboy. She'd even overlooked the fact that he ate his weight in free food.

"Good to see you, Ms. Lila." Rett grinned. Ms. Lila and Dakota's dad were like two giddy teenagers in love, despite being in their sixties, and he was happy for both of them. "Congrats again to you and Chief Jones. I can't think of two people who deserve a second shot at love more."

"That's sweet of you, love." The British ex-pat's accent deepened, and her cheeks flushed. She grabbed a menu. "Table for one?"

"Actually, I'm meeting Sinclair. She's running a little late."

His face warmed in response to the older woman's hiked brow and knowing expression.

"You and Sinclair, huh?" Lila Gayle grabbed a second menu. She made her way to a booth at the back of the café. The booth that had always been preferred by teenage lovers when he was in high school because it offered the most privacy.

"We're going over plans for this prewedding event Dex and Dakota want. That's all," he clarified. "So we won't require the lovers booth."

Secret hookups no one else knows about don't count.

"I've never called it that, darlin'." Lila Gayle shrugged innocently. Her sparkling blue eyes danced as she tried to hold back a grin. "You did. The reason I brought you back here is because I thought it would be quieter. But if you'd prefer to sit elsewhere—"

"No, this is fine. The plans are kind of a surprise, so maybe it is best if we sit back here."

"Let Oliver and I know how we can help." Ms. Lila smiled softly. "We're so excited about Dakota and Dex making a life together in her childhood home. It's nice to know that the next generation will know that house was always filled with love."

Had she guessed Dakota was expecting? Either way, he'd committed to keeping his mouth shut, so he would.

"I've missed your cooking, Ms. Lila. What're the specials today?"

She rattled them off, then went to greet a small group that entered the café.

Rett pulled his phone from his pocket and set it on the table. No new messages from Sinclair. He'd keep himself occupied by going over some real estate listings for a client. During his seven years in real estate, he'd always worked solo, and he'd done well. But at the request of his broker-in-charge, he'd been mentoring Natalie—a young agent who'd been struggling—and they'd formed an informal partnership.

She was showing his listings and handling anything his clients might need while he was away. And Rett shared new leads with her, mostly referrals from past clients.

He typed a few quick emails on his phone and sipped the cherry lemonade Ms. Lila set in front of him without him having to ask for it. And because she was Ms. Lila, who'd been like a second mother to him, she'd brought him a small dish of shepherd's pie, in case he was hungry while he waited.

Nearly a half hour after their meeting time, he heard the distinct twang of Sin's voice as she greeted Ms. Lila and was directed to his booth.

He set down his phone, standing as Sin approached. Despite his faults, he was still a born-and-bred southern boy. His grandmother would be disappointed if he didn't stand when a lady joined him at the table.

"Sorry I'm late." Sin sounded frazzled. She tucked a few strands of her honey-blond highlights behind one ear. "I've been showing beach houses to a couple from Ohio. I was beginning to doubt whether I could find a place that suited them both."

"But you did." Rett smiled. It wasn't a question. He could see the excitement in her eyes.

"Got the contract in my hot little hands." She tapped her designer bag and did a little wiggle of her hips that made him swallow hard.

"Congrats, Sinclair. We should consider this a celebration, as well as a planning meeting." He gestured toward the other side of the booth. "Have a seat."

She slid into the booth, and he did, too.

"Hope you didn't hurry on my account, Sin. I could've kept myself busy a bit longer, or we could've rescheduled."

"I make it a point to respect other people's time," she said. "But once the Murphys agreed they wanted to put in an offer, there was no way I was letting those two out of that house until they'd signed the contract. I sent it to the listing agent from my phone."

"I would've done the same."

"Thanks for understanding. Now, let's eat. I'm starving." Sin picked up her menu.

They placed their orders. Country-fried steak, homemade mac and cheese, and fried green tomatoes for him. Black-eyed peas, fried green tomatoes, and a cucumber salad for her.

"Where do we begin? With the wedding or the prewedding party?" Rett sipped his lemonade. "Is that what we're calling this bachelor/bachelorette party? 'Cause it's a hell of a lot easier to say."

"Works for me." The sunlight danced off the flecks of gold and green in Sin's eyes. "As to which event takes precedence, I'd like to think we can walk *and* chew gum. Given the time frame we're working with, we don't have much choice."

Sin pulled out her leather planner and opened it to a

page with *Dakota and Dexter's Wedding* written in fancy, colorful script. Sin uncapped her pricey fountain pen.

She glanced over at him. "It's the wedding folks remember, so I'm going to ensure that my best friend gets her dream wedding."

"We've only got a few weeks to make that happen," Rett said.

It was a tall order, but if anyone could pull it off, it was the fierce, former class president seated across from him. Sin had taken her duties seriously, managing every fundraiser, charity drive, and event like a drill sergeant. She might leave a trail of folks cursing the day she was born in her wake; but Rett had no doubt Sinclair Buchanan would get the job done. He just hoped they'd both survive the next several weeks.

"It's six and a half weeks at this point." Sin turned to a calendar in her book. "Every day, every hour, counts."

Damn. There she was again giving him that scolding schoolteacher vibe. And he was totally into it. Yep, there was definitely something wrong with him. Maybe he had a fever.

"Okay, we've got six and a half weeks." Rett shrugged. "Where do we begin?"

A devious smile spread across Sinclair's face. "Why, Garrett, I'm so glad you asked."

Chapter Six

$\bullet\!-\!\bullet\!-\!\bullet\!-\!\bullet\!-\!\bullet$

As Sin sat across the table from Rett, she caught herself staring again. He'd always been handsome, but there was something about the full-grown Rett Davenport that was incredibly appealing.

Was it any wonder that she'd frequently been distracted by thoughts of Rett in the days since the party?

She couldn't help thinking about how delicious he'd looked in his suit. The broadness of his shoulders and the width of his thighs. The fullness of his lips. And each time, she'd quickly slid down the rabbit hole that took her back to that night they'd shared.

The memories felt so real. As if she were back there in his bed. In his arms. His lips gliding over her skin.

Sinclair shuddered. Six and a half more weeks of this just wouldn't do. Not if she was going to pull off this minor miracle and give her best friend the wedding she deserved. The wedding her mother, Ms. Madeline, would've given her, had she lived to see this moment.

Sin couldn't take away the pain of Dakota's mother not being there on the most important day of her life. But she could ensure the day was filled with so much happiness and joy that Kota would feel like her mama was looking on from above, offering her blessing and ensuring everything went perfectly.

So that's what she would do.

Being distracted by wanton thoughts of Rett Davenport and his talents in the bedroom ran counter to that aim.

"Everything good?" Rett cocked his head, his eyebrows furrowed with concern.

"Of course." Sin dropped her gaze from his, her cheeks hot and her body vibrating with energy. When her eyes met his again, the words she planned to say caught in her throat.

Before their interaction at the end of Dakota and Dexter's engagement party, Sin wouldn't have had a problem telling Rett she didn't want or need his help. But he'd been so sweet and chivalrous. And the way he'd looked at her as they sat there in her SUV. It was as if he hadn't wanted to leave.

For the briefest moment, a part of her hadn't wanted him to leave either. The same part of her brain that was curious about whether the magic they'd experienced five years ago had been a one-time thing. Or had it been something... *more*?

Sin cleared her throat and forced a broad smile.

"I realize how busy you are, Rett. You're helping out at Mama Mae's. You're a successful real estate agent. And your life is in Charlotte now. Asking you to join the crazy train I'm about to be on while I plan this wedding for the next several weeks..." Her smile and her Eastern Carolina drawl deepened. "It's a lot to ask of any man. So why don't I handle all of this? Nick, Em, and Dexter and Dakota's parents are eager to help. I'll buzz you, if we need reinforcements."

"We talked about this, Sin. I *am* helping with this wedding." Rett leaned forward and tapped a finger on the table. "You said you were cool with us working together. Did I do something to upset you?"

He seemed genuinely distressed by the possibility.

Why hadn't teenage Rett been as thoughtful and kind as the man seated in front of her?

Then again, even in high school, Rett had shown flashes of decency. Which made it even more disappointing when he'd humiliated her by doing something like putting a whoopee cushion on her chair before a big class assembly or calling her an empty shell of a human being.

"You haven't done anything to upset me, Rett," she assured him. "It's just..."

"What, then?" His penetrating gaze seemed to bore a hole right through her.

"Why is it so important for you to be involved in planning this wedding?" Sin asked pointedly.

"Dex has been like a brother to me most of my life, so I'd *really* like to do this for him. He and Dakota are family. This trip home has kind of made me realize how much I miss being this involved in my family's life."

"You didn't much like Dakota when they dated in high school," Sin reminded him. She'd been indignant when she'd discovered that Rett had tried to talk Dexter out of getting serious with Dakota early on. That had been the start of their contentious relationship. Things had spiraled from there. "Why the sudden change of heart?"

"I *never* disliked Dakota." His brows furrowed. "Honestly? I was jealous of their friendship. At first, I was glad Dex had found himself a running partner so he wouldn't drag my ass out of bed before sunup."

"Same." Sin couldn't help laughing. "I actually hooked

the two of them up so Dakota would have someone else to run with."

Garrett chuckled bitterly, then he frowned.

"Suddenly Dakota seemed to be taking up every spare moment of Dex's life. So yeah, I was jealous and kind of an ass." He shrugged. "It felt like she'd hijacked my best friend. It wasn't until he lost Dakota that I truly understood how much she meant to him. There was a giant hole in his life the entire time they were apart. I'm thrilled they're together and that they're about to become parents."

"Wow." They said the word simultaneously, then looked at each other with surprise.

"Most of our high school friends have long been married with kids." She shrugged. "So I don't know why it seems so wild that Dex and Dakota are about to become parents." She glanced up at Rett, her brows furrowed. "Do you ever feel like everyone else is leaving us behind?"

Sin shifted in her seat uncomfortably. Where had that question come from? And why had she chosen to share that particular vulnerability with Rett, of all people?

Her mother's incessant question echoed in her head.

When are you going to settle down and give us grandchildren like your sister? I'm not going to live forever, you know.

Terri Buchanan's reminder that she wouldn't live forever hit Sinclair hard. There was an ever-present awareness that her mother could have another heart attack, and maybe next time their family wouldn't be so lucky. It was a devastating possibility. And it was the only reason she'd given her mother a pass for poking, prodding, and meddling in her love life.

When Sinclair glanced up, Rett was staring at her blankly. He had no clue what she was talking about.

How could he? Garrett was a perennial fuckboy who'd *never* settle down. The man seemed incapable of a long-term attachment. All the more reason to create space between them.

The more seconds that ticked by without a response from Rett, the more embarrassed Sin was at having asked the question. She cleared her throat and returned to the subject at hand.

"Don't worry, Rett. I'll be sure to give you credit for helping with the planning."

"You think I'm only in this to earn some kind of friendship points with Dex and Dakota?" Rett's nostrils flared. "Sweetheart, who hurt you?" He swigged his lemonade.

Sinclair's eyes widened and she sucked in a deep breath. Rett had always had a gift for going for the jugular when trading insults while playing the dozens in high school. Apparently, he hadn't lost his edge. She wanted to lash out in response, but the truth was she had insulted him...even if that hadn't been her intention.

Be nice, Sinclair. You promised Dex and Dakota.

"I didn't intend to upset you, Rett. I just thought—"

"That I don't actually give a shit about making a meaningful contribution to this wedding." Garrett's gaze dropped to his hands balled into fists on the table. He looked up at her again, his expression marred by a deep frown.

The anger, she understood. But the look of abject disappointment in Rett's dark eyes cut her in a way she wouldn't have anticipated. His feelings were *genuinely* hurt.

"I didn't mean to imply..."

He narrowed his gaze and folded his arms. A move that silently called bullshit on her excuse before she could even launch into it.

"Okay, I was wrong, and I'm sorry." Sinclair tucked her hair behind her ear.

A server arrived with their piping hot meals. When she walked away, Garrett picked up his utensils and ate in silence. He wouldn't even glance in her direction.

Sin's chest squeezed, and she genuinely felt awful about hurting Rett. Neither of them had had much regard for each other's feelings in high school. This was new territory for them.

She took a few bites of her cucumber salad. But her gut churned with guilt, and she couldn't enjoy her meal. Sin set down her fork with a clang, and Rett finally glanced up at her.

"You're right. It was awful of me to think you didn't really want to be involved in the planning. I can't apologize enough, Rett." She placed a gentle hand on his wrist.

He leaned back against the booth, without comment, tugging his hand from beneath hers.

"Two heads are better than one, right? I've already started a to-do list for both events. After we eat, why don't we brainstorm any additional items I might've left off the list? Then we can divide and conquer."

"You're desperate to get rid of me, aren't you?"

Sin's cheeks heated. She shifted her gaze to her bowl, picked up her fork, and speared some cucumber slices. "We only have a few weeks to make this happen."

"That's not what this is about. It's about that night in Raleigh."

Flames licked at Sin's face, and suddenly it was harder to breathe. She glanced around to see if anyone overheard him.

"We agreed *never* to talk about that," Sin whispered.

"I agreed not to tell anyone else about it." Rett put down his fork and steepled his fingers. A sly grin curved one edge of his mouth. He clearly felt the shift in energy, too.

"I never agreed not to discuss that night with you. Starting with the fact that it was rude as hell for you to dip without saying goodbye."

Sinclair rubbed her forehead, then forced herself to meet Rett's accusatory gaze. This conversation was the exact reason why she'd avoided him for the past five years. It churned up all of the conflicting feelings she had about Rett and about their night together. Embarrassment that she'd given in to her reluctant attraction to the man who'd been plain awful to her in high school. Shame over the way she'd walked out on him. A burning curiosity about seeing Rett again.

All of which made her feel she lacked control of the situation and herself. A feeling she abhorred. A feeling she'd learned to mask by keeping her chin high, her shoulders pulled back, and by feigning disinterest or even disdain.

But Rett was being open and honest with her about his feelings. Starting with the fact that her actions had genuinely hurt him. So he deserved the same.

One night of angry, albeit amazing, sex had been easy. Interacting with her former hate crush like adults— rather than spiteful teens trying to one-up each other... not so much.

"Not my finest hour." Sin smoothed the napkin draped over her lap. "But I thought it would be best if we avoided the awkward morning-after conversation."

See? She'd been doing him a favor. He should be grateful. Most fuckboys would be.

"What awkward conversation is that *exactly*?" He clearly wasn't giving up on this uncomfortable line of questioning.

"You know." She shrugged. "That whole song and dance where we exchange cell numbers and you claim you'll call, but we both know you won't." She stuffed a forkful of cucumber slices in her mouth and chewed.

Rett looked at her with what she was pretty sure was pity. She'd never felt smaller.

"I guess that explains who hurt you." Rett leaned forward, placing his arms on either side of his meal. "For the record, I'm not that dude. If I say I'm going to call…I do. Even if it's just to thank a woman for a lovely evening. And if I have no intention of calling, then I don't claim I will. I'm thirty-seven, Sin. I've outgrown all the game-playing. Besides, I happen to find honesty refreshing. You should try it sometime."

Okay, now she was *pissed*. She dropped her fork with a clang again. Rett cocked his head and raised one eyebrow, clearly amused by her indignation. Which only made Sin angrier.

"How dare you sit here tryna get all high and mighty with me, Garrett Davenport." Sin did her best to keep her voice low.

She did *not* do unseemly drama. Which was why she'd made it her business not to date local boys after her breakup with Teddy.

Thank God her ex had at least moved to Wilmington and hadn't returned to the island after his parents retired and moved to Florida.

"As if you're some choirboy," Sin continued. "Maybe I would've at least stayed until the morning if you hadn't been so awful to me in high school."

"If I was so awful, why did you come to my room that night, Sin?" Rett asked. His question seemed sincere, and that pained, vulnerable look had returned to his dark eyes. "And why'd you kiss me the night of the high school dance?"

"I didn't kiss you. *You* kissed *me*, and I kissed you back."

"You did a little more than kiss me back, sweetheart. As I recall, you climbed on my lap and dry humped me. If I hadn't put the brakes on, we'd probably have a kid together right now."

She couldn't argue the point. If he'd kept going, she wouldn't have stopped him.

"And you still haven't told me *why* you kissed me back that night. Or why you came to my hotel room five years ago, if you really believe I'm the kind of person who only does shit for my friends so they'll *think* I'm a decent guy."

Sinclair huffed. She'd floated in here on a hot air balloon. In less than thirty minutes with Rett, she'd gone through a full range of emotions. Now she felt completely deflated.

The next six and a half weeks are going to be so much fun.

He was still staring at her, his arms folded as his meal got cold.

"I don't know why I kissed you the night of the dance," Sin admitted. Her voice was faint and the fire in her belly moments ago had been doused by the wounded puppy dog look on Rett's face. "Maybe it was because that was the night Dexter and Dakota first..."

She didn't finish. It hadn't been a secret. They'd both known *exactly* why their friends had ditched the dance early. Dakota had strategically planned her and Dex's first time together while her parents were away on a college tour with her sister. Still, it felt wrong to say the words aloud.

"Maybe I was feeling left behind." Sin shrugged. "Or maybe it was those cheap-ass wine coolers you brought to the dance."

Rett chuckled bitterly. "How do you think I summoned the courage to kiss you?"

Courage? As in it was something he'd wanted to do, but couldn't muster up the nerve? The thought cycled through Sin's brain for a moment before she patently rejected the idea that a guy as cocky and arrogant as Rett Davenport had been would require a boost of courage to kiss her. He'd managed just fine to kiss half the girls at their school.

"And at the hotel?" Rett pressed.

You were a delayed rebound.

Was that even a thing?

It didn't matter. Because looking into Rett's eyes, she wouldn't hurt him any more than she already had by telling him the truth.

Her sister had mentioned in passing that Teddy and Gwen had just had their first child. Leanne hadn't even seemed to notice how Sin had been affected by the revelation.

She realized she was better off without Teddy in her life. Yet she'd spent five years dropping hints about marriage and hoping he'd finally grow up and put down roots. Hearing the couple's happy news felt like a punch in the gut.

The call from her sister had come after Rett's proposal that they sleep together, just to let off a little steam and to ease the tension they were both feeling about their upcoming real estate test. One hour later, she'd shown up at his hotel room.

Definitely *not* her finest hour.

A week ago, she might've smugly tossed that bit of information Rett's way. But now, she couldn't help thinking it would hurt him even more. Despite the animosity she'd felt toward Rett in their past, the man she'd been getting to know over the past few days didn't deserve that.

Sin pushed her salad aside.

"When you broke the ice and suggested that we have lunch and then dinner together, it was nice reminiscing over the past. Remembering all of the fun times the four of us had together. The few occasions when you weren't a jerk to me back then." She offered a small smile. "I missed the old days and my friendship with Dakota. You gave me a chance to reconnect to some of my happiest memories at a time when I really needed it."

Rett reciprocated with a half-smile of his own as he stroked his beard. "It was nice reliving those memories."

God, he is an incredibly handsome man.

Not that she hadn't noticed in high school. But now...there was something about that grown-man look. Rett had a little weight on him, though he was clearly still in good physical shape. There was a hint of gray in his beard and at his temples that he wasn't trying to cover up. That spoke volumes about his confidence. And for the briefest moment, she wished this table wasn't between them so she could scale his lap like she had the night of the dance.

Sinclair shut her eyes, a chill running down her spine.

Nope. No, ma'am. No way. No how.

What happened between them five years ago had been amazing. Mind-blowing. And supremely memorable. But it hadn't been anything more than sex for either of them. If it had, it wouldn't have taken five years and a wedding to force them to cross paths again.

Garrett visited Holly Grove Island at least once a month. If he'd wanted to see her again, he'd known where to find her. And she could've reconnected with him just as easily.

Don't get caught up in your feelings because your best friend is getting married.

That's all this was. Dakota and Dex were taking the next steps in their lives together, and she was feeling left behind. Just like the night of the dance. Maybe it was the same for Rett, too.

Sin picked up her fork and broadened her smile. "So first we eat, then we make a plan."

Rett nodded. "Sounds good to me."

Sin would focus on the work that lay ahead. Reading more into any lingering attraction between her and Rett would be a huge mistake. For both of them.

Chapter Seven

•--•--●--•--•

Garrett walked Sin to her SUV after their working lunch. Sinclair could be a little stubborn and sometimes came off as pushy. But the woman had a brilliant, organized mind, and she knew *exactly* what she wanted. He admired that.

Unlike Sin, he'd drifted through life during his twenties and hadn't discovered what he was truly good at until he'd turned thirty. Even then, he hadn't gotten serious about his life and career until a few years ago.

Sinclair hit her alarm, and Rett opened the door for her, offering her his hand. When she stepped up onto the running board, a hint more of the tawny brown skin of her thighs became visible when the skirt shifted.

Rett quickly forced his eyes to meet hers again. He was not here to dwell on the plumpness of Sin's perfect ass, the curve of her hips, or how soft the skin of her thighs appeared.

He was here to help plan and execute Operation DexKota: the perfect wedding and prewedding event for their best friends. Dexter and Dakota deserved this after the bumpy road that had finally brought the two of them back together.

"So I'll see you in Wilmington on Friday afternoon?"

There he was again, confirming the timeline they'd already established. He was trying to prolong his time with Sinclair, and he wasn't even sure why. The woman had insulted him and tried her best to ditch him little more than an hour ago.

But he hadn't let her get away with it. He'd called her out on it, and she seemed genuinely contrite about assuming he was the Tin Man who had no heart.

He and Sinclair had spent the past hour developing a solid plan for the wedding and prewedding event, and he'd enjoyed his time with her. They'd gotten into a comfortable rhythm and had even shared some laughs. It reminded him of the day they'd spent together in Raleigh.

It had begun when Rett had invited Sinclair to join him for lunch during the break in their real estate workshop. At first, things had felt weird. They'd spent the first few minutes feeling each other out after not seeing each other for years. Still, it had ended well enough that he'd invited her to join him for dinner later that night, and she'd agreed. Dinner had gone much more smoothly—perhaps because they'd shared a bottle of wine. Neither of them was drunk, but the wine seemed to lessen the tension between them. By the end of the night, he'd been determined to shoot his shot.

He'd invited Sinclair back to his room.

Sin immediately shot him down. But an hour later, she'd shown up at his door.

Rett ran a hand over his head and sighed. He still didn't know what had made her change her mind. Nor was he buying her excuse for why she'd fled his room and acted as if their night together had never happened.

But all of it only proved what he already knew. Sinclair

was a high-maintenance drama queen, and that wasn't his style.

So why couldn't he stop thinking about that night?

"Yes. Our appointment is at three. That'll give us plenty of time to drive out there." Sinclair reached for the door handle, but he held on to the edge of it and stepped a little closer.

"I was thinking…"

He expected her to respond with her usual retort when they were teens. *Well, that certainly can't be good.*

It had probably been a harmless joke to Sin, like the many times he'd teased her. Only it had fueled his feelings of inadequacy.

Dex, Sin, and Dakota had all been academic stars. But he'd been barely keeping his head above water. Trying to follow what was going on while also combatting the storm of emotions over his father's death and his mother's re-marriage had formed a hard, flaming ball in his gut. His emotions had then spiraled out of control when his mother got pregnant with Izzy.

"Yes?" Sinclair studied his face as she sifted her fingers through her hair.

"Wilmington is four hours away. Doesn't make sense for both of us to drive out there. We should carpool instead."

Sinclair cocked her head. "I guess you're right," she said, finally. "But I'm driving."

"Fine." He held up his hands in surrender, relieved that no further convincing was required. "Pick me up at Mama Mae's around eleven?"

"Make it ten fifteen. I don't want to be in a rush." Sinclair plucked her planner out of her bag and scribbled a note in it before returning it. "Anything else?"

"No, ma'am." He closed Sin's car door and stepped back, waving as she pulled out of the parking lot.

In two days, Rett was going to spend eight hours confined in a vehicle with Sinclair Buchanan—*voluntarily*.

Clearly, he was a masochist. But he couldn't help wanting to spend more time with Sinclair—the woman who still had an unmatched talent for driving him wild.

———

When Rett returned to his grandmother's house, Mama Mae opened the door before his foot hit the bottom stair.

"Well, lunch must've gone well." His grandmother didn't attempt to hide her giddy grin.

He knew where this conversation was going, and he wanted no part of it.

"It did." He shrugged off his jacket. "Sin was built for this. I wouldn't be surprised if the woman has her entire life planned down to the minute."

"What's wrong with that?" Mama Mae asked, one eyebrow cocked. She took his jacket and hung it up herself. "Sounds like the woman has it together to me. You don't think that's an admirable trait?"

"Of course," Rett said. "Particularly since we have a limited window of operation. It helps that Sinclair is clear on what she believes Dakota wants and is determined to make it happen. If there is one thing Sinclair isn't, it's indecisive. That was probably the most productive meeting I've ever been part of. She should teach a master class."

"That's wonderful, sweetheart. Then you two are going to enjoy working together on the wedding."

"I don't know about that." Rett rubbed the back of his neck. "After all, she is still Sinclair Buchanan. As frustrating as she is—"

"Beautiful?" Mama Mae was grinning like the Cheshire Cat.

Rett shook his head. "No, Gram. We are *not* doing this." He made his way to the kitchen to get a glass of water.

"We're not doing *what*, sweetheart?" she asked in her best faux innocent voice.

He held back a laugh. The last thing he wanted to do was encourage Mama Mae.

"We're not doing this matchmaking thing. I'm only in town for a few weeks while I help you work on the house and help Sin with the wedding. And I am not—I repeat— I am *not* looking to get involved with anyone. Least of all Sinclair the-annoying-beauty-queen Buchanan."

"Sure, baby." She patted his arm dismissively with a sly smile. "Whatever you say. You hungry?"

"No, ma'am. I ate plenty at Ms. Lila's." He patted his gut. "I couldn't eat another bite."

"But I made your favorite. Guinness beef stew made in the slow cooker." She practically sang the words.

Rett inhaled the savory scent. How had he not noticed it before? Seriously, Sin was throwing his brain out of whack. The sooner they got through the planning of this wedding and he returned to Charlotte, the better off he would be.

"Okay, maybe just a little now." He held up his thumb and forefinger. "But best believe, for dinner, I'm going in."

His grandmother chuckled heartily. She'd always loved feeding him and Dexter. "Good. I'll fix you a bowl. Then you can tell me what you and Sinclair have cooked up for the wedding."

———

Rett sat at his grandmother's kitchen table and ate a second bowl of beef stew. The two of them chuckled over the fact that Sinclair had insisted on calling it Operation DexKota.

"The woman is efficient; you have to give her that." Mama Mae grinned. "But then Sinclair has always been a smart cookie." She tapped the side of her temple. "I was surprised when she didn't go off to college like Dakota. She probably could've gotten into any school she wanted."

"Probably," he agreed, finishing up the last of his second serving. He was going to have to start hitting the gym if he stayed around here another week or two. Otherwise, they'd have to roll him down the aisle for the wedding.

"But she stayed here on Holly Grove Island and helped her father, the mayor, with the hardware store—despite her mother's objections." Mama Mae gathered their plates and took them to the sink. "That girl loves this island and the folks who call it home. I think she'd be perfectly content to spend the rest of her life here."

"Maybe."

Where is Mama Mae going with this? Because with Mama Mae, there's *always* a point.

"I'm sure her mama had some sort of grand plan for her. Some prestigious career or marrying into money, like her sister did. But Sin has always known her own heart and mind. Did what felt right for *her*. And she's done just fine for herself." Mama Mae scrubbed the dishes in the hot, soapy water in the sink because the outdated little cottage didn't have a dishwasher.

"It seems she has," Rett agreed, still not sure what the point was of this conversation. "Good for her."

"Exactly." Mama Mae turned to look at him, her warm brown eyes softening. "A smart, decisive woman who knows her own mind, doesn't beat around the bush, and takes no bullshit...well, that's *exactly* the kind of woman I've always imagined would best suit you, Rett. You two are perfect for each other. And you're obviously still sweet on her."

Rett nearly choked on the glass of water he was chugging. Those were nearly the same words his cousin Dexter had said a few months ago, not long after Dakota had first returned to town. He coughed and Mama Mae came around the table and patted his back until he was fine.

"Why does everyone keep saying that?" he muttered, mostly to himself.

His grandmother chuckled and shook a finger at him. "That should tell you something, son. Like maybe the real reason you're hanging around here is to spend time with Sinclair."

"With respect, Mama Mae, that's ridiculous. The woman drives me nuts. She thinks she knows everything and that she's always right." His cheeks warmed, and he wasn't sure if it was because he had, in fact, been looking forward to spending time with Sinclair or because he felt badly about lying to his grandmother about it.

"Knowing Sinclair, she probably is." There was a hint of admiration in his grandmother's voice. "But you know what I always say. If someone gets under your skin that much, there's gotta be something to it."

"There is. She's exasperating. End of story." He drank his water slowly this time.

Mama Mae laughed harder. "Well, bless your heart."

It still amused him when northerners mistook *bless your heart* as a sincere expression. Occasionally, it was. However, Rett was a born-and-bred southern boy. So he understood the complex connotations of the phrase.

This time, it was Southern for: *You poor sucker. You won't even see it coming.*

Rett sighed. "You're not listening to a word I'm saying, are you?"

"I heard what you said, son, and methinks the man doth protest too much." Mama Mae chuckled as she sat opposite him.

She was making Shakespearean references. This wasn't good.

"And more importantly"—she pointed one of her bony fingers at him—"I can hear all the things you *aren't* saying. And I can read those expressions of yours as clearly as yesterday's tea leaves."

There was no point in arguing. He couldn't remember winning a single debate with his grandmother. Even when he thought he'd won, she'd turned it into a gotcha moment that proved the point she'd been making all along. And at the age of eighty-two, Mama Mae was as sharp and spry of mind as ever. So he wasn't about to try to pull one over on her. But he didn't have to admit to anything either.

"Whose idea was it for you two to ride all the way out to Wilmington together?"

"It was Sinclair's idea to go to this event venue in Wilmington where her cousin works," he said defensively.

"And did she invite you or did you invite yourself?"

"I…I didn't invite myself…*exactly.* I just wanted to be a part of planning this thing for Dex and Dakota," he said. "I am the best man. And normally, the bride's mother and sister would be involved. But Ms. Madeline's gone and Shay's in Cali. Only seemed right that I give Sinclair a hand."

"And did Sinclair suggest you two ride together?"

"Okay, okay." Rett held up a hand. "I can see how this might look…suspect. But it just makes good sense. It'll give us time to game-plan the wedding. Besides, I care about the planet. No point in driving two cars."

He sounded like a guilty teenage boy. No wonder his grandmother nearly fell out cackling. He shook his head and sighed. Mama Mae was right. He'd maneuvered himself into spending eight hours alone in a car with Sinclair. And that wasn't even counting the tour of the venue itself.

Nothing is happening between you and Sin. Just go on this tour, then come back home, and everything will be fine.

He repeated the words to himself as Mama Mae chattered on about tea leaves, stars aligning, and him and Sinclair being perfect for each other.

Rett loved his grandmother. Her words of wisdom and patience and Dexter's insistence on being a big brother to him were the two things that had saved him from going down a dark path after the death of his father.

But neither Mama Mae nor Dex were always right. And this time, his grandmother couldn't be more wrong. Sin was a woman who knew exactly what she wanted, but what she wanted sure as hell wasn't him.

Chapter Eight

— · — ◆ — · —

Sinclair pulled into the driveway of the little cottage on Hummingbird Way that Annamae Davenport had owned for as long as she could remember. She pulled her large SUV in behind Rett's GTO. It was a strong, black, sexy, well-built car. Much like the man himself. Not that it mattered, because she was never going down that road again. No matter how much she might've been fantasizing about it this past week.

She picked up her phone and sent Rett a quick text message.

I'm here.

She waited. One minute passed. Then five. Still no response. She called his phone. It rang and rang before finally rolling over to voice mail. Sin considered blowing her horn, but that would only annoy Mama Mae and everyone else on the street.

"I swear, this man is gonna be late for his own funeral," Sin muttered as she turned off the idling engine and climbed out of her SUV. She straightened her blouse, smoothed down her skirt, and checked her makeup in the vehicle's oversize side mirror. Then she made her way toward the front door, her heels clicking against the concrete.

The adorable little cottage was nearly a century old. And right now, the place looked the worse for wear. It wasn't in danger of falling over, but compared to the new builds and renovated properties that dotted the street, Mama Mae's place was definitely the sore thumb. It was a shame, because it had the potential to be the most adorable house on the block. A feat she could easily help Mama Mae achieve.

Helping her real estate clients renovate their properties and get obscene prices for them was her gift.

Sin lifted her fist to knock on the door when it suddenly swung open.

"It's about time. Do you have any idea how long I've—" Sin gasped. "Ms. Annamae! I'm so sorry. I thought you were—"

"My grandson? Well, I certainly don't get that every day." The barely five-foot-tall woman chuckled. "Come on in, sweetheart. It sure is good to see you."

The older woman wrapped Sin up in a bear hug that took her by surprise. Ms. Annamae was as fiery and independent as she was sweet. Sin had always loved that Mama Mae had never been a "typical" grandparent. Nor had she allowed herself to be confined by the social expectations for an older southern woman.

To say that Mama Mae was a rebel would be an understatement. And while that had raised many eyebrows on the island, it had only made Sin admire the woman.

"It's good to see you, too, Ms. Annamae," Sin said when the older woman finally released her.

"Enough with this 'Ms. Annamae.'" Garrett's grand-mother frowned and waved her hand dismissively. "You're family 'round here. Call me Mama Mae."

"Yes, ma'am." Sinclair checked the time on her phone and then slipped it into the pocket of her skirt. She folded her arms. "I assume that grandson of yours still isn't ready."

"He is running a bit late, and I'm sorry for that. But don't blame Rett, it's my fault. Or at least it's this old cottage's fault." Mama Mae sighed, glancing around.

The Craftsman-style bungalow had lots of charm and character, but the old place and the furniture that filled it were lovingly worn. Sin couldn't help envisioning the updates she'd make to the cottage, if Mama Mae was her client.

"I just received my water bill and it was atrocious because my bathroom sink has been leaking and the toilet won't stop running. I made the mistake of mentioning it to Rett this morning over breakfast and he insisted on fixing both."

Mama Mae smiled softly. The love for her grandson was evident. "He had to go off the island for some parts, so he just finished up not too long ago. He went to grab a shower before you two have to be cooped up in that fancy Lexus of yours for four hours."

"Well, that was considerate of him." Sinclair smiled and the older woman chuckled. "But he was late for the engagement party, too. I'm seeing a trend here."

"You are...because that one was also on me." Mama Mae sighed. "Rett insisted I lie down because I had a bit of a cold. But I had several flats of plants that had to be put in the ground that day so..."

"Rett did your planting before the party?" Sin asked.

"He did." The woman's smile was warm. "I know he can

be a little rough around the edges, but Rett is just a big ol'
teddy bear. The sweetest, kindest man you'll ever meet."

"Oh." Sinclair winced, her neck and face suddenly hot.
She'd been angry with Rett for being late to the party. Why
hadn't he told her he'd been helping his grandmother? She
would've understood. But he hadn't said a word.

"Sin, sorry I'm late." Rett trotted down the stairs. "I
had a few things to take care of, then I had to hop in the
shower. I have no idea where my phone is, or I would've
called you." His words were hurried. But he still hadn't
mentioned that he'd been helping his grandmother.

"It's okay." She shrugged. "As long as we leave within
the next thirty minutes, we're fine. So if you need a little
more time . . ." She indicated his bare feet.

"Great. Give me five more minutes to put on my socks
and shoes and find my—"

"Here's your phone, Sonny." Mama Mae produced the
phone from the pocket of her apron. "You left it on the side
of the tub."

"Thanks, Gram." He accepted the phone and leaned
down to kiss his grandmother's cheek. "After all this time,
you're still taking care of me."

"We're still taking care of each other." She smiled fondly.

"Always have. Always will." He winked at his grandmother.

The genuine affection between the two of them warmed
Sinclair's heart. Her grandmother had passed when she
was quite young. Rett was lucky to still have Mama Mae
in his life.

"I'll go back to the car then," Sin said.

"You'll do no such thing," Mama Mae insisted. "It's
been forever since I've had company here. Sit down for a
bit and let's chat."

"What about me?" Rett sank onto the stairs and put on a pair of socks. "Don't I count?"

"This will always be your home, Rett. So no, you don't count as company." Mama Mae threaded her arm through Sin's. "You finish getting dressed. I'll entertain our guest. Go on, now," she added when he seemed reluctant to leave the two of them alone.

Rett drew in a deep breath, put on his other sock, and jogged back up the stairs.

Mama Mae whisked her into the kitchen and turned on her vintage red teakettle. She joined Sinclair at the table.

"There's something I've been wanting to talk to you about," Mama Mae said in a hushed tone. She obviously didn't want Rett to overhear her.

"Yes, ma'am?" Sinclair sat up bone straight, unsure of what to expect.

"I haven't mentioned it to Rett, but I'm thinking of selling the old place." Mama Mae glanced around wistfully. "The upkeep is becoming a bit much for me, and I don't need this much space. Just as long as I have someplace to have a small garden."

"Yes, ma'am," Sin leaned forward, her voice also lowered. "I can certainly understand that. And at this point in your life, I'd imagine that single-floor living would be nice, too."

"It would take some pressure off these old knees." The woman rubbed the offending joints beneath the table. "The house has long been paid for, so with the prices houses around here have been fetching, I'd imagine this old place would net me a sizable return, if I put a little money into it."

"Yes, ma'am, it would." Sinclair pulled out her phone. She scrolled to an album of before-and-after photos of the projects she'd renovated and sold in the past few years. She handed the phone to Mama Mae.

"These are impressive, Sinclair. What I've heard about you is no exaggeration." Mama Mae handed the phone back when she was done. "If anything, they didn't tell half the story."

"That's kind of you, Mama Mae." Sin glanced around the worn, dated kitchen. The lovely old cottage had good, solid bones. It just needed a loving touch to bring it into the modern age while maintaining the home's unique character.

She could definitely do that. But she couldn't imagine that Rett, who was also a Realtor, wouldn't object to Mama Mae giving her the listing.

The teakettle whistled, and Mama Mae got up, waving Sin off when she'd volunteered to grab it. The woman returned to the table with two cups, lemon slices, and a bowl of sugar. Sin added sugar and fresh squeezed lemon juice to her tea and sipped it. The older woman watched her intently, as if carefully debating her next words.

"I'd love it if you could give me some ideas about what you'd do to renovate this place, and what kind of return I can expect on the investment. But I understand if you can't without a contract in place."

"For you, Mama Mae, I'll make an exception." Sin smiled, then took another sip. "But what about Rett? He didn't seem keen on the idea when I suggested it earlier."

"I know." The older woman nodded. "But he did bring your card home to me. If he'd been truly set against it, he could've tossed it in the bin."

Sin doubted Rett would see things that way.

"Don't you worry about Sonny. I can handle him just fine." Mama Mae chuckled, then added with a wink, "Got a feeling you could handle him just fine, too."

"Yes, ma'am," Sin said proudly, then checked her watch. She finished her tea. "Speaking of which, I'd better round up my wedding planning co-captain or we will be late."

Sin reached for her cup to take it to the sink, but Mama Mae insisted she leave it.

"One more thing, Sinclair," Mama Mae said. "Best not mention this to Rett just yet. I'll talk to him later."

"Yes, ma'am." Sin nodded. "Now, I'm off to gather your grandson. I promise not to keep him out too late."

"Well, that's disappointing," Rett said with a sly smile as he trotted down the stairs. He looked especially good in a pair of slim gray pants and a pale blue button-down shirt. He straightened his navy-and-gray-striped tie, then grabbed a jacket out of the front closet. "Ready, planning princess?"

"That's real estate queen to you." She tipped her chin. "The event planning is just a hobby. Something I do for friends." She checked the time. "Let's hit it, playboy."

"You two have a good time!" Mama Mae called. "Don't come rushing back on my account. I'll be just fine."

Rett extended his arm to Sin, helping her down the steps in her tall, designer high heels. Then he insisted on helping her into the SUV.

This man smells absolutely divine.

What was that scent anyway? Cedarwood, maybe? Whatever it was, it smelled like a little slice of heaven. Sin had the sudden desire to bury her nose in his neck and inhale.

Being cooped up in this SUV for eight hours with Rett, who looked and smelled amazing and was evidently leading the race for Grandson of the Year, was going to be pure torture.

This was going to be the longest day of her life.

Chapter Nine

———•—•—•———

Rett walked out of the meeting with Sin's cousin—an event planner at a popular wedding venue in Wilmington—with a notebook filled with ideas. He and Sinclair had several new concepts in mind for both the wedding and the prewedding event. It'd been a long drive for an hour meeting, but seeing the space had inspired lots of new ideas, so it had been worth it. And the drive up had turned out to be enjoyable.

About forty minutes into their drive, filled mostly with awkward silence as the radio played softly in the background, the song "Candy Rain" by Soul for Real came on. He'd asked her to turn it up, and it'd kicked off an hour of a truly bad sing-along that was loads of fun. They'd played song after song that one of their little group had been obsessed with at some point in high school, and it naturally led them to reminiscing over the past, much as they had that day at lunch five years ago. He and Sin both seemed to relax, and they'd laughed so hard about some of the wild adventures the four of them had had together that his cheeks were sore.

"Since we're here, I'd love to swing by the farmers

market before it closes." Sin stuffed her planner back in her bag.

"Looking for anything in particular?" Rett asked.

"I'd like to browse the flower stands and get some ideas for the floral arrangements. Also, my parents return on Sunday. I'm making my dad my North Carolina lemon pie. It's his favorite."

"Don't suppose your trusty wedding planning co-captain could get in on a little of that action?" Rett grinned.

"That depends."

"On what?"

"On which version of you I get on the ride home," Sin joked. "The charming hometown boy from the past few days or..."

Rett frowned, and his shoulders stiffened.

When Sin noticed his reaction, her bright, easy smile vanished instantly, and she, too, seemed tense. She cleared her throat. "We should go before all the good market stalls close."

They climbed inside Sin's SUV, neither of them speaking. The vehicle felt eerily quiet, given the chatty laughter that had filled it earlier.

Rett rubbed at his beard and frowned. His afternoon with Sinclair had been enjoyable. They'd accomplished everything they set out to do, and they'd managed to have fun doing it. But then, just like in high school, they'd been getting along fine, but one of them just couldn't seem to resist ruining the mood. Something they'd been equally guilty of.

"I shouldn't have said that." Sin turned toward him, her cheeks and forehead flushed. "Things were going great between us and I just had to—"

"Be honest?" Rett turned toward Sin. A knot clenched

his gut as the words formed in his brain. It was an apology that was long overdue. "I acted like an immature jerk in high school, and I'm really sorry about that. I wish I could go back and change things. That's something I've been wanting to tell you since that night at the dance," he admitted.

Sin shook her head. "I don't understand."

"I was totally into you, and I couldn't get up the nerve to tell you. Pushing you away was my way of convincing myself I didn't care that you'd never be interested in someone like me." Rett's gaze met hers squarely. "It was childish, and I've regretted it for a really long time. So I'm saying it now. I'm sorry I gave you a hard time. I'm sorry that I acted like an arrogant ass to mask my own insecurities. You didn't deserve that."

Sin stared at him, blinking.

Well, that's a first.

He'd rendered the beauty queen speechless. Something it seemed better not to make note of during his big apology.

"Thank you, Rett. Hearing you say that…It means a lot." Sin tucked her hair behind her ear. "And yes, you were awful to me at times. But at times, I've been pretty spiteful to you, too."

Now, Rett was the one who was shocked. Sinclair was apologizing to him?

"I was Sinclair Buchanan, Miss Holly Grove Island and daughter of the mayor. So maybe I was a little full of myself and outdone by the fact that—"

"I didn't fall at your feet like every other guy in our class?" Rett smirked.

"Something like that." Sin's mouth curved in a soft smile, and all Rett could think about was how incredibly beautiful she was and that he'd really like to kiss her again. "Maybe I had sort of a crush on you, too. Putting you down was my way of saving face and proving that I didn't care one iota about the boy who'd rejected me. So I'm sorry for that, too." Sin chuckled bitterly. "We were both pretty awful to each other, weren't we?"

"We were," Rett agreed.

"But that was two decades ago. We're different people now. Better, more mature people. So why don't we make a fresh start, beginning right now?" She extended her hand.

"Deal." Rett felt a deep sense of relief. His shoulders relaxed, and the knot in his gut eased. He squeezed her hand, and electricity seemed to dance along their palms. "Why don't we celebrate our fresh start with dinner at The Copper Penny? My treat."

"After the farmers market?" The sunlight glittered off the shades of green and gold in Sinclair's hazel eyes. "Sure. I could eat."

Rett fastened his seat belt and faced forward again. It felt good to finally level with Sinclair about his feelings for her back then. But he wasn't quite ready to be honest with her—or himself—about the feelings he had for her now.

———

Sinclair strolled past another stall at the farmers market. It turned out that bringing along a handsome, six-foot-three man who both charmed the women working the stalls and happily carried her bags wasn't such a bad idea after all.

"You sure you don't need me to carry anything?" Sin asked.

"I'm good. Just watch out..."

Before Rett had finished his warning, she'd bumped into another shopper. A woman with two small children in tow.

"I'm so sorry, ma'am. I wasn't paying attention to..." Sin froze as she scanned the woman's face. She was suddenly unable to speak.

Gwen. Mrs. Teddy Walker. The name she'd written in that damn scrapbook more times than she could remember.

"Ma'am?" Gwen laughed nervously as she swept her unfortunate bangs off her forehead. "It hasn't been that long, has it?"

However long it had been, it hadn't been long enough.

Was it too much to ask for her to live the rest of her days without ever seeing Gwen the traitorous backstabber again?

Sin wanted to tell her former "new bestie" that and a whole lot more. But she didn't want to scare the two adorable little children whose hands Gwen held on either side. The handsome little boy looked so much like Teddy. And the gorgeous little girl was a good mix of both of her parents.

Both children stared up at her expectantly.

"Mommy, who is that lady?" the little girl asked as she tugged her mother's hand.

"An old friend," Gwen said without hesitation, her tone heavy with remorse. "A friend I've missed terribly."

Sin gritted her teeth, her eyes stinging as she met her former friend's gaze.

How dare Gwen stand there behaving as if she was hurt over the dissolution of their friendship? It was *her* betrayal that had destroyed their relationship.

"I don't think your friend can talk, Mommy," the little boy whispered.

Sin's face went hot. She was standing in the middle of the market like a stone, making a fool of herself.

"Gwen, I got you a bottle of water and a...Sinclair?" Teddy stood beside his wife and children. A sleeping infant was strapped to his chest in one of those fabric baby slings. When they'd dated, he'd mocked other men for wearing such a thing. "What are you doing here?"

"Shopping, like everyone else here," Sin said finally. Her shock and embarrassment morphed into flat-out anger. She stood taller, her spine straight and her chin tipped. "It is a public market, after all."

"Hey, babe. Introduce me to your friends?"

Garrett. She'd nearly forgotten he was there.

Rett slipped his arm around Sin's waist. His warm, soothing voice slid over her, easing the tension in her shoulders.

She leaned into him, thankful he was there. "This is Gwen Walker. You were already gone when she lived on the island. And you remember Teddy Walker. We went to school together."

"Sorry. Can't say I do," Rett said with an easy smile as he reached out to shake both of their hands.

Teddy grimaced and his shoulders crumpled. His ears turned red, the way they always had whenever he was angry, embarrassed, or both.

Maybe it made Sin a ridiculously petty person, but Teddy's ego being bruised by Rett's brush-off brought her a perverse sense of joy.

"What a lovely family you have." Garrett smiled at the two children, who stared up at him in fascination.

Gwen thanked Rett for the compliment and introduced their three children.

Sinclair tuned out. She didn't need to know their names.

Didn't want to hear about their seven years of marital bliss. Her brain was in a fog as their conversation floated over her.

She concentrated on just three things: Hold on to Rett. Don't fall over. Smile. *That* was the limited capacity of her current mental and emotional bandwidth as she stood there, pretending not to be crushed by seeing her ex and former friend with their band of babies.

Living the life she'd imagined would be hers.

"It was wonderful to see you, Sin," Gwen said. "I often think about you. You were a good friend, and I'm sorry about how things turned out. I'm glad to see you so happy. You two look good together."

"Yeah, it was good to see you both again," Teddy parroted but with far less conviction than his wife.

"Thank you," Sin managed to say, the knot in her gut tightening like a clamp. Her head felt light. "You, too."

Okay, so that was a bold-faced lie.

She wasn't glad to see Gwen, Teddy, and their 2.5 children. And she certainly wasn't thrilled to see them both so damned happy.

"Sin, are you all right?" Rett asked quietly, tugging her closer. Neither of them had moved an inch as the Walker family turned and walked away.

She swallowed hard and pulled free from Rett's grip. Sin blinked back the tears that burned her eyes. Tears she refused to let fall. Gwen and Teddy didn't deserve them.

"I'm fine, thanks. But if you don't mind, maybe we could skip dinner and head back." Sin raked her fingers through her hair. "It's been a really long day and I'm tired."

"Of course." Rett's eyes were filled with concern. "But you need to eat something. How about if we place a to-go order?"

"Fine." Sin hurried toward the parking lot. She was eager to start the long, grueling trip back to the island. Unfortunately, she wouldn't be very good company.

Sin dug into her designer bucket bag for her phone. She lifted it from the little pocket she stored it in but accidentally dropped it deeper inside the bag.

Perfect.

Nothing was going right today.

Sin dug around in the bag until she felt her phone.

"Sinclair!"

She glanced over her shoulder at Rett, who'd fallen a few steps behind her. Rett dropped everything he was carrying and lunged forward. He grabbed her waist and yanked her toward him, just before a car went flying by. A young woman was texting while driving.

Sin's heart beat wildly. Fear, then anger filled her chest. She considered taking off her shoe and hurling it—along with a few choice curse words—at the car that nearly plowed her down.

"Sin." Rett gripped her shoulders and held her at arm's length. "Are you all right? Is anything hurt or bruised?"

"Just my pride." She huffed. "And my strawberries." She pointed to the quart of strawberries spilled on the sidewalk.

Garrett heaved a sigh, then laughed. He pulled her into a bear hug that would've made Mama Mae proud. "God, Sin, you just took ten years off my life. I'll buy you more strawberries. I'm just glad you're okay. I can't believe I almost..." he stammered, then cleared his throat. "I can't believe we could've lost you just now."

Sin's ear was pressed to Rett's chest, and she could hear his heart thumping. He seemed more shaken by her near-death experience than she was.

It was unexpected and surprisingly sweet. She settled into his hug, enjoying its warmth and comfort. She breathed in his cedarwood scent, her eyes drifting closed momentarily.

"I'm okay. *Really*," Sin said, finally.

"You're shaking." He rubbed a slow circle on her back. "You sure you're all right?"

So maybe she wasn't as okay as she imagined.

"I will be, thanks to you." The racing of her own heart slowed a little. Sin glanced up at him. "Why don't we place our order at the bar when we arrive? I could use a stiff drink. That is, if you wouldn't mind driving home?"

"Sure, I'll drive." Rett seemed reluctant to let her go. Maybe he was afraid she'd wander into traffic again, like an unsupervised toddler.

Rett gathered her bags, and she stooped to collect the berries and toss them in the trash.

"C'mon, we'll get you some more strawberries. Hopefully, you don't have any more exes lurking inside." He winked and offered her his arm.

"Amen to that." Sin slipped her arm through his, not bothering to ask how he'd known Teddy was her ex. As she fell in step beside Rett, she was just grateful he'd been there.

Chapter Ten

—•—•—

Rett sat across the table from Sin at The Copper Penny restaurant in Wilmington. His heart had barely recovered from the moment he'd seen that kid barreling toward Sinclair in that blue sedan. He honestly didn't think he'd ever forget it.

He'd heard that a person's life often flashed before their eyes in the face of death. But every memorable moment he'd spent with Sin seemed to flash before his as the car headed straight for her. Even more surprising, glimpses of the future flashed through his brain.

Him escorting Sinclair down the aisle at Dexter and Dakota's wedding. Her waking up in his bed.

Moments that had yet to happen.

Everything transpired so quickly. In an instant, he'd dropped everything and pulled her to safety. To him. His heart hadn't stopped thumping since, though his heartbeat had finally slowed.

I almost lost you.

Those were the words he'd nearly uttered to Sinclair. Where the hell had that come from? Sinclair wasn't *his*. And there were no prospects of her ever being his. So why did he feel the near loss so deeply even now, an hour later?

Because you're a decent human being. End of story. Nothing to see here.

"So go ahead and ask me." Sinclair sipped her second drink.

She was considerably more *relaxed* than when they'd arrived. The weight of everything that had happened finally hit her, and she'd wanted to sit down and eat rather than get takeout.

"Ask you what?" Rett sipped his water with lemon.

He'd limited himself to one house draft of pale ale, even though he could've used something stronger.

"Why I ever dated Teddy Walker?" Sinclair said, as if the question should be obvious.

"I don't know enough about the guy to pass judgment." He set his glass down and leaned back in his seat.

"But you do remember him," she noted with a sly grin. "Despite pretending you didn't."

Rett chuckled. Knowing Teddy Walker, the fact that he'd claimed not to remember him would ruin Teddy's entire day. And yes, he got a small thrill from that.

"I remember him," Rett said. Teddy was about as shallow as a cookie sheet; an uninspired follower who'd do anything to be part of the popular crowd. "Wouldn't have put the two of you together in a million years. You deserve better, Sin."

Her gaze dropped from his. "I wish you'd been around to tell me that before I wasted five years on him."

Rett nearly choked on his water. "You spent *five years* with Teddy's sorry ass?"

Sin narrowed her gaze at him.

"Sorry. No judgment. I'm just…surprised. Like I said, you deserve better."

"Deep down, part of me always knew that." Sin studied the dwindling contents of her glass. "But I was madly in love. I ignored the signs that urged me to run the other way and kept pushing forward. Dropping marriage hints. Planning a future as Mrs. Teddy Walker. I guess I should be glad he never took the hint. That it wasn't me he wanted to build a life with."

There was a sad, faraway sound in Sin's voice. Rett wanted to reach across the table and squeeze her hand, but he feared she'd suddenly become self-conscious and stop talking. And he didn't want her to. He wanted to know why she'd gone for a guy like Teddy when she hadn't given him the time of day. Was it because Teddy was popular in high school, like Sin and her friends, while he was branded as an outsider? Or maybe it was because Teddy came from money and he didn't?

"How long after you two ended things before he married her?" Rett asked.

"Not long." Sin laughed bitterly and swiped a finger beneath her eyes. "They were dating within a month and married within a year. But wait…there's more." She held up a finger. "Teddy met Gwen because she was my closest friend at the time. We met at the gym in our building and became fast friends. The three of us often hung out together. And the capper? It was Gwen who suggested I give Teddy a hard ultimatum about marriage and be willing to walk away if he refused to put a ring on it. Within a few weeks of the big breakup, she and Teddy were dating."

"Wow. That was cold." Rett rubbed his jaw.

So little Mrs. Sunshine was actually a coldhearted, manipulative, back-stabbing, man-stealer. He hadn't expected that.

"As furious as I am with them for what they did, I'm also grateful." Sin's voice was quiet.

"Why?" Rett studied her eyes, brimming with sadness and something else he couldn't quite distinguish.

"Because the only thing worse than being played for a fool is to actually be one. And I would've been a fool to marry Teddy. He wasn't a bad person, but we just weren't right for each other, no matter how badly I wanted us to be. Teddy obviously realized that long before I did. My marriage ultimatum was the escape hatch he'd been hoping for."

"Or he could've been man enough to tell you that while he cared for you, he wasn't in love anymore. Or that he wanted something or someone else. What they both did was a trash move, Sin. Shouldn't surprise me, though. Teddy Walker was a wannabe leader, but in reality, he was a desperate follower who lacked a moral compass." Rett set his water down roughly.

Maybe Sinclair wasn't the only one with Teddy Walker–induced trauma. When he laid eyes on the man's smug face, he was instantly taken back to the days Teddy and his loser friends had teased him for being confused by algebra.

Teddy hadn't been the ringleader. But he'd joined in wholeheartedly, teasing Rett and making him feel stupid for his learning differences. Then he'd cast Rett looks of apology when they'd passed each other in the hall between classes.

That made Teddy even more reprehensible than the others. He'd known what they were doing was wrong. Yet he'd participated in their bullying bullshit anyway.

The moment Rett recognized Teddy, he'd wanted to punch that stupid smile off his face. Especially when it became obvious there was history between him and Sinclair. Rett realized it the moment he saw Sin standing in the middle of the market speechless, looking as if she'd seen a ghost. But it quickly occurred to him two things would hurt Teddy more: acting as if he didn't remember him and pretending he and Sin were together.

So that was what he'd done, and he'd enjoyed seeing that smug look slide right off of the other man's face.

"Maybe telling me the truth seemed cruel to him," Sinclair said. "Maybe it's my fault that he didn't feel like he could come clean with me about his feelings. Maybe I put too much pressure on him with my constant hints about weddings and babies. Maybe—"

"Sinclair, sweetheart…" Rett placed his hand over hers. He couldn't bear another moment of Sin blaming herself for what clearly wasn't her fault. "This wasn't on you. They were both grown-ass people fully capable of being honest with you. Instead, they manipulated you into doing the dirty work for them. That was pretty shitty behavior." Rett squeezed her hand. "I'm sorry Gwen and Teddy hurt you, but I'm glad neither of them is in your life anymore."

Sinclair stared at him, blinking. She looked as confused as he'd been in algebra class.

"Thanks, Rett." Sin's smile was soft and warm. She slid her hand from beneath his and gripped her glass but didn't lift it to her mouth. "My brain realizes I shouldn't blame myself for what went down with Gwen and Teddy. But seeing them and their kids today…" Her voice faded. She gulped the last of her drink, then sighed. "It still hurts, and I can't help blaming myself. Maybe I needed a reminder that it wasn't my fault. So thank you for saying it."

Rett nodded. He was glad she hadn't ended up with Teddy. Still, his chest ached for her. "Been a long day. Ready to head back?"

"Yeah, sure." Sin stood, and without thought, he stood, too. She smiled but seemed surprised by the gesture. "Can you request our checks? I'm going to run to the powder room."

Rett's gaze dropped to Sin's perfectly curvy bottom as she sashayed away. He squeezed his eyes shut and cursed under his breath.

Not gonna happen, brother.

Rett hailed the server to request their bills, since Sin had insisted they go Dutch.

In a few hours, they'd be back to town. And in a few days, he'd be back in Charlotte, away from Sin and from Holly Grove Island.

Chapter Eleven

———•——•——•———

As Sinclair approached their table, Rett's eyes lit up the moment they met hers. He stood quickly, a broad smile animating his handsome face. Sin's heart swelled and her pulse raced.

His reaction was genuinely *sweet*. Something she didn't think she'd ever say about Rett Davenport. In high school, she considered him rude and thoughtless. But these past few days, he'd been nothing but kind and considerate.

Sin was still finding it difficult to wrap her head around that. She'd agreed to dine at the restaurant partly because she was mortified by the possibility of getting barbecue sauce on the leather seats in her Lexus. But mostly, because she'd taken comfort in Rett's companionship, and she had wanted an excuse to spend more time with him.

Rett held up her jacket so she could slip her arms into it.

She thanked him, then tied the belt at her waist. "Did the server bring the bill?"

"She did." He sounded sheepish. "It's been taken care of."

"Did she forget to split it?" Sin frowned.

"No," he said simply, gesturing toward the door.

"You didn't have to do that, Rett."

"I know, but I wanted to. Now c'mon. Let's get you home." He gestured toward the exit.

Arguing the point seemed futile. Besides, it was nice of him. "Thank you, Rett. Next time, dinner is on me."

"Sure, if you want." Rett placed a hand low on her back, guiding her toward the exit. He chuckled. "I promise not to order the lobster."

Sin laughed, too, and the mood instantly felt lighter. Still, she couldn't help noticing the electricity that flowed through his fingertips and into her skin, despite the layers of clothing between them.

Her skin tingled, as did those parts of her anatomy she was trying hard not to think about. But her mind wandered back to the place it had gone several times this evening. Remembering how amazing it had felt to have Rett's strong hands on her bare skin. The fluttery excitement in her belly as he'd trailed kisses down her chest. How it had felt to have him inside her.

Sin shivered. The visceral memories of Rett's lips and hands sliding over her skin felt as real now as they had in his hotel room.

She'd tried to scrub that night from her brain. Pretend it had never happened. She'd failed abysmally. And now that she and Rett were spending time together, that night was living rent-free in her head. She couldn't stop thinking about it or him.

Sin glanced at Rett. Was he thinking about that night, too?

They were two reasonable adults. What would be the harm if they hooked up again? Nothing serious. Just pure fun and a little tension relief. Like before.

Rett stopped and held his hand out.

That shook Sin from her temporary daze. He wasn't asking for her hand. He was asking for her keys because she'd asked him to drive home.

Sin unlocked the vehicle. "Thank you, Rett."

"For dinner? Honestly, Sin, it was no big—"

"Not just for dinner. For insisting on helping with the wedding. You might've noticed I'm not big on asking for help." She smiled sheepishly and Rett chuckled. "But now, I realize how much I need your assistance. It was nice having you here today. And at the market, you saved me from the most humiliating moment of my life without me even asking. I didn't expect that." She tucked strands of hair behind her ear that a gentle breeze had blown across her face.

"I'm full of surprises." Rett winked and his dark eyes twinkled. He looked so handsome and somehow larger-than-life.

Why hadn't she noticed that before?

Instead she'd teased him. Called him the Jolly Mean Giant and countless other not-so-nice names as they'd gone toe to toe playing the dozens. She'd told herself it'd all been in good fun, but had he been as hurt back then by her cruel comments as she'd been by his?

She studied Rett's hungry stare, his expression filled with longing and desire as he glided his tongue along his lower lip. Sin shuddered at the memory of Rett's kiss and of the way his tongue had felt gliding against hers.

A thousand thoughts rushed through Sin's head as they stood there, neither of them speaking. But the thought she couldn't shake was that she wanted to kiss Rett again. To experience the comfort of his embrace and the passion that had filled her body and made her feel alive again after Teddy and Gwen's betrayal had left her battered and bruised. Feeling dead inside. Wondering if it would ever be her turn. Feelings that had resurfaced as she helped plan her best friend's wedding.

Sin gripped Rett's jacket, lifted onto her toes, and pulled his mouth down to meet hers. When she parted her lips, Rett swept his tongue between them. Searching her mouth. His hands glided around her waist, molding her lower body to his as he deepened their kiss.

Rett was *such* a good kisser. Something she'd discovered the night of the dance.

He backed her up, his body pinning hers against the vehicle. Rett angled her head and claimed her mouth, setting her entire body afire. Her nipples beaded against his hard chest. His length grew taut against her belly.

Rett kissed her until she felt feverish and breathless, her knees trembling.

Suddenly, Rett pulled away, his chest heaving. He stared down at her, his hands still resting on her hips. "It's getting late. We'd better head back."

"Or not," Sin said calmly, despite the thudding of her heart. Her eyes searched his as she smoothed a hand down his chest. She wanted Rett. He obviously wanted her, too. They'd made peace with their past, so why not give in to their desire for each other?

Rett's eyes widened. "You're suggesting—"

"Yes." She leaned into him.

Rett groaned, his eyes drifting closed momentarily. He dragged a hand over his head and groaned. "I'd love to take you up on that offer, Sin, but I can't."

"The girl who keeps calling you." Sin's cheeks flamed. "You two are involved?"

She hadn't even thought to ask if he was seeing someone.

"No, it's nothing like that. We work together." His large hand cupped her cheek.

She couldn't resist leaning into the warmth of his hand. "Then what is it?"

"You've been drinking and..."

"You think I'm drunk?" Sin laughed incredulously. "Seriously, Rett, what southern girl can't handle a couple of drinks with that much fried food to soak it up? I'm fine. I asked you to drive out of an abundance of caution. It'd be pretty hard to plan this wedding from a jail cell. Or worse," she added.

"I believe you, Sin. But—"

"But *what*?" She tried not to sound as insulted as she felt by his rejection.

"Sweetheart, you've had a hell of a day." Rett's tortured voice was filled with compassion. "The kind of day that can prompt a person to make really bad decisions."

"You're saying you're a bad decision?" Sin smirked.

He cringed. "If you'll regret it later, yes."

Sin's chest felt heavy. Rett had honestly been hurt by her disappearing act five years ago, and she felt awful about it.

"I'm sorry about the way I reacted that night, Rett. I just sort of panicked. But I don't need you to protect me from my own choices. Not tonight. And not five years ago, when I was having a slight meltdown after learning that Gwen and Teddy had had their first child."

Rett massaged his forehead and frowned.

Shit.

She hadn't intended to blurt those words out, but she'd been so focused on making her point. And maybe she was just a tiny bit tipsier than she thought.

"Five years ago, I had no idea you were having a life crisis, Sin." His firm lips grazed her temple as he whispered in her ear. "Tonight, I do."

Rett was determined to be a consummate gentleman. Mama Mae would be proud.

Sin forced a smile, despite the embarrassment that heated her face and neck. "Can't blame a girl for trying, right?"

"No, I don't suppose I can." Rett opened the passenger door and offered her his hand.

Sin accepted it and climbed inside the SUV. The only thing worse than being rejected by Rett was having to take a four-hour car trip with him afterward.

Not awkward at all.

Rett adjusted the mirror and driver's seat to accommodate his long legs and large frame. He pulled out of the parking space and headed toward home. "You sure you're okay?"

"I asked. You answered. It's fine." Sin shrugged. "Seriously, the sex was good and everything, but I'm not about to fall to pieces because you turned me down."

"Good, because I always hate when that happens." Rett's tone and expression were facetious. "And about what happened in the market earlier. No one could blame you for being upset by that encounter." He hesitated a moment, then continued. "The other day, you asked if it ever felt like everyone was leaving us behind. I understand how you feel."

Sin's spine stiffened. It was one thing to be rejected by Rett, but now he was patronizing her, too? She'd like to hold on to a modicum of her pride. "I realize you're trying to make me feel better about today. But you don't need to pretend that—"

"I'm not bullshitting you, Sin. I didn't answer your question then because it wasn't something I'd considered before. So I didn't have an answer. I've been thinking about it since then. It made me realize that things have been different since Dex and Dakota have been back together."

"Different how?"

Rett rubbed his jaw clearly uncomfortable with the

conversation. "I'm not saying I suddenly want marriage and kids. But seeing how happy Dex is..." Rett shrugged. "I don't know. Maybe some of us just aren't cut out for domestic bliss."

"*Us*?" Sin tilted her head and folded her arms. "Speak for yourself, buddy. I plan to get married someday."

"Complete with the house and kids?" Rett glanced over at her, with one brow raised.

"I can buy my own house," Sin said. "As for the kids...I don't know. *Maybe*?" It was more of a question than a declaration, and for good reason. She honestly wasn't sure. But she was clear about not wanting to discuss the topic with Rett Davenport, of all people. "Right now, I'm focused on my career. I plan to become a broker-in-charge and have my own team."

There were countless female real estate agents, but a serious shortage of women in leadership roles in the industry. Sin was determined to be part of a wave of change in that regard, and she was working hard to get herself a seat at the table. Thankfully, the owner of her brokerage, Douglas Henley, agreed.

Since neither Doug's son nor daughter were serious about the business, he'd been grooming Sinclair to run the agency when he retired in a year or two, and she already had her broker-in-charge license. But she didn't want to wait until Doug's retirement—which he kept putting off. She wanted to become a partner in the firm *now*. To see her name on the brokerage she'd help catapult to record earnings over the past five years.

Sin was *this* close to convincing Doug of the wisdom of allowing her to buy in as a partner. She was sure of it.

"That's great, Sin. From what I hear you're one of the top agents around here."

"*The* top agent," Sin corrected with a smile.

"My bad, Top Gun." There was a hint of admiration in Rett's voice. "I've heard what a badass you are. Heard you even sold Higgins's Bait Shop for a small mint."

"Can't take full credit for that one." Sin laughed. "Mr. Higgins wouldn't put a penny into the place, nor would he go down on the price. That one actually sold despite my advice."

"Sounds like Old Man Higgins." Rett laughed, too. "Still, you're putting up incredible numbers, and you're Holly Grove Island's darling. So if anyone can do it, Sin, you can."

"Thank you?" Sin said, her head cocked.

"You don't think I'm being sincere?" he asked.

"Sorry, I know we've made nice and everything, but it's a learned reaction to a Rett Davenport compliment." Sin's tone was light. "You pulled that one on me too many times in high school. You'd start off with a compliment that seemed genuine. Only I somehow ended up as the punch line."

"I know. But even then, the compliment was always sincere. You'd give me this look...like the last thing you wanted was a compliment from me. I'd instantly revert to my comfort zone of being—"

"The class clown?" Sin had used that term about Rett often. But this time, it wasn't an insult. She recognized the vulnerability he'd been feeling then. And she was kicking herself now for not seeing it *and him* more clearly.

"I didn't think I was too good for your compliment," Sin continued. "I was afraid it was the setup to some joke. To be fair, it usually was."

"You're right, and I'm sorry."

"Apology accepted." Sin smiled softly. "I'm starting to

understand how we got caught up in this vicious cycle of resentment and hatred."

"I never hated you, Sin." He covered her hand on the console with his much larger one and gave her a brief smile before returning his attention to the road.

Warmth seemed to flow from his hand into hers. Her belly fluttered and her breath caught in her throat. Apparently, the man couldn't even touch her hand without her going into full hormonal-teenager-with-a-killer-crush mode.

Sin gently slid her hand from beneath his and turned on the radio, tuning into a college station that played jazz—a genre she'd been introduced to when Dex, Nick, and a few of their friends had formed a band a little more than a year ago and began playing at The Foxhole—a local hangout on the island—once a month.

"You're a jazz connoisseur now?" Rett asked. "Thought you were a country music girl."

"Can't I be both?" Sin asked.

"You can indeed." He grinned.

"Besides, I didn't think you could handle my country music playlist."

"Now who's being judgmental?" Rett raised a brow. "I happen to like country."

"What country artists do you listen to?" Sin folded her arms in disbelief.

"Jimmie Allen, Kane Brown, Kacey Musgraves, Florida Georgia Line, Maren Morris, Mickey Guyton, and hail to the queen, Ms. Dolly Parton—a genuinely badass, brilliant woman who I'm pretty sure is in line for sainthood."

"Not bad, and you're not wrong about Dolly Parton." Sin studied Rett.

He was tall and handsome. He had a large frame, but a fit physique and attention-grabbing assets: a strong chest, broad shoulders, and a rather impressive backside. At least three women—including their server—had flirted with him at the restaurant. Rett had been polite and cordial but offered nothing more than a friendly smile. They weren't a couple and they hadn't been on a date, but he'd given her his full attention, recognizing that after seeing Teddy and Gwen, she'd needed a friend.

Is that what she and Rett were now? Friends?

"All right, country it is." Sin pulled up a country playlist on her cell phone and the smooth, rich vocals of Kane Brown singing "What's Mine Is Yours" poured from the speakers.

"*That's* the girl I know." Rett grinned. "The one who introduced me to country music."

"Which you absolutely hated," Sin noted.

"I know, and I still love my R & B and hip-hop. But I think my resistance to country music was more about it being my stepfather's favorite music. I resented Hector, and I didn't want to have anything in common with him. I started listening to it when I worked at a bar where they played nothing but country."

"You were a bartender?"

"No." Rett chuckled. "That's one of the few jobs I haven't had. But I did date the bartender. Does that count?"

"No." Sin held back a smile. "So if you weren't the bartender, you were the...bouncer." Sin snapped her fingers as they said the word simultaneously. She waved a hand, indicating his physique. "Of course, you were."

Sin could see how Rett could be intimidating enough to be a bouncer at a bar. But the more she'd gotten to know him, the more she realized Mama Mae was right. Rett was a big, cuddly teddy bear despite those rough edges. Only that didn't track with his feelings toward his mother and stepfather when they were in high school.

He'd been angry with his mother, resentful of his stepfather, and had practically ignored his younger sister. From what she'd seen at the engagement party, Rett's relationship with his mother and stepfather had improved considerably. But there still seemed to be distance between him and Izzy.

"There's something I've always wanted to ask, but if you don't want to talk about it, that's fine," Sin said.

"Shoot."

She slipped off her shoes and turned toward Rett, as much as her seat belt permitted.

"Mr. Ramos seems like such a kind, sweet guy. I never understood why you hated him or why you were angry with your mom for finding love again. If that's not too personal."

"It is." An uncomfortable silence settled over the cabin. "And it's something I don't talk about much." He sighed. "But maybe I should."

Sin couldn't help thinking about Rett's earlier words: *That's the girl I know.*

But despite all of the time they'd spent together as teenagers, they hadn't really known each other at all. If they had, perhaps they would've been friends—not enemies. They couldn't change the past, but maybe they could at least forge a friendship now.

After all, now that Dex and Dakota were about to get married, it would be impossible to keep avoiding each other. So it was time they put some effort into getting to know each other.

Sin lay a hand on his forearm. "If you'd like to talk about it now, I'd really like to know."

Chapter Twelve

Garrett probably should've passed on discussing his family with Sin. Despite one hot night five years ago and a pretty incredible kiss Sinclair might not even remember in the morning, they weren't exactly friends. Particularly not the kind who poured their hearts out to each other about messy family shit.

Yet, there was a part of him that wanted to be completely open with Sinclair about this. He wasn't even sure why. Maybe it was less about who she was and more about where he was at this point in his life.

He'd made his share of mistakes. But the thing he regretted most was how he'd blown up his family back then. Second would be not telling Sinclair the truth about his feelings for her when he'd kissed her the night of the dance. Then again, she hadn't given him much of a chance before she'd declared the kiss a horrible mistake they should never speak of again.

So why did he want to talk to her about this now?

"It's okay if you don't want to—"

"Seriously, woman, do you *ever* stop talking?" Rett asked, only half-joking.

He quickly took in Sin's wide smile and glittering hazel eyes. Her giggle lightened the heaviness in his chest. Something he'd felt in her company more and more this past week.

"The gift of gab is my secret weapon. It's both my offense and my defense. But don't tell nobody. That's between us." Her Eastern Carolina accent had deepened. She pursed her lips.

The same lips that had suggested they get a hotel room and stay in Wilmington overnight.

You did the right thing. Stay focused, man. Stay focused.

"My stepdad is a good guy. He's been a good husband and my mom's best friend. And he's been an amazing dad to my little sister and to me... as much as I'd let him. But I had a tough time when my parents split up. I was around ten years old, and until then I'd been genuinely happy. I didn't understand why my mother suddenly kicked my dad out. As far as I was concerned, he was a great father. We were always going on some cool adventure together, and when he'd help me with my homework, he had a knack for explaining tough subjects in a way I could better understand."

A knot tightened in Rett's gut, and his throat suddenly felt dry and tight.

He hadn't talked about his father in a long time. But he'd learned long ago that the grief would never go away. He'd just gotten better at masking the pain.

He'd learned to stuff those feelings deep down in his chest rather than acting out, like he had when he was an angry, lost teenager blinded by the pain of losing his father and laying the blame at his mother's feet.

"I loved my mother," he said. "But she worked long shifts at the hospital, so I spent a lot more time with my dad. He had a little business as a carpenter and a handy-man. He'd bring me along on jobs sometimes. That's where I learned how to do the basics around the house."

"Like fixing Mama Mae's leaky faucet?" Sin said.

"Yeah. My dad was great at fixing things but a terrible businessperson. The bulk of the financial responsibilities fell to my mom. She wanted him to give up the business and get a full-time job. He insisted he could make the business work. But finances were just one of the reasons their marriage fell apart." Rett frowned. "My mom was just really good at hiding her pain. I had no idea she was so unhappy in the marriage. I thought she was cranky because she worked all the time, you know? I didn't see how the two things were connected. I only knew I loved my dad, and I didn't want him to leave. That she was the reason he did."

"He was your hero. Any child in your position would've felt the same." Sin's words were reassuring.

"I wanted to go with him. If I had, who knows? Maybe I would've been with him on his bike that day."

"I'm sorry about your dad, Rett." Sin placed a hand on his forearm. Her warmth seeped through his skin, even through his jacket. "I can't even imagine how devastating that must've been for you at such a young age."

"It was." The knot in his gut hardened painfully. He cringed, remembering how he'd reacted back then.

"I blamed my mother and Hector for my dad's death, and I gave them both hell. They tried to be patient with me, but I kept getting deeper and deeper into trouble. Hanging out with the wrong crowd. Doing everything I could to make their lives miserable. After about six months, Mama Mae channeled her grief over losing her only son into trying to save me."

"So that's when you moved in with your grandmother?"

"Yeah. Mama Mae stayed on my ass. She was super strict about who I could hang out with. Which is how Dex and I got so tight. He was one of the few folks she approved of because he was so damned straitlaced and reliable." Rett couldn't help smiling. "Dex and Mama Mae kept me from going down the wrong path."

"So you weren't living with your mom and Hector when your sister was born," Sin said.

"No, and when I was fifteen I was kind of an asshole about them having a kid." Rett sighed. "It's a period in my life I'm not proud of. That's why I don't talk about it."

"What made you talk about it tonight?"

Rett kept his eyes glued to the stretch of road ahead of them rather than glancing over at the beautiful woman seated beside him.

Why had he spilled his guts to Sinclair?

Because he felt at ease with Sin, and he liked talking to her. But saying so felt too heavy and would further complicate an already complex situation.

"You told me about you and Teddy. I'm sure that wasn't easy for you. Seemed right to be just as straightforward."

"I'm glad you did. It was nice hearing you talk about your father."

"Speaking of parents...how are Mayor Buchanan and Principal Buchanan doing?" He segued, eager to talk about anything else.

Sin's father was the former mayor on the island and her mother was the principal at the middle school he'd attended.

"They're fine," Sin said. "Over the moon about having another grandbaby in the fold. Disappointed that I'm not doing my share to increase the town's population."

Rett chuckled. "Your dad wasn't fond of me, but your mom—"

"God, she hated you." Sin laughed. "But that's mostly my fault. I complained about you incessantly."

"I gave your mom plenty of reasons not to like me." Rett rubbed his jaw, thinking of all the times he'd ended up in Principal Buchanan's office. "And I did my fair share of complaining about you, too. Only Mama Mae had a different take. She figured that meant we'd end up together. That you were the one woman who'd be able to keep me in line."

"Mama Mae wanted to see us together?" Sin turned toward him, clearly amused. "Is that why she looked so pleased when I came to pick you up today?"

"Probably," Rett said. "I was afraid that's what she was chatting with you about."

"She didn't mention it." Sin's voice took on a more serious tone. She cleared her throat. "That last drink hit me a little harder than I thought. Would you mind if I took a nap?"

"Of course not."

Rett turned back to the soft jazz station. It was more conducive to sleep than "Long Live" by Florida Georgia Line blaring from the radio. The song, extolling small town life, always made him a little homesick. Reminiscing over those summers they'd all hung out together. The line about long-leg country girls in cutoff jeans made him think of Sin.

Thankfully, he'd be in town just a few more days. Then he'd return to Charlotte to decide whether to take his friend up on his offer to join his real estate brokerage in Charleston.

Rett glanced over at Sin, who'd turned her back toward him. His chest roiled with growing affection for his former hate crush. Rett sighed, pushing thoughts of himself and Sin together out of his head.

The sooner he could put some distance between himself and the long-legged country girl drifting off to sleep in the seat beside him, the better off he'd be.

———

Rett had awakened Sin when he'd exited the bridge that led them back onto Holly Grove Island. She'd popped a piece of gum in her mouth, straightened her seat, and slipped on her shoes. But she'd remained relatively quiet.

It was well after eleven at night by the time he turned onto Hummingbird Lane and pulled into the drive of Mama Mae's cottage. He parked Sin's SUV behind his GTO.

"You're sure you're okay to drive yourself home?"

"I'm fine. I swear," Sin assured him. "Thanks for coming with me today, Rett. If you hadn't been there…" Sin was clearly more shaken by her near-death experience than she'd let on. "I don't want to think about what might've happened."

"But I *was* there, and I wasn't about to let anything happen to you, Sinclair." He squeezed her tense shoulder. "So let's not think about what could've happened, okay?"

His intention had been to calm her. But a cold chill ran down his spine as the reality settled over him that Sin might've been *gone* in an instant.

"It's late. You're probably exhausted. I'd better go." Rett reached for the door handle, but Sin clutched his other arm.

"Or you could come back to my place for…*pie.*" Sin said the word "pie" coyly as she smoothed a hand down the lapel of his jacket. When her large eyes met his, she smiled.

His heart beat so loudly he was sure Sin could hear it, too. Rett could enumerate all of the reasons kissing her again was a bad idea. But he couldn't stop himself from erasing the remaining space between them when Sin leaned in and her eyes drifted closed.

He cradled her cheek. His mouth glided over her pillow-soft lips. His fingers spiked into her hair, bringing everything about that night in Raleigh back to him so vividly it felt like they were there again.

But now he knew why Sin had really come to his room that night. She'd been upset about Teddy and Gwen becoming parents. So tonight wasn't about him at all. It was Sin's emotional response to the hurt of encountering Teddy and his brood.

He wanted Sin. Had fantasized about having her in his bed again. But not this way.

Rett groaned, dragging his mouth from hers. "Look, Sin, I'm trying to do the right thing here. But I honestly don't know how many *no*s I have left in me." He studied her face. The disappointment there mirrored his own. "So maybe we should call it a night."

"Of course. Just don't forget that tomorrow you're taking Dexter to pick out the tuxedos and be fitted." Sin returned to the business-only demeanor she employed whenever they discussed plans for the wedding. As if his tongue hadn't been down her throat moments earlier.

"I'll handle it," he said. "You can count on me."

She cocked her head, eyeing him doubtfully. "You forgot, didn't you?"

Totally. But admitting that didn't seem like the best idea.

He hopped out of the SUV. She did the same and came around the front of the vehicle. Rett helped Sin into the driver's seat. He patted his phone in the breast pocket of his jacket. "It's all right here on the group calendar. Now, don't forget to let me know you got home okay."

"I will," she said. "Good night, Rett."

"'Night, Sin." He closed her door and watched her back out and drive up Hummingbird Way, back toward Main Street.

He'd be in town a couple more days. Then he'd head back to Charlotte and away from the woman who apparently still had a grip on his heart.

Chapter Thirteen

• — • — • — •

Garrett stretched and yawned, then poured himself a cup of coffee. He was exhausted from his day trip to Wilmington and the drive back last night.

"Good morning, sleepyhead." His grandmother hurried into the kitchen. "How are...oh my. You look like hell."

Rett cocked his head, one brow raised. "That's pretty harsh, Gram."

"Sorry, sweetheart, but you know I tell it like it is." She rubbed his back. "Now, tell me what's going on. Why couldn't you get any sleep last night?"

"How'd you know I couldn't sleep last night?"

"You know I'm a light sleeper. Had to be. Otherwise, I wouldnta heard you trying to sneak out of the house to hang out with those badass friends of yours." She clucked her tongue. "Thought you could get one over on Mama Mae, huh?"

Rett groaned. At one point, he'd entertained the idea that Mama Mae wasn't actually human and therefore didn't require sleep.

"Heard you tossing and turning all night. And I'm pretty sure you made yourself an entire meal at three in the morning." She chuckled. "Didn't know you still did that."

"I don't. Normally," he said. "And I didn't make an entire meal. I just had a taste for...pie." Even though the reference would mean nothing to Mama Mae, his cheeks burned, recalling Sin's seductive offer.

It was the right thing to do. It was the right thing to do. It was...

"What's got you so upset?" Mama Mae frowned. Her dark eyes were filled with concern. A look he'd seen more than he could recount over the years.

"It's nothing, Gram." Rett slid into the chair and gripped his cup.

He was thirty-seven years old. Too old to be whining to his eighty-two-year-old grandmother about the fact that he was still untethered and unsure of what he should be doing with his life. At his age, he should have it figured out.

Rett had stumbled into a great career; made good money and had a decent savings; and he owned a nice condo. He should either be content with his life or have a real plan to take it to the next level. Instead, he had a gnawing sense in his gut that he wasn't doing what he was meant to do and that he wasn't where he should be in his life.

"Sweetheart, whatever it is, you can talk to me about it." His grandmother squeezed his arm, shaking him from his daze. "You can tell me anything. That hasn't changed."

Rett nodded, relieved. He missed their long talks. "Okay. But can I get you some coffee? Maybe make you breakfast?"

"I ate," she said. "But why don't I make you some grits, eggs, and bacon while you talk?"

Mama Mae hadn't forgotten any of her old tricks. When he was younger, she'd discovered he'd been more at ease talking about difficult subjects if he didn't have to stare her in the face. So she'd get the conversation started then set about the work of cooking or cleaning. Sometimes she worked alone, but more often they worked side by side. That's when he'd been most comfortable.

"You know, I think I'd rather have hash browns than grits. I'll cut the potatoes and onions." He gulped down some coffee, then washed his hands at the sink.

Mama Mae smiled knowingly. She got the eggs, butter, and bacon out of the fridge while he retrieved the potatoes, onion, garlic, and bell peppers.

His grandmother turned on the oven and they moved silently in the cramped kitchen as they set everything up. Then they stood side by side at the counter—the only work surface in the narrow kitchen. Mama Mae lined the bacon up on a pan while he diced potatoes.

"All right now, Sonny. Spill it. I'm an old woman. I can't afford to take time for granted anymore." Mama Mae chuckled.

It was a joke. He got that. But he'd nearly cut his finger, suddenly struck by the reality that one day his grandmother—who'd had a large part in raising him—wouldn't be there. He felt a twinge of pain in his chest.

"Don't joke like that, Gram." Rett resumed dicing the potatoes. "We both know you're gonna outlive me and my kids."

"And exactly *when* should I expect these hypothetical children?" Mama Mae turned toward him, one brow cocked.

"A subject we're not going to discuss again," he said firmly.

Mama Mae clucked her tongue, then washed her hands before pulling out a mixing bowl and setting the frying pan on the stove.

"So what are we discussing? Whatever it is, it's weighing

on you heavily." Deep lines creased Mama Mae's forehead. "Is this about Sinclair?"

"No, ma'am. Why would you think it's about Sinclair?" His face was inexplicably hot.

"Seemed like there was a vibe between you two." She shrugged.

There were a myriad of concerns floating around in his head about his relationship with Sinclair. But he definitely wasn't prepared to have that conversation with his grandmother. Besides, what would be the point? He was into Sinclair, and maybe Sin was into him. But he had no intention of moving back to Holly Grove Island, and he was pretty sure Sinclair had no intentions of ever leaving. What was there to discuss?

The last thing he wanted to do was revive Annamae Davenport's matchmaking attempts. Things were complicated enough between him and Sin.

"That isn't what I wanted to talk to you about," Rett assured her.

"And how did your little trip go?" Mama Mae asked.

"It went well." Rett dumped the diced potato into a bowl, then started cutting another. "Sin was right, it was worth the drive."

"I told you she's usually right." His grandmother cackled as she cracked eggs in a bowl. "So if it isn't Sinclair, what's bothering you?"

"It's about my job."

"I thought everything was going well."

"It is," he assured her. "And I intend to stay in the real estate field. But it feels…I don't know…too easy at this point. I'm ready for a change." He put the last of the potatoes in the bowl and started slicing the onion.

"You've had just about every job there is." Mama Mae chuckled as she poured a little milk into the bowl and beat the eggs. "What kind of change are you looking for this time?"

"I know I have a history of being easily bored with jobs." It was something he'd only recently learned was common for adults like himself with ADHD and dyslexia, which had both gone undiagnosed in childhood. He'd come to terms with that, leaned into it, and made it work for him. The Ritalin prescription hadn't hurt either. "But this isn't me wanting to move on because I'm bored. I'm not just looking for a job that's more exciting. I guess I'm looking for something more challenging and fulfilling."

He'd always considered work as simply a means to an end. It was what he had to do to fund the lifestyle he wanted to enjoy. But for the past several years, he'd had a career he actually enjoyed. He still did. But it didn't feel as challenging as it once had.

"I can certainly understand that." Mama Mae nodded thoughtfully. "But the work you do is important, sweetheart. And you're good at it."

"I know it is, Gram. And I enjoy working in real estate. But a few years ago, I started volunteering on projects for Habitat for Humanity."

"Now that's a worthy cause." Mama Mae wagged a finger, smiling.

"It is. But it also made me feel connected to my dad in a way I haven't in a long time." Rett frowned. Memories of his father seemed to be fading a little more each day, and he couldn't help feeling guilty about it. "It also made me realize I'd gone a little soft." Rett chuckled, hoping to lift the mood. "Working on those projects kicked my ass, but it also gave me a purpose. I was telling a friend about it. That's when he told me about the work he's been doing renovating run-down properties—"

"Gentrification, you mean." Mama Mae folded her arms and gave him the evil eye.

"Hold on now, Gram." Rett held up a hand. "The reason I found this opportunity exciting is because they are conscious of doing a mix of projects that include affordable, single-family homes, as well as high-end projects."

Mama Mae nodded approvingly. "All right then. Tell me more about this opportunity."

"Well…" Garrett scratched his chin, delaying the inevitable. "My friend's brokerage is in Charleston. I'd collaborate on a few renovation and resale real estate projects with my friend and a few other investors."

"It does sound like a wonderful opportunity, honey. But I was hoping you'd be moving closer to home, not farther away." Mama Mae frowned.

"The drive to Charleston is just a couple hours longer," Rett noted. "And since I'd also given some thought to moving to the Bay Area, I figured Charleston was a better choice."

"*California*? Sweetheart, that's a world away."

"I know." He diced the green bell pepper. "Which made it an exciting possibility until I came back here and…" Rett paused, unsure of how to put into words the uncertainty plaguing him since his return.

He'd enjoyed vacationing on the West Coast, but he didn't like being so far from his grandmother. On the other hand, the opportunity Evan was offering in Charleston would provide the challenge he'd been longing for, a way to reconnect with his dad's memory, increased income potential in a great location, and he'd still be a relatively easy drive away from his mother and grandmother. Which made it a win all around.

So why was he still hesitant to accept his friend's offer?

Mama Mae's eyes brightened. "Sounds like my boy is missing home after all."

"I guess I have." The realization surprised Garrett. After all, he visited town regularly. But he hadn't reconnected with the townsfolk the way he had this past week. "For the first time since I left, I guess I'm feeling a little homesick. Ridiculous at my age, right?"

"No, sweetheart, it isn't. We're never too old to miss home or the people we love." Her smile deepened. "I'm sure it has a lot to do with Dexter and Dakota putting down roots here and you spending time with Sinclair." His grandmother chuckled. "Looks like the old gang is back together and you've got a bad case of FOMO."

"FOMO?" Rett diced the red bell pepper.

"Fear of missing out." She shook her head. "You *are* old."

Next, she'd be using text message speak. But Gram, who still relished her stories of seeing Santana, Sly & The Family Stone, and Jimi Hendrix perform at Woodstock, had always been far hipper than he was.

"Fear of missing out, huh?" He considered it. "Maybe. I've enjoyed hanging out with them these past few months."

"Dexter and Dakota are family," she said. "And Sin evidently means more to you than you realized."

"What makes you say that?" The question sounded more defensive once he'd said it aloud than it had in his head. Rett focused on cutting the bell pepper and avoiding Mama Mae's amused look.

"You've been hanging out with Dex and Dakota for months. Then you start spending time with Sinclair this week, and suddenly you're homesick. Don't take a rocket scientist to figure that one out, hon." Mama Mae grinned.

"I think it has more to do with the time I've been

spending with you, my mom, Hector, and Izzy—whenever she's around."

"I worry about your sister." His grandmother's tone was grave. "I think she misses her big brother, among other things."

"Judging by the way she's been dodging me? I doubt it." Rett tossed the remaining bell pepper into the large metal bowl then splashed some olive oil over the contents. Mama Mae added her favorite seasonings. "We both know I've been a lousy brother."

"Then I guess you have another reason to hang around." Mama Mae pointed a finger at him. "You're the one who broke the relationship, it's up to you to fix it."

Rett groaned. Mama Mae was right, of course.

He'd been a preoccupied teenager who hadn't had time for an annoying baby sister. By the time he moved closer to home and had come to regret not having a relationship with his younger sister, Izzy was an uninterested teenager who had zero interest in getting to know him.

Now, they were in relationship purgatory, and he had no idea how to escape.

"I promise to try." Rett spread the potato and vegetable mixture out onto a sheet pan. "But you know how Izzy is with me. I've tried talking to her. She insists everything is fine."

"Humph. You know what that word *really* means." Mama Mae raised one of her sparse eyebrows, barely hanging on after a lifetime of being plucked to death.

"Freaked-out, insecure, neurotic, and emotional." Rett's grandmother did love a good Donald Sutherland movie. Especially *The Italian Job*. "You're sure something is up with Iz?"

"As sure as I am that you're still smitten with Sinclair." Mama Mae flashed a knowing smirk.

Rett didn't have the bandwidth to argue the point. Instead, he put the potatoes in the oven and set the timer. He refilled his coffee cup, adding cream and sugar, then sat down.

"About your work problem..." Mama Mae seemed to realize he needed a reprieve from discussing Sinclair and Izzy. "You're really excited about the idea of doing renovation work—like your dad did, huh?"

Rett grinned, thinking of how much he'd enjoyed helping his father out with home reno projects. "I really am."

"Hmm..." He could see the wheels turning in his grandmother's head. "Well, it's a big decision. Why don't you take some time off, and stay here a few more weeks while you think things through? I'd hate to see you make a decision you'll regret."

"Me, too." He'd made plenty of bad choices in his life. But he'd like to think he'd matured beyond that. After all, he'd mustered the willpower to turn down Sin's invitation *twice*. "But avoiding the issue isn't the answer."

"Until you're settled in spirit, you'll never settle down and find the woman who's going to turn your world upside down. I want that for you, Rett. I was lucky enough to have that with your grandfather, may he rest in peace. Your mother has that with Hector. And it's what I pray you'll get to experience, too. Because you deserve that kind of love, sweetheart."

"You're the most important woman in my life, Gram. And I'm just fine with that."

"I promise not to tell your mother." Mama Mae smiled softly, then sighed. "I'm touched, but we both know I won't always be around. I don't want to leave this earth worried you'll end your days alone... like your father."

There was pain in his grandmother's voice that she

didn't often reveal when it came to the two men she'd lost in her life: her husband and her only son.

"I'll figure it out eventually, Gram. I always do," he assured her.

She nodded, but there was something in Annamae Davenport's determined eyes that indicated there was a plot brewing in that sharp mind of hers. He only hoped it wouldn't turn his world upside down.

Chapter Fourteen

———◆———

Always the bridesmaid, and never the bride.

It was a good thing Sinclair Buchanan looked good in all manner of bridesmaid dresses, because she had a closet full of them.

Sin sighed quietly as she stood in the middle of Beautiful Beginnings Bridal Shop. Longtime resident Gladys Drake and her family had opened the charming little boutique on Holly Grove Island a few months ago. The shop was set in what had once been a dry cleaner just off Main Street. The Drakes had renovated and modernized the space. Now the lovely little shop was overflowing with bridal gowns, bridesmaid dresses, mother-of-the-bride gowns, and countless accessories.

Sin regarded the two bridesmaids' dresses her best friend held up: one in periwinkle blue, the other in sage green. She and Dakota had spent the past hour carefully combing through the racks of bridesmaid dresses at the shop after beginning their Saturday morning adventure with breakfast at Lila's Café.

"Periwinkle is a beautiful color." Sin chose her response carefully.

Dakota scrunched her nose and narrowed her dark brown eyes. "You don't like it."

"It's a nice dress," Sin countered. "You know I'd never let my best friend pick something awful for her wedding."

"But you like that dress better." Dakota nodded toward the gorgeous lavender gown on the mannequin.

"Was I that obvious?" Sin glanced longingly at the one-shoulder dress. "I *really* tried not to be."

"And it was a valiant effort." Dakota handed the two dresses she was holding over to Calista—Gladys's youngest daughter. She slipped her arm through Sin's as they stood in front of the mannequin, admiring the dress. "But you are my best friend."

Sin leaned her head against Dakota's. After so many years apart, it felt good to have her best friend back.

"It is a stunning dress," Sin said. "But so are both of the dresses you picked."

"Then there's only one way to settle it." Dakota turned to Calista. "Sin here is going to give us a little fashion show."

"Perfect." Calista beamed. "I'll meet you over at the dressing rooms with all three selections."

"And I have a few gowns in mind that would look absolutely stunning on you, Dakota." Ms. Gladys emerged from the backroom, where she'd retreated after her last client.

"I'm not really looking for my dress today, Ms. Gladys," Dakota reminded the woman.

"I know." Ms. Gladys shrugged. "But since Sinclair here will be trying on dresses anyway, what's the harm?"

"C'mon." Sin shoved Dakota's shoulder. "Don't make me play dress-up alone. It'll be fun."

"You know I already have a bridal dress appointment," Dakota whispered to Sin.

"I know," Sin whispered back, both of them still smiling

for the sake of the shop owners. "But even if you hate them, this will give you a sense of what you like and what you don't."

"Fine. I'll try them," Dakota said.

"Very good." Ms. Gladys nodded. "Calista, let me show you the gowns I have in mind."

Dakota's heart had been set on visiting the bridal shop in Atlanta from her favorite reality show, which followed soon-to-be brides as they found their perfect wedding dress. But with the shortened timeline, it wasn't possible. So they'd made an appointment at a storied bridal shop in Charleston, South Carolina, the following weekend.

"Now, are we going to talk about your late-night adventures with Rett?" Dakota asked casually as she surveyed a wall of teardrop and sunburst earrings, pearl necklaces, crystal tiaras, sparkly belts, and a host of other bridal accessories.

Sin dropped the string of pearls in her hand. They clattered against the base of the jewelry display. She picked up the pearls and returned them to the rack, only to knock another necklace off the rack. Sin cursed under her breath, then retrieved that necklace, too.

"Wow. That good, huh?" Dakota folded her arms, her eyes dancing with amusement. "Apparently Rett Davenport has you completely discombobulated."

"I am not discom...whatever you just said," Sinclair argued, trying to ignore the fluttering in her belly. Why did the very mention of Rett's name make her feel... guilty?

Probably because it felt like her best friend could just look right at her and determine that she'd kissed Rett *twice* last night.

"What's there to talk about?" Sin shrugged. "We visited

the wedding venue and got some great ideas. We ate some excellent food. I had this amazing drink made with peach vodka, Cointreau, blueberry, and citrus."

"*And*?" Dakota hiked an eyebrow. "You've been squirrelly all morning about your trip. Which leads me to believe there's *a lot* more to the story."

"I ran into Teddy at the farmers market." Sin said the words so quickly she needed to catch her breath afterward.

"Teddy Walker, your ex?" Dakota's eyes widened, and she pressed a hand to her chest. When Sin nodded in confirmation, Dakota wrapped her in a tight hug. "Oh, honey, I'm so sorry. What happened?"

Dakota hadn't been in town when Sin and Teddy had dated, but she knew Teddy from high school. And Sin had told her friend about the relationship and the debacle with Gwen.

"I stood there in the middle of the farmers market, frozen. I couldn't think, I couldn't speak." Sin ran her fingers through her hair. "I thought I was over what happened, but seeing them together..." Sin swallowed back the building emotion. "Teddy, Gwen, and their three kids looked like one of those glossy magazine ads with the picture-perfect family come to life. Right down to the oldest boy's snaggletooth."

"Sweetie, I'm so sorry." Dakota slipped her arm through Sin's and led her toward the dressing area. They sat down on the sofa intended for friends and families of the brides. "So neither of you spoke?"

"When Teddy asked what I was doing there, I snapped. I reminded him it was a public place. But before I could embarrass myself too badly, Rett came to my rescue." An involuntary smile curved Sin's mouth when she thought of how Rett had swooped in to save the day.

"You're kidding?" Dakota was clearly amused. "What did he do?"

"My mind had gone completely blank, and I'd forgotten Rett was there. But he could see I was on the edge of losing it. He slips his arm around my waist and says in the deepest, sexiest voice imaginable, 'Hey, babe. Introduce me to your friends?'"

They both fell out giggling as Sin imitated Rett's deep voice and laid-back demeanor.

Finally, Dakota stopped laughing long enough to catch her breath. She wiped away tears. "Does Rett not remember Teddy?"

"He does, and not fondly." Sin grinned. "We both got a kick out of Teddy's bruised ego when Rett pretended he had no idea who he was."

"I'm glad he was there." Dakota squeezed Sin's arm.

"Me, too," Sin admitted reluctantly. "And not just because of what happened with Teddy."

Sin explained how Rett had saved her from being run down by a car and how he'd insisted on treating her to dinner. That he'd helped her get her head back on straight after the shock of encountering her ex and former friend. That he'd been great company and a perfect gentleman the entire evening.

She didn't mention the kisses or their past history. There was no reason to. Nothing had happened last night, and nothing would happen going forward.

Rett had been right to turn her down. Yes, it would've been fun. But then things would have been even weirder between them.

It was better if they both pretended those kisses hadn't happened. Instead, it would be business as usual between the two former hate crushes who weren't quite friends.

"I'm shaking right now just thinking about how close I came to losing my best friend again." Dakota hugged Sin tightly. "Thank God Rett was there."

Yes, indeed.

"I shouldn't have mentioned it. We can't be upsetting our little munchkin." Sin smiled.

"No, we can't." Dakota placed a hand over her still-flat belly and glanced around to make sure neither Ms. Gladys nor Calista were within earshot. "I still can't believe we're having a baby. That I'm going to be a mom."

The light in her best friend's eyes dimmed, and Sin knew exactly what she was thinking.

"I wish your mom was here, too," Sin said. "I know it's not the same thing, but we're all here for anything you need, Dakota. Everything is going to be fine. I promise."

Dakota offered her a smile that didn't quite reach her eyes. "Thanks, Sin."

Calista swept into the dressing area, both arms laden with garments, apologizing for taking so long. "These are for you." She hung the periwinkle, sage-green, and lavender bridesmaids' dresses in one dressing room for Sin.

"And these are for our beautiful bride-to-be." Ms. Gladys carried the bridal gowns with almost a sense of reverence. She hung a white ball gown, a cream-colored trumpet silhouette dress, and an A-line dress in a pale shade of peach in Dakota's dressing room.

"I know these two aren't traditional colors." Calista laughed when Dakota and Sin exchanged curious looks. "But both colors have become increasingly popular with brides."

"I hand selected these gowns for you, Dakota," Ms. Gladys said proudly. "The cream and peach will look lovely against your skin. You're going to love them once you give them a try."

"Thank you, Ms. Gladys." Dakota smiled politely at both women.

"Did you see those colors?" Dakota whispered once the women walked away.

Sin stood, pulling her friend to her feet. "If I have to try on three colors, so do you."

"Fine. But baby bump or no, I'm strutting down that aisle in a *white* dress." Dakota pointed emphatically.

"Take it easy, mama bear." Sinclair giggled. "No one is gonna make you wear anything you don't want to."

Sin tried on the periwinkle dress first, then helped Dakota get into the white confection of a ball gown.

Dakota stepped onto the fitting platform and frowned. "It was pretty on the hanger. On me...not so much."

"It looks like it's trying to swallow you," Sin said, and they both giggled. Sin twirled. "What do you think?"

"It's...nice. But we can do better," Dakota said.

"Change clothes!" They both sang the hook to the Jay-Z song and laughed. In high school, they'd often responded to each other with song lyrics. Something they'd started doing again since they'd renewed their friendship.

Sin tried on the sage-green dress next and Dakota tried on the cream-colored trumpet silhouette gown. Both were better, but still not quite right.

"I don't love the dress, but I do like this color." Dakota smoothed her hands over the silky cream-colored fabric.

"That color does look good on you," Sin admitted. "Makes me wonder what you'd look like in that last dress. The one you planned on skipping."

"Fine. I'll try it on," Dakota said. "On one condition."

"What?"

"Tell me what's *really* going on between you and Rett."
Dakota folded her arms.

Sin's face went white hot, her cheeks burning.

"I knew something was up." Dakota shook a finger.
"The vibe between you and Rett at the party was all high
school hate crush 2.0. But he *insisted* on helping with the
planning, and the two of you have been seeing a lot of each
other. Then there's the way you were blushing, and your
eyes got all dreamy when you talked about Rett earlier.
What's going on? Spill, lady. *Now*."

"Geez. Isn't it too early for your hormones to be spik-
ing?" Sin walked into her dressing room and pulled the
curtain closed.

"You haven't seen hormones yet, sweetie." Dakota swept
the curtain aside just as Sin was unzipping the dress. "This
is only the beginning. And don't think I won't squeeze
my growing ass into that tiny dressing room with you
because I will."

"Okay, all right." Sin huffed. "I'll tell you…after you
go back to your dressing room."

Dakota smiled triumphantly, then closed the curtain.
She returned to the dressing room beside Sin's. "Okay.
Let's hear it."

Sin returned the sage-green dress to its hanger. "Last
night, I kissed Rett. Twice."

"Seriously?" The excitement in Dakota's voice was kind
of adorable. Too bad she'd have to disappoint her friend by
telling her nothing would come of it.

"Yes. I may also have suggested that we get a hotel
room in Wilmington."

"You did not!" Dakota returned to Sin's dressing room,
practically bouncing on her heels.

"I did." Sin still couldn't believe she'd done it. Or that Rett had turned her down.

"What did you say was in that drink again?" Dakota asked.

"I wasn't drunk," Sin said. "Honestly. But Rett turned me down anyway."

Dakota's eyes widened. "You're kidding?"

"I'm not." Sin stepped into the lavender dress, turning so her friend could zip her up.

"That was gentlemanly of him." Dakota zipped Sin's dress, sounding surprised.

"He said he realized how upsetting the day had been, and he didn't think I was in the right state of mind. He was afraid I'd regret it."

"Rett made the responsible decision. Maybe it would've been different if you two had been together before but—"

Sin's skin flushed, her face suddenly hot as she averted her gaze from her best friend's. She lowered her chin to her chest as she smoothed the fabric over her hips, then turned around. "What do you think?"

"About the dress? Excellent choice." Dakota leaned forward, her voice lowered. " About Rett? I think you two have been together, haven't you?"

Sin swallowed hard, her heart racing. Did she owe Dakota an accounting of what had happened between her and Rett last night, five years ago, or that night in high school?

Absolutely not.

But when Dakota and Dex had gone on that business trip to New England, Sin had pressed her friend about what had happened between her and Dexter. It would be pretty damn hypocritical of her to be upset with Dakota for prying when Sinclair had practically perfected the art of being all up in other folks' business.

So she told her friend the truth about *everything*.

Dakota stood there blinking, staring at her in disbelief.

"I can't believe you didn't tell me this." She slapped Sin's arm.

Sin rubbed at the stinging skin. "I kept my part of the bargain, now it's your turn. Try on the next dress."

Dakota grumbled as she returned to her dressing room to try on the peach wedding dress. Sin sat on the little sofa outside the dressing rooms, patiently waiting for her friend to change.

"I always told you that you and Rett would make a great couple." Dakota's voice was muffled. Presumably by the fabric of one dress or the other.

"And this is why I never told you," Sin interjected.

"You realize that all that bickering between you two in high school was just immature foreplay, right?" Dakota laughed.

"I'm not denying the attraction," Sin said. "But what happened that night was just two single adults blowing off a little steam. Nothing serious."

"You sure about that?" Dakota peeked her head through the curtain. "Because what I saw in your eyes a few minutes ago had *serious* written all over it."

"Yes, I'm sure." Sin ran her fingers through her hair, tugging it over the shoulder bared by the dress.

"You two have a lot in common." Dakota's voice wafted above the curtain.

"We're both real estate agents," Sin conceded. "The list pretty much ends there."

"You're ambitious, independent, impatient. Rett's adventurous, creative, and strong-willed. You're opposite sides of the same coin. I can't believe you can't see…"

Dakota's voice went silent.

"Dakota, are you okay in there?"

Her friend's response was delayed, and Sin heard sniffling. "Yes, I'm fine. I just..."

Sin stood, her heart beating faster. "Kota, you're scaring me, sweetie. What's wrong?"

Dakota swept aside the curtain and stepped out wearing the pale peach gown. Her friends' eyes were teary as she took her place on the platform in front of Sin.

"Oh my God, Dakota." Sin pressed her fingers to her lips, her heart swelling with happiness for her friend. "That dress. You look—"

"I know, right?" Dakota sniffled. "So it isn't just in my head. This dress is actually—"

"*The one*." Sin's eyes welled with tears as she choked up seeing her friend in the dress.

The pale peach color was stunning against Dakota's dark brown skin. The high waist and A-line silhouette complemented her hourglass figure, and it would easily accommodate the growth of her belly over the next six weeks.

"Oh, honey." Sin's voice broke and tears leaked from the corners of her eyes. "You look exquisite. Do you love it, too?"

"I honestly can't believe how perfect this dress is. The shape, the design, the fit, the color...I love *everything* about it." Dakota stared at her reflection in the mirror. Tears wet her cheeks as she smoothed her hands down the voluminous satin skirt. "You know this town better than anyone, Sin. Will it be a scandal if I wear a color other than white or off-white?"

"Sweetheart, that dress is gonna have folks talkin', all right. But for all the right reasons, because you're gonna be a showstopper," Sin assured her friend. "And anyone who can't see what a perfect choice this dress is, is not someone you wanna be takin' fashion advice from."

"Leave it to you to put things in perspective." Dakota swiped a finger beneath her eyes, and laughed. She turned sideways and studied herself in profile. She arched her back and rubbed a hand over her belly. "It'll still look good if I've exploded by then, and I'm waddling like a penguin, right?"

"Sweetie, you'd look amazing in that dress no matter what. I promise you."

Dakota studied herself in the mirror. "Do you think Dexter will like it?"

"Dexter is gonna love it, hon." Sin's eyes pricked with tears again and her voice wavered. Her chest welled with emotion just imagining Dexter seeing the love of his life in this dress for the first time. "Because he loves you and this little one more than *anything* in the world. He's been waiting his whole life to marry you."

Sin sniffled and squeezed her friend's hand, both of them emotional. "Now, the only question you need to answer is this: is this dress *the one*?"

Dakota nodded with a smile. "It is. It's absolutely perfect."

They both laughed and Calista handed them tissues so they could dry their tears.

"I told you." Ms. Gladys's dark eyes twinkled. "You look so amazing in this dress. Like it was meant for you." The older woman squeezed Dakota's hand and patted it before going to greet customers who'd just stepped inside the shop.

"Now that we've found the dress, let's find the right accessories," Sin said. "I'm getting a Princess Tiana vibe from this dress. What do you think of a tiara?"

"Let's try it," Dakota said. "But let's also try a traditional veil and something a little more bohemian, like a flower crown. I've always wanted to try one of those."

"You've got it, babe. I'll be right back." Sin made her way toward the wall of wedding accessories, her heart bursting with joy.

Dakota deserved this, and Sin was truly happy for her. But the tiniest hint of envy lodged in her gut, and she hated herself for thinking that way. Maybe she was still in shock over running into Teddy and Gwen flaunting their brood and their stupid marital bliss. But a little voice at the back of her head wondered if she would ever be the one standing on the platform, preparing to marry the love of her life.

Chapter Fifteen

•◆•

W hat do you think?" Rett asked his cousin, who stood in front of a mirror at the tux shop. Though, honestly, there was no need to ask. Dexter's narrowed eyes and pursed lips conveyed his sentiments well enough.

"I don't like it." Dexter turned to the side in the mirror and craned his neck to see the back of the tux. "Actually, that doesn't begin to express my utter hatred of this look."

"You're not a tails kind of guy." Rett shrugged. "It's not the end of the world. There are dozens of other styles of tuxedos here that don't include an unnecessary appendage."

Dexter dragged a hand across his forehead. He turned to Rett. "But this is Dakota's day, right? I mean, it would only be for a few hours. It's not like I'd have to wear the thing to work every day for the rest of my life."

"It is her day." Rett nodded, then poked a finger into his cousin's chest. "But it's your day, too. And while you might only be wearing that thing for a few hours, the photos and video will last a lifetime. Trust me on this."

Rett chuckled when Dex's eyes went wide and he frowned.

"Relax, cuz. Kota wouldn't want you to spend your special day wearing anything you don't feel comfortable in. Besides, I'll bet the tails were Sin's idea. So I'm calling an audible."

"What do you have in mind?" Dex folded his arms.

The salesclerk approached them with a wide smile. "I brought you a selection of cummerbunds to—"

"Definitely *not* those." Rett held up his open palm, halting the guy midsentence.

"Agreed. And for the record, cummerbunds *definitely* feel like a Sinclair kind of thing." Dex chuckled.

"But when Miss Buchanan made the appointment, she was quite clear, sir. There are supposed to be cummerbunds. She provided specific instructions about the width and possible color selections." The man seemed terrified of running afoul of *Miss Buchanan*.

Rett couldn't help chuckling about that. He also couldn't help imagining *Miss Buchanan* standing in front of him in the thigh-high stockings and garter belt she'd worn that night five years ago, threatening to punish him for being a very bad boy.

Geez. Rett pressed a palm to his forehead. *Get out of my fucking head, Sin.*

"What?" Dex asked.

Shit. Had he said that aloud?

"No cummerbunds. Period." Rett cleared his throat and ignored the outraged look on the clerk's face. "Now. Close your eyes. Envision your ideal wedding tuxedo."

Dexter raised an eyebrow and frowned.

"Just try it, D. Everyone will be happy in the end, I promise."

"Okay…" Dex propped his chin on one fist. "If it were totally up to me…"

Dexter rattled off his short, simple list of must-haves for his ideal wedding tuxedo. The salesclerk set the cummerbunds down, pulled a pad and pen from his pocket, and took notes.

"That sounds magnificent," the clerk said. His eyes roamed the small tuxedo shop, then his gaze settled on one rack. "You can take that one off. I'll bring a couple of options to try."

"Perfect." Rett clapped his hands, startling the man. "And you let me worry about Miss Buchanan." He winked. "I promise to take the L for this, if it goes sideways. But I'm counting on a win here."

"Yes, sir." The man walked toward the rack of tuxedos and Dexter returned to the dressing room.

Rett parked himself on a small sofa.

"Part of me still can't believe we're shopping for tuxedos for your wedding and that you're going to be a dad. Where did the time go?" Rett asked.

"I know we're approaching forty. But it feels like just yesterday when we were hanging out at the beach as kids, imagining what our lives would be like," Dex said through the dressing room curtain.

"Even then, you knew you wanted to be with Dakota. That you wanted to have a family with her. After all you two have been through, how does it feel now that it's all coming full circle?"

"Amazing and...terrifying." Dex chuckled. "Not the part about getting married. The part about being a dad. Don't get me wrong, we both *really* want this baby. But I lay awake at night thinking about all the things that could go wrong."

"Nothing is going to go wrong," Rett said.

He shouldn't promise things he had no control over. He

strictly held to that in his business life. But if he could, he'd sacrifice his own life to ensure Dakota and their baby would be all right. Because Dexter and Dakota meant that much to him. But all he really could do was be there to support his cousin. And right now, blind assurance was what Dexter needed.

"And when the baby comes, we're going to have this tiny little human who'll be completely reliant upon us not to screw up their lives." Dex sighed, as if the weight of the world had been placed upon his shoulders. His anxiety was palpable, even through the heavy curtain.

"What if I suck at this dad thing? I mean, I love my father, and he was a solid parent. But we both know he isn't going to win any father-of-the-year awards. What if my kid feels the same about me?" Dex poked his head through the curtain. "Or worse, what if my kid hates me?"

"First, it's an unwritten law of the universe that every teenager hates their parents at some point in their lives. So we can't deprive the kid of his universal right." Rett gave his cousin a teasing half smile. "Second, you're going to be an amazing dad. I have no doubt about that."

"I'm grateful for your unswerving confidence, and don't think I'm not excited about the baby, because I am. But did you know Black women are more likely to suffer complications during childbirth? Our age compounds those likelihoods."

Rett was starting to worry Dex might hyperventilate in the dressing room. "No, I didn't know. But I do know you're the kind of guy who's going to do everything in your power to ensure Dakota and the baby get the best care possible. And I know that we'll all be here to support you in that. So stop attracting all this negative energy to your aura, man."

Dex's mouth curved in an amused half grin. "When'd you get so...new age?"

"Since I dated a woman who owned a yoga studio." Rett chuckled. "But right now, we're not talking about me."

"Here you are, sir. I believe these tuxedos fit your description." Jim, the salesclerk, hung two gray tuxedos on the hook inside Dexter's dressing room.

Dexter tried on the charcoal gray first. It was nice, but not enough to make Dakota and Sin overlook the fact that they'd ditched the tails.

"Try the other one." Rett hoped it would be a winner. Otherwise, he'd have Sin and Dakota ready to tan his hide. Though the image of Sin in that garter belt holding a crop...He shuddered and loosened his collar because suddenly it was hot in the little shop.

"C'mon, pal. We have a whole-ass outfit to put together before we meet the girls for a late lunch, and I, for one, am absolutely..." Rett's words trailed off when his cousin stepped out of the dressing room. "Wow." Rett folded his arms and tilted his head. "That one looks good. Much better than the Mr. Belvedere number the girls picked out."

Dexter faced the mirror. He straightened the collar of the shirt and smoothed down the jacket's lapels. "I like this one, too. But since I'm chucking the bow tie and wearing a regular necktie, it won't look too casual, will it?"

"I don't think so." Rett rubbed his bearded chin. "But maybe Jim can help with that." They both turned to the clerk. "Any ideas?"

"As a matter of fact, yes," the man said. "Let me pull a few things together."

"See? What did I tell you? The tux situation is working out fine." Rett dusted a stray thread off Dexter's shoulder, then clapped a hand on his back. "Everything will work out fine with the baby, too. You're so optimistic when it comes to everyone else. Hell, you had faith in me when just about no one else in my life did."

It surprised Rett that he was getting a little choked up thinking of that period in his life and what a staunch advocate his cousin had been for him. When things seemed to be at their darkest, Dexter had always been in his corner, believing in Rett, even when he hadn't believed in himself. He'd never be able to repay Dex for everything he'd done for him. But he wouldn't stop trying to, either.

"That goes both ways, cuz." Dex's warm smile was reflected in the mirror they both faced.

Somehow, it lessened the weirdness of the deeply emotional moment.

"Then believe me when I say this whole husband and father thing…you're gonna knock this shit out of the park. I'm talking Hank Aaron greatness here." Rett elbowed his cousin, and it seemed to ease the tension in Dexter's shoulders.

"Okay, but if we're going strictly by home run stats, Josh Gibson's numbers are even better," Dex said as he eyed himself in the mirror. "Unfortunately, he died a few months before Jackie Robinson broke the color barrier in the major leagues. But he was an absolute monster in the Negro Leagues."

"Fine. You'll be the Hank Aaron, Jackie Robinson, and Josh Gibson of dads. How's that?" He raised a palm, and his cousin slapped it.

"That's one hell of a father," Dex said. "You really think I can live up to that?"

"What do you wish your kid knew right now?" Rett turned to Dexter.

Dex turned toward him, a wistful expression on his

face. "I'd want my kid to know how much I love them and how much I love their mom. That we couldn't be more excited to have them in our lives. And that nothing is more important to me than being a good husband and father."

"Look at that." Rett's chest tightened. He couldn't help thinking of his own father and how much he still missed having him in his life. "You're already three times the father either of us had. This kid is damn lucky to have you for a dad."

Dex nodded his thanks and gripped Rett's shoulder before facing the mirror again. He lifted the pants legs, which were a little too long as he stood there in his socks. "So, how are things going with you and Sinclair?"

Vivid memories of his mouth gliding over Sinclair's, the lush feel of her lips, and her heavenly scent—something floral, lilies maybe, and a hint of passionflower—commandeered his brain. Rett cleared his throat and tugged at his collar, which suddenly felt too tight. "Surprisingly good so far, actually."

"Really? Because I'm pretty sure Sin was shooting laser beams from her eyeballs when you arrived late to the engagement party and she had to rearrange her agenda." Dex laughed.

"If she ever evolves to develop that capability, there are gonna be a lot of dead folks around this town." Rett laughed, too. "But seriously, we've made a concerted effort to bury the hatchet and work together for the sake of the two people we both love. In fact, things between us got better that night."

Dexter raised a brow in disbelief. "Really?"

"Honestly. We had a great day in Wilmington, and we actually managed to agree on a few things."

"I still can't believe Sin invited you to join her. She

could probably handle planning this wedding in her sleep."
Dexter eyed him suspiciously.

"She didn't exactly invite me. But we're supposed to be
working on this thing together, so I kind of—"

"Invited yourself." Dexter grinned. "And let me guess
whose idea it was to carpool."

"Okay, yeah, it was mine. Am I the only person on
this island who cares about the fate of this planet?" Rett's
face felt hot.

"C'mon, man, I live in the Outer Banks. With the sea
levels rising, you know I care about the environment. But
the more interesting question is when did *you* become
concerned about the environment? Around the time you
decided it would be best if you and Sin carpooled?"

"No," Rett said defensively, then admitted, "I dated a
marine biologist for a hot minute while she was in grad
school. But again, not the point."

Dexter went into a deep belly laugh that startled poor
Jim, who was gathering belts and shoes from an acces-
sory rack.

"What's so funny?" Rett demanded.

"You are." Dex wiped tears from his eyes and pointed a
finger. "You've got it *bad* for Sinclair. It's like high school
all over again but without the pimples."

"What are you talking about?" Rett didn't see what was
so funny.

"You've found every possible reason to be around Sin,
though you two claim to despise each other." Dex shook his
head. "You're both adults, man. If you're into Sin, *tell her.*"
He poked a finger in Rett's chest. "But do not, and I mean
do *not,* screw things up with her and ruin our wedding."

"It's not like I'm manufacturing reasons to be around
Sin," Rett countered, unamused. "My best friend fell in

love with her best friend. It's as simple as that. As for how we got along... Well, you know Sin. She has a way of burrowing beneath your skin and setting up shop. I don't even think she tries to do it. It's just how she is."

"And how is she, exactly?" Dex asked.

"Pushy, stubborn, single-minded." Rett counted each trait on his fingers for emphasis. "She *always* thinks she's right and never wants to concede."

"Kind of like you?" Dexter raised one eyebrow. "Yeah, I could definitely see how that would be annoying."

"Still not funny, dude." Rett gave his cousin his serious voice, but it only made Dex laugh more.

"Sounds like the perfect match, if you ask me." Dex shrugged. "Then again, I guess it would be kind of weird dating the female version of yourself."

"It's a good thing Dakota would kill me if I ruined that pretty face of yours before the wedding." Rett folded his arms and frowned. "Forget all those nice things I said about you. You're going to be a damn annoying dad."

"Annoying I can live with." Dexter grinned. "Can you live with not shooting your shot with Sinclair this time?"

Rett's eyes widened. He hadn't told Dexter about what had happened between him and Sin the night of the dance or five years ago. How could Dex possibly know he had regrets about not telling Sin how he felt about her back then?

Maybe for the same reason he could so easily read Dex. They were best friends, and they knew each other well. Maybe a little too well. Because the last thing he needed was more folks trying to get in his head.

"Look, even if I was interested in Sin, which I'm not saying I am, I'd probably have better luck dating a honey badger. Besides, I've been giving it a lot of thought and I'm considering relocating."

Dex's expression turned dead serious. "Where?"

"Charleston. Evan, the friend who got me into real estate, relocated down there a couple years ago. He's flipping houses down there with a few investors, and he's eager for me to join his team."

"When?" Dex frowned.

"Soon."

"Why?" Dex asked. "I thought things were going well in Charlotte."

"They are." Rett sank onto a chair, then shrugged. "But when Evan suggested adding renovation to the mix...it was the first time I've been excited about real estate in a long time."

"Sounds like an intriguing proposition," Dexter acknowledged. His brows furrowed and he rubbed the back of his neck. "But I was kind of hoping you'd be sticking around more, not moving farther away. Take on the role of Uncle Rett."

"Wouldn't I be Second Cousin Rett?" he teased. "Besides, you have two brothers who've already perfected the role of being an uncle."

"True, but you know you're more like a brother to me, Rett, and we've always been closer. My brothers are already married with kids of their own. Who else is gonna be the fun, forever bachelor uncle to my kids?"

They both laughed, but then an uncomfortable silence settled over them.

Moving back to Holly Grove Island had never been on Rett's list of things to do. But this extended trip home had made him aware of just how much he missed his family. And it had reminded him of all the reasons the island had been a great place to grow up.

The lengthier stay had permitted him time to visit some

of his old hangouts—like Lila's Café and Helene's Home-made ice cream parlor. And though it was too cold to swim, he'd gone for walks on the beach with his grand-mother. He'd forgotten how calming it was to sit and watch the waves. But Evan's offer to join him in Charleston was tempting, and Charleston was on the water, too. And it wasn't like he wouldn't come back to visit. He just wouldn't visit as often.

"Look, G, you know I'll support you, whatever you decide. But at some point, you need to ask yourself what it is that you're *really* in search of. Maybe if you're honest with your-self about that, you'll find what it is you're looking for."

His cousin meant well; maybe even had a valid point. But today was about Dex preparing for the next chapter in his life with Dakota. Not trying to diagnose why Rett had spent his entire life in search of something he'd probably never find. He wouldn't hijack this meaningful moment with his own bullshit. If he hadn't figured his life out by now, chances were he never would. Still, he couldn't get Mama Mae's words out of his head.

I don't want to leave this earth worried you'll end your days alone... like your father.

"Think about what I said." Dex squeezed his shoulder, then turned to Jim, who'd come over with a handful of accessories.

Dexter's advice echoed in Rett's head.

You're both adults, man. If you're into Sin, tell her.

He and Sin had gotten off to a rough start, but they'd ironed out the past and were in a much better place. He'd enjoyed his time with Sinclair, and he wouldn't mind spending more time with her. But Sin only seemed to want a repeat of that night in Raleigh: sex without commitment. Nothing more.

As much as he would enjoy the sex, experience had taught him that with Sin, that wouldn't be enough. Maybe that was the thing that scared him. The likelihood of being rejected by Sin if he leveled with her and with himself about wanting more than just sex.

"This is *exactly* the semiformal look I was hoping for," Dex said. "What do you think?"

Rett glanced up. He'd been so busy with his own thoughts he hadn't been paying attention to Dex and Jim.

Dexter was wearing a three-piece, pale gray suit with a white shirt and gray print tie.

"Great job, Jim." Rett stood and clapped his hands together as Dex stared into the mirror and straightened his tie. "That's definitely the one. It's *perfect*."

Dexter nodded. "Let's hope the girls agree."

Rett assured his cousin they would, then stepped onto the nearby platform so Jim could fit him for his matching suit. But he couldn't get Sinclair or Dexter's advice out of his head.

At some point, you need to ask yourself what it is that you're really in search of. Maybe if you're honest with yourself about that, you'll find what it is you're looking for.

Could it be that what he'd been looking for was someone he cared for enough to stop running?

Chapter Sixteen

———•◦•———

Sin pulled down Hummingbird Way and parked on the street a few doors from Mama Mae's little cottage. She was relieved Rett's car wasn't there. Yet, a tiny part of her wouldn't have minded seeing him again.

Rett had returned to Charlotte the day after they'd taken Dakota and Dexter for their wedding fittings. At first, she'd been furious that Rett hadn't been able to follow simple instructions and just get Dex fitted for one of the formal tuxedos she and Dakota had selected. But the moment Dakota had seen the photo, she'd had tears of joy, agreeing that the suit Dex selected felt much more like him. Like *them*.

Even Sin had to admit Dex looked good in the light gray, three-piece suit. In fact, he and Rett both did. So maybe Rett wasn't half-bad at this whole co-planning thing, after all.

Sin got out of the SUV with her portfolio in hand and approached the house, as she would with any other prospective client. She made note of items that required attention if Mama Mae was serious about putting her house on the market. The driveway needed to be repaved, the clapboard needed repainting, and the front gutters had to be replaced. The little deck at the back of the house had a few boards that needed to be replaced, and the entire deck needed to be restained.

Mama Mae had a lovely garden. But investing in new landscaping would enhance the house's curb appeal.

Finally, she rang the front doorbell.

"Sinclair! I'm so glad you could come today." Mama Mae welcomed her with a warm hug. "Come on in. Can I get you some coffee or tea?"

"Tea, please. The kind you gave me last time would be wonderful." Sin removed her shoes, then followed the older woman inside the house. Classic soul music drifted from an old speaker. And Sin's stomach rumbled in response to the mingling of savory scents. "It smells good in here. You've been cooking up a storm."

"I was hoping you'd join me for dinner," Mama Mae said. "It's the least I could do."

"I hope you didn't go to all of this trouble for me."

"It was no trouble, sweetheart. You know how much I love to feed folks. We have that in common. But I don't have much of anyone to cook for these days." The older woman's voice wavered and the sadness behind her smile broke Sinclair's heart.

Will that be me one day? Loving to cook but having no one in my life to cook for?

"It would be lovely to have your company." Mama Mae smiled.

Sin had looked forward to going home and finally getting off her feet after a long day of showing a few properties on a nearby island. She'd planned to eat leftovers while bingeing episodes of *Schitt's Creek*. But being treated to a hot, home-cooked meal sounded much better.

Besides, Mama Mae would be disappointed if she turned down her offer after all the trouble the woman had gone to. Sin liked Rett's grandmother. It would be nice to spend a couple hours with her. She could watch television alone on her sofa any other night.

"I'd love to stay for dinner. But first, I need to earn my keep. Is it okay if I do a walkthrough and make some notes?"

"Go right ahead, sweetheart."

"Is any room out of bounds?" She'd had her share of surprises when she hadn't asked that question.

"Not at all. You need to know what you're working with, right?" Mama Mae grinned.

"And you're sure Rett won't be upset that you want me to list your house?"

"It's like you said, Sinclair, real estate is local. Besides, this is business, and you're the top seller around here. If we decide to move forward, trust me, Rett will be onboard with the deal." Mama Mae squeezed her hand. "I need to finish up in the kitchen. Call me if you need anything."

Mama Mae cranked up the stereo as Al Green crooned the opening bars of "Love and Happiness."

Sin couldn't believe Rett would be happy about the news. But she'd tried politely ignoring Mama Mae's requests to consider listing her cottage. The older woman was nothing if not persistent. She'd called Sin's broker, Doug, and requested that Sin come out and take a look at her property. So here she was, trying her best not to upset the applecart and ruin her best friend's wedding, which was just four weeks away.

She'd just have to trust Mama Mae to handle her grandson's bruised ego.

The cottage had a fairly small footprint, but the house

had good bones and lovely Craftsman details. There was the large, welcoming porch with its deep, overhanging eaves. A light-filled living room with a grand fireplace as its focal point. Built-in shelves flanked the fireplace: the kind of feature that buyers searching for a house with character adored. The dining room had a sweet window seat with built-in drawers. The kitchen was tiny, and the appliances were outdated. But the cozy breakfast nook just off the back deck was adorable.

It wouldn't take much to update the place. But once she did, the home—filled with character and set in a prime location just a stone's throw from the beach—would command top dollar.

She made her way up the narrow stairwell. At the top of the stairs there was a bedroom in either direction. A small, light-filled guest bedroom was situated on the left side. On the right was the much-larger primary bedroom. But since Mama Mae had chosen to take the first-floor bedroom, this room was Rett's.

Sin pushed open the partially closed door and scanned the room. Her stomach tensed and a zip of electricity trailed down her spine.

Rett didn't live here anymore. And this was something she'd done in the countless other homes she'd listed for sale. So why did stepping into Rett's old bedroom feel like an invasion of his privacy?

She crept around the room carefully, as if she were in a museum or an old historic home where all of the furniture and personal items were behind a velvet rope, designed to keep gawkers from touching them. Her hand hovered over the collection of items on the heavy oak dresser. Yet she couldn't bring herself to touch any of it.

The evaporated bottles of cologne, hairbrushes, and

other personal items likely dated back to when Rett was a teenager. Because the scent he'd been wearing the three times she'd been with him was something far more sophisticated and definitely expensive. Rett's taste in cologne had evidently evolved, as had his choice of clothing and footwear.

She opened the door to the tiny closet—a not-so-great original feature of these old homes—and peeked inside. It overflowed with clothing that Sin recalled seeing Rett wear as a teen. Oversize shirts, baggy pants, and track suits that were hallmarks of Black street fashion at the time. She trailed a hand down the worn black-and-white biker jacket Rett had practically lived in during the cooler months back then.

"Can I help you with something?"

Startled by Rett's voice, Sinclair turned around quickly. She dropped her heavy portfolio, and it crashed on top of her foot. Sin squealed in pain.

Shit. She was busted, embarrassed, and pretty sure she'd broken a bone in her foot.

Smooth, Sinclair. Very smooth.

———

Rett had been annoyed, maybe even a little angry, to find Sinclair Buchanan in his grandmother's house rummaging through his things. But when she'd dropped her portfolio and yelped in pain, guilt tugged at his chest.

"I didn't mean to startle you." He stooped down to pick up the padfolio. "I just didn't expect to find you here."

"Snooping in your ode-to-the-nineties closet?" Even in pain Sinclair managed to make a snappy comeback.

He couldn't help laughing because she was right. He'd

been meaning to get rid of this stuff, but he hadn't ever quite gotten around to it. Besides, Mama Mae seemed to like keeping his old room just as it had been before he'd left home for his short stint in college, followed by a series of gigs that had taken him all over the country.

"Actually, I was surprised to find you here. *Period*," he clarified as he handed the leather-bound pad back to her. Rett glanced down to the floor, where a few sheets had fallen out. He picked one up and perused the words written in Sinclair's curvy, neat script.

Even the woman's handwriting was sexy.

He narrowed his gaze, then frowned, his eyes meeting hers. "Wait...you're assessing the house. *This* house." He pointed to the floor below him for emphasis. "My grandmother's house," he added, as if it hadn't been clear enough to both of them exactly which house he was talking about. "Why?"

"It's probably better if Mama Mae tells you why I'm here." Sin gently tugged the papers from Rett's hand and stuffed them back in her portfolio. "I assure you I wouldn't be doing this without her permission. She's well aware that I'm—"

"Going through my stuff?" Rett folded his arms over his chest.

"You know how this works, Rett. If you're as good an agent as everyone says, you go through your clients' closets, too."

"I do, but I don't fondle their things." He smirked.

"I was not...*fondling* your jacket." Sin raked her fingers through her hair as she stared him down. "I was assessing—"

"My jacket?"

"The amount of space in the closet, of course." She

seemed to mentally congratulate herself for coming up with that save. "You know how important closet space is to modern buyers."

He cocked his head. "I'd talk to Mama Mae about this, but she's gone. Left a note saying she needed to run to the store."

"She didn't tell me she was leaving," Sin said.

"Maybe she did, and you couldn't hear her over the blaring music. That's probably why you didn't hear me either," Rett said. "According to the note, Gram had to grab something at a big box store off island. I'm not sure when she left, but she'll be at least a half hour."

"And what are you doing here?" Sin's tone was accusatory. As if this was some plot to get her alone.

"She invited me for dinner tonight. In fact, she insisted on it." As soon as the words left Rett's mouth, it hit him. Mama Mae was up to her matchmaking again.

Rett loved his grandmother, but sometimes the woman could be too much.

"I'm here for... a business reason... but she invited me to stay for dinner," Sin said.

"Of course she did." He sighed. "Now, let's talk about this *business reason* you're here." He nodded toward her portfolio.

"Mama Mae—"

"Isn't here. I'll talk to her when she gets back. I want *you* to tell me why you're here." He hadn't meant to come off so pushy, but his patience was growing thin.

Sin sighed. "As you've probably deduced, she wants me to consider listing her house. And she wants my suggestions for renovations that could help her get top dollar for her home, because that's my specialty."

"Mama Mae has never once talked seriously about

selling her house." A tight band spanned Rett's forehead. "Why wouldn't she discuss a move this big with me? And why would she want you to sell it when I could handle the sale?"

"You know real estate is local. Yes, you grew up here, but that's not the same as knowing and understanding the market and the people who are buying here now." Sin sounded apologetic.

"It's not like I've been away from the island for years," Rett countered.

"It's not the same, and you know it. If this wasn't your grandmother's home, you'd be more objective about this." She folded her arms. "If a friend was selling her house, would you insist on selling it when you're four hundred miles away or would you recommend that she find a local agent with an excellent track record?"

How dare Sin be rational and make a logical argument.

"This is different—"

"It really isn't," she said abruptly, putting an end to the bullshit in her very Sin way. "It's simple. You're just being sentimental. But I can understand why it would be upsetting to hear this from me. So I should go and let you and Mama Mae talk about this privately."

Sin started to walk away in her fancy high heels, but then winced. She lifted her foot and leaned on the dresser. "Son of a biscuit, that hurts."

Rett did his best not to laugh at Sin's colorful exclamation.

"Let me take a look at it." He lifted her by the waist, and she gasped in surprise or maybe outrage. He set her on the edge of the dresser. Rett swiped aside the old cologne bottles and the dust that had settled around them so he could slide Sin back farther.

He studied the nasty bruise atop her foot. "Is it okay if I look at it?"

Sin nodded, reluctantly. Her pain had evidently taken precedent over her pride.

Rett gently glided his fingers over her bruised skin to see if anything felt amiss. He wasn't medical personnel, but he'd suffered enough breaks, fractures, sprains, and bruises as a kid to give his own Ted Talk on the subject.

"Can you move your foot?"

Sin winced as she circled her foot.

"Can you flex it for me?" he asked.

Sin did. "I think it'll be fine, just sore for a few days. Thank you."

Her voice had softened, and there was a heat in her gaze that hadn't been there moments earlier. He felt it, too. In fact, he felt it whenever he was near Sin. Whenever he thought of her. And he'd been thinking of her a lot. Imagining what it would feel like to stand as close to her as he was right now.

Rett intended to step back and help her down from the dresser, but he was frozen in place. He was mesmerized by Sin's hazel eyes. Drawn to her sensual lips and the rise and fall of her chest with each shallow breath.

Instead of stepping backward, he stepped forward. His eyes still locked with hers, he captured her mouth in a kiss. He'd half expected her to shove him away and say he'd missed his chance that night two weeks ago. But she didn't.

She slid her arms around his waist, tugging him closer as she tipped her chin, giving him better access to her warm, sweet mouth.

Cinnamon.

After all these years, the scent of cinnamon still made

him think of Sin smacking her Big Red gum—mostly because she'd gotten a kick out of how much the sound annoyed him.

Rett cradled Sin's face and deepened the kiss, eager for more of her taste. More of her touch. He savored her soft murmurs, which escalated along with the intensity of their hot, hungry kiss. Rett kissed Sin as if he'd been waiting his entire life for this moment. And maybe he had.

Sin pulled his hands from her face, and his heart stopped momentarily, fearing that she was pulling away. Instead, she placed his hands on her thighs.

He glided his hands reverently over the soft, silky skin of her outer thighs, exposed when Sin's skirt had shifted upward. His fingertips glided beneath the fabric, inching higher as they continued their heated kiss. Until he palmed her round bottom, pulling her tight against him.

Sin widened her legs, her thighs framing his as their bodies pressed together. Her nails dug into his skin through the fabric of his shirt as Sin flattened her body against his, sending his pulse racing.

Rett's entire body was filled with heat, like a dormant volcano roaring back to life and threatening to erupt. He couldn't get enough of Sin's kiss, and his body ached for her touch. His heart thumped hard in his chest and he could hear the thrum of the blood rushing in his ears.

His desire for Sin coursed through his veins, making a pathetic liar out of him. Because he'd promised himself this wouldn't happen again. That he wouldn't give her another chance to walk away, discarding him the way she had five years ago. Like he hadn't mattered.

Yet he couldn't stop wanting her. And he couldn't shut down the little voice in the back of his head that wanted Sin to want him, too.

He shifted his stance, allowing some space between them. Without breaking their kiss, he cupped the soft, wet space between her lush thighs. Swallowed her soft moan in response to his touch. He rocked his hand back and forth, and his palm glided against silky, wet, *bare* skin.

Rett pressed his mouth to the shell of her ear and whispered. "Crotchless underwear? Fuck, Sin. You're *killing* me." His painfully hard dick twitched and leaked in response to the discovery. "Did you wear these for me?"

"I...uh..." Sin stammered. "They're not just for sex, you know. It's important that your lady parts get some air."

"Did you just say *lady parts*?" Rett hadn't intended to embarrass Sin, but he couldn't help the roar of laughter that tore through his chest.

How could Sin be maddening, unbearably sexy, and so damn adorable all at once?

"*Yes*. And since she's mine, I can call her whatever I want." Her cheeks flushed and her Eastern Carolina accent deepened. "You may find this hard to believe, Rett Davenport, but not everything is about you."

"Hmm..." He stared at her, wanting to see every nuance of her expression as he glided a finger through the opening of her sexy underwear, plunging it into her heat. He whispered in her ear. "You gonna tell me *this* isn't about me either?"

Sin cursed and moaned, moving against his hand. Creating friction against the taut bundle of nerves. She was evidently done playing his little game, and there was only one thing on her mind.

Pleasure.

Rett kissed Sin again, his tongue gliding against hers as he pumped two fingers inside her and teased the hardened nub with his thumb. Until her body went stiff and her inner walls spasmed around his fingers. Her breath came in hard, sharp bursts. Sin clutched his wrist in an act of surrender as she breathed his name. The sound so sensual it nearly made him come apart.

He stepped back, slowly retracting his fingers, slick with her arousal. His heart still raced, and his breathing was labored, too.

Sin slowly opened her eyes again, meeting his gaze. He loved watching this woman come undone. More importantly, he loved being the one who made her come undone. Loved hearing the way she called his name, her southern drawl intensified.

They stared at each other for a moment, their breath mingling. Neither of them speaking. Then Sin hooked her fingers in his belt and tugged him toward her. She was unfastening his buckle when the slam of a door downstairs startled them.

They both sighed. Sin's eyes reflected the disappointment that gripped Rett's chest.

Mama Mae had returned.

He needed to talk to his grandmother, but walking down those stairs right now with the front of his pants tented wasn't an option.

Sin slipped down from the dresser, slightly favoring her injured foot. She straightened her skirt. Then she turned toward the mirror and wiped the smudges of lipstick from around her mouth. She ran her fingers through her hair.

"I'll go down and help Mama Mae with the groceries. Give you some time to take care of...*that*." Sin glanced down at the ridge beneath his zipper. She grabbed her portfolio, then walked toward the door gingerly. "I'm fine." She held up a hand before he could object. "But you should wipe that lipstick from around your mouth."

Rett rubbed his mouth with the back of his hand and leaned against the dresser. The scent of Sin's arousal still drifted in the air, mingling with her perfume and his cologne.

His grandmother had the olfactory nerves of a beagle hound. So he'd definitely need to hop in the shower before hugging her.

Rett picked up the leather weekend bag he'd dropped by the door and fished out fresh clothing. Then he headed toward the shower downstairs.

Four more weeks until the wedding.

Then he'd be on his way to Charleston. Somewhere a nice, safe distance from the maddening but irresistible Sinclair Buchanan.

Chapter Seventeen

●—●—●—●

Sinclair stood at the kitchen counter, where Mama Mae had put her to work making a salad. She smiled broadly and hoped her expression didn't reveal that she'd been making out with the woman's grandson moments earlier.

"There you are, sweetheart!" Mama Mae beamed when Rett swept into the room, freshly showered, twenty minutes after Sinclair had come downstairs. "How was your shower?"

"Good." Rett cleared his throat.

Cold? Her lips curved in an involuntary smirk. But Sin honestly did feel bad that the sudden interruption had left Rett with a raging hard-on. Because she'd been fully prepared to help him...handle it.

Rett kissed Mama Mae's cheek. "What's for dinner, Gram?"

"Chicken-fried steak, macaroni and cheese, black-eyed peas, and Sinclair is making us a salad so we can at least *pretend* to eat healthy." Mama Mae winked at her.

"Sorry again for startling you, Sin." Rett leaned against the counter. "I didn't expect you to be in my room. I hope your foot is okay."

"I'll be fine, thank you." Sin glanced in Rett's direction but didn't meet his eyes. She slid the cucumber into the salad bowl. "Nothing a hot bath and a little Epsom salt won't cure."

"Sorry about your foot, Sinclair." Mama Mae frowned. "My little surprise backfired a bit. But I'm hoping you'll both think it was worthwhile in the end."

"You hope we'll both think *what* was worthwhile, Gram?" Rett asked. "And since when are you selling this place? You never mentioned it. I realize you don't owe me an explanation, but we usually talk about things like this."

"I know, sweetheart, and that's why I asked you to come here this weekend." Mama Mae dried her hands on the apron hanging around her waist. "But *after* dinner. So could you grab a few glasses and get the sweet tea out of the fridge?"

Rett gathered the items, as his grandmother requested, then set them on the table. "Can you at least explain why you'd bring Sinclair in to handle the sale?" He gestured toward her.

Sin sucked in a quiet breath and her spine stiffened. Still, she tried not to take it personally. After all, wouldn't she have had the same reaction if her grandmother had called someone else in to handle what she excelled at? And by all accounts, Rett did excel at his job.

Mama Mae gave her a warm smile. "Because around here, she's the best, Sonny. It's as simple as that."

"But I—"

"You're a top seller, too. I know, and I'm proud of you. But Sinclair is tops on Holly Grove Island. Besides, the place needs some serious TLC, as you well know. If I'm gonna fix it up and sell it, I need to do this right. Sinclair has the experience and insight for this kind of thing. Now...no more business talk until *after* dinner." She waved him off. "Come on, let's have a nice meal together."

Rett frowned but nodded, accepting the serving bowl she handed him. "Yes, ma'am."

Rett and Mama Mae were so dang cute together. He obviously adored the woman. And something about that made the man exponentially more attractive.

Still, being nice to his grandmother didn't preclude a guy from being bad news. And maybe Rett wasn't the jerk she had once thought him to be, but he wasn't the type of man she'd pictured herself ending up with either.

Garrett Davenport had never been the kind of boy you took home to mama. Given his rumored dating history, he wasn't the kind of man you gave your heart to, either. He was the guy who was tons of fun and amazing in bed, but if things got too serious, he'd turn tail and run. Sinclair didn't need another man like that.

It was a lesson her past had taught her well. One she'd never, ever forget.

———

Rett tried to keep his eyes off of Sinclair as he sat across from her at his grandmother's dining room table. But damn if she wasn't even more beautiful than when he'd last seen her two weeks ago.

And whenever their eyes met, his mind replayed the sensual look on Sin's face as she came hard around his fingers not an hour ago.

Maybe it was a good thing his grandmother had returned when she did. In fact, maybe there was a reason the universe was trying so hard to keep the two of them apart.

And maybe that reason was because hooking up with Sinclair before the wedding was a terrible idea that would only lead to disaster.

Sin seemed to be doing her level best to avoid his gaze, too. A task made particularly difficult by the fact that they were seated across from each other.

Which was probably why his grandmother kept shifting her gaze between the two of them. The last thing in the world he wanted was for his grandmother to be on the scent, thinking there was more to this thing with him and Sinclair.

"How are your sister and her family doing, Sinclair?" Rett asked, determined to play it cool. Like sitting here with Sinclair was no big deal. Because it shouldn't be.

Sin looked surprised that he'd addressed her directly. "Perfect in every possible way." The light in her eyes dimmed, and he had the strangest desire to reach out and squeeze her hand. "She has a perfect husband, three perfect kids, and a perfect life in DC. According to my mother." Sin muttered that last bit beneath her breath.

"I'm sure your mother doesn't mean anything by it." Mama Mae squeezed her arm. "Terri just wants you to have an amazing life—"

"And I do," Sinclair said abruptly, then sighed. She shook her head. "I'm sorry, I didn't mean to cut you off. It's just that…it infuriates me that my mother doesn't get that my life can be good and whole *without* a husband and kids. I'm not against either, of course. But it isn't my life's goal. I have plans for myself, and I'm doing some really impressive things right now. All she seems to see is my single status and empty womb." She turned toward Rett. "Sorry. We're having dinner, and that was totally TMI."

"It's okay, sweetheart. We're all family here," Mama Mae said before Rett could respond. There was so much compassion in his grandmother's expression. Sin's shoulders relaxed, and her scowl eased. "You have every right to be upset. It's tough being compared to someone else whether it's explicit or implied." His grandmother glanced over at him.

Being compared to someone everyone else thought of as perfect was a feeling Rett knew well. Another thing he and Sin apparently had in common.

Rett placed his hands flat on the table on either side of his plate and leaned forward. "Sin, you're perfect the way you are. You know that, right?"

A slow, almost bashful grin slid across the mouth he'd kissed earlier, and something in his chest tightened in response.

"Of course," Sin said with a playful smirk that made him and Mama Mae chuckle.

"Then you're good." He shrugged nonchalantly. "Like Gram said, your mom means well. But what you want for your life and what she wants for you are obviously not the same right now. Maybe they'll align eventually. Maybe they won't. Either way, you're brilliant in so many ways. Don't let anyone make you feel like less because you've chosen a different path."

Sin's eyes were filled with gratitude and something that almost felt like affection. That last part was probably in his head, but a guy could dream.

"Thanks, Rett. That means a lot."

Mama Mae was grinning from ear to ear. "I knew you two would work well together."

"On what?" Rett eyed his grandmother suspiciously.

But instead of answering him, she reached for the Sweet Tea Cake. "Cake, anyone?"

"Please," he and Sin said simultaneously. They exchanged a quick look before turning their attention back to Mama Mae. She handed each of them a slice of cake.

"So, now that we're done with dinner, can we talk about the house sale?" Rett didn't want to come off as the asshole grandson who was worried about the family assets. He trusted Mama Mae knew him well enough to know that wasn't the case. He had no expectations about the house or anything else his grandmother owned. But he was worried about her sudden decision and the motive behind it. "I mean, you're good, right?"

"I'm as fit as a three-hundred-year-old Stradivarius violin, Sonny." She pointed a finger. "Don't you worry. I ain't goin' nowhere anytime soon."

"Good to know, Gram." Rett chuckled. "So why sell the cottage?"

Selling the cottage was something his mother had been hinting at for the past five years. But his grandmother wouldn't even entertain the idea. Now she suddenly wanted to move?

"You love this place," he said, when she didn't respond. "When Mom asked you to move in with her and Hector, you said the only way anyone would get you out of this house was—"

"Feet first," Mama Mae said, tickled. "And I meant every word at the time. But things are different now, sweetheart. So I've decided to take your parents up on their generous offer. I'm going to move into the mother-in-law suite on their property once it's been renovated."

"Okay." It saddened him to think of his powerhouse grandmother being incapable of living independently. Despite her painted-on smile, he recognized how hard it must've been for her to admit that. "Tell me, what's been going on?"

Mama Mae's eyes were teary. She glanced down at her hands folded on the table.

"I still lead an active life, but I've got a few more aches and pains these days. The stairs are hard on this old girl's knees, and the upkeep of the yard has gotten to be too much. I've lost patience with all of the repairs and maintenance this old place requires. I only kept it this long because I needed to know you would always have a place here on the island that felt like home." She shrugged. "Now that you'll be leaving, you won't be returning home as often. And when you do, your relationship with your mother and Hector is much better now. I'm finally ready to let go of the place, so someone else can begin making their own happy memories here."

"What do you mean about Rett leaving?" Sin asked. "You're talking about him returning to Charlotte, right?"

Rett narrowed his gaze at his grandmother, and she shrugged. He cut the moist slice of cake with his fork and took a bite. "I'm considering relocating."

"Why?" A splash of crimson streaked across her nose and cheeks when he met her gaze. "I mean...I thought things were going well for you in Charlotte. Why leave when you're at the top of your game?"

"Sonny here is always in search of his next great adventure." Mama Mae patted his arm. "He hasn't mastered the fine art of contentment just yet."

"But with Dexter and Dakota settled here now, I thought you'd come home more often." Sin sounded disappointed, which was curious. Whenever he'd hung out with Dexter and Dakota, Sin had been notably absent. "Do they know? I mean...they'll probably be really disappointed."

"Dex knows, so Dakota probably does, too," Rett said. "And I'm not moving to the other side of the world. So I'll still come home a few times a year."

An uncomfortable silence settled over the table as each of them quietly ate their cake.

"I'm not leaving until after the wedding, Gram. I can help with the repairs to the house. You know I love doing that stuff for you," Rett said.

"I know, and I'm counting on your help." Mama Mae grinned. "That's why I've made a special arrangement with Douglas."

"My broker?" Sin asked.

"Yes." His grandmother nodded. "I'm willing to pay a higher commission if Sin does her renovation design magic and you do as much of the work as you can, Rett. Then the two of you will split the commission."

"You want us to work together to sell the cottage?" Rett was trying to wrap his head around his grandmother's proposal.

"And Douglas Henley, the owner of my agency, agreed to this?" Sin asked.

"Yes." Mama Mae chuckled. "Call Doug. He'll fill you in on the details."

Rett and Sin sat in stunned silence. He couldn't say what was going through Sin's head. But spending more time with Sinclair felt like a dangerous game.

"I get that you're the top seller around here." He turned to Sin. "But if Gram is gonna do a complete renovation on the place, maybe we should bring in an—"

"Interior designer?" When a sly smile lit Sin's eyes, he already knew he was beat. "Apparently, you didn't notice the certification on my business card. Before I stumbled into a career in real estate, I'd planned to go into interior design." She shrugged. "Blame it on all those reruns of *Designing Women* my mom made us watch as kids. I wanted to be Julia Sugarbaker with a hint of

Suzanne Sugarbaker's glamour. My sister *was* Suzanne. Period."

"Besides, I've seen a portfolio of her work, and I'm sold." Mama Mae cast him a defiant look, then flashed Sinclair a reassuring smile.

Sin's grin widened.

Great. Now his own grandmother was teaming up with Sinclair against him.

"Okay, fine. Sin's qualified. But you want us to work on this project together, and I only planned to be on the island a few more weekends. Doesn't give us a ton of time," Rett said.

"Then take your leave a few weeks earlier so you'll have the time to dedicate to this project. I know it's a lot to ask of you"—his grandmother raised her hands before he could object—"but if Sinclair can get the figure she estimates for the house, it'll be worth it. Besides, if you're looking for a challenge…this place is it. It'll be like the old days." A sad look came over her. "Remember when you were a little boy and you'd help your father out on his contract jobs? Nothing made you happier." Mama Mae smiled softly. "You always said you would work on houses when you grew up, just like your dad."

Memories of those days scrolled through his mind, like an old movie reel, and gripped his chest. His father hadn't treated him like a nuisance. Instead, he'd taken the time to show him how to do things like painting and small repairs. He'd even given him a kid-size tool belt of his own.

Working on those projects were the moments when he'd felt closest to his father. That was why Evan's proposal to collaborate on flipping real estate in Charleston appealed to him so much.

Rett heaved a sigh. Taking on a house renovation in the

midst of Dexter and Dakota's upcoming wedding was a big ask. But then, his grandmother hadn't asked much of him. In fact, his stubbornly independent grandmother hardly ever asked anyone for anything. Instead, she'd generously given of herself, her time, and her resources to anyone who needed them.

How could he say no?

Still, he didn't appreciate that Annamae Davenport had manipulated him and Sin like pieces on a chessboard. So he wouldn't let her off that easily.

"I'll think about it, okay, Gram?"

"So will I," Sin chimed in. "I'll give you my decision next week. In the meantime, I should head home and get started on some of the ideas I have for the renovation…just in case," she added hastily.

Mama Mae smiled the way she did when they went fishing together on Holly Grove Island Sound and she'd gotten herself a big red drum on the hook. "Of course, sweetheart. Let me put together a plate for you to take home."

His grandmother started collecting the dishes, and he and Sin helped put away the leftovers as Mama Mae made Sin a to-go bag.

"Why don't you help Sin out to the car with her things," Mama Mae suggested after hugging Sin good night.

Sin didn't need the help. But Rett complied anyway, carrying the portfolio and the grocery bag of leftovers Mama Mae had packed. They walked out to Sin's SUV, parked a few houses away.

Before she moved to get into the vehicle, Rett turned to Sin and lowered his voice. "Look, I realize this isn't what you signed up for. I also recognize that my grandmother can be a hard person to turn down. If you don't want to do this, just say the word and I'll walk away."

"You're willing to walk away from this deal and just let me have it?" Sin tightened the belt on her short coat, a puzzled look on her gorgeous face.

"If this is what Gram really wants...then yeah." He shrugged. "It was never about the money. She means *everything* to me, and I'd do just about anything for her."

"That's sweet, Rett." Sin's eyes shone with admiration. "But if I decide against working on the project, I'll tell Mama Mae myself. She'd be disappointed, but I know she'd respect my honesty."

"You know my grandmother well." He put Sin's things in the backseat, then opened the door and helped her inside.

"Look, Sin, about earlier—"

"I know." Sin sifted her fingers through her hair. "This is a complicated situation that just got a lot more convoluted by your grandmother's insistence that we partner on this deal." She met his gaze. "So maybe we should take a step back and focus on the wedding and the cottage. After that, you're leaving anyway."

"Then we agree." His brain knew this was the best decision, but his heart and body disagreed vehemently. Hopefully, his easy smile masked his disappointment. "Good night, Sinclair. Don't forget to let me know you made it home. Otherwise, Mama Mae will worry."

"I will. Good night, Rett."

Rett watched as Sin turned her vehicle around, then headed home.

Sin was right. Neither of them needed additional complications in their lives. So they'd focus on giving their friends an incredible wedding and perhaps collaborate to renovate and sell Mama Mae's cottage. Then he'd be off to Charleston or whatever awaited him next.

Chapter Eighteen

The next morning, Sinclair greeted Lila Gayle with a warm hug, said hello to a few more of the locals like Estelle and David Addison, and a group of older gents that included Dakota's father—Chief Jones—and a few of his fishing buddies. Then she slid into the booth across from her broker, Doug, who was already halfway through a large plate of steak and eggs with a side of pancakes.

"Started without me, I see." Sin folded her arms on the table.

Douglas chuckled, then patted his gut. "I was hungry. I would've ordered for you, but I wasn't sure what you wanted."

"Answers." Sin sat up ramrod straight and pinned Doug with a glance. "Tell me about this arrangement you made with Mama Mae."

"Oh...well..." Doug rubbed a hand over his thinning hair and sighed. "I know it's an unusual arrangement. But Annamae Davenport is influential with the senior set around here. If...no, *when* we make her happy with this project, she'll sing our praises to the rest of her friends at the senior center. Might even write up a nice article for that

Outer Banks retirement magazine she contributes to from time to time. It'll be a real boon to the agency."

"And what exactly do I get out of the deal, aside from having to deal with her grandson, who is pissed that Mama Mae didn't give the listing to him outright?"

"A rather tidy commission." Doug smirked, taking another bite of his steak. "And just who do you think all of those seniors are going to be requesting as their listing agent?" He chuckled. "If you think you're the agency's It Girl now, just wait until we get a lock on the retiree market."

Sinclair tapped her fingers on the table as she watched Doug inhaling his steak—which she was pretty sure was a no go on the restrictive diet his cardiologist had put him on. Lila Gayle stopped by the table to take her order, but Sin only wanted coffee. Her stomach was doing flips and her heart was thumping. She didn't have an appetite.

"So what was it you wanted to see me about, Sinclair?" Doug seemed to sense the shift in Sin's energy. Her knee bouncing beneath the table was likely a dead giveaway. "Must be a pretty big deal, since you wanted to meet outside of the office."

She drew in a deep breath, rehearsing the speech in her head that she'd practiced on the drive to the diner. "I'd like to discuss my future with the agency."

Doug frowned, his wiry eyebrows—in a mix of brown and gray—lowered. Deep furrows stretched across his forehead. His fork clattered against the plate when he dropped it. Doug wiped his mouth with a napkin and leaned back against the booth. "Your future is with Henley Real Estate Associates, Sinclair. You know that." He flashed an uneasy smile. "In fact, I'm counting on you to run the agency once I retire."

"Which might be another five or ten years," Sinclair reminded him.

"True." He nodded. "But you've already got your broker-in-charge license, and you'll have a ton of experience under your belt by then."

Sin loved Doug, she honestly did. He was like a second father to her. He'd given Sin her start in real estate and taught her his secrets to becoming a top producer. But she had a vision for her career, and she wouldn't allow her affinity for Doug to keep her in a holding pattern. After all, she brought a lot to the table, too. Henley Real Estate Associates was a lot more successful now than it had been ten years ago, and she was a big part of the reason why.

Sinclair added cream and sugar to the cup of coffee Lila Gayle had poured for her. Then she sucked in a deep breath, leaned forward, and leveled her stare with Doug's.

"I don't want to run the agency at some indefinite future date, Doug. I want to be a partner *now*."

Doug's eyes widened and he nearly spit the coffee he was drinking across the table. "You want to be a partner?" he echoed.

"That's right." Sin sipped her coffee calmly while she waited for Doug to recover. "And don't act so shocked. I've been dropping hints about this for months."

"I know." Doug rubbed the back of his neck. "But I didn't think you were serious."

"Well, I am. And I'm not asking for a free ride here. I'd buy my way in, starting with handing over my share of the commission on this project as a down payment." Sin smiled sweetly. "And don't worry, I realize that's only a small portion of what I'd need to come up with. But I'm good for the rest."

She'd been saving for the past five years. This was an

investment in her future that she was more than willing to make.

"I'm sure you are," Doug muttered. He sighed heavily. "Maybe we can revisit this conversation in a year or two. Who knows, maybe by then..."

"Or maybe I could just take the money and start my own agency." Sin shrugged.

Doug's eyes grew as wide as saucers. He frowned. "Okay, fine. But first, you handle this project for Annamae. Make her happy and then we can talk..." He hesitated.

"Partnership." Sin finished Doug's sentence for him with a grin.

"Yes," he said as if the thought was causing him physical discomfort.

Sin slid over to Doug's side of the booth and gave him a big hug and kissed the old man's cheek. "Thank you, Doug. This is going to be a huge win for both of us. I promise."

"All right, all right." Doug chuckled, then picked up his fork. "I believe you. Just do your best work yet with Annamae's cottage and make nice with her grandson. Then we'll iron out the details." Doug poured more syrup on his pancakes. "Now, are you gonna order something or am I going to continue to eat alone?"

"Sorry, I have a project to plan and two houses to show off island this morning." Sin drained the last of her coffee and picked up her purse. "But I'll see you in the office on Monday."

"You're more of a workaholic than I ever was, Sinclair Buchanan." Doug chuckled, then sighed. "About this deal of ours...best keep it between us for now. Bianca and Allen won't be thrilled about it."

No, she couldn't imagine that Doug's children would be

too happy about it. But she'd earned this opportunity and was willing to lay out a load of cash to make it happen, while neither Bianca nor Allen had any interest in helping with the agency.

"Of course." Sin said her goodbyes to Doug, Lila Gayle, Chief Jones, and his buddies.

If she had to spend the next several weeks working closely with Garrett on this project, at least it would be worth it.

———

A week and a half later, Sinclair stood in the middle of the gutted living room in Mama Mae's cottage. Rett's grandmother had taken a few pieces with her when she'd moved in with his parents. The rest of the furniture and knick-knacks had been placed in storage, sold on consignment, donated, or given away.

Rett was more traumatized by seeing his grandmother's home all packed up and her things being donated than Mama Mae was. Sin wouldn't have pegged Rett as senti-mental and nostalgic. But it was one more way he'd surprised her.

It'd been aggravating to debate with Rett over why they should donate one item or another from Mama Mae's giveaway pile. But she couldn't help being amused and sometimes moved by his sweet, funny stories about why each item meant so much to him.

Eventually, they made their way through it. His grand-mother had given them carte blanche on the design, so she and Rett worked together to create a renovation plan. They'd update the kitchen and bathrooms and give the first floor of the old Craftsman home the open concept most buyers wanted. He'd been particularly insightful with suggestions about kitchen and bath design choices that worked for the space.

Sinclair was able to snag a top-notch general contractor whose current job had stalled because of permit issues, so they'd be able to get started on the project sooner than expected. And today was demolition day.

To save money, Rett was handling most of the demolition himself. He'd enlisted Dexter, Nick, and Em to help. But it was late afternoon, and the only car still there when she arrived was Rett's GTO.

Sin went inside and walked over to the fireplace. Cardboard covered the glass-tiled facade, original to the home. She bent down to peek behind the cardboard to see if the tiles were still intact.

"We covered it before we began demo."

Sinclair stood quickly, startled by the sound of Rett's voice.

Rett's clothing, hair, and skin were streaked with dust. A light sheen of sweat covered his forehead, and he smelled like a man who'd been working all day. Yet, he somehow managed to look enticing in a gray sleeveless shirt that showed off his muscular arms and a pair of tattered jeans that had seen better days but looked good on him.

Sin stepped back and dragged her fingernails through her hair. She needed to put space between her and the man who seemed to have a gift for making her hot and bothered.

"Didn't mean to scare you." Rett glanced down at her high heels. "How's that foot?"

"Much better, thank you." Sin ignored the flush of heat up her neck when their eyes met. She glanced around the space. "You got quite a bit done today."

"We did." He followed her gaze around the room. "Took

down those two interior walls and dismantled the deck to make room for the addition."

"The kitchen cabinets and appliances have been removed, but I didn't see them in the dumpster," Sin noted.

"We're donating them to a charity I work with that provides housing for families in need."

"You volunteer on home building projects? Since when?" Sin asked.

"A few years now." Rett shrugged. "My broker signed our team up to help build a house for the family of a local vet who was a double amputee. Being on a construction site on a hot-ass Saturday in July was the last thing I wanted to do." He chuckled. "But it reminded me how much I'd enjoyed working on building projects with my dad." The corners of his mouth lifted in a soft smile, but there was sadness in his eyes.

"When I was a kid, I'd help my dad out on small projects. He'd get this proud grin on his face and muse about how we'd have our own father-and-son contracting company someday."

Sin placed a hand on his forearm, gritty with dust. "I'm sure Mama Mae didn't realize how tough this would be for you. If you don't want to do the work, we can add it to the contractor's list."

Yes, it would eat into the profits. But she couldn't stand to see the pain in his eyes now. And Sin could only imagine what Rett must be feeling when working on his grandmother's house with his father's absence looming over him.

"I'm good. Promise." Rett's smile looked forced. "Besides, I think my dad would be happy about me working on the old place." He glanced around the room. "So, we stick to the plan."

Sin nodded reluctantly, then noticed his arm. She brushed her thumb just below a jagged cut to his skin. "You're hurt. What happened?"

"Em tagged me with the nails in a wall stud she was carrying to the dumpster." He nodded toward the open space where the wall had previously stood. "It was on me. I wasn't watching where I was going."

"Did you clean the wound?" Sin retrieved her purse and rummaged through it, aghast when Rett shrugged in response. Sin pulled a tiny pouch from her purse with alcohol wipes, adhesive bandages, and other first aid items. She guided him toward the kitchen by his elbow. "We've gotta clean this up."

"It's fine," Rett objected. Still, he permitted her to lead him to the sink, where she washed and dried her hands. "I had a tetanus shot like two years ago."

"Stop squirming," Sin said when he reacted to the sting of the alcohol wipe. Once she thoroughly cleaned the cut, she carefully applied a large adhesive bandage. "Change that a couple times a day. And keep an eye on it, so it heals right."

"Yes, ma'am." There was heat in Rett's eyes as he stared at her. "Thank you." He held up his arm. "I appreciate it."

Sin cleaned up the mess and washed her hands again. "Are you staying at your mom's, too, during the renovation?"

"No, actually, I'm going to be your neighbor." Rett ran a hand over his head. "I'm staying at Dex's condo for the next few weeks in exchange for repainting the place."

"You already moved into the building?" Sin was surprised Dakota hadn't mentioned this.

"Just last night."

"Oh." She smoothed down her skirt and tried not to react to the fact that Rett was now living a couple of floors below her. "I know you've got a lot going on, and I hate to add to that, but I could use your help prepping for the prewedding event this weekend."

"Of course. Wouldn't dream of slacking off on my duties as best man." Rett flexed the arm she'd bandaged. "Dex is so excited about this wedding. Nick, Em, and I were *this* close to gagging the dude if he'd gushed about marrying the love of his life one more time."

Sin laughed. "Could they be any cuter? I'm so happy for them."

Rett chuckled. "Despite my annoyance with him today, I am, too. Seems the whole town is ready for those two to finally get their happy ending."

"Better late than never, right?" Sin smiled.

"I guess so." There was something in Rett's eyes that made her belly flutter.

Sin returned to the living room and slid the small pouch back into her purse.

"I better go. I have a couple more showings this afternoon. Could we meet at my place on Thursday evening around seven? I'll send you a text message with my unit number."

"Sin, be careful out there," he called to her retreating back. "I know you can take care of yourself, but—"

"I'm always careful when meeting perspective clients. My office knows exactly where I'm going and who I'm meeting with. But thank you, Rett. I appreciate it."

Rett was just being polite. So why did his genuine concern for her make her spine tingle and her heart expand in her chest?

She needed to get out more. Maybe get a life while she was at it. Then maybe she'd be planning her own wedding instead.

Chapter Nineteen

·—◆—·—◆—·

Rett leaned against the bar at Blaze of Glory, waiting to get the attention of the bar owner—Michael Blaisdell, known to everyone in town as Blaze.

The man scratched the reddish-blond scruff on his chin. Retired from the marines, Blaze still wore his hair in a military fade with a short, spiky top.

"Another round?" Blaze's blue-green eyes shifted to the tables out on the patio where the rest of their group chatted and laughed. The bonfire still blazed out on Holly Grove Island Beach, where they'd all been earlier after an evening stroll.

"Please. Add it to my tab, then close it out." Rett checked his watch. "According to the prewedding festivities drill sergeant, this will be our last round of the night." He nodded toward Sinclair.

Sin stood a few feet away deep in conversation with Dakota's older sister, Shay, and the bride-to-be, who wore a tiara and a sash declaring she was *The Bride*.

Blaze chuckled. "Sinclair Buchanan knows what she wants, and the woman means business."

"That's for damn sure." Rett couldn't help staring at Sin.

She looked amazing. Her frilly, blush-colored dress grazed her thighs and had a sheer, knee-length, polka-dot overlay. The outfit was sexy, flirtatious, and romantic—much like the woman wearing it. The woman he hadn't been able to get out of his head.

Sin glanced up and met his gaze. A slow smile lit her hazel eyes. She quickly returned her attention to her friends.

Rett thanked Blaze when he handed him another glass of the overpriced fizzy water he'd been drinking all night. He and Sin had agreed, as the event cohosts, to go easy on the drinks.

The things we do for our friends.

"Looks like the next wedding bells in town will be ringing for you and Sin." Blaze grinned slyly.

Rett coughed, nearly choking on his seltzer. "What on earth makes you say that?"

"Seriously, man?" Blaze grabbed glasses and set them up on the lower portion of the bar. "You know you've been staring at her all night, right? If not, you're in even deeper than I thought."

Rett's face heated. Had he really been that obvious, or was Blaze giving him shit just for the hell of it? He sipped his drink. "I'm cohosting the event. Just looking for cues on our next move, that's all."

He sipped more of his drink and ignored Blaze's unconvinced look and subsequent laughter.

"Whatever you say." Blaze poured their drinks. "I'll bring these over in a bit. Should I call a ride share service, so everyone gets home in one piece?"

"We're good. Sin insisted on renting one of those chauffeured party buses." Rett had objected to the additional expense at first. But when he'd come up with the idea to do a Holly Grove Island town hop rather than a bar hop on the mainland, the bus had been a godsend. "The driver will be here in half an hour."

Blaze nodded behind him. "Incoming."

Rett turned around in time to see Sinclair strutting toward him in tall, flesh-tone, open-toe high heels that made her shapely legs look impossibly long. "What's up?"

"The driver's running a few minutes behind, but he's on his way." Sin set her empty glass on the bar, and Blaze handed her another sweet tea. She thanked him, then turned back to Rett. "Your idea about doing an island hop was a stroke of genius. Everyone really enjoyed it."

"Dakota and Dex not only fell in love with each other again, they both fell in love with Holly Grove Island again. Seemed like the best way to celebrate both." Rett shrugged. "But I'm glad everyone enjoyed it. Maybe this joint event thing isn't so bad after all."

The joint bachelor/bachelorette party had kicked off with a picnic at Holly Grove Island Park open to everyone in town. The event was catered by Lila's Café and featured ice cream from Helene's Homemade. Then the wedding party hopped onto a rented party bus and headed to The Foxhole for live music and the first round of drinks. Next, they'd done one of those paint parties at the new art gallery. They'd had a bonfire on the beach. Now they were ending the night with another couple rounds at Blaze of Glory's.

Sin glanced over at their best friends, who were sharing a sweet kiss away from everyone else. She smiled. "It was totally worth it. Look how happy they are."

Dexter looped his arms around Dakota's waist and whispered something in her ear. She smiled from ear to ear and placed a discreet hand on her belly.

Seeing the two of them so in love warmed his chest. But

he also felt a twinge of envy, and it took him by surprise. What the hell was going on with him lately?

Rett glanced over at Sinclair. Her eyes were misty. They were voyeurs in a private moment between their unsuspecting friends, which seemed to have moved both of them.

Their eyes met. That feeling he couldn't quite explain stirred in his chest again. He flashed her an awkward smile. She returned it, then took a huge gulp of her drink.

"So being back home...Has it made you miss the island?" Sin asked, her gaze on their friends at the back of the room as Dexter's brother Steven told an animated story about their adventures as kids.

Steven had been married to Kristen for nearly a decade. The dude was probably just glad to have a night out with his wife while the kids were having a sleepover at their grandmother's.

Rett considered Sin's question. How honestly did he want to answer it? How honest was he willing to be with himself? He'd been surprised by how much he missed the slower pace of island life and hanging out in town with close friends. He missed the black cherry and cherry vanilla ice cream floats from Helene's Homemade and taffy from Sweet Connections. He missed breakfasts at Lila's Café. Missed the beach and fishing on the sound with Dex or Mama Mae.

During his regular visits, he'd focused on spending time with his grandmother. He would chauffeur her to errands on the mainland. Or he'd have dinner with his mom, Hector, and Izzy. He hung out with Dex whenever their schedules permitted, but he rarely saw anyone else or got to go to any of the local hangouts. But helping to plan the wedding events plus renovating Mama Mae's house had forced Rett to engage with the community in a way he hadn't in years.

He'd reconnected with family and old friends at the engagement party. And after just a few weeks back home, he felt like a part of Holly Grove Island again. It had given him a renewed appreciation for the town he couldn't wait to escape as a teen.

It had also churned up a mixture of nostalgia and longing that felt foreign and...uncomfortable.

"Being back home has been...nice," he said finally. He avoided Sin's discerning stare and the tiny smirk that called *bullshit* as obviously as if she'd said it aloud.

"Well, you certainly seem happy to be home." She shifted her gaze toward the table in the back. "And your family is thrilled to have you here."

"True." His chest expanded as he thought of the dinners with his parents and Mama Mae or meals at his aunt Marilyn's over the past few weeks. Of how much fun he'd had joking and catching up with Dexter, Em, and Nick on demo day at Mama Mae's cottage. It'd even been fun spending time with Dexter's two younger brothers—Steven and Ellis—and getting to know their wives and children, who ranged in age from two to eight. The kids had been a handful, but they'd also been fun. For the first time, he'd seen the appeal of being the fun uncle. "I've enjoyed spending time with them, too."

"But you're still leaving." Sin's hazel eyes regarded him carefully. There was a hint of disappointment in her tone.

Or maybe he just wanted to believe it mattered to Sin whether or not he stayed.

"This is a layover, not a destination," he said. "My family understands that."

"Understanding it doesn't mean they're okay with it." Sinclair's eyes dimmed momentarily. She finished the last of her sweet tea, then set the glass on the counter. "I'd better start winding things down or they'll behave like a bunch of toddlers when you tell 'em it's time to leave the playground. Can you ask Blaze to settle up everyone's tabs?"

"I'm on it." Rett didn't acknowledge Sin's observation about his family's disappointment over his decision to move. What would be the point? He couldn't control how anyone else felt about his choices. Instead, he watched the generous sway of Sinclair's hips as she strolled toward the outdoor patio of the rustic bar, which took advantage of Blaze of Glory's beachside location.

When he turned to ask Blaze to settle up their accounts, the older man stood behind the bar with his arms folded and a smirk on his whiskered face.

"Save the commentary, man, and just settle up everyone's accounts, all right?" Rett said before Blaze could speak.

"Yes, sir." Blaze chuckled softly as Rett walked away.

Rett didn't acknowledge the man's implied *I told you so* either.

It didn't matter that he still had a thing for Sinclair. They'd decided nothing would come of it. The only thing that mattered was that the two of them worked well together.

They'd pulled out all of the stops to make this event happen and to give Dexter and Dakota their dream wedding, despite the shortened timeline. And though it was still early in the process, he and Sin had worked together seamlessly during the planning phase of the renovation project. But the wedding would happen in two weeks, and in four more weeks, they'd be done with the house. Then he'd be on his way.

Until then, he would keep his eyes from wandering and keep his imagination in check.

———

Rett set the last of the items he and Sinclair had hauled up from her SUV in the home office of her condo. He'd carpooled with Sin so he could help her haul everything they'd need to the event and back. It was nearly one in the morning, and they were both exhausted. He was going to hit the shower and then go to bed as soon as he returned to Dex's condo.

"Is that everything?" Sin glanced at the collection of extra blankets and various party favors lined up against a wall in her office.

"It is, and thanks to you, tonight was a huge success."

"I couldn't have pulled this off without my planning co-captain." Sin's grateful smile tugged at something in his chest. "You were invaluable, Rett. I'm sorry I doubted you."

"We misjudged each other about a lot of things, Sin. But that's in the past." Rett shrugged, his gaze lingering on hers.

Their eyes locked, but neither of them spoke. In the moments that felt like minutes, he couldn't help thinking about how incredible Sinclair was and how much he'd like the chance to finish what they'd started that day at Mama Mae's place. The hungry look in Sin's eyes and the way her teeth sank into her lush lower lip made him wonder if she was thinking the same thing.

Rett cleared his throat, breaking the awkward silence. "I'm gonna hit the shower, fall into bed, then sleep for twelve hours straight."

He turned and headed down the hall.

"Same." Sin trailed him toward the door. "Between the wedding planning and renovating Mama Mae's house . . . we deserve it. And there's one more thing we deserve. Wait here." Sin went to the kitchen and pulled out a chilled bottle of champagne. She held it up, then set the wine on the counter while she retrieved two flute glasses and a bottle opener.

"A nightcap?" Rett raised a brow.

"A toast to celebrate a successful day of events and our best friends being one step closer to wedded bliss." Sin smiled broadly.

How was it possible that Sinclair seemed to get more beautiful every single day?

Suddenly, the chorus of "A Song for Mama" by Boyz II Men played.

"That's my mom's ringtone." She checked the delicate gold watch on her wrist. "It's almost one. My mother *never* calls this late." Panic settled into the furrows between her brows. "Sorry, I need to take this."

"Of course. I hope everything is okay."

"Me, too."

"Mom? Are you okay? Did something happen to Dad?" Sin asked when she picked up the phone. Sin listened quietly for a moment, then huffed. "What else was I supposed to think, Mama? You're calling me way past your bedtime."

Rett leaned against the kitchen counter as he watched Sin. Her expression and tone had gone from worried to annoyed, then agitated. Her cheeks and forehead were flushed. She sat at the breakfast bar and turned her back to him.

"You couldn't have called in the morning to give me fashion advice about what to wear to church? Let me guess, this has something to do with you chatting up Devon James at the park. I already know what's going on in that head of yours, Mama, and I need you to listen to me carefully. I am *not* interested in Devon, nor any of the other guys you've tried to set me up with. I'm perfectly capable of finding my own man, thank you."

Something in Rett's gut tightened. This was a very personal conversation between Sinclair and her mother; one he shouldn't be privy to. But it set his teeth on edge to think of Sin with that pompous ass Devon James. His father owned several rental properties on the island. Dev was an arrogant, self-centered bastard in high school. From what Rett had heard, that hadn't changed.

Rett walked around the counter and placed a gentle hand on Sin's shoulder.

She muted her phone while her mother prattled on about Devon James. "Sorry, I'm trying to wrap up this conversation about how I'm a hopeless spinster whose reproductive organs are in danger of decaying."

Sin was being sarcastic, but Rett could hear the sting in her voice and see the pain in her eyes. He fought back the urge to take her in his arms and kiss her. Remind her she was a fucking goddess: married, single, divorced, or anything in between.

Instead, he rubbed the back of his neck. "It's okay. I'm exhausted and you probably are, too. I'm going to head downstairs, hop in the shower, then go to bed. Rain check?"

Her shoulders sagged and she frowned. "Are you sure? I won't be long, I promise." Sin unmuted the phone to reply to her mother. "Yes, I'm still here. No, my answer hasn't changed. I'm not interested in Devon, and I never will be." She muted the phone again. "Sorry."

"Don't be. And don't let your mom get in your head. You're a strong, accomplished woman who knows what she wants. We forget that sometimes when dealing with our parents and grandparents." He dropped a kiss on her cheek. "Good night, beautiful."

A soft smile lifted one side of Sin's mouth and her gaze warmed. He'd seen that look in Sin's eyes before, but he still hadn't deciphered it.

Was it friendship, or maybe even affection?

"Good night, Rett."

He cranked up the painted-on smile intended to mask his disappointment over the unexpected end to their perfect night.

Chapter Twenty

——•—•—•——

Thirty minutes after finally ending the call with her mother, Sin found herself outside of Dex's condo. She raked her fingers through her hair, damp from the shower, and fluffed it a bit. Sin readjusted the basket filled with champagne and a midnight snack balanced on her hip. She opened the door Rett had left unlocked, as promised. She'd told herself she would just leave the basket for Rett. But wasn't the point of this that they celebrate their accomplishment together?

Her heart raced as she stepped inside the condo, which smelled like fresh paint. She locked the door behind her, her eyes scanning the great room where all of the furniture had been pushed to one side and draped with tarps.

"Rett?" she called as she ventured into the space.

He stood on a stepladder in the great room wearing headphones, paintbrush in his hand. She could faintly hear the music from a distance. He wore black basketball shorts and not much else.

Sin set the basket on the counter and walked toward him. She pulled out her phone and added a reply to the series of text messages that had brought her there at nearly two in the morning.

I'm right behind you.

He pulled his phone from his pocket and read the message. Then he powered down the headset and slipped it around his neck before climbing down.

"Hey." He stood in front of her, his voice low and incredibly sexy. Like he'd awakened from a deep sleep.

"Hey." Her heart beat faster.

Rett was a big, solid guy. But he was obviously in shape. His arms and chest were muscled. He didn't have a six-pack, but his stomach was toned. Her gaze followed the trail of hair on his belly that disappeared below his waistband.

"Let me wash the paint off my hands and grab a shirt." Rett disappeared down the hall toward the primary bedroom.

"Sure."

Don't get dressed on my account. I was enjoying the view.

Sin glanced around. Rett had painted the kitchen, and he was starting on the great room.

"Sorry about that." Rett tugged on a faded black The Roots concert T-shirt. "Thanks for doing this." He nodded toward the basket and folded his arms, his biceps flexing with the movement. "You'd think we'd both have collapsed into bed after the week we've had. But I'm wide awake right now. Maybe a drink will help."

Sin tore her eyes away from his arms and the way the move emphasized his strong chest. She shifted her gaze to his handsome face. "I was wired after my shower. Partly excited about how well today turned out. Partly aggravated with my mom for ruining my high. And for interrupting our well-deserved celebration toast." Sin indicated the ladder. "You apparently put your sleeplessness to good use."

"Figured I'd do the prep work and cut in the corners. Then I'll be ready to paint."

"I'm surprised that you've already started painting." Sin glanced around the space. "I doubt Dexter expects you to tackle this job while planning his wedding *and* working on Mama Mae's house."

"Thought it would be best to knock out the painting as soon as I could." Rett left the rest unspoken. He apparently wanted to skip town quickly, once his obligations were fulfilled.

"I didn't realize you were in such a hurry to leave." Why did Rett's eagerness to leave feel like a sharp blade being inserted between her ribs? "Have you decided where you're going?"

"I've narrowed it down to a couple options." Rett seemed to be purposely vague. Then again, he hadn't planned to tell her he was leaving. Mama Mae had spilled the beans, and Rett hadn't seemed happy about it. He shoved his hands into his pockets, seemingly eager to change the subject. "So you brought us a nightcap?"

"Yes." Sin lifted the bottle of chilled champagne, a champagne bottle opener and stopper, and two flutes from the wicker basket. She set them on the counter. "And just in case you're hungry…" She pulled out a small charcuterie tray with meats, cheeses, fruit, and olives.

"Now that you mention it, I'm starving." Rett slapped a hand on his belly, and Sin couldn't help thinking of how good he'd looked without that T-shirt.

Sin shook off the thought and set the food out on the counter. "Glad I'm not the only insomniac with the munchies around here."

"Guess that's something else we have in common." Rett declined the champagne opener she offered. He twisted off the foil. "That takes all of the fun out of drinking champagne."

Rett popped the cork. Despite expecting it, the sound startled Sin, and she laughed, her heart racing. She picked up the two flutes and Rett filled them.

Sin handed Rett a flute of the fizzy liquid. He accepted it, his eyes locked with hers.

There was something so warm in his dark eyes, but there was a hint of apprehension there, too. Perhaps it was the same hesitance she'd felt when she'd picked up her phone to text him, asking if he was still up. She hadn't expected Rett to reply, but she'd been glad he did.

Sin held up her glass, and Rett did the same. "Here's to a lifetime of happiness for our amazing best friends."

A twinge of emotion choked her up, and her eyes stung with unshed tears. Sin felt silly for reacting that way, but Dex and Dakota were her closest friends, and she loved them dearly. She honestly couldn't be happier for them. And yet, a part of her felt a little sad, too.

"To Dex and Dakota." Rett clinked his glass against hers, their eyes still locked. "I can't think of two people more perfect for each other."

"Here, here." Sin took a generous sip of the bubbly champagne that tickled her nose.

Rett sipped his champagne. He nibbled on a square of sharp cheddar cheese, his dark eyes trailing down her body before meeting her gaze again.

"Just two more weeks until the wedding, and we'll be about halfway done with the renovations by then." Sin rattled off the words, feeling a sudden need to fill the awkward void.

"I should be done with the painting here, too." Rett glanced around the space.

"Is Dex anxious to rent the place?" Sin asked.

"He said I can stay as long as I'd like. But this is an income property for his growing family. I don't want to take advantage of his generosity."

"It's not exactly rent-free," Sin noted. "You are painting the place. And are these new?" She indicated the black undermount sink and matte black faucet.

"Yep. One of those touchless models. The first one I've installed." Rett smiled proudly.

"Sexy and practical." Sin sipped more of her champagne. She waved a hand in front of the sensor, triggering the water. "Now I am jealous."

When she looked up, Rett's heated stare sent a jolt of electricity down her spine. Her neck and face were suddenly hot.

"So, since Dex isn't rushing you, you're just anxious to leave town," Sin pressed.

"I've been here a lot longer than I expected. Figured I should be ready to take off once we're done with the house." Rett sat on the edge of a stool.

"Being prepared is admirable." Sin plucked a grape from the plate and popped it into her mouth. A million thoughts churned in her head.

Why was she taking Rett's eagerness to leave so personally? And why had it been so important to her that they share this toast tonight?

Sin's heart thumped in her chest, the sound reverberating in her ears.

You know why, Sinclair Buchanan.

In the weeks since the engagement party, she'd come to know Rett in a way she hadn't before. Their relationship had evolved from a hate crush to a tentative friendship. And maybe, if he hung around, it could become something more. And while she wasn't quite sure what that something more might be, she did know what it was she wanted from Rett tonight.

Rett drained his glass, then refilled it. He reached for her glass, but she shook her head, her heart racing. Rett set down the bottle and sipped his champagne. "You're gonna make me drink alone, huh?" he teased with a deep chuckle.

Sin set her glass down and swallowed hard. Her hands trembled, and butterflies flitted in her stomach as she met his gaze. "I don't want you to blame the champagne for this."

Sin clutched Rett's T-shirt, pulling him closer until his mouth crashed into hers.

Glass clinked against the granite, then Rett was cradling her face in both his hands. He took control with a kiss that was eager and demanding from the start; not tentative, as their earlier kisses had begun. The passion and desire that had been brewing between them these past few weeks seemed to burst into flames.

Rett's hard, hungry kiss sent ripples of need through her body. Deepened the ache she already felt for him. Her nipples, hard and tight, pressed against his firm chest, heightening the euphoric sensation of their dizzying kiss. Her sex pulsed with her growing desire for this man.

Rett dropped his hands to her waist and dragged her body against his. He groaned softly, his hardened shaft pinned between them.

He gripped her bare thigh, pulling her leg over his as he glided a hand beneath her skirt and squeezed her bottom, clad in skimpy, sheer mesh fabric. Rett pulled her tight against him.

"Is this why you really came here, Sin?" She could hear Rett's smirk in the words he whispered between their hot and heavy kisses. His fingers bit into her flesh as he tugged her closer.

"Yes," she admitted, her voice rough. Her growing hunger for Rett packed into that single word. There was no point in denying it. She ached for his touch. Her mind was already lost in the tactile memory of how it had felt to have Rett inside her. "I want you, Rett. Now. *Please.*"

He trailed kisses down her neck. "You rushin' me, Sin?"

"Think of it as eagerness. You, sir, should be flattered." She held back a giggle as Rett's beard grazed her skin.

"I am." He cradled her face, his eyes meeting hers. "But I've waited five long years for another shot at this. So I plan to take my time and enjoy every single minute. That okay with you?"

There was something so sincere in Rett's gaze and in the rich timbre of his voice that washed over her like warm honey. Something beyond the immediate hunger in his dark eyes that sent a shudder rippling through her body and made her sex pulse.

Did Rett feel anything more for her than just the physical attraction raging between them?

A part of Sin desperately wanted to know the answer to that question. But the part of her brain charged with protecting her heart was too afraid to find out.

Stop overthinking it and just enjoy the moment.

She and Rett had shared one incredible night together because there hadn't been any expectations. No wondering about what the future held. That was what she wanted again. And she wouldn't ruin this moment by trying to make this something it wasn't.

What they both wanted was sex; plain and simple. Given

their divergent career and life plans, sex without commitment was all she could expect from Rett. And if she wanted this to happen tonight, she needed to be okay with that.

Sin swallowed hard, ignoring the little voice that inquired whether she *really* was okay with it. She sank her teeth into her lower lip, her eyes locked on his as she nodded in response.

"Good." He lifted Sin, and she wrapped her legs around him instinctively, her sandals falling to the floor.

She looped her arms around Rett's neck, holding on to him as he moved swiftly to the bedroom. The room was dark except for a small lamp beside the bed.

He lay her on the bed, the covers already pulled back, as if he'd just rolled out of it. Rett pulled his shirt over his head and tossed it to the floor, followed by the shorts he was wearing commando.

Rett was well-endowed, to put it mildly. And she would enjoy riding every single inch of that bad boy.

His knowing grin indicated he hadn't missed her reaction to seeing him naked again. Sin ignored his smirk. She sat up and tugged the camisole over her head, tossing it to the floor onto his pile of clothing. Then she lifted her bottom enough to shimmy out of her skirt and add it to the pile.

Her skin heated beneath Rett's appreciative stare as she sat on his bed nearly naked, his gaze roving over her skin and landing on her beaded nipples, aching for his touch.

"You are so fucking beautiful, Sin." He whispered the words with a sense of awe. Her skin flushed, and there was a fluttering in her chest.

"So are you." Sin wrapped her arms around him as he lay above her. Her heart swelled as she gazed up at him, her fingertips pressed to his back. "Inside and out. I'm sorry I didn't see that before."

Rett's expression shifted from abject lust to something more. He seemed stunned by her apology; but so was she. Sin hadn't expected to say those words, but she'd uttered them with the utmost sincerity.

Garrett was so much more than she'd imagined. Had she taken the time to truly see him back then, maybe they could've been friends. Perhaps even something more.

Rett captured her mouth in a sensuous kiss. His large hands cradled her face as he kissed her with a passion and intensity she hadn't ever felt before. Sin's skin was on fire, and she trembled with her rising need for him.

Rett broke their kiss, leaving her breathless as he trailed kisses down her neck. He covered one of her nipples with his warm mouth, his tongue flicking over it again and again, like fingers strumming a guitar. Winding her up more.

Her legs widened and she whimpered softly as he licked and sucked the hypersensitive bud, then moved on to the other. Then he trailed kisses down her stomach and over the sheer, black mesh fabric—the last remaining barrier between them.

Suddenly, he lifted his head. His eyes twinkled with a mischievous grin. "You gonna tell me again you didn't wear these for me?"

She shook her head. "No."

"Good." His grin widened. "But I need to hear the words." He spread her open, his tongue swiping the sensitive flesh through the opening in her crotchless underwear and making her shudder.

"What words?" She propped herself up on her elbows, her eyes drifting shut as she got lost in the mind-blowing sensation of his warm tongue against her skin.

"You know what words." He stopped, and she practically whimpered in protest.

So he was playing hardball. *Fine.* After all, he was worshipping at the altar of Sinclair, the least she could do was stroke the man's ego—both figuratively and literally.

She met his gaze. "I wore these for you. In fact, I bought them for you," she admitted. "But it's not my fault. Savage X Fenty was having a sale, so I stocked up."

Rett pressed a kiss to her sensitive flesh, his thumbs still spreading her. His chuckle rumbled against her skin. "Remind me to thank Rihanna."

Before she could respond, he'd dived in, kissing and sucking, delicately at first, then with increasing urgency.

Her whimpers turned into moans and then curses. Until finally he'd taken her over the brink, and she found herself calling Rett's name, her body tense and her legs trembling.

Sin lay back on the pillow, trying to catch her breath as Rett pressed soft, sensuous kisses to her inner thigh.

He lay beside her and kissed her shoulder. Then he nuzzled her neck. "Anybody ever tell you how fucking amazing you look falling apart like that?" he asked in a husky whisper before pressing a warm kiss to her ear.

Sin shook her head, not trusting her voice. She turned on her side and cradled his cheek. Rett was incredibly handsome. So much smarter than she'd given him credit for. He was sweet and protective of the people in his life. And she'd come to truly care for him.

She quickly brushed the realization aside.

They weren't in a relationship. This was only sex. Just like before. Losing sight of that would create false expectations, and one or both of them would get hurt.

Sin kissed his lips, salty with the taste of her.

Rett climbed off the bed and rummaged in the side zipper of his duffel bag on the floor. He returned with little foil wrappers. He kept one and tossed the rest onto the nightstand.

Before he could rip it open, Sin held out her open palm. His mouth pulled to one side in a wicked grin that always did things to her.

Sin ripped the foil packet open and rolled the condom down his shaft to the base. She pressed a kiss to his chest, then scooted back onto the bed. She stared up at Rett as he hovered over her and pressed himself to her entrance, slowly easing inside as he cursed quietly.

Pleasure rolled up her spine as Rett inched deeper inside. Her breath hitched. She held on to him, her nails biting into his skin when he hit bottom, then slowly began to move his hips with a steady rhythm.

Their mingled sounds of pleasure increased in frequency and volume as he brought her closer to the edge. She was overloaded with sensations. The friction of his steady movement against her already sensitive clit. The hair on his chest brushing against her sensitized nipples. The delicious angle he was hitting when he'd thrown one of her legs over his hip.

The building sensations culminated in an explosion of intense bliss at her core. Sin called Rett's name, much louder than she should have at such a late hour. But her pleasure-addled brain hadn't been capable of applying reason. She fell apart in Rett's arms, her stomach tensing and her sex pulsing as he continued to move his hips.

Suddenly, his body stiffened, and he arched his back, the muscles tensing beneath her fingertips as he drove deep inside her, her name on his lips.

Rett rolled onto his back, pulling Sin to his chest. He tugged the covers up over them and stared at the ceiling, his chest rising and falling.

"God, that was amazing." Rett was still breathless.

"Even better than I remembered." She pressed a kiss to his chest. "And I remember that night being pretty spectacular."

Rett brushed his lips over hers. "And we're just getting started."

Sinclair practically purred with anticipation. "I like the sound of that."

This day had been perfect, and Sin wouldn't let anything ruin it. Not even the little voice in the back of her head that poked at her again, reminding her that Rett was leaving soon. Warning her of the distinct possibility that when he did, she would be the one who'd be hurt.

Chapter Twenty-One

— • — • — • —

Rett stared in the mirror after discarding the second condom. Or was it the third? His heart was still racing after making love to Sinclair again. He'd taken her in the bed, up against the bedroom wall, and over a chair. After five years of dreaming about being with Sin again, he'd been determined to work out all of his fantasies and the frustrations over their false starts these past few weeks.

Now he was bone tired, even though his mind was still racing. Rett cleaned up and slipped on a pair of underwear he'd grabbed from his bag. But when he returned to the bedroom, Sin was gone. Her clothing was gone from the pile on the floor, too.

He cursed under his breath and dragged a hand down his face. It was that night in Raleigh all over again.

Maybe it shouldn't have bothered him then, because there were no expectations for anything more. But he'd been sure things were different this time. They'd developed a friendship and mutual respect. Maybe even admiration for each other.

Or maybe he'd been wrong.

Rett climbed into bed, angry with himself for being so perturbed by Sinclair's hasty retreat. He sighed, remembering he needed to lock the front door behind Sinclair. But before he could climb out of bed, Sinclair returned with a large serving platter that contained their flutes, the champagne bottle, and the charcuterie tray and crackers.

"Hey." He smiled softly at the woman he'd come to admire so much these past few weeks. She was wearing his Roots concert T-shirt, which he hadn't noticed had also disappeared from the pile. "I thought you—"

"Left?" She frowned. "No. And I shouldn't have ghosted you before. I just didn't think you'd want me to stay." She handed him the tray and climbed into bed. "But that's no excuse. I'm sorry." She kissed him. "Then again, I just assumed... maybe you'd rather I not stay now."

"I want you to stay." Rett kissed her again. "I did then, and I do now."

A soft smile lit Sin's eyes, and it warmed his chest.

They had a late-night picnic in bed, eating mostly in silence. Then Rett put away their dishes and climbed back into bed. He slipped an arm around Sinclair, glad she'd agreed to stay.

"So about this being a complicated situation we should take a step back from..." Rett dropped a teasing kiss on her neck.

"We can handle this." Sin's eyes drifted closed as she tilted her head, providing better access to the soft skin of her throat. "We've both been working tirelessly on behalf of the people we love. We deserve a little fun."

Is that all this is? A little fun?

He honestly didn't know anymore. He only knew he wanted Sinclair and that he enjoyed being with her. Maybe he should accept that as blithely as Sinclair evidently had.

Only... he couldn't.

Rett kissed Sin's temple and said good night.

He lay there in the dark, the sound of his heart thumping in his ears as he cradled Sin, who'd drifted off to sleep in his arms. But the thoughts swirling in his head kept him awake with the same question he'd been wondering for the past few weeks.

What if he and Sin could become something more?

———

Rett awoke, feeling groggy and tired. He'd drifted off in his sleep, holding Sinclair in his arms.

Sinclair.

Rett sat up quickly and surveyed the room, which was still mostly dark, thanks to the heavy curtains. But sunlight beamed from a small crack between the panels of fabric. It had to be at least noon.

This time, Sin was definitely gone. Her clothing, which she'd neatly folded on the chair, was no longer there.

Rett groaned. They'd shared a moment last night. Something deeper than sex. But he wasn't sure exactly what that was and what it meant.

He was leaving in a few weeks. Yet he couldn't stop thinking of Sin and their night together. And he couldn't stop the persistent thought that had taken root in his brain.

Maybe what he was feeling for Sin was the thing he'd been searching for.

He needed to talk to Sin. Now. Before he lost his nerve.

———

Garrett inhaled deeply as he stood in front of Sinclair's door. Pans clanged in the kitchen and the smell of food wafted from beneath her door. He raised his fist and knocked.

Everything went still. For a moment, he wondered if Sin would answer. But finally, her soft steps padded toward him. She opened the door.

"Rett, hey." Sin glanced down the hall. She pulled him inside and closed the door behind him. The confident, assured Sinclair Buchanan seemed nervous, almost shy. "Can I get you some coffee?"

"Please." He shoved his hands into his pockets. "Though I'd hoped to be the one bringing you coffee...in bed."

Sin flashed him a nervous smile, her cheeks flushed. She tucked a few loose strands of hair behind her ear. "You were dead to the world. Didn't seem right to wake you."

He stepped closer. "I was dead to the world because you wore my ass out last night." He raised his hands in surrender. "Not that I'm complaining."

"Good. Because it wasn't the Garrett. The Garrett was great."

Rett chuckled at Sin's reference to Drew Barrymore's "The Chad was great" line in the first *Charlie's Angels* movie.

He looped his arms around her waist. "Good, because the feeling is mutual."

Sin slid out of his grasp and went to the kitchen. She grabbed a mug and made him a cup of coffee, her back turned to him. "I thought it would be better not to be seen slinking out of your place doing a walk of shame."

"Why should you be ashamed?" Rett gripped the counter. "We're both single. What's wrong with us seeing each other?"

Sin handed him the mug, then set a spoon and containers of cream and sugar on the counter. The flush of her cheeks had deepened. "We're not dating, Rett. We hooked up."

"Again." He spooned sugar into his coffee.

"Still not the same." Sin fiddled with the messy bun atop her head. They stood facing each other, arms folded. "And yes, I'm a modern woman who does what she wants. But that don't mean I want all of Mayberry to know about it." Sin shrugged. "You know how it is here. News travels fast."

Rett's heart raced and his mouth went dry. He stepped closer, resisting the urge to pull her into his arms again. "Would that be such a terrible thing, Sin?"

Chapter Twenty-Two

• • •

A knot tightened in Sin's stomach and her throat felt parched. What was wrong with her?

She was Sinclair Buchanan: a woman who was never at a loss for words or opinions. Yet, in this moment, she didn't know what to think or say. She was shaken, more by Rett's open, heartfelt expression and the hint of vulnerability in his coffee-brown eyes.

"You're a guy. People won't make the same assumptions about you," Sin said. "And while I realize that's their problem, not mine, I'd much rather have folks in town talking about what I've accomplished in my career or my contributions to the community. Not gossiping about who I'm sleeping with...*slept* with," she added quickly.

Rett placed his hands on the counter on either side of her. "Sin, last night was..."

"Amazing." Her response was instinctive. "Still..."

"Then why'd you leave?" Rett rested one large hand on her hip. She could swear that electricity flowed through his fingertips.

She forced her eyes to meet his, despite his closeness and the difference in their heights. "I just told you why, Rett. I—"

He captured her mouth in a kiss. But this kiss was different. The hunger and passion that made her nipples bead and her sex grow damp and heavy were certainly there. But this kiss was unhurried and deliberate. Filled with a tenderness that made her belly flutter and her heart swell.

Sin wanted to pull away. To remind him this wasn't what they were about. They were about carnal lust that filled a physiological need. No questions asked. Nothing expected beyond a good time and multiple orgasms. But Rett's slow kiss—hungry and passionate without the greedy desperation of their earlier encounters—made her feel things she wasn't supposed to feel with a man like Rett. A man who wasn't serious about his life and career. He was simply passing through. Flitting from one adventure to the next. So this feeling...*whatever it was*...had to be some ridiculous, passing phase.

Sinclair pulled away, her chest heaving and her face stinging with heat.

Her eyes met his. "What was that?"

"If you don't know, I've been doing it wrong up till now." Rett shoved his hands into his pockets. The fabric across the front panel of his pants stretched, emphasizing the outline of what lie beneath.

She shuddered at the tactile memory of everything that had happened between them.

"You know what I mean." Sin forced her eyes to return to his. "That wasn't our usual I-can't-wait-to-get-you-outta-those-clothes kiss. That was a..." Her words trailed off and she pressed her fingertips to her lips involuntarily.

"The kiss of a man who *really* likes you and would maybe like to see you again?"

She nodded wordlessly, glancing away from the sincerity in his expression, which filled her with an unexplained warmth. Her reaction was silly. She was behaving like an infatuated teenage girl. Yet it felt as precarious as the riptide that pushed unsuspecting swimmers out to sea.

"Good. Because I *do* really like you, Sin. And I'd like to see you again." Rett lifted her chin, forcing her eyes to return to his.

Sinclair studied his face. Maybe Rett wasn't asking for a relationship.

"So what you're asking for is a repeat of last night," Sin said carefully, the tension in her shoulders easing. "Now that might be my favorite idea you've come up with thus far. But we need to be discreet about this whole thing or—"

"I'm not interested in being your dirty little secret, Sin. I'd like to take you out."

"On a date?" Sin's pulse quickened. "Here on the island?"

"You make it sound like I'm asking you to rope a wild steer or something." Rett looked at her curiously, his arms folded.

"Aren't you?" Sinclair propped a fist on her hip.

Trying to pin Rett Davenport down in a serious relationship was as precarious an endeavor as trying to rope one of the feral horses—descendants of Spanish mustangs— that had roamed free in the Outer Banks for hundreds of years.

"Have you ever been in a serious relationship, Rett?"

"Of course." He straightened the collar of his white polo shirt. "Serious just isn't what I'm usually looking for."

"Well, I am." Sin's tone softened. The admission surprised her, and her cheeks heated with embarrassment. The last thing she wanted was to come off to Rett as desperate or needy. Yet, now that the words were out there, she might as well be honest with him and herself. "Since Teddy, I've been focused on my career. But a part of me still holds out hope that I'll eventually find the kind of love Dakota and Dexter have. So yes, we had fun and we enjoy each other's company, but anything beyond that…" Sin shrugged.

Rett winced, and a twinge of guilt tugged at her chest.

"I didn't intend to sound so harsh." Sin liked Rett. A lot. Maybe too much. "But we've never pulled punches with each other. Now isn't the time to start."

The oven timer sounded, and Sin was grateful for the reprieve. They both needed to take a breath and think about this rather than simply reacting to raw desire and crazy chemistry.

Last night had been intense and a little wild. That was expected. What she hadn't expected was to feel so many emotions. When they'd been together in Raleigh, it had been strictly physical. But last night was different in a way she couldn't explain.

And the kiss he'd just given her intensified the emotions she was already grappling with. Feelings that terrified her. Because Rett had no intention of staying on Holly Grove Island once his grandmother's renovation was complete.

Sin turned off the blaring buzzer.

Don't fall for the trap, girl. Dakota's wedding and pregnancy have you caught up in your feelings.

Sin slipped on her black oven mitts and removed the fresh, hot biscuits she'd made from scratch. Cooking calmed her and helped her clear her head. It was her personal form of meditation. She'd been too restless to sleep after she'd returned to her condo and showered. So she'd made candied bacon and fresh buttermilk biscuits to go with the homemade peach preserves she had a taste for.

She set the pan of hot biscuits on the stove.

"Did you say something, Sin?"

I said that out loud? "I was talking to myself."

Sin turned her back to Rett and sighed. What was going on with her today?

Before Rett had come to town, she'd been content with her life. She hadn't dated in months and she'd been completely focused on her career and her renewed friendship with Dakota. But now her best friend was getting married and having a baby, and she was feeling some weird form of loss that was throwing her off her game.

When she'd climbed out of Rett's bed that morning, she'd taken a moment to watch him as he slept. She couldn't help thinking of how good it had felt lying in his arms. Part of her wanted to stay and spend the day in bed with him. But the little voice in the back of her head charged with keeping her heart intact reminded her not to expect anything more from Rett.

So what had compelled the quintessential bachelor to suddenly behave like a romantic suitor when she was proposing the perfect undercover, no-obligation, headboard-banging arrangement?

"I respect that we've always been honest with one another, Sin. Painfully so." Rett rubbed his jaw and furrowed his thick brows. "But I'm approaching forty. Do you honestly believe I'm not capable of being in a relationship?"

"Wouldn't know. Until recently, we hadn't really seen much of each other."

"Actually I'd say we've seen an awful lot of each other over the past five years." Rett's gaze trailed down her body and lingered on the hem of her thigh-length skirt.

Her skin warmed, and not because she was still standing in front of a hot stove. Sinclair turned off the oven and removed her gloves.

"So what?" She shrugged. "We've seen each other naked—"

"Twice." Rett held up two fingers victoriously, his eyes glinting in the sunlight. "Most recently just a few hours ago."

"Be that as it may." Sinclair folded her arms, partly out of frustration with Garrett's logic. Partly to hide the beading of her nipples in response to his seductive stare. "I'm sure you've seen plenty of other women naked in the past five years, most of whose names you probably don't remember."

"Also harsh," Rett said.

"Didn't hear you say it wasn't true, though." She raised an eyebrow. "Eggs?"

"You're fixing me breakfast?"

"Sweetie, you had *me* for breakfast just a few hours ago. At some point I'm pretty sure my head was spinning, and I was speaking in tongues. Making you a little somethin' to eat doesn't feel like a very big ask," Sin said. "Over easy okay?"

Rett nearly choked on his coffee but recovered quickly. He coughed. "Yes, but not runny, please. Thank you."

Sin nodded toward the breakfast bar, indicating that he should grab a seat. Then she melted butter in a skillet.

"As I was saying, us sleeping together a couple times over five years doesn't mean we suddenly *know* each other. You know?"

Okay, maybe she was rambling, but something about Rett had always rattled her. And though she was loath to admit it, this man who was incredibly handsome, extremely desirable, and oh-so-capable-in-the-bedroom still drove her crazy. Only now he drove her wild in ways she couldn't have imagined back then.

"Let's take sex out of it for a moment," Rett said calmly.

I'd rather not. In fact, I'd prefer that we were having sex right now rather than this painfully awkward conversation.

"Okay." Sin cracked one egg into the skillet and then the other. She sprinkled on a little salt and pepper before covering the skillet to ensure the eggs cooked all the way through. "Let me get our plates together, then we can talk."

Sinclair plated their eggs, once they were done, along with the candied bacon and a few biscuits. She handed Rett a plate and sat beside him at the counter. "My homemade peach preserves are there. Got strawberry in the refrigerator, if that's what you'd prefer."

"Peach is fine, and this all looks great, thanks." Rett didn't begin eating. He was obviously waiting for her. After she'd taken her first bite, he dived into his meal. "Wow, Sin. Dex, my mom, and Mama Mae have always raved about your cooking, but *wow*. Everything is amazing. And these have got to be the best biscuits I've ever had."

His effusive praise for her food warmed her chest. She was a southern woman who loved cooking. Nothing made her happier than seeing people she cared about enjoying food she'd made from scratch as a labor of love.

They ate breakfast in companionable silence, which Sin found comforting. Then her phone beeped and a text message from her mother scrolled across her lock screen.

Saved you a seat at church.

Sinclair typed a quick reply.

Sorry. I won't be there today. Something came up.

It took less than a minute for her mother to respond.

Cool. I'll let God know.

Sinclair rolled her eyes, knowing her mother was only half kidding. Terri Buchanan could just add that to the laundry list of reasons her youngest daughter was still an unmarried heathen.

When they finished eating, Rett gathered their dishes.

"Just leave them, hon. I've got it," Sin said.

"You cooked. I'll clean. It's only fair," he insisted as he stacked the dishes.

"Thank you, Rett." She'd let him have this. Then maybe he'd let go of this absurd idea of them dating.

Rett rinsed their dishes. "By the way, is this the part of the program where we start using pet names for one another?" His lips twisted in a sexy smirk that sent electricity up her spine.

"Pet names? What are you talking about?" She folded her arms. "Everyone on this island calls you Rett."

"You just called me *hon*. And earlier, you called me *sweetie*," he noted with a self-satisfied grin.

"You're a born-and-bred southerner. You should know I'm just as likely to call the grocery clerk or the mail carrier hon, sugar, or sweetie whether they're male or female. I wouldn't go taking run-of-the-mill southern terms of endearment to heart." She joined him at the sink, then opened the dishwasher and began loading it as he handed her the dishes.

"True." Rett dried his hands on a cloth. "But if you didn't like me, you wouldn't call me hon or sweetie. And if you didn't enjoy spending time with me and weren't considering my proposal, I doubt you would've skipped church to make me breakfast." He folded his arms and leaned against the counter. "Which means you *are* considering it."

Dammit. Wannabe Sherlock Holmes was right. She was considering his offer, wasn't she?

Sinclair heaved a sigh as her gaze met his, then she started the dishwasher.

She really hated that Rett was standing in her kitchen looking like a smug, six-foot-three tower of mouthwatering deliciousness. Handsome face. Hair graying slightly at the temples. Gray threaded through his well-groomed beard. Broad shoulders. Muscled arms and a thick-but-toned ass and thighs. And that was fully dressed.

But Rett was right. This wasn't just about their physical attraction. She enjoyed spending time with him. In fact, she looked forward to it. And maybe a tiny part of her was curious about what it would be like to date her high school hate crush. Despite the little voice in the back of her head warning her nothing good could come of it.

A flurry of additional texts from her mother lit up her phone. Sin picked it up. The first message began:

> Since you're not seeing anyone and work keeps you too busy to meet any nice men, I took the liberty of rounding up a few possibilities.

The remaining messages were the equivalent of a dossier on three eligible bachelors: Devon James, who was apparently on the other side of that empty seat her mother had saved her in church. The second was the current mayor's son, who was back for a visit. The third was her brother-in-law's lobbyist coworker, whom her mother had encouraged to join her sister and brother-in-law when they came to the island for Dakota's wedding.

"Dammit, Mama," Sinclair muttered under her breath, her stomach and jaw clenching and her temperature rising. Her fingers flew across the screen as she typed out her reply.

Stop. It. Mother. Now. Please. I don't need...

"Sin, wait..." Rett put his hand over hers before she could finish typing her message. "I wasn't trying to get in your business, but I couldn't help seeing your mom's message. I assume those photos are dudes she's picked out for you."

"Yes." Sin huffed and her bangs fluttered. "No matter how many times I tell her I'm not interested, she just doesn't get it." Sinclair paced the floor. "Is it that difficult to accept that I'm okay with being single? That I have no intention of settling for just anyone." She glanced at Rett and cleared her throat. "No offense."

"None taken." He hiked an eyebrow and folded his arms in a move that indicated he did, in fact, take offense at her comment. "But I have a proposal that could work for both of us."

Sin turned to Rett with her arms folded and an eyebrow raised. "What kind of proposal?"

"Your mother is doing all of this because she thinks you aren't seeing anyone."

She wasn't. "Okay?"

"What if you were seeing someone?" Rett asked. "Then your mom would stop bugging you about not dating."

"No offense..." She'd found herself saying that a lot during this conversation "But my mom isn't very fond of you, Rett. In fact, the entire time we've been working together on the wedding and the renovation, she's been warning me that you'd try to get into my panties."

"Guess she wasn't wrong about that, but in my defense...crotchless, so..." He shrugged.

Sin laughed, and it was like Rett had hit the release button on the pressure valve created by her mother's "helpful" text messages. She studied Rett's face and cocked her head. "You're seriously proposing we date to get my mother off my back?"

"That's why you'd be doing it, yes," he confirmed.

"And why would you be doing it?" Sin asked.

Rett stared at her, as if the answer should be obvious. His expression seemed so sincere. "I like being with you, Sin. And I'd like to explore whatever is happening between us." He cupped her jaw. "My gut tells me you do, too."

Sinclair opened her mouth to object to Rett's interpretation of her feelings, but he covered her open mouth with his, his tongue gliding against hers as he slid his arms around her waist and dragged her body against his.

Her objections died on Rett's lips—pressed to hers— as their kiss escalated. Sin's skin felt flushed and her pulse raced. Her skin tingled and her nipples felt painfully tight as they scraped against his hard chest.

Her body ached with her growing desire for this man. The man who'd been worming his way into her heart, little by little, over the past few weeks. Making her feel things for him she hadn't thought possible. Things that could only lead to her getting hurt when Rett packed his bags and rode the GTO out of town in a few weeks.

Yet she couldn't fight his gravitational pull and extract herself from his orbit. Maybe a part of her didn't want to.

Chapter Twenty-Three

———•—•—•———

Rett broke their kiss, pulling back enough to study Sinclair's face. Her hazel eyes slowly drifted open and glinted in the afternoon sunlight. She studied him as if he was a confounding puzzle.

"You're willing to do the whole dating thing when I'm offering to keep things casual between us with no expectations?"

After all this time, Sinclair still made Rett feel something he couldn't quite explain. This time, he wanted to explore those feelings rather than pretending they weren't there. So here he was, doing what he'd been too gutless to do in high school. When he'd been afraid that beloved beauty queen Sinclair Buchanan, whose life seemed practically perfect in every way, could never be interested in someone as lost and broken as he'd been back then.

Rett was shooting his shot with Sinclair, despite knowing there was a good chance he'd go down in a fiery blaze.

"Absolutely." He grazed her cheekbone and pressed another kiss to the lips that tasted of homemade peach preserves. Then he pulled back, needing to see her expression. "Last night hit different than it did five years ago for me,

Sin. I know it did for you, too. Or you wouldn't have stayed the night."

"Of course it was different." Sin's cheeks flushed. She dropped her gaze from his momentarily, stammering in response. "We know each other better now. We've developed sort of a friendship. But that doesn't mean we...that I..." Sin's objections died. She stared at him, blinking. Then she sucked in a deep breath. "Okay."

"Okay? As in, yes?" Rett studied Sin's face.

"Yes." A lopsided smile played across Sin's face. "Thank you for doing this for me, Rett."

"I'm no saint, sweetheart. Yes, I'm doing this to take the pressure off you with your mom." Rett tightened his grip on her waist. "But I'm also doing this because I need to know if there's something more here. I think you need to know, too."

Sin didn't object. But being Sin, she wouldn't confirm his suspicions either. She just stared at him with a sassy little smirk that made him want to toss her over his shoulder and take her to bed.

Rett dipped his head and captured Sin's eager mouth in a heated kiss. He tightened his grip on her waist, crushing her lush curves against his body. Their night together replayed in his mind, the sights and sounds so vivid it felt like he was back there again.

His new favorite thing was hearing Sin call his name, her body trembling as her nails dug into his skin. The feverish way she kissed him back told him all the things that stubborn Sinclair Buchanan—a woman who hated to be wrong—wouldn't say.

A fondness had grown between them these past few weeks. Still, a part of Sin couldn't seem to let go of the image of him as the angry, insecure teen he'd once been.

Or maybe she was worried he'd play some rotten joke on her, as he had long ago.

He was to blame for that, but he'd do whatever it took to make Sin see the man he was now. A man who wanted and needed her. And that maybe she felt the same about him.

Sin tugged Rett's shirt from the waistband of his pants and slid her warm palms up his bare back. She grazed the skin with her fingernails, and the sensation went straight to the part of him pinned between them and standing at attention. He ached to be inside her. To hear Sin call his name as he found his edge. Freefalling into the deepest, most profound sense of ecstasy he'd ever known.

But more importantly, he needed Sin to see that he was worth taking a chance on.

Rett lifted Sin onto the breakfast counter she'd just wiped down after their meal. She gasped as she grasped his shoulders. He sat on the barstool in front of her and spread her knees, his palms gliding up the insides of her thighs as she stared at him with wide eyes.

"Rett, what are you doing?"

"Eating dessert." He tugged aside the damp fabric shielding her sex. When his thumb brushed against the hardened nub, she shuddered and sucked in a deep breath. Rett lowered his head and lapped at her glistening flesh.

"But we're in my kitchen." Sinclair's chest heaved with quick, shallow breaths.

He didn't stop, but he did gaze up at her as she watched him intently.

"Can you think of a better place to eat?" he asked, before running his tongue over her glistening flesh again in long, slow deliberate passes, avoiding the place she wanted him most. He spread her wide with his thumbs and tasted her.

He took Sin higher and higher with his fingers and
tongue until she gripped the back edge of the counter,
and her body stiffened. She cursed, calling his name again
and again. Until she was pleading for a reprieve from the
intense pleasure.

Rett slid Sin onto his lap, so she straddled him. He
cradled her warm, languid body against his. Sin rested
her head on his shoulder, her breathing quick and shallow.
When it had evened out, Rett planted a long, slow kiss on
her soft lips. He broke the kiss, reluctantly, cupping her
cheek as he studied her dreamy gaze, flushed skin, and full,
lush, kissable lips.

As much as Rett wanted to carry Sin to bed and make
love to her, there was something he wanted even more. For
Sin to realize he was serious about being with her. And he
knew exactly how to prove it.

"Come to dinner with me tonight at my mom's."

"As your date?" Sin's dreamy eyes widened.

"Seems like a good idea to start off with a friendly
crowd. And my family adores you, especially Mama Mae
and Izzy."

"You're sure they won't have a problem with me crashing your family dinner?"

"I'll ask my mom to set an extra place for you, if it
makes you feel better," he said between kisses to her neck.
"But trust me, they're going to be thrilled I'm bringing you
to dinner." He dropped another kiss on her shoulder.

Sin's back tensed, but she nodded. "As long as your
mom doesn't mind."

"Then I'll pick you up in"—he glanced at his watch—
"three hours. And this time, I'm driving." He kissed
her again.

"Yes, sir." Her adorable little smirk reminded him he was

still hard and the damp, warm space between her thighs was pressed against him there. Sin frowned. "Wait…does that mean you're leaving? *Now*?"

"Afraid so, sweetheart." Rett stood, his hands beneath her round bottom as he let her down until her bare feet met the floor. "I have to meet the carpenter over at the house. He's installing those built-ins we want for the first-floor main bedroom extension. Otherwise, he won't be available for at least two weeks. "

They'd decided to have a window seat flanked by built-in shelving installed to accent the window overlooking Mama Mae's backyard. And since they were going high end with the reno, they'd installed a fireplace in the equally large secondary bedroom upstairs. Now they needed a custom fireplace mantel. So they'd called in a top carpenter in the area: an old friend of his dad's. Which was why the man was both willing to work on a Sunday and give them one hell of a deal.

"Right. I forgot." She frowned, her disappointment evident. "I'll see you later then."

"Can't wait." Rett forced a smile, though his body was screaming for him to sweep Sin up in his arms and carry her down the hall to her bedroom. He pressed another quick kiss to her lips. "Lock up behind me?"

Sin looked slightly amused by his constant worrying over her. But she simply followed him to the front door.

"Dakota and Dexter," Sin blurted suddenly.

"What about them?"

"What do we tell them?" Sin asked.

"The truth. We're attracted to each other and exploring our options." Rett put a hand on the doorknob but didn't open the door. He turned to Sin. "Anything you'd like to divulge beyond that is up to you."

Rett took the stairs down the two flights to Dex's condo. He heaved a small sigh of relief. Getting Sin to agree to go out on a few dates was one thing. Making her see that something deeper was happening between them was a much taller task. But Sin was special, so she was worth the effort.

Sinclair was an accomplished real estate professional, an inventive interior designer, and a gifted cook. She was passionate about her work and taking care of the people in her life. A good daughter, a supportive sister, and a loyal friend. And she loved Holly Grove Island and its residents.

As they'd worked together to arrange their friends' pre-wedding festivities it felt as if Sin had reintroduced him to the town where they'd grown up. He'd been slowly falling in love with Holly Grove Island again. Maybe he was falling for Sin, too.

Chapter Twenty-Four

Sinclair sucked in a quiet breath to calm the butterflies dancing in her belly in response to the knock at the door. She smoothed down the sunny yellow eyelet fabric of her sundress. Then she ran her fingers through her shoulder-length hair, flat ironed and worn in soft beach waves.

She was being silly. This wasn't a blind date with some stranger. She was going out with Rett. Someone she'd known more than half her life. They'd spent plenty of time together these past few weeks. And Rett had seen every single inch of her body in all its naked glory.

Why was she suddenly so nervous about going out with him?

Rett knocked again, shaking Sin from her daze. She opened the front door. The moment she saw Rett's smiling face, the nervousness faded away.

"Sin, you look...amazing." Rett kissed her cheek. "Yellow looks good on you."

She appreciated that he'd taken care not to ruin her lipstick. "Thank you. Are those for your mom?" She indicated the bouquet of flowers he clutched.

"No, these are for you." He held out the lovely bouquet

of roses, lilies, and hydrangea in delicate shades of pink, white, and peach accented by fresh greenery. "The flowers for my mother and Gram are in the car."

"They're beautiful. Thank you." Sin accepted the large bouquet, inhaling its heavenly scent. "Let me put them in water, then we can go."

Sin arranged the gorgeous flowers in her favorite vase and placed them on the table in her front hall, then they left.

Rett had routinely been thoughtful and considerate, but as he opened the passenger door to the GTO for her, things felt more intentional than him simply being a gentleman. When they arrived at his mother's house, Rett rang the doorbell, then extended his open palm.

Sin stared at it for a moment. They'd kissed, had sex, and had done countless other things together. But they hadn't held hands. The gesture felt strangely intimate and extremely public: a declaration that they were together.

She swallowed hard, then slipped her palm in his.

Rett kissed the back of her hand and smiled.

Sin's heart fluttered, and a giddy smile warmed her cheeks.

"You two are so darn adorable together. I always knew you'd make a good match," Rett's mother Ellen said with a wide grin as she swung open the front door. "And I can't remember the last time I saw Rett look this happy."

"Hey, Ma." Rett handed the larger bouquet to his mother and kissed her cheek. "I'm a little old to be getting the Rett-brought-a-girl-home treatment," he said in a teasing tone.

"Maybe if you'd ever brought anyone home, I'd be over it." She pinched his arm. "But this is a first. So I don't care how old you are, I'm going to enjoy it."

"You've never brought a girl home?" Sin asked incredulously after accepting a warm hug from Ellen. "*Ever?*"

"*Never*," Ellen answered for him. "Which makes this an extra special occasion." She winked. "Go on in. They're all out there on the sunporch. The pot roast still has a few more minutes. I'm just going to put this stunning bouquet in a vase. I'll join you shortly."

"Your mother is just trying to make me feel special, right?" Sinclair whispered when Ellen walked away. "I'm not really the first woman you've brought home to your parents, am I?"

"My meet-the-parents standards are pretty high." Rett shrugged, a sheepish expression on his handsome face. "You're the first person I've wanted to bring here."

A knot tightened in Sinclair's gut. Rett had paid her the highest compliment in bringing her here for their first date, even though she already knew his entire family.

"Ready?" Rett threaded his fingers through hers this time when he gripped her hand.

Sin nodded and let Rett lead her through the house and onto the large, three-seasons room off the backyard. Hector grinned broadly as he stood to greet them.

"*Hola*, Rett." Hector grinned at his stepson, who bumped fists with him. "*Hola*, Sinclair! How wonderful of you to join us." The bear hug he gave her reminded Sin of the warm hugs her father always gave. "You have no idea how much joy you have brought to my wife and to Rett's grandmother." The older man nodded toward Mama Mae, who sat in the corner beaming.

"I told you these two were meant to be together," Mama Mae said proudly, after thanking Rett for the flowers. "I felt it here and here." Mama Mae slapped a hand on her belly, then placed a hand over her heart. "My intuition ain't never let me down yet."

"Was it your intuition or you coercing them into

renovating your house together?" Hector chuckled, laughing harder when the older woman gave him the evil eye.

"Mama Mae, is that true?" Sin asked in mock surprise.

"Snitches get stitches," Mama Mae said in a husky whisper as she pointed to Hector.

"All right, all right!" Hector held up his hands in surrender, still laughing. "I did not know it was supposed to be a secret."

"Forgive my family," Rett said. "Apparently, it's Let's Clown Rett Day and nobody told me." He glanced over at his younger sister, Isabel, seated on the far end of the sofa. "Hey, Iz."

"Hey," she responded flatly, not bothering to glance up from her phone.

Sinclair glanced over at Izzy. She was feigning nonchalance, but beneath the act, Sin sensed that Rett's younger sister was hurt and perhaps angry. Sin felt bad for both siblings.

Rett and Hector had moved on to talking about the off-season trades made by the Carolina Panthers.

Sin let go of Rett's hand and joined Izzy on the sofa.

"Hello, Isabel." Sin beamed. "How's it going?"

"Good. I just finished all my exams and I got a paid internship at Holly Grove Island Arboretum and Aquarium," Izzy said nonchalantly as she turned toward Sin on the sofa.

"Congratulations, Izzy! They only award two of those internships each summer, and the competition is pretty stiff. Good for you."

Em's friend Kassandra Montgomery was the director of the program. Every spring she was beside herself trying to choose the final two candidates.

"Thanks, Sin." A genuine smile lit Izzy's dark eyes. She

lowered her voice. "My family doesn't seem to think it's any different from when I worked summer jobs at Helene's Homemade or Sweet Confections, you know? They don't get that—"

"It's a major deal you busted your ass to make happen?"

"Exactly!" Izzy folded her arms. "It's so frustrating."

"I understand how you feel, believe me. My parents are the same way. I'm kicking ass and taking names. Working toward my goal of owning my own brokerage. But all they're worried about is when I'm going to get married and bear some grandchildren." Sin huffed, too.

"That sucks," Izzy said.

This isn't about you. You're supposed to be consoling Izzy, not joining the pity party.

"Have you explained to your family why this is such a big deal?" Sinclair kept her voice low so only Izzy could hear her.

"I shouldn't have to break it down for them, right? I'd be like fishing for compliments or something, you know?"

"I know it feels like they should understand, Izzy. But your parents are both busy people, so some things might escape their notice. Not because they don't care, but because they're overwhelmed with everything that's going on in their lives." Sin nudged the younger woman's shoulder and gave her a big smile. "At least give them a chance."

Ellen walked out onto the porch. "Dinner's ready. The table will be set in a few minutes. Izzy, would you mind helping me?"

Izzy stood and shoved her phone into the back pocket of her shorts. "Sure, Mom."

"I'd be happy to help, too." Sin followed Izzy and Ellen inside.

Izzy showed Sin to the powder room, where she could

wash her hands. Instead of leaving, Izzy asked, "Have you told your parents how you feel? Maybe they don't know how much their comments about marriage and kids bother you."

The question took Sin by surprise.

"My mother is *very* perceptive, and it's not like I've hidden my annoyance." Sin wet her hands, then squirted soap in her palms. "Besides, I've asked her repeatedly to stop playing matchmaker."

"Maybe you need to be more direct with your mom about *why* you don't appreciate her pushing you into marriage and motherhood." Izzy's eyes widened with recognition. "Is that why you're suddenly dating my brother? So your mom will give the matchmaking a rest?"

"I...uh...why would you—"

"I'm not mad about it." Izzy's words halted Sin's stammering. "Hook up with my brother all you want. I'm just glad you're not serious about him or anything."

Sin dried her hands on a frilly towel. "Why?"

"My brother has no intention of hanging around here." Izzy shrugged as she examined her nails. "Honestly? I'm surprised he's stayed this long." The younger woman raised her eyes to Sin's. The pain in them was palpable. "Look, Sin, I like you. You're decent people. And I'm not saying Rett is a bad guy, because he isn't. He just isn't the guy you can expect to be there for you. And I don't want to see you get hurt." Izzy turned and walked away. "See you in the kitchen."

Sin nodded, unable to form an audible response.

She already knew this about Rett, didn't she? By his own admission, he hadn't been looking for anything serious. So why did it hurt to hear Izzy repeating what she already knew about Rett? And if what his sister said was true, why was Rett so insistent they should explore this relationship?

Chapter Twenty-Five

•—◆—•

Rett sat on the verandah with his family after dinner. He and Hector had washed the dishes and put everything away. He was talking to his mother about her job. Yet he couldn't help sneaking glimpses of Sin as she chatted with his grandmother.

Mama Mae genuinely adored Sinclair, and Sin's warmth and admiration for his grandmother felt authentic, too. In fact, his entire family seemed taken with Sinclair—including his sister. Izzy clearly liked Sin more than she liked him.

Gnawing guilt rose in his gut over the disconnect between him and his sister. It was his fault, and he'd always regret that. He'd tried to fix things with Izzy, but she had no interest in repairing their relationship.

Still, it made his heart swell to see his sister—who often seemed sullen—smiling and laughing with Sin. Usually, Izzy had ditched them to go hang out with her friends or disappeared to her room by now. But she'd been so busy chatting with Sin and Mama Mae that he hadn't seen Iz look at her phone once in the past several hours.

"It's nice to see how well Sin fits into *la familia*, eh?"

Hector shoved Rett's shoulder and gave him a knowing grin. "It can be a nightmare when your wife and mother don't get along," he said in a low, teasing voice only Rett could hear.

"Sin and I are just feeling each other out. I promise you that neither of us is even thinking about the 'M' word."

"My apologies." Hector patted his chest with a beefy hand as he tried unsuccessfully to tamp down his smile.

Rett mulled over his stepfather's words. "Must've been tough for you, marrying a woman whose kid hated you." It pained him to say the words, but it was no secret how he'd felt about Hector back then.

The other man sighed deeply. He seemed to be measuring his words. "Let's just say our love was tested by fire." Hector chuckled softly, but Rett could hear the pain that lingered in those awful memories.

Hector had always been so kind and patient with Rett, even when he'd been at his worst.

"I'm sorry, Hector. You're a good guy, and I'm glad you came into my mom's life…into *our* lives. I'd never seen her truly happy until you came along. Good thing you two didn't let her badass kid run you off," Rett said with a wry smile.

"Your mother is a remarkable woman, son. Wild horses wouldn't have dragged me away, as long as Ellen was willing to have me." A soft smile curved one side of Hector's mouth as he glanced over at his wife in the midst of an animated conversation with Sin, Izzy, and Mama Mae. "Been nearly twenty-five years, and I love her even more now."

"She's lucky to have you," Rett said. "We all are."

Hector's brown eyes widened in surprise. "Thank you, *mijo*. You do not know how much it means to hear you say that."

"I think I do. Sorry it took me so long to say it."

Hector squeezed Rett's shoulder. Then he approached the ladies and tried to persuade them to play a game of Taboo.

When Rett glanced at Sin, she was staring at him. Her smile was tentative, and a burning question flickered behind those hazel eyes. Rett sighed, wondering what his mother or Mama Mae had said to put that look on Sin's face.

———

Rett and Sin waved goodbye to his family as he backed out of their driveway. They drove the first few minutes in silence.

"Thanks for coming to dinner on such short notice," Rett said. "I shouldn't be surprised you charmed the pants off everyone tonight. I'm pretty sure every single one of them is in love with you."

"Your family is amazing. I knew your mom was smart, but I had no idea she was so brilliant. And yet she's so down-to-earth. And I always knew Hector was friendly, but he's this giant teddy bear. The way he loves on your mom and sister, his warmth and respect for your grandmother, his obvious affection for you...the man is adorable. And your grandmother..."

Sin burst into sudden laughter, as if remembering something Mama Mae had said earlier.

"Mama Mae is one of the most hilarious people I've ever met. But she's also wise and supportive. Your sister is great. It takes a minute for her to warm up to folks, but she's a bright, sweet kid with a dry sense of humor. She just wants..." Sin's words trailed off. "Like I said, your family is amazing. I had a wonderful time this evening. Thank you for inviting me."

Sin seemed to be deep in thought and uncharacteristically quiet as she watched the familiar scenery sail by the window. An awkward silence echoed in the cabin of the GTO.

"What was it you were saying about Izzy?" He couldn't help thinking that whatever it was she'd stopped herself from saying was the cause of Sin's sudden silence.

"Nothing," she said quickly. Though it didn't sound like nothing. "But I have been thinking. More like wondering, actually." She wrung her hands in her lap—a very un-Sin-like thing to do.

Sinclair was one of the most confident women he knew, which made how shaken her confidence seemed to be by her mother pressing her to get married and produce grand-children a notable exception.

"All right." Rett covered her hands with his much larger one and squeezed. "Ask me anything. I have nothing to hide."

"You said you want to explore this." Sin turned toward him. "Why if you just plan on leaving anyway?"

Rett returned his hand to the wheel. A particularly curvy stretch of road lay ahead. He hesitated before responding. "My plans are pretty fluid right now. Seems like the perfect time to see where this goes."

"And what if we decide we'd like to keep seeing each other? Would you stay?"

"I'd strongly consider it."

A few weeks ago, his answer would have been a resound-ing *no*. After all, he'd spent his teenage years dreaming of how he'd make his great escape from their tiny island town. But the past few weeks had made him see the town in a different light. Before, he'd only seen the things he'd wanted to escape from. Now, he could clearly see all of the reasons to stay.

Holly Grove Island was a haven from the rest of the world. The slower pace of life here was calming. And island residents genuinely cared about their neighbors. Characteristics he'd loathed as a teen but appreciated now.

"Would you ever consider leaving the island?" Rett asked.

"No." Sin's answer was quick and decisive. "I realize it isn't fair of me to ask if you'd stay when I won't consider leaving, but I can't help how I feel." Her voice wavered.

"I respect your honesty." Maybe it made him selfish, but Rett wanted to be with Sin *and* to move forward with the opportunity in Charleston. He doubted that either of them would be interested in a long-distance relationship. So he'd have to make a choice.

"Given that we both know you'll eventually want to leave, perhaps we should reconsider my proposal to just make this about living in the moment without expectations. That way no one gets hurt."

Rett pulled into the parking garage of their building and parked in one of the spaces assigned to Dexter's condo. He took Sin's hands in his.

"That would be the safe thing to do," he acknowledged. "But I've played it safe with relationships my entire life, Sin. I'm not interested in doing that with you."

"Why is this different?" She studied his expression in the limited light of the parking garage as they sat in his car.

"Because it's you, Sin." He swept the hair from her face and tucked it behind her ear. "I missed my chance with you in high school. I don't intend to make that mistake again."

"Oh." The softness in her gaze warmed his chest.

"I don't know how this will turn out. But I know I don't want to spend the next twenty years regretting not finding out. Does that answer your question?"

Sin nodded, her eyes shimmering in the darkness. She pressed her mouth to his.

The sweet, almost tentative kiss made Rett's chest expand with his growing affection and deep admiration for Sinclair. It was clear that regardless of what happened between them, he would never be quite the same.

Chapter Twenty-Six

•—•—●—•—•

Sin followed Rett inside Dex's condo. The overnight bag she'd thrown together hastily and had insisted on carrying herself felt heavy on her shoulder. It was filled with full-size bottles of her pricey but luxurious shower gel, hair care, and skin care products. But the weight of the bag was more psychological than physical.

She was making a conscious choice to spend another night with Rett. But this time, she didn't have the emotional shield of telling herself it was only sex. That it didn't really mean anything to either of them. Because clearly, something more was brewing between them.

It had been coming on slowly over the past several weeks. Little shifts in her perception of Rett that had shown her how wrong she'd been about him. He wasn't the selfish, arrogant monster she'd believed him to be. Rett was confident but not cocky. Self-assured but not arrogant. And the sacrifices he'd been willing to make for Dexter and for Mama Mae proved that he was more selfless than selfish.

She'd even been wrong about Rett not being family-oriented—a trait that was important to her in a prospective mate. Yes, he'd had a rough relationship with his mother and Hector. But he'd gone to great lengths to repair it. Which was why it bothered her that Rett hadn't resolved things with his sister.

Rett put her bags in the bedroom. When he returned, he held up his phone.

"My Mom and Gram have already sent me text messages insisting I bring you for dinner next week." Rett looked up from his phone with a lopsided grin. "They're more concerned whether you'll be there next week than if I will."

"You're being a drama king." Sin laughed. "Your family adores you."

"No, they love me," he corrected. "They adore *you.*"

It was one silly date. Still, Sin was overwhelmed by the warmth and affection Rett's family had shown her. She'd always wanted a close relationship with Teddy's family. His father was nice enough, but his mother and sister had never liked her. And if she was being honest, she hadn't much cared for them either. But she'd been willing to make the effort for Teddy's sake. Neither of them had shown her the same consideration. So Sin couldn't help being moved by the fondness Rett's family had shown her tonight.

A ding indicated Rett had received another text message. He smiled at first, but then frowned. He turned the phone toward Sin so she could read the message.

It was a seven-word message from Izzy.

If you hurt Sin, I'll cut you.

"You wanna tell me again I'm just being a drama king? My sister *literally* likes you more than me." His tone was teasing, but the furrowing of his brows indicated there was more pain behind his words than he was willing to admit.

So perhaps there was a member of Rett's family who

actually did prefer her to him. But maybe she could help fix that.

"You've made amends for the past with your mom and Hector. Why not with Izzy?"

"What makes you think I haven't tried to make amends with my sister?" Rett's frown deepened. He set down his phone, grabbed a beer from the fridge, and chugged from the bottle.

"Because it's evident the wound is still fresh." Sin tried not to react to his annoyance with her question. Rett was obviously pained by his broken relationship with his sister.

"Well, I *have* tried to fix things with Iz."

"What *exactly* have you done to smooth things out?" Sin pressed, undeterred by Rett's increasing crankiness.

"Everything but stand on my head." Rett drained the glass bottle and set it on the counter with a clink. "My sister is as stubborn as a mule. Don't let that cute face fool you— that girl can hold a grudge like nobody's business."

"Don't see any family resemblance there," Sin muttered.

Rett narrowed his gaze and folded his arms as he leaned against the kitchen counter. "I've tried to engage her in conversations. I've bought her ridiculously expensive stuff for her birthdays and holidays. I've invited her to do a movie night or dinner. I even offered to help her buy a car. She shuts me down every single time."

"Okay." Sin nodded thoughtfully as she stood in front of him with her arms folded, too. "But have you ever apologized?"

"Yes." Rett sounded indignant, but then quickly began to backtrack. "I mean, I've told her I'm sorry I wasn't around when she was a kid and that we're not close now. That I'd like to fix things between us. She rolls her eyes and walks away every single time." Rett shrugged. "What else am I supposed to do?"

"Those sound like nonapology apologies. I *hate* those." Sin shuddered. "Don't tell me you're sorry my feelings were hurt. Tell me you're sorry you were a selfish dickhead. That you regret what you did, and you'll never make that mistake again. And mean it. That, my friend, is a *real* apology."

"Isn't that what I said?"

"No. You made it sound like you were both the victim of unfortunate circumstances. As if the situation was unavoidable." Sin propped one hand on her hip, the other waved in the air. "But that's *not* what happened. *You* made a choice that affected everyone else around you. Admit that. Take ownership of your role in the heartbreak Izzy experienced when the big brother she adored wanted nothing to do with her."

"You spent a couple hours with my sister and suddenly you have the problem all figured out?" Rett glared at her, his growing annoyance flickering in his dark eyes. "You know, it's not like you have the perfect relationship with your sister, either," he noted, the reminder cutting deep. "Your mother, either, for that matter. If it's so easy to fix things with family, why haven't you figured out how to fix your own family issues?"

Sin stared at Rett, blinking. Surprised by how much his words stung.

She was tough as nails and not easily shaken. She'd been brilliant at playing the dozens as a kid and she'd gone toe to toe with Rett many a day as teens.

So why was she suddenly speechless, standing there with a knot in her gut, and her eyes burning with unshed tears?

"You're right." Sin lifted her chin, finally finding her voice. "It wasn't my place to say anything. Not my pig, not my farm." She headed for his bedroom to retrieve her bags.

"So now I'm a pig?" He followed her to the bedroom.

"Well, I'm sure as hell not referring to Izzy." She turned to face him. "If the mud fits, wallow in it."

There was the slightest hint of amusement in his dark eyes. But his expression sank when she hitched her overnight bag on her shoulder. "You're leaving?"

She stared just past his shoulder; her arms folded. "I've clearly worn out my welcome."

"Sin." Rett lifted her chin. "We're having a small disagreement. It's no big deal, and it's no reason for you to leave."

"Maybe *that's* the problem." Sin poked a finger in his chest. "It's no big deal to you, but it is to me. And it's a huge deal to Izzy. She's bitter and angry, and she's hurting. And yes, after a few hours with your sister, I *do* understand exactly how she feels. Because, as you so kindly pointed out, I've got complicated family shit of my own I'm dealing with. So I can relate in a way you obviously can't."

Sin huffed, taking a step back. "But by all means, you keep being an arrogant bonehead more invested in being right than fixing things with your sister. Because, after all, it's been working out so well up till now."

They stood there in silence, her heart beating rapidly. She raked her fingers through her hair. "I should go. Give you some space tonight."

She made her way past him and down the hall.

Rett trotted ahead of her and stopped.

"I don't need space, Sin. I need you here with me. And despite my defensive, asshole response to you trying to be genuinely helpful, I could *really* use your insight where Izzy is concerned." Rett pressed a hand to his chest. "I'm genuinely sorry for being a complete dickhead just now. This thing with my sister...it's a sensitive subject. But that doesn't give me license to take it out on you when all you were doing was trying to help. I'm sorry for being a defensive jerk about it, and I promise, it won't happen again."

Sin stared at Rett, her head cocked as she mulled over his apology.

"Make sure it doesn't, or Izzy's threat will be the least of your worries." She pointed a warning finger at him.

"I don't doubt it." Rett reached for her bags.

Sin handed them over and followed Rett to the bedroom where he set them down.

He turned to her. "Hungry?"

"Starving. I thought you'd never ask. Those crab cakes your mama made were hitting. I hope one of those made it into the bag." Sin took a step toward the kitchen.

Suddenly, Rett's arms snaked around her waist from behind and he pulled her body against his as he nuzzled her neck, making her giggle. He turned her in his arms, his eyes meeting hers. "I really am sorry, Sin."

"I know." She pressed a quick kiss to his lips. Then she called dibs on the crab cake and raced him to the kitchen.

———

Rett and Sin sat at the barstools devouring the leftovers they'd divvied up as they chatted about Mama Mae's renovation project and Dexter and Dakota's wedding—just two weeks away.

"Speaking of Dakota and Dex..." Rett said.

"I know," Sin mumbled through a mouthful of his mother's banana pudding. "I've been debating whether I should call or text or if I should just wait until I see her for lunch later this week.

"Gossip travels at the speed of light around here. My mother is probably on the phone with Aunt Marilyn right now," Rett said, referring to Dexter's mom. "And then she'll tell Emerie, who'll tell Nick, Dexter, and the entire town. Which means Dakota will already have heard fourth or fifth hand by then. Trust me, you do not want to upset a hormonal woman."

It was a lesson he remembered clearly from when his mother was pregnant with Izzy.

"You're right. I'll send her a text message tonight and tell her we can talk details at lunch on Wednesday," Sin said.

"Good plan." Rett rested a hand on the soft skin of her exposed thigh. "And I'm ready to hear your suggestions on my dilemma with Izzy."

"Good, because I have the perfect idea. But I need to know if you're willing to go with a grand gesture."

"I was prepared to bribe Iz with a car, remember? Whatever it is, I'm willing to at least consider it."

"First, Izzy deserves a genuine, heartfelt apology. Have you ever told her the things you told me about how badly you took it when your parents broke up and your dad died?"

"She knows what happened," he said gruffly, his throat dry.

"But has she ever heard the story directly from you?" Sin stroked his stubbled cheek, her tone and expression softening.

"It's not something I like talking about." A knot tightened in his gut just thinking about having that conversation with his sister. "I'm still not sure what made me open up to you about it, frankly. But I am glad I did."

"You'll be just as glad once you talk to Izzy," Sin assured him. Something in her confident tone and expression made him believe her. "It'll help her see where your head was at and what you were feeling at the time. She needs to understand that it wasn't her you were rejecting. You were trying, the only way you knew how, to hold on to your dad by not relinquishing his memory. If you're as open and honest with Izzy as you were with me, I think you'll discover that your sister has more compassion than you give her credit for."

"I won't make excuses," he said. "I was a shitty big brother. End of story."

"Maybe you need to cast a bit of that forgiveness you're seeking from Izzy in your own direction," Sin said softly. "You're a human being. We make mistakes. And you were a kid dealing with a lot of trauma on your own as best you could. Don't be so hard on yourself, okay?"

Rett's chest swelled with affection. He tugged Sin off her stool and wrapped her in a bear hug as she stood between his open legs. Rett buried his face in the sweet coconut-and-vanilla scent of Sin's hair and shut his eyes against the pained memories that filled him with guilt and regret. "Thank you, sweetheart."

Sin pulled back to meet his gaze, her eyes misty. She smiled. "Don't thank me yet. You haven't heard the rest of my plan."

"This is gonna cost me, isn't it?" Rett chuckled.

"You better believe it." She grinned. "But it will be worth every cent. Now, do you mind if I hop in the shower first?"

"Not at all. That'll give me a chance to straighten up the kitchen."

"When you're done here...I wouldn't mind if you joined me." Sin didn't wait for Rett's response. She didn't need to. He wouldn't dare turn down her invitation.

Spending his days and nights with Sinclair was something he could definitely get used to.

Chapter Twenty-Seven

•—•—•

Sinclair couldn't believe her best friends' wedding day was finally here. She fanned her eyes, glistening with tears, so she wouldn't ruin her makeup.

"Dakota, sweetie, you look absolutely stunning," Sin finally managed, raw emotion clogging her throat. "I know people say this all the time, but I honestly have never seen a more beautiful bride."

"Do you really like it?" Dakota's eyes brimmed with tears, too, and her voice trembled slightly. She smoothed her hand over her small baby bump, unnoticeable beneath the voluminous tulle fabric and underskirt in the high-waisted dress. The soft, warm peach color popped beautifully against her friend's brown skin. "I don't look bloated and swollen or—"

"*Preggers*?" Sin whispered as she swiped away the wetness from the corner of her eyes. "Only that amazing glow would give that away. Because you look absolutely radiant."

"That, sweetheart, is called *love*." Lila Gayle approached them, in a lovely, soft gray, tea-length "mother-of-the-bride" dress. She squeezed Dakota's hand and air-kissed her cheek. "I'd recognize that look anywhere."

Lila Gayle had become Dakota's stepmother a little more than six months ago. Sensitive to Dakota's feelings about her late mother, Lila Gayle had planned to take a backseat at the wedding. But Dakota had insisted that her new stepmother be a part of the process and wear a mother-of-the-bride gown. Lila Gayle, who had no daughters of her own, had been moved to tears by Dakota's gesture.

It was one of the many sweet and wonderful moments they'd experienced while planning the wedding. Moments that had both warmed Sin's heart and also made her the slightest bit envious of her best friend. Because in just a few more minutes, Dakota was finally going to walk down that aisle and marry Dexter—her childhood sweetheart.

Lila Gayle and Dakota were two women who'd found their soul mates. Sin was truly happy for them. But she wished she could rub her best friend's back and get a little of that magic for herself.

"You're right, Ms. Lila." Sin smiled as she blinked back a fresh wave of tears. "That's love, if ever I've seen it."

"You should know." Ms. Lila grinned. "One can't help noticing that you have a radiance about you whenever you're with Garrett. And you two have been spending quite a bit of time together." Lila Gayle's British accent deepened, along with her smile.

"That's exactly what I told her." Dakota shared a know-ing smile with her stepmother. "Sin has no idea how deep in she and Rett are."

"Are we talking about the fact that Sinclair has apparently fallen in love with her hate crush, Rett Davenport?" Dakota's older sister, Shay, fussed with the train of the bride's gown.

Everyone else in the room giggled. Sinclair snapped her mouth shut, her cheeks warm. She wanted to make it clear she had no intention of falling in love with Garrett. But that would've defeated the purpose of them dating so publicly. So she forced what she hoped was a bashful smile and kept quiet.

"Sinclair Buchanan speechless?" Shay grinned. "Wow. That boy put it on you, for sure." Everyone in the room laughed again.

Sin was five seconds away from saying something when Shay glanced at her watch, then clapped her hands.

"Showtime, ladies. Let's go!"

Ms. Lila and Marilyn—Dexter's mother—gave Dakota an air-kiss before making their way out to where everyone was gathered for the outdoor ceremony on the beach. Shay handed the fragrant bouquets of white, blush, and peach-colored roses, peonies, and dahlias to each bridesmaid. The stunning arrangements had been prepared and delivered by Kassandra Montgomery, whose mother owned Montgomery Florist. Kassie often helped her mother out on the weekends, on top of her job at the Holly Grove Island Arboretum & Aquarium.

Sin straightened Dakota's tiara, then held her friend's hands in hers. "You ready, babe?"

"Yes. I can hardly believe today is finally here." Dakota sucked in a deep breath. "It feels like I've been waiting for this my entire life."

"I know." Sin squeezed her friend's hand and blinked back tears. "I couldn't be happier for you and Dex."

"And I couldn't be happier about you and Rett." Dakota leaned in and lowered her voice. "You're perfect for each other. You always have been. I hope you two finally figure that out."

"I...we..." Sin stammered.

"And here's yours." Shay handed Sinclair her bouquet. "C'mon, Dad's waiting for us."

Sin lagged behind them, grateful for the change of subject. She gave Chief Jones and his daughters a moment. Today was bittersweet for the three of them. Dakota's mother, Ms. Madeline, had died six years ago. Dakota and her mother had been very close, and her absence loomed large over the day's proceedings.

Tears filled Oliver's eyes as he regarded his youngest daughter in her wedding dress, and he didn't bother hiding them.

"Baby girl, you are so beautiful. Your mother would've been so proud. And I know she's happy for you and Dex." Chief Jones hugged Dakota, then wrapped an arm around Shay, too.

"The three of us are *not* going up that aisle crying." Shay extracted herself from their group hug and dabbed her tears with one knuckle. She sniffled. "So let's get it together so we can get to the part where there's an open bar and lots of cake."

That made them all break into laughter. Oliver wiped his eyes with a hankie, which he stuffed back into his breast pocket. Dakota and Shay fanned their faces.

Sinclair took her place in line, right after Shay, but just before Dakota and Chief Jones. She tried her best to stay focused on the wedding, but she couldn't help replaying Dakota's words in her head.

I couldn't be happier about you and Rett. You're perfect for each other. You always have been. I hope you two finally figure that out.

The past couple of weeks, during which she and Rett had been publicly dating had been…fun, to say the least. They'd gone to his parents' again for dinner, gone to dinner and a movie with Dex and Dakota, and attended a town concert, all while working on the wedding and the house renovations. Yes, the man was amazing in bed, as Shay had alluded. But the past few weeks had been about so much more than that. She'd really gotten to know Rett—in a way she hadn't before.

He was a clever, innovative thinker with a keen eye for design. And he'd saved a ton of money on the project by installing cabinetry himself and adding some flourishes that made them feel custom-made. He'd installed the flooring and done the painting himself, along with dozens of other small projects. Sometimes, Sinclair had dropped by Mama Mae's house, just to watch Rett work. Then there was her growing realization that Rett was really sweet and funny. Thoughtful and protective.

Sin liked Rett more than she was willing to admit to him or Dakota. Or even to herself. Partly because Rett Davenport wasn't the man she'd imagined herself ending up with. Partly because she feared that she wasn't enough to make him stay. No matter how much she wanted him to.

Sin took a deep breath and stepped out into the warmth and sunshine of the stretch of Holly Grove Island Beach that was exclusive to the resort. She began her slow descent down the aisle in a one-shoulder dress in a hue just slightly darker than that of the other bridesmaids. She gripped the bouquet tightly and focused on walking with her head held high while not tripping over the floor-length hem of her gown. She'd planned on staring straight ahead at the stretch of the Atlantic Ocean, just beyond the officiant. Instead, her gaze locked with Rett's. A warm smile slid across his handsome face, and her heart beat double-time.

Rett looked so striking in his light gray three-piece suit, a white dress shirt, and a lavender print gray necktie. He had a fresh cut—a low fade with just a little height on top—and his beard and mustache were perfectly trimmed.

He put his hand over his heart, his smile deepening. A message meant just for her.

Sin's belly fluttered and her nervous smile relaxed into a more genuine one as she took her place beside Shay at the head of the aisle.

Electricity traveled up her spine, and her skin tingled. Because even as the entire room had turned to watch Dakota and Oliver make their way up the aisle, Sin could feel the heat of Rett's gaze.

Sin thought of all the moments she and Rett had shared since he'd returned to town. And she couldn't help wondering if Ms. Lila was right and that Rett was falling for her, too.

———

Rett scanned the ballroom as he leaned against the bar. His mother and Hector were on the crowded dance floor swaying to "Always and Forever" by Heatwave. In a few months, they would celebrate their twenty-fifth wedding anniversary. Yet they stared into each other's eyes like young lovers, as in love now as they had been from the very beginning. Perhaps more so.

It had taken him a long time to come around, but he admired them. And he was truly happy for them, just as he was for Dexter and Dakota.

Rett glanced over to where the newly married couple stood talking with Shay and her husband, Howard. His cousin's arm was looped around his wife's waist as he held her close. Their body positioning signaled that they were a single, impenetrable unit. The energy between Shay and her husband was the complete opposite.

Shay's and Howard's smiles seemed forced, and their

shoulders were stiff. Neither Shay nor Howard looked happy, but it seemed important to both of them to *appear* as if they were. And while Dexter and Dakota couldn't keep their hands off each other, Garrett couldn't remember seeing Shay and Howard touch.

Trouble was definitely brewing between those two.

Seeing their discomfort in the midst of the celebration of Dex and Dakota's love felt like a cautionary tale. A reminder that half of all marriages ended in abysmal failure. Rett didn't like those odds. It was one of the many reasons why he hadn't ever envisioned himself standing at the head of the aisle, as Dexter had today, waiting for his bride.

He hadn't seen a healthy marriage. How could he be expected to emulate one?

His parents had divorced. His grandfather died when he was quite young. His aunt and uncle had maintained a cold, seemingly loveless marriage for the sake of their children.

Rett sighed, glancing over at his mother and stepfather again. His mother laughed at something Hector said, then she leaned in and gave him a quick kiss.

No, he had been privy to a healthy, loving marriage. He just hadn't allowed himself to recognize it for what it was.

What his mother and Hector had was real. He was convinced that the love Dakota and Dexter shared was, too. And for the first time, a part of him longed for that kind of love.

His gaze shifted to where Sinclair was chatting with Nick and Emerie. Rett's mouth tightened in an involuntary smile, and warmth filled his chest. Sinclair looked stunning in that dark lavender dress. She raked her manicured fingers through her ombre blond and brown hair, which hung just past her shoulders in soft waves. Sin laughed and pressed a hand to Nick's shoulder. An innocent gesture. Yet he wished he was the one standing with Sin instead.

Over the past few weeks, they'd spent a lot of time together. Working on the renovation over at Mama Mae's. Enjoying a home-cooked meal in Sin's kitchen or his while they made plans for the wedding. Watching a movie or making love in his bed—where she'd spent nearly every night for the past two weeks.

Today had been absolutely perfect. But it had also been a very long day. And he couldn't wait to end it with Sinclair in his bed again.

The first bars of "Not Another Love Song" by Ella Mai came on and Rett drained the last of his drink. He walked over to Sin.

"Hey, beautiful." Rett placed a hand low on her back. "Dance with me?"

She nodded and placed her much smaller hand in his.

They excused themselves, then he led her to the center of the dance floor. Rett slipped his arm around her waist. They moved together in silence for a few minutes as Ella Mai sang about having feelings for someone while being hesitant to admit it. It was a song he'd been listening to a lot lately. And he was beginning to understand why he was so drawn to it.

"You look gorgeous." He leaned in so she could hear him over the music.

"Thank you." She grinned. "And you might have mentioned it a time or two. Not that I'd ever tire of hearing it."

"Good, because I don't think I'll ever get tired of saying it." He spun her around, then pulled her closer, their bodies swaying together. Rett pressed his lips to her ear. "As much as I love seeing you in this dress, I can't stop thinking about how much I'd like to see you out of it."

"Garrett. Sinclair."

Rett stood ramrod straight, both of their heads turning in the direction of the stern voice he recognized as her mother's. He nodded at the older woman. "Mrs. Buchanan."

"Hey, Mama," Sin said, her back tensing a little beneath his fingertips. "Are you and Dad leaving now?"

"Yes, I'm quite tired," Terri said. "But now that the wedding is over, I thought maybe we could make arrangements for the two of you to come to *our house* for dinner. Since your dinner with Ellen and Hector is evidently a standing engagement, how about you come to our place on Friday night week after next, once we've returned from watching the kids in DC?"

"I...uh..." Sin stammered, glancing up at him.

"We'd love to join you for dinner, Mrs. Buchanan." Rett spun Sinclair before pulling her into his arms again.

"Wonderful." Terri bid them good night, kissed her daughter's cheek, then turned and left.

"Why did that feel like the equivalent of being called into the principal's office?" Rett chuckled. He should know. Sin's mother—a retired school principal—had called him into her office many times over the years.

"She's upset about me throwing a wrench in her matchmaking plans." Sin rolled her eyes. "She'll get over it."

"You mean she's pissed that you're seeing me," Rett said. It was no secret Terri Buchanan didn't much like him. And with the number of times he'd ended up in her office in middle school, he couldn't exactly blame her.

"I wouldn't take it personally." Sin's warm smile lit her eyes. "But are you sure you're okay with going to dinner at my parents'? If not, I understand. After all, you're working on the house and on your big move."

"Of course I'll come," he said. "If I don't, she'll doubt this is real. You'll be right back to trying to duck your mom's matchmaking attempts."

Rett didn't address Sin's not-so-subtle inquiry about his relocation plans. Something he'd found himself doing frequently. He'd also been dragging his feet on responding to Evan in Charleston. He was stuck in place. Not prepared to move elsewhere, but not ready to commit to life on the island either.

He and Sin were caught in a catch-22. She needed to know he was committed to staying before she'd open her heart to him. But he needed to know Sin was all in before he'd commit to staying on Holly Grove Island.

"My mom can be tough, so I appreciate the sacrifice," Sin said. "I promise to run interference, and I know my dad will, too. Even when I complained about you in high school, Dad would try to help me see your side of things and to be patient with you." Sin smiled fondly. "Maybe that's because my dad was a bit of a hellion back in his day. A local politician mentored him at a time when he really needed it. He's never forgotten that. It's why he's so big on giving back to Holly Grove Island. And it's why he raised me to do the same."

Message received loud and clear. Sinclair Buchanan was never, *ever* leaving this town.

"You're an asset to the island," Rett said. "Your dad must be proud."

Sin's smile widened and her eyes sparkled again. She pulled him down for a quick kiss on the lips. The first she'd given him in such a public place.

The past few weeks had been busy, and the work had

been hard. But Rett couldn't remember feeling happier than he did now, holding Sin in his arms.

"About tonight," Sin said. "I thought maybe we could spend it at my place."

They'd eaten at her place, hung out there, even had spontaneous sex. What they hadn't ever done there was sleep together. Something about Sin offering to let him share her bed felt like a monumental shift in their blossoming relationship.

"I'd like that." Rett pressed another kiss to her lips. They continued their dance as the DJ shifted to "No Sleep" by Janet Jackson featuring J. Cole.

Excellent choice.

Because when they got back to Sin's place, sleep was the last thing in the world that would be on his mind.

Chapter Twenty-Eight

———•—•—•———

Sinclair stood in front of the mirror of the bathroom just off her bedroom, where Rett lay tangled in her Italian-made, Egyptian cotton sheets, fast asleep and naked as the day he was born. It had taken every ounce of willpower she could muster to extract herself from his arms and get dressed for work.

She'd spent most of the past week in Rett's company, and she'd been enjoying every minute with him. Being with Rett put her at ease. He was funny and sweet. And as much as she bristled over it, she appreciated how protective he was.

Maybe she'd only agreed to take their relationship public as a way of pissing off her mother—who hated Rett— and to get her to stop with the constant matchmaking and pressure to get married. But her relationship with Rett had quickly escalated to much more than that.

No, that wasn't true. The relationship had begun as more than that. They'd developed a friendship and mutual respect for each other over the past few months. It made her belly flutter to realize she felt something deeper than friendship or lust for Rett.

Was it possible she was falling for him?

Sin shut her eyes and inhaled deeply.

Do not fall for another unavailable man, Sinclair Buchanan.

There had always been something holding Teddy back from truly committing to their relationship. As much as she'd like to put the blame squarely on Gwen's shoulders, the truth was that she'd lost Teddy, if she ever really had him, long before Gwen came into the picture.

Rett already had one foot out the door. She'd only be setting herself up for more pain and disappointment if she gave her heart to a man whose mind and heart were clearly elsewhere.

Since Teddy, she'd managed her expectations. She'd focused on her career and dated for fun, while keeping an eye out for the elusive Mr. Right—the man who would check off all of the little boxes on her dream guy checklist. She hadn't been willing to put her heart on the line again. And she'd always been content with her life. But seeing how happy Dexter and Dakota were together and her escalating feelings for Rett had made her wonder if she really did want more.

Sin heaved a quiet sigh and glanced toward the bedroom where Rett lay asleep.

Maybe, with the right guy, she could focus on her career *and* have a loving, romantic relationship.

Sin tiptoed into the bedroom and selected a pair of simple gold hoops from her jewelry chest.

"Leaving?" Rett's gruff morning voice startled her. One arm was flung over his eyes, and the sheet was settled precariously low on his waist, exposing the fine trail of hair down his belly leading to parts she knew all too well.

You've got an early morning meeting. There's no time for that.

Sin tore her eyes away from Rett's bare chest. "I have

a standing quarterly meeting with Douglas. He likes to go to the Krispy Kreme over in Nags Head. It's the only time Ruth lets him have doughnuts."

"You're telling me you're opting for doughnuts when you could stay here and have..." Rett made a clicking sound with his tongue and indicated the part of his anatomy currently tenting the sheet.

"You, sir, do not play fair. I'm already dragging ass this morning after *someone* kept me up all night." Sin tried to ignore the growing ache between her thighs. "Please, don't make leaving any harder than it already is. And feel free to stay and sleep in. I had a spare key made. It's on the kitchen counter."

Rett tilted his head, his eyes wide. "You're giving me a key to your place?"

"So you can lock up when you leave," Sin added quickly, not wanting it to seem like a big deal. "Dex and I have always held emergency spare keys to each other's condos. Since you're staying in his place... for now... and because we leave here at different times in the morning, it made sense to give you a key."

His mouth curved in a slow smile. "Thank you for trusting me. I'll take good care of it, I promise."

His words seemed loaded. Like he was talking about more than a spare key to her condo. Sin shook the thought from her head, remembering how she'd attributed a deeper meaning to the actions of her ex. She'd seen what she'd wanted to see.

She wouldn't make that mistake again.

"I know you will." Sin was grateful when her phone suddenly rang. It was Felicity, the receptionist at the brokerage, calling from her cell phone. "I have to take this. But there's coffee in the kitchen."

Rett gave her a quick kiss, then ducked into the bathroom.

Sin answered her phone. "Good morning, Felicity. What's..." Sin stopped at the sound of her friend crying. "Fliss, honey, are you all right?"

Sin paced the floor as the woman cried hysterically. The tension in Sin's shoulders rose with every second that passed.

"No," the other woman finally managed through her tears. "I'm not okay." There was another long pause and more tears. "Sin, he's gone."

"Who's gone, sweetie? Did Meatball run away again?" Sin asked of the woman's dog, who was a little escape artist.

"No...it's Douglas. He apparently had a heart attack late last night and died in his sleep. His wife called me this morning."

"No, that's not possible. I just spoke to Doug yesterday before he left the office. And this morning we have a date at Krispy Kreme." Sin's head was throbbing, and it felt like the room was spinning. "So he can't possibly be... *gone*," she said adamantly, her eyes welling with tears.

"I know, honey. It seems impossible. He seemed so vibrant and healthy—"

"No!" Sin said again louder, this time. She pressed a hand to her forehead. "No, no, no," she repeated the word again and again. Maybe if she said it enough, it would be true.

After her mother's heart attack several years ago, Sin's biggest fear was losing her parents. More so, since Dakota's mom died six years earlier. But until now, she hadn't realized just how much Doug meant to her. That he was a father figure to her, too. And that she wasn't prepared to lose him, either.

"I'm so sorry, Sin. I know you two were really close.

He thought the world of you. You were like a daughter to him." There was a soft smile in Felicity's voice.

That was the moment Sin lost it.

Her shoulders shook and tears ran down her face. She sank to her knees on the carpet, her legs no longer able to support her weight. The sound of her own wailing seemed to echo in the space around her.

Suddenly, Rett was there, kneeling on the floor in front of her. "Sin, sweetheart, what happened?"

Sin couldn't speak. She couldn't move, her limbs felt too heavy. All she could do was sob, consumed by her grief, knowing she'd never see her friend and mentor again.

———

Rett's heart pounded in his chest. He'd just gotten done brushing his teeth when he heard Sin scream *no* repeatedly. He'd opened the bathroom door just in time to see her collapse to her knees and drop her phone.

"Sin, baby, talk to me." He held her shoulders as she bowed her head and sobbed uncontrollably. "What's wrong? Are you hurt?"

Rett heard a faint voice and caught a glimpse of Sin's phone on the floor. According to the caller ID, it was Felicity, the receptionist from Sin's office.

He picked up the phone. "Hello?"

"This is Rett, right?" The woman on the phone sniffled.

"Yes. I'm Sin's...friend." He glanced at her. "What's happened?"

The woman explained that Douglas was gone, adding, "He was like a second dad to Sin. This is a blow for all of us, but it'll be hardest on her. I'm going to reschedule her appointments for the rest of this week and arrange for another agent to be on call for Sin's clients."

"Thank you, Felicity." Rett glanced over at Sin. "And I'm really sorry for your loss."

Rett ended the call and tossed the phone on the bed. He turned to Sinclair. "Sweetheart, I'm so sorry about Douglas. I know how much he meant to you."

"I can't believe he's gone." Sin glanced up at him with wide eyes, almost as if she'd forgotten he was there. She dragged the back of her hand across her face. "Doug can't be gone. He can't be." Sin shook her head in disbelief. "We're supposed to have doughnuts this morning and…and….this has to be a mistake. He can't not be there. He can't be…"

Sin dissolved into tears again, and buried her face in her hands, her shoulders shaking.

Sinclair was wrecked by the news and seemingly in shock. Her eyes were red, and mascara streaked her tear-stained face. The abject pain in her expression, echoed in her sobs, broke Rett. He was overwhelmed with memories of the devastating loss of his father.

"C'mon, baby. Let me get you back into bed." Rett scooped Sin up in his arms.

He laid Sin in bed, removed her shoes, and helped her get undressed. Then he helped her into the white T-shirt he'd planned to wear. Rett retrieved the packet of makeup-removing cloths he'd seen her use from the bathroom, but when he held the packet out to her, Sin just stared blankly, tears gliding down her face.

"It's okay, sweetheart. I've got you." Rett took a few of the cloths, which looked like baby wipes but smelled like cucumber, and gently wiped away her makeup.

Whenever they'd gotten ready for bed, side by side, Sin

followed her makeup removal with a full skin-care routine. But for now, this would have to do.

He tucked Sin beneath the covers, and she curled into a ball with her back to him. Rett climbed onto the bed and kissed her wet cheek.

"I know this must feel like the most awful day of your life, and I'm so sorry. But I'm here, Sin. Whatever you need, just ask."

Sin threaded her fingers through the hand that lay on her side and tugged it around her.

If what Sin wanted was for him to lay there and hold her, that was exactly what he'd do.

Rett slipped beneath the covers and cradled Sin against him, his chest pressed to her back as she cried herself to sleep.

Chapter Twenty-Nine

It had gotten late, and Sin was still in bed. She'd awakened briefly after a bad dream, but Rett had gotten her back to sleep. He'd tried to get her to eat something, but she wouldn't. And now evening had fallen, and Sin was still sleeping.

He was worried, so he'd called Mama Mae, who insisted he get some food into her.

Rett didn't want to leave Sin alone, not even long enough to grab an order from Lila's Café. So he called in reinforcements.

I'm here.

Rett scanned the two-word text message and returned his phone to the back pocket of his jeans. He hit the buzzer, which permitted visitors to enter the main entrance, then he waited until he heard the knock at the front door.

"How's Sin doing?" Izzy asked as she stepped inside of Sinclair's condo, her gaze shifting around the place.

The delicious aroma of homemade chicken and dumplings, pot roast, chicken pot pie, and homemade banana pudding from Lila's Café wafted from the large paper bag Izzy held.

Rett's stomach grumbled, reminding him he hadn't eaten since the grilled cheese sandwich he'd made himself for lunch. "She's sleeping so peacefully I hate to wake her. But she hasn't eaten anything all day."

"Poor Sin." Izzy glanced in the direction of the hallway. There was a moment of awkward silence, then Izzy said, "Well, thanks for the burger. I'll grab it and go."

Izzy set the bag on the counter and rummaged through it.

"Thanks for bringing the food over, Iz. Can you stay a little while? Maybe eat with us?"

"I doubt Sin wants company right now," Izzy noted.

"Well, right now, it's just me. And I could use the company. Besides, this would give us a chance to talk." Rett studied his sister's face. It was the first time he'd really noticed the features they had in common. Her eyes and nose were reminiscent of his own. "C'mon, Iz. *Please*?"

Izzy worried her lower lip with her teeth and sighed. "Where can I wash my hands?"

He pointed to the powder room, relieved his sister had agreed to stay.

He'd wanted to talk to her since his conversation with Sin. But the wedding and the renovation had kept him busy. And the couple of times he'd tried to talk to his sister, she'd claimed to be too busy for a chat. This might be his best shot at clearing the air with Isabel.

Rett checked on Sin. She was still sound asleep. Then he washed his hands at the kitchen sink and laid out Izzy's burger and fries and his pot roast meal on plates. They ate together in near silence for several minutes before he put down his fork and turned on the barstool toward his sister.

"Iz, there's something I've been wanting to talk to you about."

"Yeah?" She stuffed another fry in her mouth without looking at him.

"Izzy." Rett touched his sister's arm, and she glanced up at him. "I know things haven't been good between us. I realize that's on me. But you're my little sister, Iz. I care about you."

"Oh, so *now* you care about me?" Izzy put down her burger and wiped her hands on a napkin. "After twenty-two years of giving zero fucks about me, you suddenly have a damn to spare and I'm just supposed to...*what*? Jump up and down like some yapping poodle and be grateful for whatever crumbs of affection you toss my way?"

"Isabel, I know I was a shitty brother. I fully own that. But I had a *really* hard time dealing with my parents' divorce, my dad's death, and Mom getting remarried. I was angry, and I blamed Mom for my father's death."

Izzy frowned, but there was compassion in her dark brown eyes. "It's awful how your dad died, Rett. And I'm sorry you lost him that way. But how could you possibly blame Mom for what happened?"

Rett pushed his plate away, his appetite suddenly gone.

"It was irrational; I realize that now," he admitted. "But back then I held Mom responsible because if she hadn't divorced my dad, he'd never have owned that bike. And he wouldn't have been careening down the switchbacks and slaloms of the Appalachian Mountains in Virginia."

Pain flooded his chest when he thought of his father dying on that mountain and of how his reaction to his father's death had hurt his mother, Hector, and even Izzy. He wished he could go back and do things all over again.

"It was unfair of me to blame Mom. And it was wrong

of me to reject Hector and then you when you came along. But at the time, it felt like accepting you and your dad was a betrayal of mine. I held on to that anger and hatred and blame because it felt like the only ties I had left to my father. The only way I could prove I still loved him. I realize now that my dad would never have wanted me to be angry and resentful or to make my mom's life miserable. But by the time I'd figured that all out...I'd already destroyed our relationship"—he gestured between them—"and I am so sorry for that, Izzy."

Rett sucked in a deep breath, choked up over discussing the loss of his dad and that dark period in his life.

Isabel placed a gentle hand on his wrist and studied his face. "I didn't realize...I mean, I guess I didn't understand how deeply your father's death affected you. It just seemed so long ago, you know? I couldn't understand why you weren't over it. But I can see it still hurts, even now."

"Yeah. It does," he said.

"I'm really sorry about your dad, Rett. But it sucked for me, too." She tucked her long, curly brown hair behind one ear. "I had a big brother I adored, but you could barely stand to be around me. And whenever you were around, I could feel the resentment. Do you know how hard it is to grow up knowing your only sibling wishes you didn't exist?"

Izzy's words felt like a Samurai sword being run through his gut. He felt every ounce of the pain in her trembling voice. And he hated himself for being the person who'd caused it.

"I'm sorry I hurt you, Iz. I'd do anything to fix the past, but I can't. All I can do is try my hardest to fix things going forward. You're my baby sis and I love you. But I understand if you can't forgive me; I just hope that one day at least you won't hate me."

"I don't hate you, Rett." Tears streamed down Izzy's

cheeks, and Rett handed her a napkin. "I'm hurt and angry because I love you. I just never understood why my big brother didn't love me back." His sister broke down, her shoulders shaking quietly.

Rett stood, wrapping Izzy up in a big hug as she cried on his shoulder.

Finally, Izzy pulled out of his embrace, her face was streaked with mascara. Her nose and cheeks were red.

"Okay, so we both want things to be better." Izzy shrugged. "What do we do now?"

"Start over." Rett was grateful his sister was finally open to giving him another chance. "I wasn't capable of being the brother you deserved then, but I promise to do everything I can to be that man from now on."

Izzy wiped her face with the back of her hand. "By leaving again?"

Another shot to the gut.

Rett ran a hand over his head and sighed. "Izzy, no matter where I am, I'm still going to be your brother, and I'll still love you. And if you need me—for anything—just say the word, and I'll hop on a plane."

"What if what I need is for you to be here?" Izzy looked at him pointedly. "Because how can we be expected to make up for all the time we've lost if you're hundreds of miles away?"

Rett frowned. Izzy wouldn't take kindly to him pointing out the obvious: cell phones, video chats, and rapid travel methods made it easy to establish and maintain a close relationship with a sibling or friend, despite the geographic distance between them.

"And what about Sinclair?" Izzy asked.

Rett's heart beat rapidly as he thought of Sin, just down the hall. "Things with me and Sin are...*complicated*."

"Mom says you're in love with Sin, but you're scared to death to finally settle down." Izzy smirked in response to his widened eyes. "So Mom is right. You really are—"

"Like I said, Iz, it's complicated." Rett lowered his voice, hoping his sister would do the same. But he didn't bother denying it. "And I haven't committed to going anywhere. Not yet."

"We might've called a truce tonight, but I meant what I said, Rett. You hurt Sin, and I'll kick your ass. So *don't* screw this up. *Comprendes*?" She jabbed a finger in his direction.

"The last thing in the world I want to do is to hurt Sin."

"Good. Because I really, *really* like her, Rett." Izzy hopped down from the stool. "I'd better go. I told Mama Mae I'd be back soon. It's movie night."

"One more thing," Rett said. "Mom and Dad's twenty-fifth anniversary is coming up soon."

"Yeah?" Izzy looked shocked he'd referred to Hector as *Dad*.

"Why don't the two of us plan something special for them?"

"An anniversary party?" Izzy smiled. "That'd be cool. We should make it a surprise party. But we don't have a lot of time to plan."

"No worries. We have the queen of quick party planning to help us out once she's feeling better." Rett winked.

"I'm in. I'll put some ideas together and text them to you." Izzy's eyes danced.

Maybe Mama Mae wasn't far off about Sin usually being right. She had been about Izzy needing a genuine apology from him. It wasn't an instant fix for their relationship, but this was the most hopeful he'd been about it, and he was grateful for that.

"Perfect." Rett tapped the counter. "Can't wait to see what you have in mind."

"Hello, Isabel. Good to see you." Sin walked into the room. Her voice sounded a little weak, and her wet hair was pulled back into a ponytail. She wore a T-shirt and shorts.

"Sin, I'm sorry about your boss." Izzy crossed the room and wrapped Sinclair up in a bear hug. "If there's anything I can do for you...anything at all...don't hesitate to call."

"Izzy brought us chicken noodle soup, chicken pot pie, and banana pudding from Lila's Café." Rett stayed rooted in place, but he scanned Sinclair carefully.

Despite all the sleep, she looked exhausted. There were shadows beneath her reddened eyes and her nose was red and irritated. He stood there, fighting the overwhelming desire to gather Sin in his arms and promise her everything would be okay.

"Thank you, Isabel." Sin squeezed the younger woman's hand, uncomfortable with the fuss Izzy and her brother were making over her. "Sorry to drag you out of the house so late."

"You would've done the same for me." Izzy smiled. "I have to go. It's movie night with Mama Mae, but I'll check on you tomorrow." Izzy gave Sin another big hug, then she hugged Rett before bidding them both a good night.

Izzy hugged her brother? What a pleasant development.

Rett locked the door behind his sister, then sat on the barstool beside Sin. His eyes were filled with worry. "Are you sure you're okay to be out of bed, sweetheart?"

"Physically? I'm fine." Sin shrugged, embarrassed that Rett had seen her fall to pieces the way she had earlier.

"I checked on you when Izzy first arrived with the food. You were out cold. When did you wake up?"

"I heard voices, and thought I'd hop in the shower. Do you mind?" She indicated his plate. The savory smell of Rett's pot roast was too tempting to pass up. When he gestured toward the plate, she picked up his fork, speared a piece of his now-cold pot roast, then popped it into her mouth and chewed. "Hmm...good."

"You can help yourself to the pot roast, or I can heat up the chicken noodle soup or the chicken pot pie," Rett offered.

"Both," Sin muttered through a mouthful of pot roast. Her empty, rumbling belly took precedent over etiquette and decorum. "I'm starving."

"Let's start with the soup." Rett kissed her cheek, his scruff scraping against her skin.

He poured the soup in a bowl and heated it in the microwave.

"So you and Izzy seem to be in a better place. Did you two have your talk?"

"We did. You were right, Sin. Izzy needed to hear the story from me." Rett put a hand over his heart. "Thank you for pushing me on this. And for suggesting Izzy and I work together to plan a twenty-fifth anniversary party for my parents."

"Then at least something good has come out of this awful day." She'd awakened earlier, hoping this had all been a bad dream. It hadn't. Staying in bed all day hadn't changed a thing. "Wait...Have you been here all day?"

"Didn't want you to wake up alone, especially after the nightmare you had earlier."

"You didn't have to do that, Rett. You had a busy day planned over at the house."

"I sent Mama Mae over to manage the contractors. She's enjoying bossing the crew around a little too much." He chuckled. "And I was just going to paint the upstairs. I can do that later this week."

"I really appreciate what you did for me today, Rett." Sin smiled softly. Her heart was filled with gratitude and deep affection for the man who had become increasingly important to her. "Sorry you got stuck babysitting me today."

Dakota and Dexter were two days into their honeymoon in Turks and Caicos. Her parents had returned to DC to watch the kids while Sin's sister accompanied her husband on an international business trip. So he probably felt obligated to stay with her.

Rett used a pair of oven mitts to place the hot bowl of soup on a place mat in front of her. He handed her a soup spoon.

"I *wanted* to be here for you, Sin. Besides, like Iz said, you would've done the same for me." He crooked a finger beneath her chin. "Why is it that you give so much to everyone else, but expect so little in return?"

Why was she willing to go to hell and back for everyone else while insisting they shouldn't do the same? It was a question she wasn't prepared to delve into.

She shifted her gaze from his. "My soup is getting cold."

Rett sighed quietly, sinking onto the barstool beside her. He gestured toward her bowl. "If you're still hungry once you've finished, I'll heat up the pot pie."

Sin ladled a spoonful of Lila Gayle's delicious, made-from-scratch chicken noodle soup into her mouth. The savory, homemade broth melded with the flavors of the shredded, perfectly seasoned chicken and carrots. There was something about Lila Gayle's chicken noodle soup that always made Sin feel better. She devoured the soup and then the chicken pot pie.

Once she was done, Rett insisted on rinsing the dishes and

straightening up the kitchen. He turned out the kitchen lights and stood in front of the stool where she was perched.

"It's late. I should get you into bed, beautiful." He kissed her temple.

It was a sweet gesture that felt incredibly intimate. Something that would be shared not by casual lovers, but by two people who were deeply in love.

Is that what we are?

Sin swallowed hard, pushing the question out of her head. It was too much to think about right now on a day when her world had imploded. Instead, she focused on the pleasure they'd shared and the comfort she'd found in it.

"I like the sound of that." She grasped his shirt, tugging him down until his mouth met hers. Her kiss was anxious and greedy. His response was slow and measured.

Rett pulled back, his eyes studying hers. He cupped her cheek. "Sin, if you're doing this because you think this is all we are...I can be so much more than this, if you'll let me."

Sin swallowed hard; her cheeks were suddenly hot. Her eyes pricked with tears. She bit her lower lip, unable to voice the words that echoed in her head.

I'm terrified of being hurt again.

Rett seemed to understand all the things she couldn't say. He brushed his lips against her forehead, then took her by the hand. "It's okay, babe. C'mon, it's been a long day."

He tucked her into bed, then took a shower and climbed into bed with her.

Sin burrowed into the warmth of Rett's embrace as he cradled her against him, his broad chest pressed to her back. The tenderness he'd shown her wrapped itself around her, like a cozy blanket. Sin drifted off to sleep, her heart filled with gratitude, affection, and an overwhelming sense of connection to the man who held her in his arms.

Chapter Thirty

◆━◆━●━◆━◆

Rett stood admiring his old room at Mama Mae's cottage. They'd added a built-in window seat in this room, too; installed a proper walk-in closet worthy of a second primary bedroom; created an en suite bathroom; updated the lighting; and added a few flourishes, including a fireplace. Buyers were going to love this space. In fact, he was a little jealous that he wouldn't get to enjoy any of his hard work, since they were putting the house on the market as soon as it was ready.

He sealed the can of paint and gathered the paintbrushes to clean them. His phone rang. It was Evan, calling from Charleston. Rett wiped his hands on a rag and answered the phone on speaker.

"Hey, Ev. What's up?"

"I know you said you need time to think about it, man. But I'm looking at the photos you sent of your grandmother's house, and I had to call. I *need* you on my team, Rett. The place looks incredible. In this market, we can make a killing working together." Evan spoke so quickly he barely drew a breath. "How soon can you get down here?"

Rett froze, his temples suddenly throbbing. "We're not

done with my grandmother's house," he said. "Got side-tracked by permit issues and a few other things. Why?"

"Because if you're in, I'm ready to bid on some of these properties." One thing Evan Diamond did not lack was enthusiasm.

"That's exciting." Rett mustered up about as much enthusiasm as someone being informed that they needed a root canal. "But I can't say for sure when we'll wrap up work on the house. Then, of course, we'll have to sell it."

"The house looks phenomenal, and real estate there is moving quickly. Price it right, and you'll have a bidding war on your hands," Evan said. He paused a moment, seeming to sense Rett's hesitation. "I get that you're not sure when you'll be ready to move down here. But maybe you could come down for a weekend. We'll explore the city, and I promise you a good time. Plus, I'll show you some of the properties I'm considering, and we can discuss how I'd see things going with this. I think you're going to be impressed."

Rett had been looking for a position that offered a new challenge, a little more excitement, and an ocean view. What Evan was offering certainly fit the bill. But as much as he liked Evan, going into business with a friend could get messy quick. Besides, after the week Sin had had, he wasn't about to leave her alone while Dakota and Sin's parents were out of town.

"Can't come down this weekend." Rett rubbed his jaw. "A friend... someone important to her died. She's returning to work today for the first time in a week. I wouldn't feel comfortable leaving her right now."

"Sorry about your friend's loss," Evan said. "But I didn't realize you were involved."

"She's a really good friend," Rett said.

He and Sin had officially been dating for more than

three weeks, and Rett still wasn't quite sure what to call their little arrangement.

"She must be pretty damn important if you're putting a business opportunity like this on pause for her." Evan chuckled. "Tell you what, think about it and get back to me on this as soon as you can, all right?"

"Definitely. Thanks, man. I'll be in touch." Rett ended the call and heaved a sigh. A few weeks ago, he wouldn't have thought twice about heading down to Charleston to meet with his friend. But now, there was so much more to think about. How would leaving now affect his relationship with Izzy? And what would happen with him and Sin?

"Seems like you've put down more roots here than you thought." Mama Mae chuckled.

"Gram, what are you doing up here?" Rett asked. "And why on earth did you climb those steps?" He moved a few items off a box and swept away any debris before settling her onto it.

"I wanted to see how things were looking up here." She glanced around, her eyes watery. "Makes me wish we'd done this a long time ago."

Rett surveyed his work. The place looked damn good. "Me, too."

"I also brought you lunch." Mama Mae pulled an insulated bag out of her much larger purse. "Had some chicken casserole left from dinner."

Rett kissed Mama Mae's cheek and thanked her. After washing his hands, he sat on one of the other boxes and accepted the food and a fork.

"So how much of my conversation did you overhear?" Rett asked before shoveling a spoonful of food into his mouth.

"Enough to know you're torn about walking away from

Sinclair." Her tone was warm. "Understandable, given that you two seem happy together."

They were. But he didn't feel the need to say that part aloud.

"I know Sin has lived here her entire life, but maybe—"

"You're thinking of asking that woman to follow you to Charleston or California and then to wherever the wind blows you next?" Mama Mae gave a bitter laugh. "Guess you don't know Sinclair as well as I thought you did."

Sinclair's resounding *no* when he'd asked if she'd ever leave the island echoed in his head. Still, he couldn't help hoping that, given the right incentive, Sin might be persuaded to change her mind.

"You once said you'd never leave this house, Gram. Circumstances change," he noted. "People change."

"True. And if you were talking about moving to one place and staying put...maybe Sin would consider it. But, sweetheart, Sin isn't a nomad kind of woman. And at this point in her life, I doubt she's interested in becoming one."

Rett sighed, taking another bite of his food, knowing Mama Mae wasn't wrong. He pushed the thought from his mind, wondering instead how Sin was doing on her first day back at work since Douglas's death less than a week ago.

Douglas had groomed her to run his firm once he'd retired. But she'd been struggling with the idea of taking over the helm after his sudden death. Rett hoped everything was going well.

———

A knot tightened in Sin's gut when she pulled into the parking lot of her firm and saw the red Mercedes-Benz with the license plate Queen B33.

Bianca.

Given Douglas's plan to make Sinclair the broker-in-charge when he retired and his plan to offer her a partnership in the firm once they'd completed the sale of Mama Mae's home, Sinclair had expected his wife, Ruth, to be there to make the transition official. Douglas's daughter, Bianca, hadn't stepped foot in the office in more than two years. So Sinclair certainly hadn't expected to see her today. The twinge in Sin's gut reminded her that wherever Bianca was, drama would ensue.

"Good morning, Felicity." Sinclair slid off her sunglasses and clipped them onto her bag. "How are you holding up?"

"Not great." Felicity rose to hug Sin. "How about you?"

Sin gave her head a subtle shake but didn't elaborate. It would only evoke a tide of tears from both of them.

"I saw Bianca's car in the parking lot. I'm surprised to see her here," Sin said.

"So was I." Felicity glanced anxiously in the direction of Doug's old office. She squeezed Sin's arm. "I have a really bad feeling about this."

The knot in Sin's stomach tightened, and her back tensed. *So do I.*

"The meeting is scheduled to begin in thirty minutes, so I guess we'll soon find out." Sin glanced around the office. "Where's Ruth? I'd love to say hello before the meeting begins."

"She isn't here, and according to Bianca, Ruth isn't coming. Bianca will be handling the meetings."

Sin cursed under her breath. This wasn't going to be good.

"You said *meetings.* I thought there was only one meeting."

"Bianca wants to meet with a few of the agents privately—starting with you. She asked me to send you into her office as soon as you arrived," Felicity said.

"*Her* office?" Sin asked indignantly. "You mean Doug's office?"

Felicity pointed toward the office, and Sin narrowed her eyes. Doug's brass plate was gone. A black nameplate etched with white letters read *Bianca Henley, Broker-in-Charge.*

Sin's pulse raced and her temple throbbed. She turned to Felicity. "Bianca can't manage herself, let alone a high-volume office of this size."

"I know." Felicity squeezed Sin's hand. She was the only other person in the office who'd known about the partnership offer and that Doug wanted Sin to run the firm once he'd stepped away. "I'm so sorry, Sin," she whispered.

Sin swallowed the anger, frustration, and string of curses brewing in her chest. "It's okay, Fliss. Everything will be fine."

Sin hugged the other woman again. Then she tipped her chin, her head held high, and strutted toward the office that would *always* be Doug's—no matter who occupied it.

She tapped on the door lightly. There was no answer, so Sin knocked again.

"Come in," Bianca said, already sounding annoyed.

"Lord, please don't let this day end with me catching a case," she whispered under her breath before turning the knob to the door and stepping inside.

Sin gasped. Bianca had taken down all the photos that had decorated Douglas's office. Photos of family, team members, and clients. The walls were cold and blank; much like Bianca.

"Good morning, Bianca." Sin made a mental note not

to fold her arms or stare at the woman with a hatred of a thousand burning suns. "You wanted to see me?"

"Sinclair Buchanan," Bianca said her name with a flourish, as if she were announcing her on a game show. She gestured to the chair on the other side of the desk. "Have a seat."

Sinclair preferred to stand, but she was trying her best not to be obstinate. She slid into the seat opposite Bianca.

"We didn't get to talk at your dad's funeral. So I didn't get to tell you how sorry I am for your loss." Sin meant every word. No matter what she might think of Bianca, she couldn't imagine the pain of suddenly losing her father.

"Thank you." Bianca propped her chin on her fist and sighed. "Look, there's no easy way to say this, Sinclair, so I'm just going to say it." Bianca sat back and steepled her fingers. "I know my father thought very highly of you and had discussed making you a partner in the firm and the successor to the throne, so to speak. But that was just Dad's way of goading my brother and me. He wasn't *seriously* going to put you in charge of our family's firm."

"Then why did he mentor me for that very reason?" Sinclair asked.

"Well, he made no *formal* provisions for such a transfer of power in his will. Therefore, our family took a vote on the matter. I'm sorry to tell you that we've chosen *not* to make you the broker-in-charge. I'll be assuming the role instead, as should be."

That had been clear from the nameplate on the door. Still, it was devastating to hear. But she refused to let Bianca see how upset she was. "That's your right, I suppose."

Bianca frowned, seemingly disappointed not to get more of a reaction. "We respect your contribution to this office, of course. So you're welcome to stay with the firm. However, we'll need to revisit the commission split arrangements with all of our agents, including you."

Sin's jaw clenched so tightly she nearly cracked a molar. Her hands balled into fists on her lap and she reminded herself to remain calm.

Bianca is just trying to get a rise out of you. She knows who makes the most money for this office.

"There's a reason your father raised my commission split to where it is now, Bianca. He did it for the same reason any broker gives his top-earning agent a more favorable split. So they'll stay on and keep making the firm money."

"A lot less money," Bianca noted.

"Less of *something* is a whole lot better than more of nothin', sweet pea." Sinclair's Eastern Carolina twang deepened, and she was pretty sure her head was rocking from side to side. But Bianca had just taken away her dream of running the brokerage and now she was messing with her money. So at this point, she didn't care.

Bianca's face turned red. "You're good, Sin. But you're not the only game in town...or even in this office. It's the brand my father built that funnels clients into this brokerage. And in the current market, the real estate practically sells itself. A newbie would do just as well, if they were given the best leads."

"Are you implying I was given some sort of unfair advantage here? Or are you just that clueless about how a profitable real estate office works?" Sinclair folded her arms and stared at the other woman.

"Look, Sinclair." Bianca stood, leaning on the desk. "I don't know what kind of hold you had over my father, but there's a new Queen Bee in town, and you're looking at her. So you can either get on the train, or you can get off at the next stop." Bianca folded her arms and stared down at Sinclair.

"Why wait for the next stop?" Sin stood, too. The sound of her heartbeat drummed in her ears, but she remained calm. "I'd like to get off of this train wreck right now. Consider this my formal notice that I'm ending my contract with the agency. And don't worry, I'll follow it up in writing."

Bianca looked stunned that Sin had the nerve to push back. That she'd gone so far as to quit. But she quickly recovered. "To be clear, I didn't ask you to leave the agency. This is your choice. However, out of respect for my father, my family and I would like to offer you a generous parting gift."

The woman produced an envelope from the desk with *Sinclair Buchanan* handwritten in what she recognized as Ruth's handwriting. That made Sinclair's heart sink, but she held her shoulders back and tipped her chin.

Sin accepted the envelope and opened it. There was a generous five figure check inside.

"In exchange for?" Sin raised a brow, unfazed by the dollar amount. She didn't trust Bianca Henley any further than she could throw her.

"You would just need to sign this." Bianca slid a stack of papers across her desk.

Sin scanned the document then shoved both the document and the check back toward the other side of the desk. "A noncompete agreement? *Hell* no."

Sin walked toward the door, but Bianca scrambled to get in front of her.

"I understand you're upset. You expected to run this place and now things are changing. But don't make a rash decision you'll regret. We're the top firm in the area. If you stay, yes, your wings will be clipped a tad. But you'll still be able to soar. If you go with a competing firm... well, let's face it. No other firm is truly our competition." Bianca laughed bitterly. "Like you said, a little of *somethin'* is better than a whole lot of nuthin'."

Oh no this heffa didn't.

"I need to get out of here. Now." Sin said the words more to herself than Bianca.

"My dad gave you your little career." Bianca's voice was sharp. "He sponsored your real estate education and he has always treated you like family. In fact, he couldn't stop going on about what a phenomenal agent you are and how much you reminded him of himself. Now you're just going to have a tantrum and walk out because you're not getting your way?" Bianca huffed indignantly. "Don't you think you owe it to my father to stay on and help his family continue his legacy?"

"No," Sin said simply. "Any debt I owed to your dad, I've paid back tenfold. And as for what your father would've wanted...he already made that quite clear. He wanted *me* to run this firm. And it's never been clearer to me why he did." Sinclair maneuvered around Bianca, but the other woman shifted in front of Sin again.

"Sin, don't be so rash. Everything's negotiable. You're a real estate professional. Surely you realize that."

Sinclair had tried to stay calm, to keep things professional. But she was two seconds away from kicking off her heels and removing her earrings.

She shook a finger in Bianca's direction. "If you block me from exiting this office one more time, *Queen Bee*, I swear on my Grandma Fanny's grave that I'm gonna shove the broomstick you rode in here on right up your ass. You'll be sneezing splinters for a week."

"Fine." Bianca stepped aside and smoothed down her skirt. "Have it your way. But the only reason you've been such a top producer is because you were riding the coattails of this brokerage. If you walk away, you'll be struggling for scraps in a small pond."

"Then why are you so desperate for me to sign a non-compete clause, I wonder." Sinclair made her way to the door, not waiting for the other woman's reply.

Sinclair gathered her things and said her goodbyes with her head held high and dry eyes, despite her friend Felicity's tears. Then she climbed into her SUV, cranked up Jimmie Allen's song "Underdogs" on repeat, and drove toward her condo.

She'd kept it together, like she had a steady tap of ice water in her veins, because she refused to give Bianca the satisfaction of thinking she'd broken her. But now that she was alone, the reality of what had happened was setting in.

She no longer had a job. No, it was much more than a job. It was a career that she'd spent the last several years carefully cultivating. A career she'd focused on, setting everything else aside—because it had been that important to her. Now, in an instant, it was gone. And what did she have to show for it?

Sin touched her cheek and discovered it was wet with tears. The muscles in her shoulders and back were knotted, and it felt like a rock was sitting in her gut.

Just breathe. Everything's gonna be fine.

Sin was anxious and stressed, but she had a good idea of how to burn off some of that tension and anxiety. And she knew just the person to help her find that release.

Chapter Thirty-One

◆━━◆━━◆

Tires crunching on Mama Mae's gravel drive and the slam of a car door indicated that someone was there. Rett turned down the 1990s and early 2000s hip-hop playlist thumping from his Bluetooth speaker as he finished painting.

He peeked out of the front window. It was Sinclair's SUV. He checked the time. She was scheduled to be in an important meeting at her office. So why was she here?

Rett slipped his phone into the back pocket of his army-green cargo pants and trotted downstairs to meet her. She was standing in the great room, her eyes glassy and red-rimmed.

"Sweetheart, what is it?" Rett's heart raced, all of the terrible possibilities flashing through his brain.

Sinclair didn't answer. Instead, she fell into his arms, silent tears wetting his shirt.

He kissed the top of her head and rubbed slow circles on her back, not pressing her for an answer. She'd talk when she was ready; not a moment before. That much he knew.

And while his heart broke for whatever pain Sin was evidently feeling, he was grateful she'd come to view him as a source of comfort.

Sin sniffled, muttering her apologies for getting makeup on his white T-shirt, already splattered with paint.

"I don't care about the shirt." He cupped Sin's cheek. "I care about you. What's wrong?"

"I'd rather not talk about it right now."

"Okay." He kissed her forehead. "What do you want to do?"

The corners of her mouth lifted in a sexy half grin. "Do you really want to know?"

"I don't know." Rett chuckled. "Do I?"

She leaned into him. "What I'd love to do right now is...tear something up. Like totally and completely destroy something. I wish we had another project like this going on and it was demo day."

That had been the last thing he'd expected Sin to say.

Rett chuckled. "No offense, sweetheart, but you don't strike me as the demo day type."

"Hey, I've helped with a few renovation projects." She smacked his chest.

"Ouch!" He laughed harder. "That was design stuff. Or moving and sorting things. Not tearing out walls."

"Why? Because I'm a woman?" she asked indignantly, one hand on her hip. "After all, Em helped you on demo day."

"True. But Em wasn't sporting five-hundred-dollar heels, a designer suit, and a pricey manicure at the time." He grabbed her wrist and held her hand up in case she needed a reminder.

"Fine. I'll go home and change. Problem solved." She glanced around the place, which was looking pretty amazing, if he said so himself. "There has to be something I can do around here." She turned to face him. "What are you working on today?"

"Painting," he said. "I'm putting the finishing touches on the bedroom upstairs."

"I can do that," she said.

"Have you ever painted before?"

"Not that I recall." She shrugged. "But it can't be that hard, right? Just show me what to do, and I'll do it."

Rett dragged a hand down his face.

What the hell had happened today?

"Babe, you're sure you wouldn't rather just talk about whatever is bothering you?"

"Later. I promise." She sighed. "So about this painting—"

"I have a better idea. Go home, get into some comfortable clothing you don't mind being completely destroyed. Then meet me at my mom's house in about an hour. I have a demo project for you after all."

"Perfect." Sin's eyes danced. "Should I pick up lunch?"

"Mama Mae has that covered." He kissed her. "See you in an hour."

Sin turned to walk away. For now, whatever weighed on her so heavily seemed to have been lifted from her shoulders.

Rett liked being the person Sin could turn to. The person from whom she sought comfort and solace. And he liked that Sin had gradually become that person for him, too.

But the wedding was over, and they were a few weeks from completing Mama Mae's reno project. Then he'd need to make a decision: stay and make a new life on Holly Grove Island that would hopefully include Sin. Or move on to the next great challenge in his life and career.

As he watched Sin drive off, he was pretty damn sure his heart had already decided.

———

Rett stood at the back window of his parents' home, sipping coffee and watching Sinclair swing a sledgehammer like it was nobody's business. She'd been at it for more than an hour, tearing down the interior walls of an old, outdated mother-in-law suite on his parents' property. Now, she was outside demolishing an old shed, and there was still no quit in his little demolition darling.

"What's going on with Sinclair?" Mama Mae stood beside him, looking on with deep concern. "And why are you in here sipping coffee with your pinkie extended like you're at an English high tea while she's out there sweating and getting dirty?" She turned to him.

"I don't know what's wrong with Sin. She isn't ready to talk about it." His gut was knotted with concern for the woman he'd come to care for more than he'd ever imagined. "And I'm in here for two reasons. One: Sin wanted to do this by herself. Two: It's safer. She nearly took my head off twice with that sledgehammer."

"Never imagined Sinclair Buchanan would be so good at physical labor." Mama Mae chuckled. "But the girl is using muscles she's probably never used before. She's gonna feel that tomorrow." She handed him a glass mason jar. "That's my special Epsom salt and essential oil mix. Have her soak in a hot tub. Use half the jar tonight. Half tomorrow. Otherwise, she won't be able to move for a week. Now, let Sin know lunch is just about ready."

Rett set down the bath salts and finished the last of his coffee. He kissed his grandmother's cheek. "Thanks, Gram."

He poured two glasses of filtered water and carried them outside, offering one to Sin.

"Ready for a break, Sledge Hammer? Lunch is nearly ready."

She nodded, and her hair, pulled in a messy bun atop her head and dusted with debris, shifted. She thanked him and drank the entire glass of water in nearly one go. Rett took the empty glass and gave her his, which she drank more slowly.

He sat on a nearby stoop. "Ready to tell me what this is all about?"

A pained look marred Sin's gorgeous face already streaked with dirt and dust. She gulped the last of her water, then wiped her sweaty forehead with the back of her hand.

"I'm not going to be the broker-in-charge at the firm," Sin said finally. "Doug's daughter Bianca has decided that, despite her father's wishes, she's much better suited for the job. His wife, Ruth, who didn't have the decency to tell me herself, apparently agrees."

"Shit. Sorry, babe." He set the glasses on the ground and pulled her onto his lap. "I realize you didn't want it to happen this way, but I know how much you were looking forward to taking the reins at the firm. I can't imagine the gut punch the news delivered. Is that why you didn't stay for the big meeting?"

"No." Sin's expression deflated further. "I ended my relationship with the agency. Once I'm done with my current contracts, I won't be working for Doug's firm anymore."

There was an aching sadness in her voice, and her eyes clouded with tears. She wiped them away briskly with her forearm and tried to stand. When he held her firm on his lap, she almost seemed relieved.

"What happened, Sin?"

"I know you'll think this was a knee-jerk reaction to being passed over to run the firm. But I could've lived with that. I might've even been able to handle working for that awful daughter of Doug's. But when she threatened to adjust my commission split...I was done."

"By how much?" Rett asked.

"Doesn't matter." Sin shrugged. "It was just the beginning of Bianca trying to make my life a living hell, so I walked."

"Good for you, hon." Rett rubbed her back.

"Is it though?" Sin's voice sounded small. Her brows knitted with doubt and perhaps fear. "Because all this time, I've been hustling and sacrificing for this *one* thing. I set aside everything else in my life for it. Now, it's gone."

"Yes, it is good. You are the smartest, strongest, most organized, and focused human being I've ever met. You can do anything you put your mind to, Sin. I'd stake my life on that." His words seemed to ease the tension in her shoulders. "You *will* come out of this on top. I have no doubt of that. Don't think of this as a setback. Think of it as—"

"A setup for something great?" Her mouth curved in a slow smile. "I like that."

Sin pressed a slow, tender kiss to his lips. A kiss that not only made him want her, but also tugged at something in his chest.

"We'd better get cleaned up for lunch." He gave her bottom a gentle slap, and they stood.

"I never realized how exhilarating it is to work on a project like this." Sin stared at the shed. "Tearing things down to rebuild them even better. And, of course, I love the design and planning parts, too. I'm kind of sad Mama Mae's house is almost done. I'd love to work on another project like that where I'm more fully involved."

What Sin was describing was exactly what Evan had invited him to partner on in Charleston. Something he had yet to share with her.

"We could be the next Mekkai and Camilla Arrington," Sin said excitedly, referring to a couple who had their own home improvement show. They restored older homes in the Chicagoland area. "I'm not talking about being TV show hosts or anything. But I am talking about doing more projects like Mama Mae's house. We're pretty incredible at this."

"We are," he acknowledged with a small smile. But Sin was hyped up on adrenaline and overflowing with emotions. What seemed like a brilliant idea in the moment might be a terrible one once she'd gained some clarity. "But why don't we talk about this later? After you've eaten and gotten some rest?"

Sin looked disappointed he wasn't as excited about her idea. She shrugged. "Sure."

He kissed her damp forehead, but she wriggled away.

"Don't! I'm sweaty and gross."

His mouth stretched in a wicked smile.

"You're thinking about showering together, aren't you?" Sin poked a finger into his gut.

"Weren't you?" He retrieved the glasses and draped an arm over her shoulder.

"I am now."

Rett was glad he'd been able to make Sin smile and alleviate some of the stress she'd been feeling. But he couldn't help wondering if all of this had come to a head for a reason.

Chapter Thirty-Two

— • ● • —

Sin lay in Rett's arms with one arm and one leg across him as they both tried to catch their breath. After they'd demoed the mother-in-law suite and the old shed, they'd returned to his place, soaked in a hot tub together, then spent the evening in his bed.

When Rett went to the bathroom, she slipped on one of his T-shirts and went to his kitchen to make them both another Long Island iced tea. Sin stretched. Her arms and legs felt rubbery and her back was sore after her day of demolition capped off by an evening of acrobat-worthy sex. She took a few ibuprofen and washed them down with water before returning to the bedroom with their drinks.

Rett was slipping beneath the covers, providing a quick glimpse of his bare bottom.

"You're still naked." Sin smiled. "Does that mean you're ready for another round?"

"Give me a minute, woman. I'm not a machine, you know." Rett grinned. "Give a brother a chance to get his stamina back up."

"Then I suggest you hydrate, darlin'." She handed him a

glass, then dropped a quick kiss on his lips before crawling into bed with her drink.

As she quietly sipped her Long Island iced tea, the events of the day and worries about her future commandeered her brain.

"It's gonna be all right, Sin." Rett set his drink on the side table and squeezed her hand.

She couldn't get over how in tune with her Rett always seemed to be. He knew when something was wrong. When she needed his comfort and encouragement. And when she needed time and space—like when she'd been swinging that sledgehammer earlier.

It was still difficult to believe that this sensitive, thoughtful soul she'd come to adore was the guy she'd hated so intensely in high school.

Rett sat up against the headboard. He turned toward her, clearly uncomfortable.

"Rett, what's wrong?" Sin set her drink down, too.

He rubbed the back of his neck. "I was thinking...if money is going to be a problem—"

"If you're asking whether I'll be able to manage my bills...I'm fine for now." Sin smiled softly. "I bought the condo free and clear several years ago. I've got a ton of equity in it. And I have a decent savings. That should give me time to decide what I want to do next."

"And what would you like to do next?" Rett threaded their fingers.

"I've been so focused on running the brokerage, I haven't really thought of any other options. There are a few smaller agencies that serve this area," Sin said. "A few have tried to recruit me in the past. But Bianca's right; they're small fish in a small pond. They don't come close to competing with Doug's firm."

"Not even with Sinclair Buchanan on board?"

"I appreciate the vote of confidence, but it'd take more than one good agent to elevate those firms. We're talking connections, referrals, marketing, and advertising dollars—none of which most of them have to spare." Sin sipped her Long Island iced tea. "They'll always be a pale imitation of Doug's agency, fighting for the scraps that fall from the big table."

It was a bleak reality that amped up the tension in her shoulders. She hadn't left herself many options. Still, she couldn't bring herself to regret walking away from Bianca.

"I was thinking about what you said earlier. About wishing we had another project to work on." Rett sucked in a deep breath. "What if we could work on more projects together?"

"You have another prospect?" Sin was intrigued.

"A friend asked me to consider partnering with him on a few renovation projects."

"In the Outer Banks?" Sin was excited about the possibility. They'd worked together surprisingly well.

"Actually, my friend is based in Charleston," he said.

"Charleston, *South* Carolina?"

"Yes." There was a hint of amusement in his voice.

"That's a seven-hour drive," Sin noted. "Is this a quick renovation project? Or are we talking about relocating there for a few months?"

"It would be an ongoing partnership and a permanent move." He studied her face. "I know you'd prefer to stay on the island, Sin, but like you said, your opportunities are limited here. If we moved to Charleston, they'd be endless. And you could do more of these reno projects that you love so much. Most importantly, we'd get to do it together."

"You're asking me to move to Charleston with you?"

"I guess I am." Rett's answer came out as a strangled whisper.

Sin stared at Rett blankly, the sound of her heartbeat filling her ears, and her face suddenly hot. She certainly hadn't seen this coming, either.

She cared for Rett. *A lot.* And it was evident that he cared for her, too.

She'd been hesitant to start a formal relationship with Rett, but now that they had, she loved how things were blossoming between them here in the cocoon of their beloved town, surrounded by the people they loved.

But now he was asking her to choose between him and the place where she'd always felt safe and happy. The place that had always been home.

———

"Rett, I'm flattered you want me to go to Charleston with you, I really am," Sin said. "I guess I'm just a little surprised by the request."

Rett stared at the gorgeous woman who'd turned him inside out these past few months. He'd blown into town expecting to stay no longer than his obligations as best man required. And he certainly hadn't considered getting involved with anyone.

Yet, here he was, enamored with this smart, beautiful, funny woman who managed to be bold and a little irreverent while also showing a hint of vulnerability. He'd fallen completely under her spell. Returning to a life without Sinclair Buchanan didn't hold any appeal.

He sifted her freshly washed brown and gold strands through his fingers, his eyes meeting hers. The words he wanted to say percolated in his chest, refusing to make their way up his throat.

"Are you okay?" she asked with a nervous smile. "You look like you've seen a ghost."

"I . . ." Rett swallowed hard and the knot in his gut tightened. He inhaled deeply, a task that suddenly seemed much harder. But when Sin had sat on his lap and poured her heart out to him earlier that afternoon, he'd come to a startling realization. And if he didn't say the words now, he might never gather the courage to say them. "I love you, Sin."

Sin's forehead and cheeks flushed, and there was panic in her hazel eyes. She looked like a cornered rabbit in search of an escape route.

Rett knew that look well. It was the same panicked look he'd gotten when a woman he'd been dating had suddenly dropped the "L" word when he thought they were just having fun.

"I told you I needed to find out if this thing between us could become something more. For me, it has." He pressed on, not permitting his hurt pride to prevent him from telling Sin how he felt this time. Rett lifted Sin's hand and kissed the back of it, then met her gaze. "I'm in love with you, Sinclair. And I don't want this to end."

Sin seemed stunned; her gaze on their connected hands. But she didn't pull away. For that, he was grateful.

"Say something, sweetheart," he said, finally, his tone hushed.

Sin raised her watery eyes to his. She turned her body toward him and stroked his stubbled cheek with her free hand. But there was a pained look on her beautiful face that knotted his gut. "Rett, I care deeply for you. And it's obvious you care for me, too."

"But?" He squeezed her hand gently and tried not to

get discouraged by how carefully she'd avoided using the word *love*.

"Really getting to know you and being together has been...amazing." A faint smile lit her gorgeous face. "But saying you love me makes this all very, very real, and a little terrifying for me, to be honest." She dropped her hand from his face and grimaced.

"Why does me telling you that I love you scare you so much?" Rett grazed her cheekbone with his thumb, bringing her gaze back to him.

Sinclair had come into his life and turned his entire world upside down. Made him feel things he'd begun to wonder if he was capable of feeling. He wouldn't give that up so easily.

"What if this relationship is just a knee-jerk reaction to our best friends getting married and expecting their first child? Maybe we've just gotten caught up in the moment."

It was a fair point, but he'd considered it. And his feelings for Sin dated long before Dakota had returned to town a year ago. Maybe she hadn't thought much about him since their night together in Raleigh five years ago, but he'd thought about her a lot.

"Dexter and Dakota's wedding is the circumstance that brought us together. But it isn't the reason I fell in love with you, Sin. Maybe you're afraid to admit it, but I know you love me, too."

Sin's eyes widened. Yet she didn't deny his claim. It was the tiniest thread of hope, but he held on to it tight, just the same.

Rett captured her mouth in a kiss that began slow and tentative, but quickly grew intense. She slid onto his lap, straddling him as her wet heat glided against his shaft.

Sin lifted the hem of her T-shirt, and Rett helped her tug it over her head and off.

He held on to her hips as she ground them against his, her slick flesh gliding over his, making him harder by the second, his desire for her escalating. He sheathed himself. Then he lifted her hips, guiding her down onto him.

Rett groaned with pleasure as his heated flesh pushed inside her. At the sensation of her soft, full breasts pressed to his chest. The heat between them escalated as they moved together, their moans and whimpers growing louder and more intense. The words they whispered to each other became hotter and more explicit until Sin clutched his shoulders and cried out his name, collapsing against his chest.

He rolled them over, their bodies still connected as he moved his hips until his back stiffened and pleasure rocketed up his spine.

"I love you, Sin." Rett kissed her ear before tumbling to the mattress beside her.

They lay together, both of them breathing heavily as they stared at the ceiling. The silence between them seemed to echo off the walls.

When he returned from the bathroom, Sin wrapped her arms around him and lay her head on his shoulder.

"I really do care for you, Rett," she said. "But my life is here. It's where my friends are, where my family is. And as much as I enjoy what we have—"

"You're not prepared to leave Holly Grove Island." Rett buried his face in her hair and rubbed a hand up and down her back.

She nodded, wetness on her cheek as it glided against his chest. "I want this, too. But you're making me choose between you and everyone and everything else I love,

Rett." Sin trailed a hand down his stomach. "And I just don't think I can do that right now."

"It's all right. I understand." He gazed up at the ceiling, his gut tied in a knot.

It would've been more accurate to say his brain understood Sin's need to stay rooted there on the island. His heart was having a hell of a time coming to terms with it.

Putting himself out there and saying *I love you* had been terrifying, and it hadn't gone the way he'd hoped. But he didn't regret telling Sin he loved her.

He'd keep holding on to that tiny thread of hope that, deep down, she felt the same.

Chapter Thirty-Three

— • ● • —

Sinclair sat on the front porch swing beside her best friend, both of them sipping icy cherry lemonade. Dakota sat with one foot folded beneath her. The other pushed off the porch floor to set the swing in motion.

"Remember all those times we'd sit here on this swing together as girls, giggling about the boys we had crushes on and imagining what our futures would be like?" Sin asked. "God, that feels like forever ago."

"I know, but not much has changed." Dakota grinned. "Because you and Rett are still very much into each other."

"Actually, it feels like everything has changed." Sin nodded toward the belly Dakota, who was practically glowing, had just rested her hand on. "I was the one gushing about how I'd be married with a houseful of babies, and you were focused on your career ambitions."

"Sin, you act as if your window of opportunity has closed. Marriage, kids . . . all of that is still possible, if that's what you want," Dakota said carefully. "Is it?"

Sinclair contemplated how to best express all of the thoughts that had been going through her head the last few years.

"I adore my nieces and nephew, and rest assured, I'm going to be the best auntie this little bug could ask for." Sin touched a hand to Dakota's belly. "But I don't know if I want kids of my own. Honestly, I'm not sure I ever really did. It just felt like what I was *supposed* to want. Does that make me sound like an awful, selfish human being?"

"No, sweetie, of course not." Dakota squeezed Sin's shoulder. "It's your life. Live it however you choose. And whatever you decide, know that I'll be here to support you."

"Thanks, Dakota. That means a lot." Sin hugged her best friend. She'd avoided getting too close with anyone else since the debacle with her boyfriend-stealing bestie Gwen, so she was thankful to have Dakota back in her life.

"Do your parents know how you feel?" Dakota asked.

Sin shook her head, her stomach in knots just thinking of how the conversation would go with Terri Buchanan, who was obsessed with her grandbabies and on a mission to have more. "It's something that has become clearer to me with each additional child my sister has." She laughed bitterly. "Like I said, I love my nieces and nephew. But being a mom is a huge responsibility, and it just isn't the life I want right now. Maybe ever."

"You should tell your mom the truth," Dakota said. "I know she's on this grandbaby kick right now, but if she knew you don't want kids—"

Sin shot to her feet and paced. "She'll swear that I don't really mean what I'm saying. That one day I'll regret not having kids." Sin moved to the porch banister, opposite the swing. "And maybe she's right. But it's how I feel now."

"Talk to your mom, Sin," Dakota said again. "I'll come with you, if you want."

It was sweet of her friend to offer but telling her mother

she'd decided kids weren't in her immediate future while seated beside her blissfully pregnant best friend, probably wasn't the way to go.

"I appreciate the offer, sweetie. Really. But I can handle my mama. It's just . . . you know how I've been with her since her heart attack. And with Doug dying of one so suddenly . . ."

"I understand." Dakota nodded, her eyes filled with empathy. "I know you don't want to do anything that could trigger another incident with your mom, Sin. But allowing things to fester between you two this way . . . it's preventing you from *really* enjoying the time you have with her. Take it from me, I'd do anything to have my mother here with me. Even though I was furious to discover that she was the reason Dex ended things between us back then. But if she'd been alive, I would've told her exactly how I felt, we would have fought it out, forgiven each other, and moved on. Because I've learned you can't take a moment of your life for granted when it comes to relationships and the people you love."

Sin returned to the swing and heaved a sigh. Her best friend was right. She was holding her tongue and walking on eggshells around her mother. The relationship no longer felt as genuine or familiar as it once had been. She missed having a close relationship with her mom.

"I'll talk to my mother," Sin conceded.

"When?" Dakota folded her arms.

"I don't know," Sin said, honestly. It was a conversation she needed to work herself up to having with her mother. "But soon, I promise."

Dakota nodded, seemingly satisfied with her answer. But then she turned to Sin with a slightly panicked look on her face. "What about Rett? Does he have plans for marriage or kids? Or has it not come up?"

"I don't know what Rett's plans are long-term." Sin shrugged. "That's part of the problem. The man flies by the seat of his pants, going wherever the wind blows. I need structure, order, stability. The prospect of living the way he does scares me to death." Sin turned to Dakota. "A friend of Rett's in Charleston wants him to partner on a few real estate deals."

Dakota stopped pushing the swing. "Is Rett going?"

"I assume so," Sin said quietly, trying to strain the pain the words caused from her voice. "He invited me to go with him and to join their partnership."

"You turned him down." It wasn't a question. "But was it because you're genuinely not interested or because you're afraid?"

Sin bristled at her best friend's direct question. One she'd been afraid to ask herself.

"Because Holly Grove Island is my home. It's where the people I care about are. I couldn't imagine living anywhere else." Sin sighed and raked her fingers through her hair. "And yes, I'm afraid. Last night, Rett said he loves me."

"That's pretty evident to anyone who has seen the two of you together." Dakota smiled softly. "So why does Rett's admission frighten you? I would think you'd be—"

"Overjoyed? Flattered?" Sin offered. "I feel all of those things, too. And I honestly want to believe Rett is in love with me. But my head keeps reminding me that my heart has been *very* wrong before. Can you blame me for not trusting it?"

"I understand what it's like not to trust your own judgment anymore after getting burned in a relationship. And you and Rett have a complicated history." Dakota squeezed Sin's hand. "But, sweetie, that man *adores* you. Rett is a man in love, if ever I've seen one."

"You really think so?"

"I do."

"I really do care for Rett," Sin said.

"I know." A warm smile lit her friend's eyes.

"I just don't know if I'm in love with him."

"Do you *really* not know? Or are you just afraid to admit it?" Dakota's question was direct, but her tone was gentle. "You don't need to answer that now, but it's something to think about. Are you two still going to your parents' house for dinner tomorrow night?"

"Yes." Sin groaned. "I don't know who I feel sorrier for—Rett or me."

"I'm surprised your mother hasn't been all over you about dating Rett."

"You know my mother. Passive-aggressiveness is her favorite sport. She hasn't taken direct jabs at him. She just keeps making little remarks intimating that Rett isn't marriage material."

"Like what?" Dakota asked.

"She keeps reminding me of all the trouble Rett got into in middle school and high school. Then there's her favorite line: 'Tigers can't change their stripes, sweetheart. No matter how hard they try.'" Sin's imitation of her mother's voice was pitch-perfect.

She and Dakota fell out laughing, a welcome distraction from the anxiety and stress she was feeling over her dilemma with Rett and her strained relationship with her mother.

Thankfully, the conversation shifted to the baby Dakota was expecting and how happy her father and Lila Gayle had been to learn they'd soon be grandparents. But the questions Dakota had asked kept playing in Sin's head.

Did she love Rett? Did he want marriage and kids?

She hoped to one day fall in love and have the kind of relationship her best friends shared. But she wasn't sure motherhood was in the cards for her. So if Rett wanted children, she wouldn't lead him on.

———

Sin pulled the piping-hot pan of homemade manicotti from the oven and set it on top of the stove. She inhaled the savory scent of her mother's famous meat sauce.

Her mother was Italian and German—born to immigrants who'd met in a class teaching English as a second language. And she loved cooking foods that reflected both sides of her family heritage. Homemade pasta noodles and sauces made from scratch that simmered all day were the hallmarks of her Italian cooking repertoire. Potato pancakes, pork schnitzel with a creamy dill sauce, and yummy strudels were some of her mother's favorite Old World German recipes.

Sin had learned to cook in the kitchen with her mother when she was barely knee-high to a grasshopper. She'd helped her mother make and dry the noodles and layer the plums on top of her mother's delicious plum tarts. Sin stored every one of those family recipes in a little box on her kitchen counter. But she'd added a number of her own recipes, most of which skewed toward soul food and traditional southern cooking, which reflected her African American heritage and recipes handed down for generations in her father's family.

When Sin turned around, her mother was staring at her. "Sinclair, what's been going on with you lately, sweetheart?"

"What do you mean?" Sin pulled off the red oven mitts and set them on the counter.

"You know what I mean. You've been different the past few months. Your father and I hardly see you anymore."

"To be fair, you two have been in DC visiting Leanne and the grands," Sin noted. "Besides, I've had a lot going on these past few months. Dex and Dakota's wedding, the renovation project with Rett—"

"*That's* the real issue," her mother said. "The amount of time you've been spending with Garrett. Honey, I hate to say it, but he's always been a bad influence. I can't tell you how many times some young girl sat up in my office, crying her eyes out because she'd gotten busted ditching school to hang out with Garrett."

"Mom, Rett was thirteen maybe. He was struggling with the loss of his dad, something he admits he didn't handle very well."

"I had several other students who'd lost a parent. It was difficult, of course, but they found positive ways to cope."

"Everyone isn't the same, Mother. Besides, that was ages ago. Rett's a completely different person now." Her sixteen-year-old self would never have believed that she'd be the one vehemently defending Rett. It was like she was living in a parallel universe.

"Well, maybe I'd know this new and improved Rett if you'd made an effort to spend time with your father and me. But you haven't. Not the way you do with *his* family." Her mother aggressively folded the heavy whipped cream into a steel bowl filled with the zabaglione she'd made and set over ice.

"So that's what this is about. You're jealous over how much time I'm spending with Rett's family."

Her mother cast a look over her shoulder. "Can you blame us? You have dinner with them every Sunday. And you're at Annamae's house nearly every day since you've quit your job. And I'm guessing Rett was behind that decision, too."

Her mother removed her apron, her lips pursed. "I'm not saying what Bianca and Ruth did was right, but if you'd stayed on with the brokerage, at some point Bianca would've gotten bored with running the firm and turned it over to you. Instead, you threw a hissy fit and ran off, like a little girl on the playground who picks up her ball and goes home because the other children won't do things your way."

"Why can't you ever support me the way you support Leanne?" Sin demanded. "She decides she wants to take a last-minute international trip and you drop everything to watch her kids. I ask you to support the fact that I didn't feel appreciated—"

"There you go, being dramatic." Her mother dismissed her argument with the wave of her hand. "Do you have any idea how unappreciated I felt as principal of the middle school? How unappreciated your father felt as the mayor of this town, which, at the time, wasn't even a paid position? Do you realize what kinds of sacrifices we had to make for you girls and for the town?" Terri folded the apron up and set it on the counter. "And why do you always feel the need to bring up Leanne?"

"Because you always do." This wasn't a conversation she'd intended to have today, but her mother had started it, so they were going to have it. "*Sinclair, why haven't you gotten married, like your sister? Sinclair, when are you going to give us grandchildren, like your sister?*" Sin mimicked her mother's tone and cadence.

"I do not…I mean…it's not the same," her mother stammered. Crimson spread across her cheeks and forehead. "You're taking what I said out of context. I wasn't comparing you to your sister…exactly. I—"

"Everything all right in here?" Her father entered the kitchen. His gaze went to Sin, then to her mother, and back again. "You good, baby girl?"

"Why do you automatically assume I'm somehow attacking her?" Her mother propped a fist on her hip.

Her father shook his head and chuckled. He kissed his wife's cheek. "Let me guess. This conversation is either about the many reasons our daughter shouldn't be seeing Rett or it's about the fact that she still isn't married and hasn't given us grandchildren."

"Both!" Sinclair said.

Her mother frowned, which only made her father laugh harder. His deep chuckle filled the kitchen.

The doorbell rang, drawing their attention.

"Looks like the guest of honor has arrived." Her dad flashed her a smile. "I'll let him in. Maybe we should table this discussion for now, hmm?"

"She started it," Sinclair muttered beneath her breath.

"I did not. I simply asked—"

"Well, I'm finishing it, at least for now. *Capisce?*" He gave his wife's bottom a playful swat, then kissed her temple. "We'll be in the living room."

Her father walked out of the kitchen, and Sin and her mother stared at each other for a few moments before returning to their meal preparations.

They hadn't even sat down for dinner yet, and Sin's stomach was already in knots. This was going to be one hell of a night.

Chapter Thirty-Four

— • • • —

Rett shook hands with Troy Buchanan, who greeted him with a broad smile. "Welcome, son. Good to see you again. Come on in."

Rett stepped inside, inhaling the savory scent of Italian food. "Something certainly smells good."

"Now you see why I've got this spare tire." Troy patted his ample belly and laughed. "Terri and Sinclair are both amazing cooks, and I'm their favorite test subject."

"Sounds like an excellent problem to have, Mayor Buchanan."

"Just Troy is fine, son," the older man said. "Have a seat, the girls will join us shortly."

While they waited, they chatted about Mama Mae's renovation project, then lamented the struggles of their favorite football team. Finally, Sin and her mother joined them. Both women looked tense, and neither of them was smiling.

There was obvious tension between Sin and her mother. He was undoubtedly the reason.

"You look beautiful, Sin." Rett smiled.

Sin's eyes lit up, and she seemed to relax a little. She

thanked him and gave him a quick peck on the lips. Something he was sure she'd done just to piss off her mother. Sin slipped an arm around his waist as she stood beside him.

"Your home is lovely, Principal Buchanan," Rett said.

"Thank you, Garrett." The woman offered a smile that barely stirred the muscles of her face. "But there's no need to be so formal anymore. Please, call me Terri."

"Yes, ma'am," Rett said out of habit.

"Well, dinner is on the table. Sinclair will show you where you can wash your hands." Terri turned and left the room, her husband on her heels.

"That didn't feel frosty at all." Rett rubbed his arms against an imaginary chill.

"She's in rare form today." Sin sighed. "C'mon, I'll show you to the powder room."

"You all right?" Rett asked as Sin hovered in the doorway while he washed his hands in the vessel sink of the ornate half bathroom.

"I'm fine. I just wish she'd at least *try* to understand my point of view." Sin slumped against the doorframe.

"And what's the topic at hand?"

"She doesn't understand why I quit the agency rather than waiting Bianca out."

"Your mom will come around, Sin. In the meantime, you've got me. And I'm backing you one hundred percent, all right?"

A smile lit Sin's eyes. She slid her hands up his chest and pressed her open mouth to his. Her tongue glided against his, making him wish they were back at her condo alone. He forced himself to break their heated kiss.

"You're trying to get me in trouble," Rett whispered, his lips brushing the shell of her ear. He nuzzled Sin's neck. "Your mother already doesn't like me."

Principal Buchanan had never been a fan of his, and truthfully, he'd given her plenty of reasons not to be.

Sin groaned loudly but didn't disagree. "I'll be counting the hours until we're back at home in my bed."

She grabbed his hand and led him to the dining room.

It was going to be a long, torturous evening if Terri's initial greeting was any indication of what he should expect.

But he was willing to endure it, and much more, if that's what it took to show Sinclair he meant what he'd said.

He was utterly and completely in love with her.

———

Sinclair picked at her manicotti—normally one of her favorite dishes. She'd lost her appetite, listening to her mother relate another tale of some troubled youth she'd tried to save during her time as an educator who'd eventually gotten arrested, died, or cheated on their spouse.

Sin clutched the fork as tension knotted her shoulders and tightened the muscles of her back. She'd stopped responding to her mother. Instead, she stared at her plate of barely eaten food while wishing the floor would open and swallow her whole. She was hurt and angry on Rett's behalf. He didn't deserve this. He hadn't hesitated to accept her mother's invitation to dinner, and he'd done it because he cared about her. She cared for him, too. So she wouldn't make him sit here and listen to another minute of this.

She dropped her fork with a clang and turned to Rett.

"Honey, I'm so sorry," Sin whispered. "Say the word and we can go."

"It's okay, sweetheart." He squeezed her hand beneath the table.

"Sinclair Buchanan, do you have something you'd like to share with the class?" her mother asked. "And why on earth aren't you eating your food? My manicotti is your favorite."

Sinclair really hadn't wanted to have this conversation with her mother. She'd expected a little needling and perhaps a snide remark or two. What she hadn't expected, and would never have asked Rett to endure, was her mother making him feel like the town reject.

Rett would never permit his family to treat her this way, and she wouldn't allow her mother to treat him badly either.

Sin glanced at Rett, and it was as if he could sense the switch flipping in her head. She'd had enough.

"Sin, don't—" he began.

She ignored Rett's plea. This was a conversation she and her mother needed to have. And since she'd done this in front of Rett, she'd dragged him into the conversation, too.

"That's it, Mother. *Enough*."

"Enough of what?" Her mother feigned innocence as she popped a bite of manicotti into her mouth.

"Enough of your passive-aggressive attacks on Rett. Implying he's a bad influence, and I could do better."

"I didn't say any of that," her mother noted. "I simply related the unfortunate circumstances that have befallen some of my past students, just as I often share the triumphs of former students." Her mother set down her fork. "If you see a correlation between that and your current...*situation*—"

"Terri, *enough*." Her usually easygoing father's voice was tense as he slapped his large hand on the table, jostling the dishes and silverware. "Rett is a guest in our home. We didn't invite him here to make him feel uncomfortable."

"I'm not trying to make him uncomfortable." Her mother folded her arms. "But I have an obligation to do what's best for our daughter."

"Yes, you *are* trying to make him feel unwelcome," Sin said. "And you don't have the right to run my life or to guilt me into marriage and motherhood."

"I'm not trying to run your life, Sinclair. I'm simply reminding you that you're thirty-five years old. Your window of opportunity is closing, if you ever hope to become a mother—"

"I don't." The words flew out of Sin's mouth before she could catch them. She hadn't planned to tell her mother this way, but she'd promised Dakota she would have this conversation, and now she was.

"Come again?" Her mother looked stunned. As if she'd declared her plans to shave her head and join the buck-naked circus. "You don't want children?"

Sin swallowed hard and shook her head. "No, I don't think I do."

"This is your doing, isn't it?" Her mother turned the full weight of her glare on Rett, her voice elevated. "You don't want children because being responsible for someone besides yourself would cramp your style."

"Terri..." Rett cleared his throat when her mother gave him the evil eye. "Principal Buchanan, I would *never* coerce Sin into making a decision like this. Besides, your daughter is a strong, determined woman who knows exactly what she wants."

Sin squeezed Rett's hand beneath the table, buoyed by his words.

"I'm not an impressionable teenager, Mother. I'm a thirty-five-year-old woman, as you've so kindly pointed out. I know what I want, and I'm finally okay with what I don't want. I've consciously made the decision *not* to have children. This isn't a position I've taken lightly. Nor should it make me some sort of pariah. It's my choice." Sin poked a thumb in her chest. "And I choose to be content with being an amazing aunt."

Her father looked shaken by Sin's admission, and her mother's eyes welled with tears. She felt badly about telling them this way. But her mother had cornered her, and the words had just spilled out. Now that they had, Sin felt relieved.

"Thank you for dinner." Sin stood, her knees wavering slightly. It was the first time in a long time she and her mother had had an actual fight. "But perhaps we should call it a night." Sin looked down at Rett, who seemed dazed.

He stood, too. "Good night, Mr. and Mrs. Buchanan. The meal was delicious. I'm sorry for any problem I've caused this evening. That wasn't my intention."

Sin grabbed her purse and slipped her hand into Rett's. They made their way to her SUV.

Rett cradled her face and frowned. "Sweetheart, I *really* appreciate that you were indignant on my behalf back there. I just wish we'd handled this a better way."

"You think this is my fault?" Sin's heart thumped in her chest. She'd just taken his side over her parents and walked out in the middle of dinner. Yet he was acting as if she was just being a temperamental diva. "Did you not get what she was implying about you?"

"Of course, I did, Sin. I expected your mother to come at me with both guns blazing, because I realized it would be hard for her to let go of my past. That I'd have to earn her respect. And I'm prepared to prove to her that I'm not that angry troublemaker she once knew. But after tonight, I'm going to have to work ten times harder to earn your parents' respect."

Sin heaved a sigh and leaned against her vehicle. She ran her fingers through her hair. "I'm sorry, I just couldn't take it anymore. Every poke she took at you felt like a sword being jabbed in my chest. I can't imagine how it felt for you."

"You know what this means, right?" Rett grinned.

"No," she said. "What?"

"It means you're a hell of a lot more into me than you're admitting." He kissed her. "Gives a brother some hope."

Sin rolled her eyes and laughed. Even in the midst of all of this, Rett had found a way to make her smile. She adored him for that.

And maybe he had a point.

———

Rett had put Sin in her SUV and watched her drive off before heading to his own car. That was when he realized he'd left his phone and keys inside Sin's parents' home.

Talk about awkward.

He dragged a hand down his face and heaved a sigh. Then he trotted back up to the front door and rang the bell.

Despite what had happened at dinner, Rett didn't believe Mrs. Buchanan was some awful, overbearing mother. Terri just had a serious blind spot where her daughter was concerned.

"Oh, it's you." Terri huffed, folding her arms.

Rett had always liked Mrs. Buchanan, even though the woman clearly didn't care for him. But she'd been fair, and she'd shown her students respect—even when their behavior hadn't merited it.

Her feelings toward him then were understandable. He'd given his mother hell over her new marriage, hadn't wanted anything to do with his new sibling, had left home to live with his grandmother, and had acted out as a teenager struggling with grief and an undiagnosed learning difference. But that was ancient history, and he'd done a lot of growing up.

He'd repaired his relationship with his mother and stepfather, and thanks to Sin, he was actively working to repair his relationship with his younger sister.

People changed. *He'd* changed.

But if Terri Buchanan insisted on seeing him as that grieving, misunderstood boy who'd been lashing out at the world rather than the man who'd matured and turned his life around, so be it.

"Yes, ma'am," he said. "I left my phone and keys inside."

She stepped aside and gestured for him to enter.

"I was hoping my daughter had come to her senses and realized she was being unnecessarily dramatic."

Terri Buchanan loathed him. *Fine*.

He could take whatever she had to say about him—implied or otherwise. But what he couldn't stand another moment of was her thoughtless comments about the woman he adored.

Rett turned to the Buchanans. Troy was seated at the table, still looking shell-shocked. Terri stood beside him.

"With respect, ma'am, your daughter isn't being 'dramatic.'" He used air quotes and the woman frowned. "She's fed up and expressing her hurt feelings. As well she should."

"So it is you we have to thank for this little outburst." Mrs. Buchanan folded her arms.

"No, ma'am. Actually, it's you." Rett felt a brief sense of satisfaction at the outrage on Terri's face. "It seems this conversation was long overdue. I was simply the catalyst."

"You've been back in town, what, all of two months, and suddenly you're an expert on what it is that my daughter needs?" There were flames in the woman's eyes, and her jaw was set.

"No, ma'am. But I do believe Sinclair is the expert on what she does and doesn't want. On what's best for her. And it's the job of anyone who loves her to respect that and to support her," Rett said with a shrug. "Personally, I don't think that's too much to ask."

"Neither do I, son," Mr. Buchanan said firmly.

Terri turned to him, her deep frown intensifying the appearance of the fine lines around her eyes and mouth.

Troy squeezed her hand. "I know how badly you wish we had grandkids here on the island. But it isn't fair to burden Sinclair with our expectations. It's Sin's life. If she marries or doesn't, has children or doesn't…that's up to her. We need to respect that. Just as you wanted your parents to respect your decision to marry me." The older man smiled softly.

His words seemed to touch his wife's heart.

Terri's look of outrage had morphed into one of sadness. Her eyes filled with tears, and she suddenly seemed far away.

The Buchanans were an interracial couple living in the South. Forty years ago, when they'd gotten married, Rett could imagine just how much pushback they must've gotten from people who'd claimed to only have their best interests in mind—including Mrs. Buchanan's family. Sin had told him that her maternal grandparents had only come around to supporting the marriage after the birth of Leanne—their first grandchild.

She dabbed at the corners of her eyes with a napkin Troy handed her. "I love my daughter very much. I want her to have everything she deserves in life. She's an amazing woman, and she has so much love to give. She'd make a terrific wife and mother."

"Perhaps she would." Rett said. "But she's also a consummate professional with a brilliant creative mind. She loves the work she does, and she's achieved a lot. She has plans for the future—beyond being a wife and mother. But you make it seem as if..." Rett held his tongue. This wasn't his business. It was between Sinclair and her parents. He'd already overstepped and said too much. "I should go."

"Go on and say what you were going to say, son," Troy urged him. "No point in trying to stick your finger in the hole now. The dam's broke."

Rett returned his attention to Sinclair's mother. Her blue eyes seemed dimmer now. The expression on her face indicated she both wanted to hear what he had to say and dreaded it in equal measures.

"I know you mean well and that you love your daughter. But when you compare her to her sister and harp on the fact that she's childless and isn't married...it makes Sin feel like her only real value to you is becoming some rich guy's trophy wife and bearing his offspring. Like none of the things she's accomplished in her life and career matter to you." Rett swiped his phone and keys off the living room table. "I need to check on Sin. Make sure she's okay. Thank you, again, for dinner, Mr. and Mrs. Buchanan."

"Terri and Troy." The older man stood, extending his hand. Rett shook it.

Mrs. Buchanan turned and headed toward the kitchen without a word.

"I'll walk you out, son." Troy trailed Rett to the front door. "I know this was an uncomfortable conversation," the older man said. "But we both needed to hear it, so thank you for speaking up. And as for my wife...you keep being the man you were today, and I know she'll come around."

"You're welcome, Mister...Troy." Rett shook the man's hand again, grateful for his reassuring words. "Please thank your wife for dinner. The food was wonderful."

"I'm pleased to hear it." Terri rejoined them. She handed him a heavy cloth bag. "I packed this after you all left. It's manicotti, one of my homemade apple pies, and a pint of brown sugar cinnamon ice cream from Helene's Homemade. Sin's favorites."

"I'll take them to her right away. Thank you."

"I packed it for both of you." Terri slipped an arm around her husband's waist.

It wasn't an apology, but maybe Terri had at least called a truce for now. If that was the best he could hope for, he'd take it.

Rett got into the GTO and glanced back at Sinclair's parents. Troy's arm was draped over his wife's shoulder as they waved goodbye.

Sinclair's parents weren't perfect. But they were still very much in love after forty years of marriage. And despite the bumps in their relationship with Sinclair, they loved their daughter and wanted the best for her.

Rett couldn't help thinking of his mother and stepfather, married for nearly twenty-five years and more in love than ever. Then there was Dexter and Dakota, whose love had endured, despite everything they'd been through. It brought things into perspective. Suddenly, the prospect of marriage and a lifetime commitment didn't seem quite so scary.

He wanted his happily-ever-after, too. And he wanted it with the woman who'd managed to burrow beneath his skin and stake her claim on his heart.

Chapter Thirty-Five

— • — • — • —

Sinclair stood in front of her refrigerator, rummaging for something to eat. Why couldn't she have waited until *after* dinner to storm out of her parents' house?

There was the rattling of keys and then the front door opened. Rett stepped inside with a large cloth bag she recognized as her mother's.

"Please tell me you have leftover manicotti in that bag." Sin closed the refrigerator door and moved toward him.

"I do. Plus, your mom sent you an apple pie." He set the bag on the kitchen counter.

"You're a saint." She clutched his shirt and pulled him down for a lingering kiss.

"For bringing you leftovers?" He chuckled.

"And for enduring whatever you had to with my parents to get them." She rummaged in the bag and put the items on the counter. Her mother must've felt badly about her behavior. She'd even tossed a pint of brown sugar cinnamon ice cream from Helene's Homemade in the bag. Sin put the ice cream in the freezer, then turned to him, her heart aching as she thought of how awful her mother had been. "I'm really sorry about tonight, Rett. I'd never have put you through that intentionally."

"It's okay, babe." Rett pulled her to him and sat on the edge of a barstool. "Your mom still sees me as the big bad wolf. She's just trying to protect her daughter. I get it." Rett cradled her cheek, his gaze open and sincere. "Because I love you, and I'd do whatever it took to protect you, too."

Her chest felt warm and a chill ran down her spine. She believed Rett when he said he loved her. And she loved him, too. But the words wouldn't come. Instead, she stared at him, her heart racing as she searched his dark eyes.

Sin captured Rett's lips in a kiss. Hoping her body would convey all of the things she couldn't find the words to say. She tugged his cotton shirt from his waistband and glided her hands up his back beneath the fabric, enjoying the feel of her warm skin on his.

She lost herself in the taste of his mouth, the warmth of his skin, and the comfort of his embrace. Everything else faded away.

Sin pulled her mouth from his and met his hooded gaze. She wanted this man in her life. But if Rett wasn't staying, at least they could have this for now. Moments together she would always remember.

"Rett, make love to me," Sin whispered against his lips when he kissed her again.

"Thought you were hungry," Rett mumbled between teasing kisses that made her ache for him.

"I am." Sin smiled against his mouth. She glided a hand up his chest. "But not for food."

Rett stared at her with a heat in his eyes so intense it unnerved her. Then he swept her up in his arms, carrying her to her bedroom.

Their kisses were frantic and urgent as they stripped each

other bare. But as he joined her in bed, what she saw in his eyes wasn't just desire. It was affection, friendship...love.

Sin's heart swelled with emotion, and her vision clouded.

Rett's brows furrowed. He cupped her cheek. "Baby, what's wrong?"

Sin gave him a watery, nervous smile. The words she wanted to say caught in her throat.

Just say it.

She studied the face of this beautiful, complicated man she'd truly gotten to know over the past few months. The man who meant so much to her now. Whom she couldn't imagine not having in her life.

"I love you, Rett." She swallowed hard and tears streamed down her cheeks. She traced his cheekbone with her thumb as she gazed at him through the haze of her tears. "And I don't want to lose you. But I don't want to leave Holly Grove Island either. Maybe if it was somewhere closer to home—"

"It's okay, sweetheart." One corner of his mouth curved in a soft smile. He kissed her palm. "We'll figure it out."

She pressed her mouth to his, grateful Rett was willing to compromise. The kiss felt more meaningful than any of the kisses they'd shared before. It was an expression of their love and affection for each other, as well as their desire. And as she and Rett made love, Sin was overwhelmed with a deep sense of love and joy.

Her legs trembled as his sweat-slick skin moved against hers, bringing them both closer to the edge. His dark eyes were fixated on hers, as if he didn't want to miss a moment of her ascent into bliss. Finally, her stomach tensed, and her sex clenched, then spasmed as intense pleasure rocketed up her spine.

Sin called Rett's name, her fingertips pressed into his

back as she arched hers, drawing him closer. Rett rocked his hips harder and faster, his brows furrowed with focus and determination. Finally, his muscles tensed, and he arched his back, punctuated by a guttural growl and a string of curses, followed by her name.

Rett tumbled beside her on the bed and gathered her in his arms. His chest heaved as he pressed a kiss to her damp forehead. The stubble on his chin grazed her skin.

They lay together in silence, catching their collective breath. Yet the lull between them didn't feel awkward. Sin felt a quiet sense of contentment. She was exactly where she was meant to be, with the person who finally felt like the right fit. And he had been worth the wait. But there were still so many details to work out.

She wanted to stay on the island. Rett wanted to move to Charleston. He'd said they would figure it out, and she believed him. But the reality was they couldn't both get what they wanted. One of them would be disappointed.

"I love you, Sin." Rett rubbed her bare shoulder. "I think I always have."

"I love you, too, Rett." Sinclair lifted her head and pressed another kiss to his lips. Her heart swelled and her tummy fluttered every time she said the words again.

"What you said tonight about not wanting kids of your own...were you just saying that to piss your mother off?" Rett asked tentatively.

"It's something I've been thinking about for a while. Becoming a mother just isn't my focus right now. There are still so many things I want to do. I've felt guilty about it for a long time. Especially with my mom pressing me to get married and give her grandchildren. But I've finally made peace with it." Sin propped her chin on her arms, folded on Rett's chest. "Why? Do you want children?"

If he wanted a family and she didn't . . . that was something they couldn't reconcile. So it was better to be honest about it now. Because more than anything, she wanted Rett to be happy. She'd like to think he wanted the same for her.

"No." He sifted her hair through his fingers, his lips curved in a smile. "I was just stunned to learn you felt the same way I do. That we're even more compatible than I thought."

Sin sighed with relief as she lay her head on his shoulder again. "Does that make me the perfect girl for you?"

"It makes you the perfect woman for me, and I have no intention of letting you go."

Sin's heart danced and her eyes filled with tears of joy. At least for tonight, she would ignore her worries about her career and the fight with her mother. Right now, her world felt right. So she would enjoy being with Rett.

They would figure out everything else later.

———

Sinclair quietly exited the bathroom and swiped her cell phone from its charger. She dropped a soft kiss on Rett's temple as he lay in bed still sleeping. Then she made her way to the kitchen. She put on the coffee, took bacon out of the fridge, and turned on the oven to make a batch of her warm, fluffy buttermilk biscuits Rett loved so much.

She put the bacon and biscuits in the oven, then washed her hands. Sin's phone lit up with her daily reminder to hit the gym. She dismissed it but noticed the missed calls and waiting voice mail from her mother. Sin sighed, mentally preparing herself for her mother's quasi-apology that wouldn't amount to an apology at all. Then she played the voicemail.

There was silence, at first. Maybe her mother had

pocket-dialed her, as she sometimes did. Suddenly, there was sniffling, and her mother's voice trembled.

Sin's heart raced, imagining the situations that could possibly bring her mother to tears.

"Sinclair, sweetheart," her mother finally said, "I'm sorry. Not just about tonight. I'm sorry about the pressure I've been putting on you to get married and have kids. I never intended to make you feel inadequate or somehow less than your sister. I just wanted you to have all the happiness you deserve. I love you, sweetheart. Please, call me back. And please apologize to Rett for me. I owe him a great deal. If it wasn't for him, I wouldn't have known how you really felt. Good night."

Sin's eyes brimmed with tears in response to the genuine emotion in her mother's voice. She was grateful for her mother's heartfelt apology but surprised Rett had apparently talked to her mother.

No wonder her mom had sent Rett home with a bag full of leftovers and a full pint of her favorite ice cream.

The oven timer sounded, alerting her that the biscuits and bacon were done. She removed both from the oven, then paced the floor.

It was sweet that Rett had stood up for her—after all, she'd done the same for him. But she hadn't wanted him to run interference, because this was a conversation she really needed to have with her mother herself.

A few minutes later, Rett made his way to the kitchen in a pair of black basketball shorts worn commando and hanging low on his waist. He wrapped his arms around her from behind as she brushed melted butter on the warm biscuits. Rett dropped a kiss on her neck.

Do not think about how good this man looks right now. Not the time.

"You made your homemade biscuits." Rett trailed kisses along her shoulder.

Her back tensed slightly. "I did."

Rett turned her in his arms, his handsome features pinched with a frown. He lifted her chin. "What's wrong, babe?"

Sin stepped out of his hold and grabbed two plates. She set them on the counter and put three biscuits and three slices of bacon on each plate. "Eggs?"

"No." Rett lightly gripped her shoulders, turning her so he could see her face. "I want to know what's wrong."

Sin raised her eyes to meet his. "What did you say to my mother last night after I left?"

Rett dragged a hand down his face as he leaned against the counter. "We talked about why you were so upset last night." He shrugged. "Why? Is your mom angry with me?"

"No. She left a tearful voice mail apologizing to me and thanking *you* for telling her how *I* really feel." Sin pointed at him, then jabbed a thumb to her chest. "Which I found rather curious, because I didn't ask you to speak for me. Nor did I give you permission to share anything I told you in confidence."

———

Shit.

Sin was pissed about his conversation with her parents.

She managed to keep her tone even, but her voice trembled slightly, and her hands were clenched at her sides. So it was safe to assume Sin was upset with him.

"I didn't go back there with the intention of having that conversation with your parents."

"Then why did you double back there after I left?"

"I left my phone and keys on the table, and I went back to get them. But when your mother said you were being 'unnecessarily dramatic,' something in my head snapped." He shrugged. "I was respectful, of course, but I couldn't let that statement stand. She could've hurled any accusation she wanted against me. I would've just let it go. But she was dismissing your feelings, and that bothered me on a deeper level than you could possibly imagine. I couldn't let it go. So I told her you had every right to be upset and why."

Sin sighed quietly and her expression softened. She wrapped her arms around his waist as she gazed up at him.

"It was sweet of you to defend me, Rett. But it wasn't a discussion for you to have on my behalf. I really wanted to tell your sister how you felt, but I didn't. Because it was a conversation the two of you needed to have." She tapped a finger against his bare chest. "I never betrayed either of your confidences. Instead, I encouraged you to talk to each other and work it out. I gave you my take on how your sister was feeling. I never told you *exactly* what she said, because that wasn't my place. Just like it wasn't yours to tell my parents how I was feeling. I'm a grown woman, Rett. I can speak for myself."

"Then why haven't you, Sin? You have no problem telling anyone else *exactly* how you feel about anything," he said. "You sure as hell didn't hold your tongue with Bianca. So why haven't you told your mother the truth? Why haven't you *insisted* she back off with the matchmaking?"

Sin picked up the plates and set them at the breakfast bar but didn't respond.

"Sin?" He called her name again. "Sweetheart, talk to me."

She glared at him. "So you can run and tell my parents that, too?"

Rett rubbed the back of his neck, his shoulders slumping. *Touché.*

Sin checked her phone. "We have to get out of here. You have to meet the landscapers over at your grandmother's house, and I have to meet with clients in a little over an hour. So let's table the discussion for now." She squeezed his hand. "I know you were only trying to help, and I appreciate it. Now, I need to hop in the shower, or I'll be late. But you should eat before your food gets cold."

Sin gave him a quick kiss on the lips, then hurried toward her room.

Rett ran a hand over his head and cursed under his breath. He hadn't meant to violate Sinclair's trust. He'd felt the need to protect Sin because she'd become incredibly important to him. He only hoped he hadn't ruined things between them.

Chapter Thirty-Six

After her client appointments, Sin pulled her SUV into her parents' driveway and climbed out of the vehicle on shaky legs. She'd been thinking all day of exactly what it was she wanted to say to her mother.

She'd been miffed that Rett had forced her hand, but this conversation had been a long time coming. So she should be grateful he'd set things in motion.

Her mother opened the door before Sin had set foot on the bottom step. Terri Buchanan looked tired and worried, despite her warm smile. "Sweetheart, I'm so glad you're here."

Sin's mother wrapped her in a tight hug that reminded her of the way she'd hugged her when she arrived home from her first day of school.

"Can we talk honestly for a few minutes?" Sin said.

"Of course, darling." A pained look deepened the lines around her mother's mouth and eyes. "But before you say anything, I completely accept the blame for my behavior."

"I'm not here to lay blame, Mama." Sin sighed. "There's plenty enough to go around. But I should've spoken up sooner. I let this thing between us fester for too long."

Sinclair joined her mother on the sofa. Her mom tucked Sin's hair behind her ear and sighed. "Don't be mad with Rett for speaking up, sweetheart. I honestly didn't realize how deeply I was hurting you. That wasn't my intention."

"I know you weren't trying to hurt me, Mom. But you did." Sin blinked back tears. "Nothing I've accomplished seemed to matter to you. All you cared about was my unmarried status and how many grandchildren I could give you."

"That's not exactly true." Her mother squeezed her hand. "But all night I've been thinking about what Rett said. So I understand why you felt that way. And for that, I'm truly sorry. It was admittedly selfish of me."

"Then why'd you do it?" Sin asked.

"Probably for the same reason you haven't told me before now how you really felt," her mother said. "That heart attack ten years ago . . . it reminded me I won't always be here for you girls. That there will be a part of your lives and your children's lives—if you choose to have them—that I'll be absent for. I guess I wanted to minimize the important moments I'd miss out on. Like seeing my baby walk down the aisle. Or become a mother." Her mother's eyes glistened with tears. "It was selfish, I know. But it came purely from a place of love."

Sin nodded, her eyes welling with fresh tears. She tightened her grip on her mother's hand. "I get that now. But all this time, it felt like you were saying I wasn't good enough. That I didn't measure up to Leanne with her powerful, connected husband, idyllic life, and angelic children."

"I see that now." Her mother cupped her cheek. "I can't apologize enough for making you feel that way. I love you very much, Sinclair. Your father and I are so proud of you. And from now on, I promise to focus on every one of your accomplishments—no matter how big or small."

Sinclair laid her head on her mother's shoulder.

"The only thing I've ever really wanted, sweetheart, is for you to be happy. I've had an amazing life with your father all these years, and I've loved being a mother to you girls. I guess I pushed you to do the same because I thought that would ensure your happiness long after I'm gone. I never stopped to consider what it is you want." Her mother rubbed her arm.

"Something Rett said struck me. I asked him if he considered himself the expert on what makes you happy. He told me that you are the expert on what's best for you. And that it was the job of anyone who loves you to respect that and support you."

"Rett said that?" Sin sat up, her heart swelling with affection.

"He sure did." Her mother grinned. "And he was right. So I promise to do just that from now on. All right?"

"I'd like that." Sin smiled, relieved that she and her mother had come to a renewed understanding. It didn't magically erase all of her past hurt feelings, but it was the bridge they both needed to get her there. And it was Rett she had to thank.

"One more thing, Sinclair. In our new spirit of complete honesty. You did *not* cause my heart attack. I know we were having a heated argument at the time, but it could've happened when I was at school or driving to work. If it had to happen, I'm glad I was here with you. You knew exactly what to do. You gave me aspirin and got me to the hospital quickly. Otherwise, I might not be here now."

Sin cringed at the memory of her mother suddenly clutching her chest and falling to the floor during their argument. She'd had nightmares about it for years. Neither she nor her mother had ever mentioned their fight being thc catalyst of her heart attack. But it had always weighed heavily on her. And she'd been terrified to repeat the error in judgment.

"Thanks for saying that, Mom," Sin said.

"It's true." Her mother lowered her gaze. "It's also true that I've been playing into that guilt a little. It was wrong of me, Sinclair, and I'm truly sorry."

Sin hugged her mother tight.

"C'mon in the kitchen, sweet pea." Her mother stood, still brushing away tears. "I'll make us a couple of marocchinos to go with the coffee cake I just took out of the oven."

Sin washed her hands and prepped the glass mugs by using a spoon to smear Nutella inside each of them. Then her mother poured a shot of espresso into each glass mug before steaming the milk and filling each of the glasses with it. Her mother finished the marocchinos off by dusting cocoa powder on top while Sin cut the coffee cake.

They sat at the kitchen table and ate.

"Garrett certainly isn't the same kid he was in high school. And perhaps I judged him too harshly even then," her mother admitted. "Rett's obviously learned from his mistakes. He's a big man with a big heart. He isn't afraid of a little hard work, and he takes good care of the people he loves. And it's quite clear he cares for you, Sinclair. In fact, I'd say he's very much in love with you." A soft smile crinkled the skin around her mother's sparkling blue eyes.

"He is," Sin admitted with an involuntary smile. "And I'm in love with him, too."

"Then why do you look so conflicted, sweetheart?"

Sin explained about Rett wanting to go to Charleston, and her desire to stay on the island and revamp her career. Her mom listened patiently and asked occasional questions.

Finally, her mother said, "I'm grateful you live so close,

especially with your sister being in DC. But love often requires compromise. If you love Garrett, and you really want to make things work between you, maybe the next chapter in your story happens elsewhere."

Sin frowned at the thought of leaving the island and the people she loved behind. But it also pained her to think of losing Rett.

"Rett believes we can work through this. But in reality, one of us wins and one of us loses. Eventually, the person who loses is bound to become resentful."

"Love is always a gamble, sweetheart. But you'll never win if you keep taking yourself out of the game." Her mother sighed. "I know how much Teddy and Gwen hurt you. But if you ask me, they did you a favor. Don't let the scars from that bad experience prevent you from giving your heart to the right man."

Rett had evidently made quite the impression on her mother.

"You think Rett is the right man for me?" Sin was stunned by her mother's change of heart.

"I can hardly believe I'm saying it myself." Her mother chuckled. "But yes, baby, I do. I ran into Annamae at Lila's Café this morning. She couldn't stop singing Rett's praises. It helped me fill in a few of the blanks and gave me a clearer perspective. I realized that maybe I'd written Garrett off at a time when what he'd needed was my support. I'll always regret that. But it's a mistake I won't make twice."

"Me, too." Sin drank the last of her marocchino, then set down her mug.

"Now, you need to decide whether you care for Garrett enough to take a chance on love again, even if it means going with him to Charleston. But whatever you decide, your father and I will support your decision."

Sin hugged her mother, then helped her clean up the kitchen as they chatted about the renovation project and how much she and Rett had enjoyed working together.

After they were done, her mother stood near the window with her chin propped on her fist, deep in thought.

"What's wrong?" Sin placed a hand on her mother's arm.

Her mother looked up, as if startled, a slow smile spreading across her face. "I know I said that love often requires compromise and sacrifice, and that's true. But what if there was a way you could both get what you want?"

Sin looked at her mom, her head tilted. "I'm all ears."

After their chat, Sin kissed her mother goodbye and headed for her SUV. As she drove toward Mama Mae's house, her mother's words about her needing to decide if Rett was worth the risk replayed in her head again and again.

He was, even if it meant making a sacrifice. And he needed to know that.

———

Music blared from Rett's headphones as he cleaned his paintbrushes in the utility sink. The renovation had gone a few weeks longer than they'd planned because of permit issues and materials on back order. But the house was finally finished.

He was glad. Yet, the end of the project felt bittersweet. Rett had enjoyed working with his hands, doing the kinds of projects he'd done with his father as a boy. In fact, he'd loved everything about the process: from planning and budgeting to demolition and construction. Now, all that was left was cleanup. Then they would put his grandmother's house on the market.

Rett glanced around and sighed. The place was all-new now, but this old house still held so many great memories. And it was still the place that felt most like home. He'd never considered himself nostalgic, but he would be sad to see the place go. He only hoped whoever purchased the home would appreciate it as much as he did.

There was a tap on his shoulder, and he jumped, sloshing the water, cloudy with paint residue, onto the floor, narrowly missing Sinclair's sandal-clad feet.

"I'm sorry." He slid the headphones down around his neck and set the plastic container of brushes in the sink. He grabbed a towel and quickly wiped the water from the plastic drop cloth covering the laundry room floor.

"I didn't mean to startle you." Sin stooped to help him clean up.

"It's okay." He gathered everything and set it aside. Then they both washed their hands in the laundry room's utility sink. A quiet lull settled over them as he took her in.

Sin wore a breezy white blouse and white shorts that showed off her gorgeous legs and thick, toned thighs— one of the many features of her body he adored. Her dark brown hair, highlighted with blond, was swept back into a messy ponytail. As always, she was beautiful.

"Sorry," they said simultaneously, followed by nervous laughs.

Rett grazed her cheek with his thumb. "After this morning...I couldn't wait to see you again."

"Then kiss me." A soft smile lit her eyes.

He slid his arms around her waist, kissing the soft, dreamy lips he'd come to adore. It had only been a few hours since he'd held Sin in his arms. Yet, it had felt so much longer. Sinclair had come to mean so much to him. He had no intention of letting her go.

Sin was the only woman he wanted in his life. The one woman he'd dreamed of spending the rest of his life with. A prospect that would've seemed terrifying a few short months ago.

Rett finally pulled himself away and cradled her cheek. "Does this mean I'm forgiven?"

"It means I hope you can forgive me. I'm not used to people going to battle for me like that because I don't usually give them the chance." She gazed up at him. "You were only trying to protect me, and I overreacted. I'm sorry, Rett."

"That means a lot, Sin. But you were right. I should've encouraged you to level with your mom instead of taking it upon myself to tell her. Lesson learned for both of us, I guess."

"Agreed. But that still leaves us with another problem." She angled her head. "How badly do you want to move to Charleston?"

Rett had been thinking about this a lot the past few days. He led Sin by the hand to the stairs, where they both sat, and he turned his body toward hers.

"Charleston is a beautiful city, but it wasn't the place itself that appealed to me as much as taking on a new challenge. I needed a change, but I wasn't quite sure what that was. Working on my grandmother's house reminded me of how much I love doing this kind of work. So yes, the opportunity to do more of this with my buddy in Charleston would be cool. But the best thing about this project was working on it with you, Sin. So if I have to choose between going to Charleston and staying here to be with you, I'd choose you every single time." He brushed his thumb over her cheek, his heart full. "Because you mean that much to me."

Sin's eyes glistened. "And as much as I want to stay here on the island, I want to be with you even more. So if you really want to go to Charleston, I'm willing to go with you, Rett."

Rett was stunned. "You'd be willing to make that kind of a sacrifice for me?"

"I would." She smiled. "But I'm proposing a compromise that'll work for both of us."

Rett was still reeling from Sin's change of heart. If she never stepped foot off this island, the fact that she'd been willing to consider moving to Charleston to be with him meant the world to him. Rett stroked her cheek. "Okay, beautiful, let's hear this compromise."

Chapter Thirty-Seven

Rett stood in the middle of Mama Mae's living room. It was a spot he'd stood in countless times before. And while they'd been able to maintain the home's historic Craftsman charm, the place looked altogether different. The new, open floor plan lent to a brighter, spacious, more modern living room, dining room, and kitchen.

The first-floor addition had allowed them to create a well-appointed first-floor primary bedroom suite. The addition on the second floor expanded the space in what was a bungalow so that there was an additional primary suite on the second floor. And the landscaping was simply breathtaking, elevating the home's curb appeal.

Today they were having an open house for just their friends and family. Then they'd take photos and list the place the following week. Rett honestly couldn't remember being prouder of anything he'd accomplished in his life. But he certainly hadn't pulled off the miraculous transformation on his own.

He glanced over at Sin, who was arranging plates of lemon bars, snickerdoodles, and brownies around the red, white, and blue poke sheet cake she'd spent a good portion of the morning laboring over. The presentation was inviting, but the woman putting it together was absolutely stunning.

Sin looked radiant in a soft green, sleeveless linen dress cinched with a wide, tan leather belt that matched her open-toe sandals. She was singing softly to Maren Morris's "The Bones," playing in the background. He couldn't help smiling as she sang the song about a relationship that could weather any storm.

That's what he would do his damnedest to build with this fierce, beautiful woman who made his heart dance, settled his soul, and lit his fire with her flirty smile that hinted at mischief.

Rett wrapped his arms around her waist and kissed the back of her neck, exposed by her fancy updo.

"How did I get so damn lucky?" he purred in her ear, and she giggled.

"I don't know how we both got so lucky." Sin turned in his arms and pressed a gentle kiss to his lips. "But I'm glad we did, babe. I love you so much."

"Love you, too." His heart skipped a beat.

No matter how many times he and Sin had said those words to each other, over the past few weeks, it still set his heart aflutter. He hoped and prayed that things would always feel this way between them. That they'd never take each other for granted.

"I thought we were invited to see a house makeover, not a make-out session," Nick said as he walked into the house.

"Oh hush, you're just a hater. Leave them alone. They're adorable." Emerie shoved her best friend's shoulder before crossing the room to hug Sin and then Rett.

"You're the first ones here." Sin slipped her arm through

Em's. "Feel free to look around and tell us what you think. We want your honest opinion. Believe me, it can't be any harsher than what potential buyers would say."

"The place looks phenomenal, Sin. You and Rett did an amazing job. You two make a great team." Em admired the refurbished fireplace.

"We really do." Sin smiled broadly, glancing back at him and squeezing his hand. "There are refreshments in the kitchen, so help yourself and make sure you check out the first- and second-floor additions to the house."

Sin turned back to Rett. "The project turned out better than I ever imagined. So I don't know why I'm still nervous."

"You want it to be perfect, and it is." Rett gestured around the space. "Gram's gonna love it, and so will everyone else, including buyers." He was struck by a wave of sadness at the thought of someone else calling the place that meant so much to him home.

Sin hugged him. "I know it'll be hard to let the place go. But you'll still have your memories. And this house will always be a part of you. No matter who owns it." Sin kissed him.

"Rett, Sinclair, I can't believe how beautiful the place looks." Mama Mae walked into the house with Rett's parents and sister, who were also marveling at the transformation.

"I'm glad you're happy with the place, Gram." Rett gave his grandmother a big hug. Her tears wet his shirt.

"You even managed to make my old furniture look good in the place." Mama Mae dabbed her cheeks with a napkin that Sin handed her.

Sin had wanted to bring in a staging company to fill the space with sleek, contemporary furniture. That had been the only expense his grandmother had vetoed. Instead, they'd used her pieces, editing them to ensure the rooms didn't feel overcrowded. Then Sin had spent a minimal budget to put pretty vases and bowls around the place, filling them with fresh flowers and fruit.

Sinclair had used all of the knickknacks Rett had been fondest of and added a few more. She'd also bought some throw pillows and slipcovers to give the old furniture a fresh look. The woman was good at her craft, and it was evident that his grandmother agreed.

Dexter and Dakota arrived, followed by Dexter's mother—Rett's aunt Marilyn. Dakota's father and Lila Gayle dropped by. Sinclair's parents, Terri and Troy, came. Lastly, a few of his grandmother's friends from the senior center popped in. They had a full house, and everyone was raving over the renovation. He had no doubt buyers would have the same reaction. Coupled with the prime location of the home, just a block from the beach, and their plans to price it just right, Rett doubted the house would stay on the market long.

"This is incredible." Mama Mae hugged each of them, her eyes filled with tears. "And I don't just mean the house. I couldn't be happier you two finally figured out you belong together."

"You were right about us being a good match." Rett slipped an arm around Sin's waist and pulled her closer. "Dex and Dakota's wedding brought us together. Collaborating on this project gave us the chance to really get to know each other."

"And to fall in love," his grandmother added proudly. "Which reminds me, I brought you a little gift, Sinclair."

His grandmother produced a tea tin wrapped in a bright pink ribbon and handed it to Sin.

Sinclair thanked her. "Is this your special blend of tea I love so much?"

"It sure is." Mama Mae's smile widened. "It's a rooibos tea with rose petals, cinnamon sticks, vanilla beans, cacao, pink peppercorns, and the special ingredient is *ashwagandha* root. I call it my love potion tea." She chuckled when their eyes both went wide. "You two were a special kind of hardheaded. Figured I needed a little something extra to make you two see just how well-suited you are for each other."

"No complaints here." Sin smiled at him, the flecks of green and gold in her eyes catching the light.

"Me neither." Rett grinned.

"Good. Because I have one more surprise for you." His grandmother beamed. "I'm gifting the house to you, Rett. There's just a bit of paperwork we need to sign, then the place is yours, free and clear. You can live in it, sell it and move to Charleston...whatever you choose."

"You're giving me the house?" Rett was so shocked he could barely speak. He hugged his grandmother, his chest tight and his heart bursting with gratitude. "That's incredibly generous of you, Gram. But this is your home. I can't possibly—"

"Don't you dare say you can't accept my gift, Garrett Davenport." Mama Mae pointed a finger at him. "I know it's *my* home. Which means I have the right to do with it as I choose. And what I choose to do is to gift it to *you*. I hope you'll stay in it and turn it into a home filled with love again, the way it was when your grandfather and I first bought the place more than fifty years ago. But I don't want to pressure you. So if you've decided to move to Charleston—"

"We're staying." Sinclair practically beamed, no longer

able to hold back their good news. She looked to him, and he nodded. "Rett and I enjoyed working together so much, we want to collaborate on more projects like this."

The rest of their friends and family had gathered around and were excited by the news.

"I'm thrilled you two are staying on the island," Chief Jones said. "But are you sure about going into business together? Working together can test even the strongest of relationships."

"We know," Sin said. "Which is why we've agreed to take this slowly and see how things go. We've also drawn up a business agreement that will make it easy to quit the partnership equitably, if that ever became necessary. But given how well we've worked together the past few months, I don't anticipate it will." She leaned into Rett and pressed a hand to his chest.

It reminded him of how Dex and Dakota had stood together at their reception: as a single impenetrable unit, and he couldn't help smiling. That's exactly what he wanted with Sin.

"And we've agreed that if working together becomes too much, it's the relationship that's most important." Rett kissed Sin, and all the women in the room responded with a collective *aww*.

"Sinclair, I know you were expecting your share of the commission from the sale of the house. But don't worry. Douglas knew I planned to gift the house to Rett. That's why the contract included the contingency to pay you a generous, flat fee for your design services, in the event I chose not to sell the house. It's equal to the commission you would've made on the sale."

"I don't know what to say, Mama Mae," Sin said.

"Say you two will live here and love each other for

the rest of your lives." Mama Mae held each of their hands in one of hers. "That'll be payment enough for this old girl."

Rett glanced at Sin. Her eyes were shiny with tears, and she wore a broad smile. She nodded.

"We will," they both said.

Their friends and family laughed and applauded. Hugged them and gave them high fives.

Rett wrapped Sin in a tight hug, his heart full.

He was more than lucky. He was happy. Happier than he'd ever been. Because he was in love with the most amazing woman. And they would live together, there in the house where he'd grown up. The place that had always felt like home.

Rett hadn't ever expected to return to the house on Hummingbird Way. But here he was, surrounded by his family and friends. And there was no place in the world he'd rather be.

Epilogue

—•—•—•—•—

Sinclair glanced around the lovely little cottage that had once belonged to Mama Mae. It was Christmas Eve, and the space, twinkling with lights and dotted with poinsettias and fresh-cut flowers, overflowed with their friends and family. The aroma of their festive holiday meal and an array of freshly baked holiday cookies permeated the house. Everyone was on hand except Rett's grandmother, who'd gone on a Christmas cruise with several of her friends from the senior center.

As Dakota and Dexter chatted with Chief Jones and Ms. Lila, Sin cradled their one-month old daughter, Olivia Madeline Roberts, who slept peacefully in her arms. The little girl had a full head of soft curls that likely explained the heartburn Dakota had suffered with for most of her pregnancy. Olivia had a good mix of her parents' features but looked very much like her maternal grandmother, Ms. Madeline.

It made Sin sad that Olivia would never get to meet the woman from whom she'd inherited her middle name. But as Sin glanced around the room, she knew this little girl would always be surrounded by love.

"Sinclair, you lay that baby in her bassinet upstairs before you spoil her rotten," Dexter's mom chided.

"Yes, ma'am." Sin realized she sounded like a pouty preteen, but she wasn't ready to part with her goddaughter, whose sweet, milky, baby-fresh scent was slightly intoxicating.

A soft smile lit Marilyn's warm brown eyes. "She's such an easygoing baby." The older woman smoothed back the sleeping infant's glossy curls. "Her dad was the same way. He even smiled like that in his sleep."

"If I had a room full of people clamoring over me, I'd be smiling, too," Em said, her arms folded as she shot a glance across the room at Nick, who was laughing with a woman he'd introduced as a new neighbor.

Sinclair and Marilyn exchanged looks.

"Someone sounds jealous." Marilyn took the baby from Sin after offering to take her upstairs and lay her down.

"Jealous of my niece?" Em asked. "You must be kidding. You know how much I adore Olivia."

"No, you're jealous of Ms. Thang over there all cuddled up with your *bestie*." Her mother stressed the word in a teasing tone.

"Am not." Em folded her arms. "And why would I be? We're—"

"Just friends," Sin and Marilyn echoed, then laughed while trying not to wake the baby.

"That's right. We *are* just friends. Have been since we were kids. Why is that so difficult for everyone to understand?" Em practically whined.

"Maybe because you're staring at them like you just lost your best friend," her mother said gently as she settled Olivia on her shoulder. "You can't spend your entire life hoping Nick Washington finally sees you as something more than a friend, honey. Men can be a little slow when it comes to things like that. Either tell the boy how you feel or move on. He certainly has." Marilyn nodded toward Nick and the woman. She kissed Em's cheek, then headed upstairs with Olivia.

Em huffed, her arms folded as she frowned.

"It's not like that with us," Em said to Sinclair, since her mother was already halfway up the stairs.

"Well, it certainly seems that way." Sin slipped an arm through Emerie's and smiled. "And there's nothing wrong with that. But your mom is right—if you have feelings for Nick, you should be honest with him about it."

Em's frown deepened, and she nibbled on her lower lip. "What if I did feel that way, *hypothetically*?" she added quickly. "And then I tell Nick, but he doesn't feel the same?"

Sinclair could feel the tension in the younger woman's shoulders.

"Then, at least you'll know. And like your mom said, you can move on. But the way things are now...it just isn't fair to you, Em. Nick gets to have you in his corner, whenever he needs you. Meanwhile, he's living his best life, dating the entire free world while you're stuck in limbo...a wishin' and a hopin'. It isn't fair."

"I guess I am pretty boring, huh?" Em said.

"I didn't say that, Em. You are *not* boring. You're loyal, funny, creative, beautiful, and absolutely brilliant. You have so much to offer, sweetie," Sin said. "And if Nick can't see that, then maybe he doesn't deserve you."

Em glanced over at Nick and his friend. She sucked in a deep breath and turned to Sin.

"You're right. And I promise to consider your advice. But in the meantime, maybe we could keep this between

us. I'd prefer if no one else knew. Not even my brother and
Dakota." Em held up a finger of warning before Sin could
tell her she was pretty sure Dex and Dakota already knew
how completely into Nick she was. "Promise me, Sin, or I
swear I'll never tell you a single thing again…*ever.*"

"Fine. I won't say a word." Sin raised a hand, as if
taking an oath in court. "*Promise.*"

Em sighed, relieved. She nodded toward the door.
"Someone's looking for you."

Sin glanced toward the front door where Rett had just
stepped inside. He looked handsome in the hooded winter
coat she'd bought him when they'd been struck by a spell of
unusually cold weather in the Outer Banks. Rett was holding
a large red box with a silver bow. They'd been dating seven
and a half months. But the way Rett smiled at her the moment
their eyes met still made her heart dance and her tummy flutter.

"Hey there, beautiful." Rett leaned down and kissed her,
his lips and nose cold.

"Hey there, handsome." Sin wiped her lipstick from his
lips with her thumb. "Did you get something else for the
baby?" She indicated the box.

She and Rett had gone a bit overboard buying things for
their goddaughter. The stack of gifts beneath the tree for
Olivia was admittedly ridiculous.

"You could say that." Rett grinned as he shoved the box
toward her.

"This is for me?" Sin asked, accepting it. "Thank you,
sweetie. I'll put it under the tree."

"Actually, this one, I think you'd better open now." Rett
had a sheepish grin on his face.

"You're sure?"

"Open it already," Terri said. "I want to see what's in
the box."

When Sin looked up, several of their friends and family were watching eagerly.

"I guess it won't hurt to open one gift early." Sin set the box on a nearby table and lifted the lid. She gasped with surprise. The box contained a small dog bed, a leash, doggy clothing, and a variety of dog toys. Sin pressed her hands to her mouth and looked up at Garrett, her eyes misty. "Does this mean..."

"Merry Christmas, baby." Rett grinned and opened his coat, revealing the black, fluffy ball of fur sleeping inside of the dog carrier strapped to his chest. "Meet Stella."

"Oh, Rett." Sin's eyes stung with tears as she scratched the sleeping puppy's head. "Is she really... *ours*?"

"She is. I hope you like—"

Before Rett could finish, Sin lifted onto her toes and kissed him. She pulled back and surveyed the adorable puppy. Only her head was visible above the carrier. "Is it okay if I—"

"Of course." Rett seemed relieved she was so excited about his surprise.

Sin lifted the puppy from the carrier, cradling her to her chest. She nuzzled her head and stroked her ears. "Hello, Stella. Welcome home, sweet girl," Sin whispered to the sleeping pup.

"She's a Havapoo." Rett shoved his hands into his pockets with a bashful smile. "Mrs. K's Havanese made nice with the neighbor's toy poodle."

Sin stroked Stella's sleek black fur, admiring the splashes of white on her chest and front paws. "What's this?"

Sinclair lifted the shiny, round tag hanging from Stella's neck. She expected the tag to bear the puppy's name. Instead, it was engraved with the words *Will you marry Daddy?* and joined by a small replica of an engagement ring.

Sin's heart beat wildly, and her eyes clouded with tears. When she looked up to meet Rett's gaze, he was no longer standing in front of her. He'd lowered to one knee and held up a small, black, velvet ring box. Sin pressed a hand to her heart as tears spilled down her cheeks. She recognized the ring with a large emerald-cut diamond flanked by two smaller emerald-cut stones set in a platinum band. It was the ring she'd fallen in love with when she'd helped Dexter pick out Dakota's engagement ring at Diamonds & Pearls Jewelry Boutique.

Stella rustled in her sleep, and Sin held her closer. "Rett, honey, it's beautiful."

His mouth curved in a smile and he reached for her trembling hand. "Sinclair, the months we've spent together have been truly amazing. Being here with you has made me happier than I've ever been. And I know, without a doubt, there's nothing I want more than to be right here on Holly Grove Island, building a life with you, Sin. The funny, brilliant, determined woman who makes every single day of my life feel like a gift I don't deserve."

Rett swiped the back of his hand across his face, his voice breaking. He inhaled deeply, then kissed her hand. "Sweetheart, will you marry me?"

Sin nodded wildly, her heart overflowing with love for the man who'd been her rock these past months. Rett supported her, challenged her, and made every day a joyous adventure filled with laughter and love. She couldn't imagine not having him in her life.

"I thought you'd never ask, Rett Davenport." Sin grinned through tears of joy.

Everyone, including Rett, laughed. Rett slid the ring on her finger, then stood and pulled her into a deep and sensuous kiss, the space around them exploding with applause.

All of the commotion woke Stella, and she wriggled in Sin's arms. "It's okay, sweet girl," Sin cooed in her ear and rubbed her back. "Everything is going to be fine. We're home now."

They spent the rest of the evening showing off her ring and accepting congratulations from their friends and family.

Over the past six months, their fledging firm Buchanan & Davenport Properties had renovated and sold the homes of three of Mama Mae's friends, in addition to slowly building traditional listings and sales. Then, after the holidays, they'd look for their first property to flip.

And now she and Rett had a wedding of their own to plan.

Sin's life had taken a path she'd never have expected. But she was overjoyed with the life she and Rett were building and thrilled about their future together here in the little house on Hummingbird Way.

Don't miss the next book in the
Holly Grove Island series!

Coming Winter 2024

About the Author

Award-winning author **Reese Ryan** writes sexy, emotional romantic fiction with captivating family drama; surprising secrets; complex, flawed characters; and all the feels. She's the host of *Story Behind the Story*—her YouTube show where romance readers and authors connect.

A panelist at the 2017 Los Angeles Times Festival of Books, winner of an inaugural Vivian Award, and a two-time recipient of the Donna Hill Breakout Author Award, Reese is an advocate for the romance genre and diversity in fiction.

You can learn more at:
ReeseRyan.com
Twitter @ReeseRyanWrites
Instagram.com/ReeseRyanWrites
Facebook.com/ReeseRyanWrites
Tiktok.com/@reeseryanwrites
Pinterest.com/ReeseRyanWrites

For a bonus story from another author that you'll love, please turn the page to read *Only Home with You* by Jeannie Chin.

Zoe Leung allowed her mother to pressure her into a safe, stable career path, but now Zoe's job search has hit a dead end, and she isn't sure what to do next. She fills her days with waitressing and volunteering at Harvest Home, her uncle's food bank and soup kitchen, while figuring out her next move. If she flirts with fellow volunteer—and her older brother's best friend—Devin James, who can blame her? He's only the subject of her lifelong crush. And finally looking at her like he returns the sentiment.

Construction worker Devin James has always thought Zoe was gorgeous, but he doesn't want to jeopardize his friendship with her brother or her family, who all but took him in when he was younger. But as much as he plans to stay focused on building his dream house, he can't stop thinking about Zoe. And the more time he spends with her, the more he realizes that the only home he wants is one with her.

FOREVER

Chapter One

Twenty-eight more months.

Devin James silently repeated it to himself with every crack of his nail gun. He moved to the next mark on the beam, lined up his shot, and drove another spike of steel into the wood.

Based on the numbers he'd rerun over the weekend, twenty-eight months was how long it was going to take him to save up for a house of his own. Still too long, but he was on target, putting away exactly as much as he'd budgeted for, paycheck after paycheck.

"Take that," he muttered, sucking in a breath as he kept moving down the line.

His dad had told him enough times that he'd never amount to anything. Devin tightened his grip on the nail gun and sank his teeth into the inside of his lip. What he'd give to get that voice out of his head. To show his dad he wasn't too stupid to do the math, and he wasn't too lazy to do the work.

He'd buy those three acres of land from Arthur. His mentor—and his best friend Han's uncle—had been saving the lot for him for three years now, and he'd promised to sell it to him at cost. Once Devin had the deed in his hand, he'd start digging out the foundation the next day. Between the buddies he'd made at construction sites and the favors folks owed him, he could be standing in his own house within six months. A quiet place all to himself on a wooded lot five miles outside of town. He'd get a dog—a big one, too. A mutt from the animal rescue off Main Street.

He'd have everything his useless old man told him he could never have. All he had to do was keep his head down and keep working hard.

He finished the last join on this section of the house's frame and nodded at Terrell, who'd been helping him out. The guy let go, and they both stood.

Adjusting his safety glasses, Devin glanced around. It was a cool fall day in his hometown of Blue Cedar Falls, North Carolina. The sun shone down from a bright blue sky dotted with wispy clouds. The last few autumn leaves hung on to the branches of the surrounding trees, while in the distance, the mountains were a piney green.

He and his crew had been working on this development for the better part of a year now. It was a good job, with good guys for the most part. Solid pay for solid work, and if he had a restlessness buzzing around under his skin, well, that was the kind of thing he was good at pushing down.

"Hey—James."

At the shout of his last name across the build site, Devin looked up. One of the new guys stood outside the trailer, waving him over. Devin nudged the protective muffs off his ears so he could hear.

"Boss wants to see you before you clock out."

Devin nodded and glanced at his watch. The shift ended in thirty. That gave him enough time to quickly clean up and check in with Joe.

He made a motion to Terrell to wrap things up.

"What's the hurry?" a voice behind him sneered. "Got to run off to Daddy?"

Devin pulled a rough breath in between his teeth. Head down and work hard, he reminded himself.

No punching the mayor's son in the face.

But Bryce Horton wasn't going to be ignored. He stepped right in Devin's way, and it took everything Devin had to keep his mouth shut.

"Isn't that what you call old Joe?" Bryce taunted. "*Daddy?* You sure come fast enough when he calls."

Devin's muscles tensed, heat building in his chest.

He kept himself together, though. Bryce had been like this since high school, putting everybody down and acting like he was the king of the hill. The entire hill was all sand, though. The guy never did any work. If *his* daddy didn't run this town, he'd have been out on his rear end ages ago.

As it was, Bryce'd been hired on as a favor to the mayor's office, and getting him fired would take an act of God. Didn't stop Devin from picturing it in his head. Daily.

Devin ground his molars together and brushed past him.

"Oh, that's right," Bryce called as Devin showed him his back and started to walk away. "Your real daddy left, didn't he?"

Red tinted Devin's vision. He flexed his fingers, curling them into a palm before taking a deep breath and letting them go.

It'd be so easy, was the thing. Bryce wasn't a small guy, but he wasn't a particularly strong one, either. Two hits and he'd be on the ground, snot-faced and crying. That was how bullies were.

That was how Devin's dad had been.

Without so much as a glance in Bryce's direction, Devin

shucked his glasses, muffs, and gloves, stowed his stuff, and headed over to the trailer. As he walked, he blocked out the sound of Bryce running his mouth. He blocked out the surly voice in his own head, too.

By the time he got to the door, his blood was still up, but he was calm enough to show model employee material, because that was what mattered.

With a quick knock, he tugged open the trailer door and poked his head inside. Joe was at his desk, big hands pecking out something or other on the keyboard.

"Hey." Devin kept his voice level. "Heard you wanted to see me?"

Joe glanced up and smiled, the lines around his eyes crinkling. "Yeah, hey, have a seat."

Devin closed the door and sat down. While Joe finished up what he was working on, Devin half smiled.

Joe was a good boss because he was one of them. He'd worked his way up the ranks from grunt to site supervisor over the last twenty-five years.

Didn't make the sight of his giant frame squished behind a desk any less funny, though.

After a minute, Joe squinted and hammered the return key before straightening and turning to Devin. "James. Thanks for coming in."

"No problem, boss."

"I'll cut to the chase. You're probably wondering why I called you in here."

Devin shifted his weight in his chair. He'd been so distracted by Bryce and then by watching Joe pretend he didn't need reading glasses that he hadn't given it that much thought. Business had been good, and Devin never missed a day. He hadn't screwed anything up that he knew of. Which left only one thing.

Something he'd dismissed out of hand, even as he'd thrown his hat in the ring.

"Uh…"

"You know Todd's retiring at the end of the month."

Devin nodded, his mouth going dry. He fought to keep his reaction—and his expectations—down. "Sorry to see him go."

"We all are, but he's earned it." Joe let out a breath. Then he cocked a brow. "Big question of the day is who's going to fill in for him as shift leader for your crew."

"You made a decision."

"Sure did." Joe kept a straight face for all of a second. When his face split into a wide smile, Devin mentally pumped his fist. Joe extended his hand across the desk. "Congratulations."

Devin didn't waste any time. He shoved his hand into Joe's with fireworks going off inside his chest.

Yes. Holy freaking hell, yes.

"I won't let you down, sir."

"Oh, believe me, I know it, or I woulda picked somebody else."

As he pulled his hand back, Joe started talking about responsibilities and expectations, and Devin was definitely listening.

He was also mentally updating all the numbers in his budget.

He'd never really expected to get the job of shift leader. There were older guys who'd put their names in. Heck, Bryce could have gotten it, and then Devin would have been looking for another job entirely.

But he knew exactly how much his pay was going to go up by. Every cent of it could go into savings. Twenty-eight months would be more like fourteen. Maybe even twelve.

One year. One year until he'd have enough for the land and the materials.

He couldn't wait to tell everybody. Drinks with his buddy Han would be on him tonight.

Arthur was going to be so proud.

Joe paused, narrowing his eyes at Devin and making him tap the brakes on his runaway thoughts. "It won't be an easy job, Devin."

Devin swallowed. "I'm up for the challenge."

"You don't have to convince me," Joe repeated, holding his big hands up in front of his chest. He set them down on the desk and fixed Devin with a meaningful look. "Just. Stand your ground, okay? Do that and I have every confidence you'll be fine."

Right.

Moving up would also mean being responsible for an entire shift crew of guys.

Including Bryce Horton.

That same hot, ready-to-fight instinct flared inside him, followed right after by the icy reminder to push it down. He smiled tightly. "Not a problem."

"All righty, then." The matter seemed settled as Joe stood. "I'll get the paperwork sorted. You start training on Monday."

Devin rose. "Thank you. Really."

Joe gestured with his head toward the door. "Go on. Have a beer or three to celebrate, you hear?"

Devin had no doubt he'd do exactly that—eventually.

With a spring in his step, he headed for the parking lot. He smacked the steering wheel of his beat-up bucket of bolts as he got in and slammed the door behind him. As the old truck lurched to life, he cranked the stereo and peeled out, triumph bursting inside him.

This was it. The break he hadn't dared to hope for but that he needed, the thing that was going to get him on the fast track to his goals.

And there was only one place he wanted to go.

The Harvest Home food bank and soup kitchen stood in a converted mill on the north end of town. Business in Blue Cedar Falls was generally good, and it had only been getting better since tourism had picked up on Main Street.

Main Street's cute little tourist district felt a long way away, though. Devin's wasn't the only rust bucket truck parked outside Harvest Home. On his way in, he held the door for a woman and her four kids who were coming out, each armed with a bag. He didn't need to peek inside to know they were filled with not just cans but fresh food, too. The kind of stuff that filled your belly *and* your heart.

Goodness knew Devin'd had to rely on that enough times when he was a kid.

He ran his hand along the yellow painted concrete wall of the entry hallway, his throat tight. He couldn't wait to tell Arthur.

But when he turned the corner, it wasn't Arthur standing behind the desk. Oh no. Of course it wasn't.

Devin's blood flashed hot. For one fraction of a second, he let his gaze wander, taking in soft curves and softer-looking lips. Dark eyes and long, silky, ink-black hair.

A throat cleared. A brow arched.

Like he'd been slapped upside the head, he jerked his gaze back to meet hers. She smiled at him mischievously, and he bit back a swear.

"Hey, Zoe," he managed to grit out. Silently, he said the rest of her name, too.

Zoe *Leung*. Devin's best friend Han Leung's little sister. Arthur Chao's beloved niece.

The one person on this earth he should *not* be getting caught checking out. Especially by her.

"Hey, Dev." The curl of her full lips made his heart feel like a puppy tugging at its leash to go run off into traffic. Only a semi was barreling down the road.

The past few months since Zoe had moved back home after college had been torture. Fortunately, he had lots of practice keeping himself from doing anything stupid around her. He'd been holding himself in check for years, after all. Since she was eighteen and he was twenty-two.

Because if he ever let go of that leash on his control? Gave in to the invitation in her eyes?

Well.

It'd probably be a whole lot easier if he just got run over by a truck.

Chapter Two

Zoe Leung's heart pounded as heat flared in Devin's eyes.

Only for it to flicker and then fizzle in about two seconds flat.

The whole thing made her want to tear her hair out.

Because she was a realist, you know? Sure, she'd had a crush on Devin since she'd realized that not all boys were slimy and gross (her brother Han definitely excluded). But she'd never expected anything to ever come of it.

To him, she was the bratty kid who used to follow her brother and his friends around all the time. Skinned knees and messy ponytails and oversize hand-me-down T-shirts did not bring any boys to the yard, and she'd made her peace with that.

Right until her high school graduation, four and a half long years ago.

Her mom had made such a big deal of it. Her last kid graduating from high school had combined with menopause in some pretty unpredictable ways. Finally, the nagging about wanting a good picture had gotten to be too much. Fed up with it all, Zoe had gotten her sister Lian to help her figure out how to do her hair and her makeup, and she'd actually worn a dress for once. It'd been a big hassle, but she'd had to admit that she felt and looked great.

At the party after, while Han and Devin and a few of their friends were tossing a football around in the backyard, she'd gone up to them to let them know the pizza was there.

She could see it all in her head so clearly. Devin had looked up. His eyes had gone wide.

Only to have a football smack him right in the head.

He'd never looked at her the same after that. Every time his gaze landed on her, it would darken. His Adam's apple would bob, and that scruffy jaw would tense, his rough, hardworking hands clenching into fists at his sides.

Exactly the way he'd been looking at her about two seconds ago.

An angry flush warmed her cheeks as he jerked his gaze away—probably checking to make sure her overprotective big brother, Han, wasn't going to materialize out of nowhere and throw another football at his head.

It was infuriating.

When he didn't have any interest in her, she could totally handle it. But now? This weird, intense game of sexual-attraction chicken he was playing?

What a bunch of bull.

The last time they'd run into each other at the drugstore, he'd done the same thing, heat building in his gaze right until the moment she'd stared back at him. She'd played it cool, hoping he'd say something. Instead, he'd grabbed the first thing he saw off the shelf and darted toward the checkout. Either the guy was super eager to get home with his novelty sunglasses or he was avoiding her.

After months of being back home spinning her wheels on her doomed job search, she was tired of spinning her wheels on whatever was going on between the two of them, too. She wasn't expecting him to drop down on one knee and ask her to marry him or anything. But she was into him, and it sure seemed like he was into her. While she was here, couldn't they, like, *do* something about it?

Enough playing it cool. Clearly she was going to have to be the one to make the first move.

Abandoning subtlety for once, she sauntered over to him. She put a little swing in her hips, just for fun. She'd come out of her shell a lot during the four years she'd been away. She could still rock a messy ponytail and an oversize T-shirt, but the snug top and short skirt she was wearing in preparation for her shift at the Junebug tonight were just as comfortable—and she knew how to use them.

"How's it going?" she asked, coming to a stop a foot away. Too close, for sure. The air hummed. He was tantalizingly warm, pushing heat into the tight space between them and making her skin prickle with awareness.

Licking her lips, she gazed up at him. She was all but batting her lashes here.

The darkness in his eyes returned as he stared down at her.

He had always been good-looking. Back in the day, it had been in a loping, gangly teenage way. His spots on the baseball and football teams had put some muscle on him, but whatever he'd been up to at his construction job had done even more. Under his jacket and tee, he rippled with muscle. His jaw had gone from soft to chiseled, and he kept his golden-brown hair shorter, too.

"Uh." He swallowed. "Good. Great, actually."

"Yeah?"

He still hadn't backed away. That was a good sign, right?

"Yeah." He nodded almost imperceptibly.

Something turned over, low in the pit of her belly.

He smelled so good, like man and hard work and wood shavings.

She wanted to ask him what was going on that was so great. She wanted to sway forward into him, tip her head up or put her hand on his broad chest and find out if it was as hard and hot as it looked.

He swallowed and shifted his weight, edging ever so slightly closer to her. Her heart thudded hard. Maybe he wanted her to do all those things, too. Maybe...

"Devin? What are you doing here?"

Crap.

The instant Uncle Arthur's gently accented voice rang out, Devin jumped back as if he'd been burned. The hot thread of tension that had been building between them snapped. A flush rose on her cheeks, almost as deep as the disappointment flooding her chest.

"Arthur! Hey, um." Devin glanced around wildly, looking at everything but Zoe. Honestly, it would have been less conspicuous if he'd come over and put his arm around her. "Do you have a second?"

"For you?" Uncle Arthur smiled, pleased lines appearing around his eyes and mouth. "Of course." He looked to Zoe. "You don't mind?"

Zoe forced a smile of her own. "Of course not."

With a smile of thanks to Zoe, Uncle Arthur led Devin back to his office. Zoe was tempted to follow and listen at the door, but that would be childish.

Instead, she sighed and retreated to the front desk. This was a slow hour. All the appointments for people to pick up goods from the food bank were over, but the soup kitchen hadn't opened for dinner service yet. Down the hall, pots and pans banged, though, so Harvest Home's two staff cooks, Sherry and Tania, must already be at work.

That didn't mean there wasn't anything to do, of course.

Ever since she'd slunk back to Blue Cedar Falls with the useless accounting degree her mom had talked her into, she'd been splitting her time between scrolling social media, waitressing at the new bar in town, and helping out here. Working at Harvest Home barely paid a pittance, of course, but she didn't mind. Uncle Arthur might be her mom's brother, but he was her exact opposite in terms of how he treated Zoe. He was cool and relaxed, and he trusted Zoe with real responsibilities. Watching him work his rear end off here—even though he was in his sixties and on three different high blood pressure medications—made her want to live up to his example.

She liked helping people. Sending folks off with whatever they needed to help get them through tough times gave her a warm feeling inside. Even the boring administrative stuff felt important.

With a sigh, she plunked behind the desk and got to it, confirming pickups, arranging deliveries, and checking in about volunteer shifts. When the crew of said volunteers helping out with supper tonight showed up, she showed them to the kitchen and placed them in Sherry's and Tania's capable hands. On the way back, she definitely did *not* linger outside Arthur's office, staring at the closed door as if she could burn through it with her laser eyes and find out what he and Devin were going on about.

Okay, maybe for a minute, but that was it.

As she returned to the front room and started in on labeling bags for the next day's pickups, the door swung open.

A telltale *tutt*ing sound announced who it was before Zoe could so much as look up.

"Zhaohui." Her mother came in carrying a box of extra

produce from their family restaurant, the same way she did every Tuesday—the one day of the week the Jade Garden was closed. She set the box down and came straight over, her tone as disapproving as ever as she snatched the marker from Zoe's hand. "You know Arthur likes black ink."

Zoe rolled her eyes. "Well, I like purple, and do you see Arthur doing the work?"

"I think the bags look great." Han had come in behind her, hauling another crate of soon-to-expire vegetables.

"See?" Zoe told her mom.

Her mom made that noise in the back of her throat that said nothing and everything as she waved a hand at Zoe and let her grab the marker back. She drifted away, and Zoe met her brother's gaze over her head.

"Hey." Han wrapped an arm around her shoulders to give her a quick squeeze in greeting. She rolled her eyes the way she was contractually obligated to as his little sister, but she appreciated the affection all the same. "How's it been today?"

"Not bad." Zoe finished labeling the bags—in dark, entirely legible purple—as she gave him a general rundown. She glanced at the clock. She didn't need to leave for her shift at the Junebug for another few minutes. Normally, with Han and her mom here to take over, she'd head out and get a few minutes of quiet in her car to decompress, but she eyed the back office again.

Before she had to make a decision, the door swung open, and her breath caught. Devin came out first. Uncle Arthur followed, patting his back. Both of them were all smiles.

As Devin spotted Han, his grin grew even wider. "Dude, I didn't know you were going to be here."

"What's up?" The two traded bro-hugs and smashed their fists together, and for a second it was like being twelve years old again, watching them and feeling completely outside it all.

Devin stepped back. "Guess who's moving up to shift leader next week."

"Whaaaat?" Han held his hand out, and they high-fived.

"That's awesome," Zoe interjected.

Devin's gaze shot to hers only to dart right back away.

Uncle Arthur clapped Devin's shoulder. "I knew it would happen."

The corners of Devin's mouth curled up, even as he shrugged and looked down.

Zoe's ribs squeezed. He might be trying to act cool, but Devin had been following her uncle around for even longer than Zoe had been following Devin. She knew the praise and faith meant the world to him.

"Your company hiring?" her mom asked Devin, her tone way too innocent. "Maybe in accounting department?"

Zoe glared at her.

"What?" Her mom put her hand over her chest. "I'm just asking." She raised her brows. "Someone has to."

Sure, sure. So helpful. Zoe clamped her mouth shut against the instinct to remind her mom that she'd been the one to push Zoe into accounting in the first place. Well, that or medicine or law, and accounting had definitely been the easiest option of those.

Zoe hadn't exactly had a strong sense of what she wanted to do, but it wasn't sit behind a desk crunching numbers all day. The fact that she hadn't been able to find a job in the field was salt in the wound. Did her mom really need to remind her of it constantly?

"I'll check, Mrs. Leung," Devin promised. He cast Zoe a sympathetic glance, and she couldn't decide if that was better or worse than him totally ignoring her.

Her mother cocked a brow, silently saying, *See?*

Zoe huffed out a breath.

Defusing things the way he always did, Han turned back to Devin. "We *have* to celebrate."

"The Junebug does two-for-one drinks before eight tonight," Zoe blurted out. Self-consciousness stole over her as all eyes turned to her, but screw it. She doubled down. "Plus, you know." She pointed her thumbs at her chest. "Employee discount."

Han looked to Devin, brows raised.

"Sure," Devin said slowly. He let his gaze fall on her for all of a second. There was that flare of heat again. But as fast as it had come, it disappeared as his eyes darted away. "Who doesn't like cheap beer, right?"

"Right," Zoe agreed. She smiled tightly.

Thanks to her entire freaking family showing up, this round of "Poke Devin Until He Cracks" was a stalemate.

But the good news was that she'd just earned herself another shot.

Chapter Three

So, how's it feel?" Han asked. "Mr. Fancypants promotion."

Devin shook his head. "I'm still having a pretty hard time believing it."

After a brief stop at home to change, he'd met Han at the Junebug on Main Street for the cheap drinks Zoe had promised them. Add in some burgers and the owner Clay's famous cheese fries, and this was basically Devin's ideal night out. He snagged another stick of greasy goodness from the basket in front of him and popped it in his mouth. It tasted like victory.

And cheese.

But mostly victory. After years of careful planning, everything he'd been working for finally felt like it was within his grasp. Arthur'd taken the time to rerun the numbers with him in his office, and twelve months was a solid projection. For years now, Arthur had been holding on to that lot on the outskirts of town for him. It was one of a handful of shrewd real estate investments he'd made decades ago. He'd been slowly selling off the rest of his plots as Blue Cedar Falls had grown and tourism had boomed, but not that one. It made Devin's throat tight, just thinking about it. The guy had so much faith in him.

Sure, he'd also somehow gotten Devin to commit to mustering up a volunteer squad from Meyer Construction to serve Sunday supper at Harvest Home—some church group had apparently made the finals in a choral competition and had to pull out at the last minute. But that was just more evidence of how much he trusted Devin.

Well, Devin was going to show him that he'd put his faith in the right man. He'd get enough guys from work to show up on Sunday—no problem. And twelve months from now, he'd make good on his promise to buy those undeveloped acres.

His own land, away from the crappy apartments where he'd grown up. Someplace quiet just for him, no nosy roommates or noisy neighbors upstairs. A home he'd build with his own two hands.

Just don't screw it up, a voice in his head whispered.

Devin bit the inside of his cheek. Ignoring the doubt in the back of his mind, he reached for his beer and took a good swig.

"How're you boys doing?" Zoe appeared at the side of their table in the corner. Heaven help him. She'd put on some lipstick or something since he'd seen her at Harvest Home. He couldn't stop looking at her red mouth, and his best friend was going to *murder him.* Oblivious, Zoe glanced between the both of them. "Y'all ready for another round?"

Devin drained the last gulp from his glass and thunked it down in front of her. "Sure am."

"Awesome."

Devin should probably be pacing himself. He had an early shift in the morning. But he was celebrating. Letting loose for one night wouldn't hurt.

Just so long as he didn't slip up and let himself look at Zoe's chest.

Crap. Too late.

He jerked his gaze away. "Maybe some water, too," he croaked.

Zoe nodded. "Probably a good call."

"Whatever he's having, put it on the house." Clay Hawthorne, owner and proprietor of the Junebug, wandered over. He clapped Devin on the shoulder, then shot a narrow-eyed glance at Han. "Not this guy, though."

"Hey," Han protested. "After all the free food I give you."

"Fine, fine." Clay held his hands up in front of his chest. "It's all on the house, but, Zoe, don't give them any top-shelf stuff, you hear?"

"Only the worst for my brother," Zoe agreed. "Got it, boss."

"You know I'm just giving you free stuff because it means I don't have to write a receipt, right?" Clay told them.

Han shook his head. "You have really got to figure that stuff out, man."

"I know." Clay scrubbed a hand through his red-brown hair. "But math is hard."

Devin gestured around. "When you get to big numbers like this it is."

"Doomed by your own success," Han sympathized.

Clay was a relative newcomer to Blue Cedar Falls, but you'd never know it. Devin didn't make it out to Main Street all that often, but whenever he did, the Junebug was hopping, drawing in the tourists that flocked to the area and locals alike. Clay seemed to know everybody on a first-name basis—or if he didn't at the start of the night, he did by the end.

He'd become good friends in particular with Han, which

was great to see. Han had been Devin's best friend since they were kids. He was a good guy—maybe the best. But he was so serious, carrying the weight of the world on his shoulders. He didn't get out a lot. The guy could use another friend in his corner.

"Tell me about it," Clay grumbled. "This place was supposed to be small, you know. Just a hole in the wall for me and maybe ten other people."

"Guess you should have told June that." Han tipped his head toward the front door, which had just swung open to reveal the lady in question.

Clay's complaining ceased, his whole demeanor changing as he lifted a hand to her in greeting. She smiled, too, broad and unreserved, as she crossed the space toward him.

Devin shook his head, rolling his eyes fondly as Clay swept June up in his arms. He'd never get over a big, gruff guy like that turning into a teddy bear whenever his girlfriend was around.

As they kissed, Devin looked away, because wow. They were really going at it. He happened to meet Zoe's gaze, and they shared a stifled laugh at the PDA.

Then Devin had to look away all over again, because sharing anything with Zoe—especially something related to kissing—was a terrible idea.

"Get a room." Han threw a napkin at Clay and June, and they finally broke apart.

Zoe swatted lightly at Han. "Don't listen to my brother," she told June. "He's just jealous."

"Ew." Han recoiled. "I definitely am not."

And okay, yeah, considering Han had dated June's sister May for approximately all of high school, that made sense.

"How's it going?" June asked, ignoring him.

"Fine," Zoe told her. "Just commiserating with Clay about how you ruthlessly turned his dive bar into the most popular spot on Main Street."

June shook her head and patted his arm. "Pretty sure that was mostly your doing." She gestured around. "Everything here was your idea. I just helped you put it all together."

"Okay, fine, it was a group effort," Clay said, his smile wry. He then pointedly steered the conversation away from how business was booming—and, Devin noticed, away from the jabs Han had been making about how he needed to get his accounting figured out.

If anybody else noticed, they didn't make a big deal of it, so Devin kept mum, too. They all made small talk for a few minutes. Inevitably, Zoe had to excuse herself to go check on her other tables. "You got everything under control?" Clay asked.

Zoe gave him a thumbs-up as she walked away. "On top of it all, boss."

"Guess we should head out." To Han and Devin, he explained, "Date night."

"Have fun," Han told them.

"And thanks again for the grub," Devin said.

Clay tipped an imaginary hat at him before turning and steering June toward the back.

Devin returned to his burger, but after a minute, it registered with him that Han's attention was decidedly elsewhere. And that he wasn't happy.

He followed his buddy's scowling gaze.

And kind of immediately wished he hadn't.

Zoe stood over by a table on the other side of the bar, her head tipped back in laughter as a group of guys gave her their orders. One of them had sidled his chair awfully close to her. Another winked.

Devin fought not to sigh.

"Don't do it," he warned.

Han's voice came out gruff and pinched. "Do what?"

"Whatever it is you're thinking about doing to those jerks."

The guy next to Zoe leaned over as if to pick something up off the ground, only there was nothing there.

Han bristled.

Zoe neatly sidestepped the creeper, but none of the tension left Han's frame.

"Seriously, dude." Devin shifted his chair to block Han's sight line. If it also meant he couldn't see Zoe anymore, well, that was just a bonus. "She can handle herself."

The opening night of the Junebug had proven that. Han had lost it on the guys leering at his little sister, and she'd put both them—and her brother—in their places.

"I know," Han grumbled. "But those guys are out of line."

He wasn't wrong, but still. "When it comes to Zoe, you think everyone is out of line."

"I do not."

"You absolutely do." Devin's throat tightened.

Han had always been overprotective. When they were kids, it was cool. No one at Blue Cedar Falls Elementary could mess with either Zoe or their middle sister, Lian. But as the girls had gotten older—and after Han's father died—Han's overprotective instincts went out of control.

"I just..." Han picked at his fries before pushing them away. "I know she's an adult, okay?"

"You sure about that?"

Han ignored him. "She's an adult, but she doesn't act like one. At her age, I'd taken over the restaurant. I was paying the mortgage, you know? She's living in the basement."

Ouch.

That wasn't exactly fair, though. Their father had died during Han's first term at the Culinary Institute in Raleigh. It'd been his decision to leave and help his mom out after.

It'd also been his decision to make sure Zoe and Lian wouldn't have to make the same sorts of sacrifices.

Devin raised a brow. "You think she shouldn't have gone to school?"

"Of course not." Han blew out a breath. "It's not even that I mind her living in the basement. It's just—those guys are dirtbags."

"Maybe dirtbags leave good tips."

"It's more than that," Han insisted. "It's like she *likes* dirtbags. You remember all the losers she brought home in high school. And none of them lasted."

"So she dated a few guys." Devin stared at Han pointedly. "*Most* people did."

Han narrowed his eyes right back. "This is not about me. Or May."

Han had been practically married to May Wu for the entirety of high school, and everybody knew it.

As Devin saw it, Han had never gotten over her, either. Just because he'd mated for life didn't mean he should expect everybody else to.

"Uh-huh."

"I didn't go nuts on Lian, did I?"

Lian had also been a lot less of a wild child than Zoe growing up.

"I'm telling you," Han insisted. "You know how Zoe and Mom would go at it. She's always been rebellious. Mom says turn left and Zoe heads right. Mom says get a job in your field, and Zoe ends up waitressing in a bar."

"In a job you got her."

"Beside the point—I just wanted to get her out of the

house, and Clay needed the help." Han picked up a fry and pointed at Devin with it. "The guy thing is just a part of it. She'll bring home anyone she thinks will piss Mom off."

Was that it?

Devin fought not to squirm. If so, how far did it go? Their mom had her opinions, and yes, she and Zoe bumped heads about them. But was Han any different with his overprotective crap?

Would Zoe do something just to piss her brother off, too?

Suddenly, Zoe going all seductive temptress on Devin back at Harvest Home that afternoon took on a whole new light.

Something in his stomach churned. He'd known better than to act on her flirtations—for a whole host of reasons. But if she'd been doing it to get a rise out of Han?

Devin took a big gulp of his water to wash down the bitterness creeping into the back of his throat.

It didn't matter. Han was Devin's best friend. If he didn't want anyone dating his little sister, Devin would respect that.

That didn't stop him from asking one final question.

"So what if she brought home someone you *did* like? Someone with good intentions, a decent job. Treated her well." Devin's voice threatened to tick upward, but he wrestled it down. "What would you do then?"

Han chuckled. "Sure. That'll be the day."

"For real, though."

"Look, I just want her to be happy. She brings home someone great, fine. But I don't see it happening. She's immature and messing with fire just to see if it'll burn. I'm protecting her from douchebag guys at bars, sure. But I'm also protecting her from herself."

"Who are you protecting from herself? Someone new?"

Crap, where had Zoe come from? She set a fresh beer down in front of Devin. She snagged the other one off her tray and held it over the table like she was seriously considering throwing it in her brother's face. "Or just me, like usual?"

Han reached out and grabbed the pint glass, but she pulled it away, keeping it out of his grasp.

"Way to prove how mature you are." Han stood.

She set the glass down with a thud. Beer sloshed right to the edge, but it didn't spill over. Clenching her jaw, she asked, "Anything else I can get you gentlemen?"

"Zo, don't be like that."

She ignored Han. "Devin?"

"Nah," Devin said carefully. "I'm good."

"Great, well, anything you need, you just let me know." She smiled at him way too sweetly.

He swallowed hard, his heart pounding. The full force of her attention on him affected him way more than it should. He didn't want Han getting a whiff of him being interested. He didn't want her getting an inkling about it, either.

Maybe her earlier flirting had been genuine. But her being sunshine and roses to him now?

Yeah. That was definitely for Han's benefit.

Which cast everything else in doubt, too.

Chapter Four

S top."

Zoe screeched to a halt with her hand mere inches from the knob on her family home's back door.

So close.

Her mother cleared her throat, and Zoe prayed for strength before turning around. "Yes, Mother?"

Her mom stood in the kitchen, brows raised, arms crossed. Ling-Ling, the shepherd mix Han had adopted after Zoe left home, sat at her heels. If it was possible, the dog bore the same judgmental glare. "How many résumés did you send out today?"

"Mom—"

"How many?" her mother repeated, firm.

Zoe blew out an exasperated breath. "I didn't, like, count."

"And why not? We paid for a degree in *accounting*, did we not?"

"Would you like me to send you a spreadsheet?"

Her mom scowled, and Ling-Ling made a little growling sound. "No need to take that tone."

Zoe could say the same herself. "Look—"

"You remember what we talked about earlier, right?"

How could Zoe forget?

"Yes, Mom." Zoe wasn't applying herself enough, wasn't taking her future seriously, wasn't considering enough options, blah, blah, blah. "Can I go now? I promised Uncle Arthur I'd open up Harvest Home for him."

The severe line of her mother's frown finally softened. "Fine." She made a little shooing motion with her hand. "Go, go."

Zoe turned to leave. "I just fed Ling-Ling, so don't let her con you into a second dinner."

Her mom never cut Zoe an inch of slack, but the dog walked all over her.

"You send me that spreadsheet tomorrow," her mom called.

"I was *obviously* kidding about that," Zoe cast over her shoulder, opening the door.

She kept walking right on through it, too, blocking out any further replies from her mother by swiftly—but gently!—closing the door behind her.

Still annoyed by the whole thing, she got into her sensible pre-owned Kia and started it up. Her fingers itched on the steering wheel, and the urge to put the pedal to the metal as she pulled onto Main Street tugged at her. She mentally shook her head at herself. The last thing she needed was Officer Dwight pulling her over and giving her a lecture, too.

As she begrudgingly maintained the speed limit, she ran over her mom's words again in her head. With every iteration, she got more worked up. Wasn't it bad enough that her mom had pressured her into going into accounting in the first place?

"Think about your future," Zoe mumbled, imitating her mother's voice. "You want good job, right?"

Fat lot of good the accounting degree had done her in that respect.

To be fair, Zoe hadn't exactly had a better idea about what to do with her life. But it would have been nice to have had some options other than doctor, lawyer, or bean counter.

She chewed on the inside of her lip. At a stoplight, she impulsively hit the button on the dashboard to make a call.

Her sister, Lian, picked up on the second ring. Long and drawn out, her voice came out over the car's tinny speakers. "Yes?"

"How did you know what you wanted to do with your life?"

"Well, hello to you, too."

"I'm serious," Zoe insisted.

Despite facing more or less the same pressure from their mother, Lian had forged her own path. She had a job as a teacher in the next town over, with a 401(k) and health insurance and everything and an apartment where no one harassed her every time she tried to get out the door.

Basically, living the dream.

"I can tell," Lian said dryly. There were rustling noises in the background. "Give me a second to think."

Zoe didn't have a second. The drive to Harvest Home took only ten minutes, and she'd squandered at least seven of them stewing. "I mean, you must have felt pretty strongly about it. Goodness knows it wasn't Mom's idea."

Lian laughed. "No, that it was not." She hummed in thought, then said, "I guess...When you know, you just *know*. You know?"

"Clearly not." Zoe groaned.

"Sorry, that's what I've got."

"You are so useless."

"Uh-huh. Which is why you always call me first when you're stuck."

"I'm not stuck." Okay, she was. Kind of.

She just didn't know what to do with her life or how to get her mother off her back. But other than that, she was fine.

No, she hadn't made any progress on Operation: Seduce Devin Until He Breaks, but she had her job at the Junebug, which was fun and paid well. Her leftover free time—when she wasn't applying for jobs or making pointless spreadsheets for her mother—she spent at Harvest Home, and it was... well, great.

She sighed. If only she could convince Uncle Arthur to take that well-earned trip to Fiji he was always talking about and let her take over there full time. She'd miss him, sure, and it wouldn't exactly be a fancy corporate accounting job. But if she could rustle up enough grants to pay herself a salary, even her mother couldn't give her a hard time about that.

As she turned into Harvest Home's parking lot, she finished up her conversation with her sister. Sherry and Tania arrived just as she was heading toward the door.

"Good afternoon, ladies," Zoe said, swinging her hair out of her face as she found the right key.

Sherry grinned. She was an older white woman who'd been cooking for Harvest Home since Arthur had founded it back in the late nineties. "Hey, Zoe."

"Arthur finally take a day off?" Tania asked. Tania was newer, hired when the place had expanded a few years ago, but now it was hard to imagine how they'd gotten along without her. She was Black and maybe twenty years younger than Sherry, and the two were a powerhouse team.

"Fingers crossed."

Tania threw her head back and laughed. "I give it an hour."

"Swear I'm going to tie that man to his recliner." Zoe shook her head and pushed open the door.

Uncle Arthur was tireless, and getting him to take an entire day off—much less a trip to Fiji—was a rare victory. She swallowed hard. The only person she'd ever known who worked harder was her dad, and everyone knew how that had ended. If he'd rested and relaxed more, would that have prevented him from dropping dead of a heart attack at forty-eight?

Who knew. Probably not.

But Uncle Arthur was sixty-five with high blood pressure. The guy deserved a break.

Heading inside, Zoe flicked on the lights and fired up the computer to check messages at the front desk. Sherry and Tania made their way to the kitchen. Absently, Zoe pulled up the volunteer schedule. It took its sweet time loading, so she called, "Any idea who's serving tonight?"

As paid employees, Sherry and Tania were the backbone of the organization's meal service, but they couldn't pull off feeding fifty people a day without an equally dedicated crew of volunteers. Businesses, churches, and schools fielded teams that came out to make the magic happen every night.

Sherry and Tania must have been out of earshot. Frowning, she wiggled the computer mouse and reloaded the schedule. Before it could come up, the door swung open. Zoe darted her gaze toward the entryway.

Only to be met with a pair of gorgeous blue eyes, a broad set of shoulders, a trim, muscular frame, and a bright smile.

"Meyer Construction, reporting for duty," Devin said.

Zoe's heart did a little jump inside her chest as she straightened up. "Oh, hey!"

"Hey." Just like he had the last time he strode through that door, he raked his gaze over her. She swallowed. She wasn't dressed to get good tips at the Junebug today. A flannel shirt over a T-shirt and jeans was hardly what she'd call sexy, but it didn't seem to matter, based on the way his eyes darkened.

"I didn't know you all were serving today."

Devin moved forward into the space, making room for a half dozen folks to file in after him. He shrugged, tucking his thumbs into the belt loops of his dark-rinse jeans. "Arthur talked me into it when I was here telling him about my promotion." One corner of his mouth curled upward. "Said it'd be a good use for my new leadership skills."

The last guy to come in groaned. "Are we ever going to hear the end of that?"

Devin stiffened and flexed his jaw. "I haven't even started yet, Bryce."

Ah, okay, now Zoe recognized the guy shouldering past Devin. The mayor's son, Bryce Horton, had been a couple of years ahead of her in school, but Lian had complained about him plenty at the time. He'd been a royal jerk, and it didn't seem like much had changed.

"Then why am I even here?" Bryce asked, pulling out his phone and plunking down in one of the chairs meant for patrons.

Devin's whole frame radiated tension, but however angry he was, he kept it out of his tone. "Come on. Kitchen's in the back."

Bryce rolled his eyes, even as he kept his gaze glued to what sure looked like a dating app he was swiping through.

Zoe resisted the urge to sneak a peek at his username—just so she could avoid it if she ever ended up on the same site.

Devin's voice dropped. "Now."

Grumbling, Bryce lurched out of the chair and followed Devin down the hall.

"Right behind you," Zoe called. She just had a couple more quick things to take care of out here.

Bryce looked over his shoulder at her and made a super-gross kissy face. Glancing back, Devin caught him, and his eyes narrowed, his hands curling into fists at his sides.

Interesting. When her brother shot his death glare at guys who were hitting on her at the bar, it made her want to strangle him. But when Devin did it?

A warm little shiver ran up her spine.

She probably shouldn't like it so much, but she did.

She swallowed, fighting to calm the flutters in her chest as she shot Bryce a glare of her own. No matter how much Devin's protectiveness gave her the warm fuzzies, she could handle herself. "Wasn't talking to you," she informed Bryce.

"Sure." He clicked his tongue and brought his hand to his ear like a phone and mouthed, *Call me.*

Devin bustled him along, thunderclouds in his eyes. The coiled strength in him gave her even more little flutters inside.

As soon as they disappeared around the corner, she put her head in her hands to muffle her groan. Getting the butterflies over this guy was pathetic. She was acting like a swooning schoolgirl with a crush again.

Sucking in a deep breath, she dropped her hands from her face. She was too old for this pining nonsense.

Resolve filled her. Devin showing up to volunteer tonight

might have taken her by surprise, but it was a golden opportunity. Han was working at the restaurant tonight, so he couldn't appear from out of nowhere, football in hand or no. Devin would have his guard down.

With so many people around, Zoe couldn't exactly seduce Devin. But maybe this was her chance to show him that she was so much more than a kid with a crush now.

And that the spark between them was real.

———

"Need any help?"

Zoe sighed and cast her gaze skyward but didn't stop busing dishes. "I thought you were taking the day off."

Uncle Arthur smiled. "Was just in the neighborhood and thought I'd stop in." He craned his neck to peer into the dining room. "Decent crowd tonight."

"Fifty-seven."

"Impressive." He pursed his lips. "Terrible, but impressive."

Nobody wanted to be put out of business more than Uncle Arthur. When his family had landed in this country nearly sixty years ago, they'd relied on soup kitchens. He'd come a long way since then, and he'd had some good luck with investments that had allowed him to found this place. He loved having a way to give back to the community here in Blue Cedar Falls that had taken him in. But if hunger and unemployment just disappeared, he'd be delighted to be out of a job.

Stir crazy and climbing the walls, looking for his next venture, but delighted.

"Late fall is always tough."

The weather here was warm enough that construction and tourism carried on year-round, but whenever the weather turned chilly, the number of people showing up at Harvest Home climbed.

"True." Uncle Arthur came over to squeeze her arm. "Knew you could handle it, though."

Her chest contracted. With no one else in her life trusting her to handle anything more than her TikTok account, that was way too nice to hear. She chuckled to hide the tightness behind her ribs. "Which is why you felt no need to check up on me at all."

"He's not checking up on you," Tania said, coming in from taking a load to the compost pile out back. "He just can't stay away from me," she teased.

"You know me," Uncle Arthur agreed indulgently, dropping his hand.

Sherry was right behind Tania. She shook her head at Arthur. "Held out longer than I thought you would."

Ignoring her, Uncle Arthur gestured toward the dining room. "I'm just going to quick make the rounds."

Zoe waved him along. On his way out, Arthur nearly bumped right into Devin, who had a crate filled with dirty dishes in his arms.

Devin's eyes lit up. "Thought you were taking the night off."

"Don't you start in on me, too." Uncle Arthur waggled a finger at him.

"You're working yourself to an early grave," Zoe called after him.

Uncle Arthur's finger shifted to point at her, but she just shrugged. She wasn't going to apologize for trying to remind him to take a break once in a while. He continued out to the dining room to do his usual thing, thanking volunteers and checking in on the guests. Sherry and Tania followed him with more milk crates to help with cleanup.

Rolling her sleeves to her elbows, Zoe started running the water.

Devin brought his crate of dishes over to her. "He's unstoppable, huh?"

"Seems it." She frowned. Her uncle definitely gave that impression, but he was getting up there, and she did genuinely worry about him.

"He's fine. There's a reason he showed up at the last possible second." Devin tipped his head toward the dining room. "He's not going to do any work. He just likes talking to everybody."

His voice was soft and full of affection.

"Right." Sometimes Zoe forgot that Devin's road to practically becoming a member of their extended family began right here at Harvest Home. Uncle Arthur didn't like to talk about it, but Devin had started out as a guest, coming by with his dad every week. Then by himself even more often than that. Sure, he'd become best buddies with Han by then, but it went deeper than that. Devin knew better than anyone how dedicated Uncle Arthur was to making people feel welcome here.

As he started unloading the dirty dishes, Devin's arm brushed hers, and a shiver of warmth ran through her skin.

Her throat went dry as she glanced up at him. They'd been working in close quarters all night, but any efforts to either seduce him or change his impression of her had taken a back seat to the task of getting dinner on the table for almost sixty people. In the end, this was the closest they'd really gotten, physically.

As if he could feel her gaze, he looked down. When their eyes met, heat flushed through her. How could a person's eyes be so blue? She got lost for a second, just staring at the gold-brown scruff on his sharp jaw, the soft red fullness of his lips, when everything else about him was chiseled and hard.

"Do you—" The huskiness of his voice only distracted her more.

"Huh?"

He pushed a plate toward her more insistently.

A different, embarrassed flush rose to her cheeks as she grabbed it and ran it under the water. "Right, right. Sorry."

He didn't need to stand so close as he passed her the next one, but she didn't tell him that. Wasn't she the one who'd started the game of trying to make him break? With the way he'd been looking at her, she'd taken it as a personal challenge to get him to make a move or at least admit that there was something brewing between them.

Now here she was, right on the cusp of cracking herself.

What would he do if she did? If she made the real first move and turned to him. Reached up to graze her fingertips along his cheek.

If she leaned forward on her tiptoes and tugged him down so she could taste his mouth...

She shuddered inside, blushing furiously as she placed another plate on the rack inside the dishwasher. She'd been harboring these kinds of fantasies since she was a teenager. It was hard to tell how much was actually possible and how much was just the same nonsense she'd been imagining for years.

Unwilling to shatter the moment, she set it all aside and concentrated on cleaning up. He seemed content to do the same. Even if his presence was making her heart do weird flips behind her ribs, she tried not to let it show.

They fell into a rhythm, like they'd been working together like this forever. That made sense—they'd both been volunteering here for years, but it still felt unfairly kismet, somehow.

"Thanks," she said after a couple of minutes. "By the way. For bringing in the folks from your company tonight."

"Happy to do it." He let out a rough sigh. "Well, for the most part."

It was clear who he was talking about.

Chuckling quietly, she shook her head. "Yeah, Bryce is still a piece of work, huh?"

"You have no idea."

The guy had barely lifted a finger the entire time he'd been here, and he'd eaten a solid dinner's worth of food meant for the guests.

"How does he get away with it?"

"You know." A dark undertone ran through Devin's words.

She shivered, reminded again of how much strength Devin kept contained inside himself. He never used it, though, no matter how frustrated he got.

It made her feel ... safe. It always had. Even when they'd been kids messing around in Uncle Arthur's basement. Any time the other boys his age had gotten too rough around her, he'd stepped in and said something.

Which was probably part of how she'd ended up with this stupid crush on him in the first place.

"Yeah, I guess I do."

People filed in and out of the kitchen, bringing new loads of dishes through. Zoe was indulging herself, spending this time rinsing plates when she should be out there directing traffic, but between Uncle Arthur, Sherry, and Tania, there were enough people running the show for her to dawdle a little longer. And the chance to stand so close to Devin was just too good to pass up.

"So you've really gotten involved here, huh?" he asked, moving to her other side to help her start loading the second washer.

She shrugged and passed him a stack of silverware. "I have the time right now. And I like helping out. Working with the guests. Getting to spend more time with Uncle Arthur."

A smile stole across her face as she talked about it all. She'd missed everyone in her family while she'd been away at college, but her uncle was the only one who didn't carry any baggage—or seem to have some sort of agenda for what she should do with her life.

Devin hummed in acknowledgment, giving her space to keep talking. It was refreshing.

"This place," she continued, trying to sum it up. "The work we do here, the people we serve. It feels important."

"I get it," Devin said quietly.

He would.

But then one corner of his mouth tilted down. "You said you have the time 'right now.' You see that changing soon?"

"Ugh." Zoe huffed out a breath as she scrubbed at a particularly stubborn spot on a plate. "I don't know. Apparently, at some point I'm supposed to get a real job."

He chuckled and passed her another dish. "What? Overrated."

"Says the guy who just got the big promotion."

"It's not that big a deal," he said, rolling his eyes, but his posture straightened slightly. It was definitely at least a medium-size deal. Humble as he might be, she hoped he was getting some satisfaction from his work.

She considered for a second before asking, "How did you know? That construction was what you wanted to do?"

It was the same basic question she'd asked Lian earlier—unhelpful as that conversation had been.

"I don't know," he answered slowly. "I didn't exactly have a ton of options."

"Smart guy like you?"

He laughed, only it didn't entirely sound funny. "I like working with my hands. Got a decent eye for it. Pay's good, relatively speaking. Arthur was able to help me get my foot in the door when I needed—when I decided it was time to find a place of my own."

There was something he wasn't saying, his voice dipping low and pulling at something in her chest. Before she could probe any deeper, though, he looked at her.

"So, how are things going with the whole real job thing, then?" he asked.

Well, that was certainly a way to kill the mood.

"Ugh. Terrible." Her mom had laid into her just that afternoon, telling her she wasn't sending out enough résumés or casting her net wide enough, prompting her to waste a good hour or two rage-scrolling Monster. "I'm putting in applications for jobs pretty much all over the state at this point. A few in Atlanta, too."

His eyebrows pinched together. "You'd really go that far?"

"I don't want to." She liked it here. She always had. Things here were easy. Comfortable. Being close to her family—when they weren't driving her up a wall or dictating her love life and her job search, anyway—was nice.

But she'd do what she had to do. She'd always wanted to get out on her own, and this extended period of being between things was making her itch to be independent again.

It wasn't like it was with her brother. Han had come

home when their father died and had taken over—well, everything. His sense of duty was giving him white hairs.

She'd choose to stay here, too, if it worked out. But she had to keep her options open. She couldn't just be *stuck* here because she couldn't make it on her own.

"We'll see how things go." She shrugged. It was such an annoying platitude, but that was her life now.

"Well, I hope you stay close." The way he said it was so genuine, she jerked her gaze up to meet his, but he was pointedly studying the dishes. After a second, he smiled, his tone lightening as he darted a teasing glance her way. "I mean, how can Han kill anyone who dares to look at you if you live far away?"

That was it. She shoved him, and he laughed, plates clanking together as he bumped into them where they were so neatly stacked in the racks. He playfully pushed back, and then what choice did she have, with her wet hands and all, but to flick some water in his face?

He sputtered, the droplets clinging to his skin in interesting ways, and her breath sped up. She went to do it again, but she must have telegraphed her intentions too clearly, because he grabbed her wrist before she could. Her heart hammered in her chest.

She stared up into his eyes, and for a second, everything around them faded, because she had seen that look before.

About two seconds before he got hit in the head with a football.

"Someone wanna tell me why we're out there doing all the work while these two are messing around in here?"

Devin straightened, pulling away from her so fast, she had to catch herself from falling over.

Apparently, playing the part of the football tonight, Bryce came over holding one measly dish, which he popped—still caked in drying potatoes—straight into the dishwasher. Struggling not to let on how flustered she was by the unwelcome interruption, Zoe plucked it out and set it in the sink, shooting him a glare.

"Thank you, Mr. Horton," Arthur said delicately as he hauled a crate in and set it on the counter. He caught Zoe's gaze, and she huffed out a breath.

Bryce's dad was the mayor. The town gave Harvest Home a bunch of money and support every year. She would do well to remember it.

But wasn't that just how a jerk like Bryce got so ... jerk-y? Everyone giving him a free pass because his father was a powerful guy?

She glanced at Devin. How did he do it? Constantly keeping a lid on himself when the guy kept asking to get punched in the face?

Before she could suss it out, a few more of the Meyer Construction volunteers came in with the last of the supper service cleanup.

Bryce gawked at the towering piles of dishes. "How are we supposed to get all this done? Some of us have places to be tonight." Winking, he elbowed one of the other guys, who subtly moved to put more distance between them. Not that Bryce noticed. With a leering smirk and a waggle of his phone, he added, "If you know what I mean."

Devin exhaled roughly. He threw his shoulders back. Instead of answering Bryce, he looked around and held his hands out expansively. "With a crew like this? We all pitch in and we'll have it done in no time."

"Uh-huh." Bryce kept scrolling on his phone.

"What do you say we put a little wager on it?" Devin's smile rippled with challenge. "We get out of here within the hour, and the first round at the bar is on me."

Chapter Five

This was going to cost Devin a small fortune.

It was worth it, though. At the hour mark, pretty nearly on the dot, his team had put the last clean pan on its shelf. The fact that Arthur, Sherry, Tania, and Zoe had thrown their backs into it, too, had helped a ton. Heck, even Bryce had cleaned a few tables. Free drinks were some powerful motivation.

Powerful, expensive motivation.

As the last guy put in his order, Clay whistled, punching in the numbers on the register.

"This sure seems like a nightmare for the bookkeeping," Devin tried in vain. "You should probably just give them to me for free."

"Nice try." Clay printed off the bill and handed it to Devin. "You wanna settle up now or start a tab?"

"Settle up now." Passing over his debit card, Devin eyed Bryce, who was standing by the pool table in the corner. Devin had promised the first round, and he was going to see it through, but he wasn't going to make it easy for anyone to try to turn it into two.

"Good choice."

He signed the slip, then joined the rest of his crew. He tried to pay attention to what they were saying, but his gaze kept drifting to the table in the corner where Zoe sat with Arthur, Sherry, and Tania. All four of them had been only too happy to take him up on the free drink offer, too, and he was happy to have them.

Probably too happy.

Working side by side with Zoe tonight had been an eye-opening experience. While her sexy waitress outfit had bowled him over the other day, this afternoon it had been her maturity—the way she'd known how to handle every situation that arose as they'd cooked and served. Even now, while he and his buddies from work stood around, shooting pool and playing darts and talking about yesterday's game, she was engaged in what looked like a deep conversation with Arthur, Sherry, and Tania. They regarded her with all the respect she deserved. Which he was starting to realize was a heck of a lot.

She'd really rolled up her sleeves tonight. She knew Harvest Home as well as he did, and despite mostly working in the front office, she wasn't afraid to get her hands dirty. Her eyes went all soft when she talked about the place, too. She might be the only person besides him and Arthur who understood it for the miracle it was.

She was funny and smart and beautiful and...

He cut off his train of thought before it could pull any farther out of the station. Jerking his gaze away from her mouth as she laughed at something Tania was saying, he took a big gulp of his beer.

Han wasn't here tonight, but the two of them had been friends for so long that the guy lived rent-free in his head. If anybody else was staring at Zoe the way Devin had been just now, Han would've been ready to deck him. Devin wasn't some dirtbag trying to get a peek up her skirt, but he needed to do a better job keeping his eyes to himself.

Before too long, Bryce gave one of the other guys a noogie before sauntering Devin's way. Devin crossed his arms over his chest, but his body language wasn't enough to keep Bryce from coming over and slapping him on the biceps.

"See you tomorrow, *boss*." He said it like an insult, but Devin wasn't going to take it that way.

"Bright and early."

The instant Bryce was gone, it was like someone had undone one of the knots in Devin's back. A few others filtered out not long after, and he thanked them each for coming out and giving a part of their day to volunteer.

Eventually, he and what was left of his crew drifted toward the pool table. They played a couple of rounds, but it was tough to focus. Every time he lined up a shot, he either had to face Zoe or put his back to her, and he had to get this under control. Being this aware of her wasn't right.

But it did give him a heads-up when she and the others started to gather their things.

Arthur was the one to approach first and clear his throat. Devin turned to find him jacket in hand.

Arthur clapped him firmly on the shoulder. "Good work tonight, Devin."

"Anytime." Then he remembered how Arthur had somehow managed to get him to agree to find a crew for this afternoon without his even fully realizing he'd committed until it was too late. "I mean, not *any* time, but..."

"I know what you mean."

Devin nodded at Sherry and Tania, who stood behind Arthur, clearly ready to go, too. "Glad you all could come out."

Tania grinned. "Any time you feel like footing the bill, you let us know."

They said their goodbyes, and the three of them made for the exit.

Which left Zoe. He scrunched his brows together. She wouldn't have just snuck out, would she? He would have noticed.

"Boo," she said from just behind him, poking his shoulder.

He didn't jump, but it was a near thing.

"Oh, hey." His voice came out rough. God, she smelled good. She was doing that thing again, getting up in his space, but unlike the other day, it didn't feel forced or unnatural. It felt like where she was supposed to be. Half hopeful and half ready to be disappointed, he asked, "You taking off, too?"

She had her flannel shirt draped over her arm and her bag slung across one shoulder, but there wasn't any sign of her keys. She cocked a brow and glanced behind him. "Actually, I was about to call winner."

Oh.

Oh, okay. This he remembered.

Devin and Han and some of the other guys used to play pool in Arthur's basement, days they couldn't mess around outside. Zoe would hang out there, too, and of course they couldn't tell Arthur's niece to scram. They only ever let her play if they needed an even number for a team. She was short and she scratched half her shots, and when she called winner, everybody had to pretend not to groan.

Unconsciously, he flicked his gaze over her form. His throat bobbed.

She was still short, but the confidence in her expression told him she'd learned a couple of things since she was twelve.

It was late. He should probably tell her he was just wrapping up here and ready to call it a night. If he was serious about not jeopardizing his friendship with Han, spending more time with his baby sister was *not* a smart strategy.

But there was something about the challenge in her eyes that was too enticing to resist.

For old times' sake...

Before he could second-guess himself any further, he lifted a brow to match hers. Without a word, he turned. He surveyed the table. His team was in good shape—just the eight ball left to sink, while stripes had three balls on the table. Sucking in a deep breath, he pointed toward the corner pocket.

He could feel her behind him as he lined up his shot. His skin tingled with awareness, but his vision went sharp. He pulled his cue back and nudged it forward, once, then twice.

The cue ball went spinning off across the felt, straight as an arrow. It rebounded, narrowly missing the ten before smacking straight into the eight. The eight shot toward the corner pocket, where it hovered for half a second on the edge before sinking right in.

He couldn't have done it better if he'd tried.

His partner held out his hand, and Devin slapped their palms together. He nodded at the guys he'd beaten. They shook their heads, but they took it just fine. He grabbed his beer and swallowed the last of it down.

Then he turned. He met Zoe's gaze again, and the heat in it went straight to the center of him.

"You want winner?" he asked, throat raw.

Her head bobbed up and down, her pretty pink mouth parted just the tiniest bit.

"Well." He swallowed deeply. This was a monumentally

stupid idea. But he was in it now. "What're you waiting for?"

———

Zoe was seriously starting to lose track of who was egging on who. After she'd called winner, the other guys Devin had been playing with decided to head out. At least one of them had shot him a knowing look. Another had patted him on the back and winked at her. She'd rolled her eyes and sent them on their way.

Was the tension between them as obvious to the people around them as it was to her? If so, it was a good thing her brother wasn't around. She glanced toward the bar. Clay didn't seem to be paying them any attention. His girlfriend, June, had shown up a little while ago with her friends Caitlin and Bobbi, and between pouring drinks for everyone and chatting with them, he had his hands full.

Zoe still didn't completely trust him not to rat her out to Han—intentionally or otherwise.

Whatever. All along, she'd said her brother should mind his own business. She was a grown woman, and she could do as she pleased.

And at the moment, what she wanted to do was Devin.

Only it wasn't quite that simple anymore, was it? Her advances had sort of been a lark at the beginning, but after spending time talking to him while cleaning up tonight, she was starting to wonder if there might be more between them than simple attraction. This wasn't a schoolgirl crush, and it wasn't leading to just a single night of fun.

As to what it was leading to?

Little sparklers fired off inside her. She'd love to have the chance to find out.

After she schooled him at pool.

She took a second to select a cue and chalk the tip as he went ahead and racked the balls. The sight of him in those jeans had her sucking her bottom lip between her teeth.

The guy was really just unfairly handsome, with that golden tan skin and clear blue eyes. The short-cropped hair that shone under the hanging lights and the scruff on his deliciously sharp jaw.

He smiled at her and gestured toward the table. "You wanna break?"

"Be my guest." That had been her plan, right? Getting him to break.

He grabbed his cue from where he'd leaned it. He set the cue ball down just to the right of center, leaned over, and lined up. She let her gaze move over his entire body as his muscles tensed.

With a sudden surge of motion, he fired off his shot. The crack of the cue ball hitting the one dead center rang out through the air. Balls scattered everywhere, while the cue ball spun in the middle of the table before coming to a halt.

"Nice."

He winked. "I've been practicing a bit."

Oh, she liked him like this. She'd always appreciated his serious side, but seeing him loose and playful and— dare she say flirty? It warmed her insides, even as it ratcheted up nervous anticipation about where this evening was going.

He called a shot and made it with ease. He sank two more before finally missing.

Zoe gripped her cue more tightly as she walked the perimeter of the table. Devin's gaze on her was distracting as hell, but she kept her focus.

He might have missed, but he'd done a good job setting her up for failure. Nice to know he wasn't going easy on her. She finally selected her shot and grabbed a bridge off the rack.

"You don't need that," Devin told her.

"Speak for yourself, tall person."

"Seriously." Then he was there, wrapping his hand around hers. "May I?"

Heat zipped up her arm. His warm scent surrounded her, and she got dizzy for a second, having him so close.

Which was her only explanation for why she let him take the bridge away. He guided her to the other edge of the table. She lined up her shot, and sure, she was closer to the ball now, but she didn't love the angles.

"I don't know." She shook her head, ready to stand and go back to her original plan, but he stopped her.

"Let me show you?" he asked.

Her whole body locked down as he stepped up behind her. He was so hot, bracketing her frame. His height swamped her, making it hard for her to breathe, and she was going to die before she even so much as managed to seduce him.

"See?" he asked.

Did he know what he was doing to her? She clenched down inside against a powerful wave of desire.

But he was still talking about pool. He placed his hand over hers on the felt, realigning her shot a few degrees to the left. Her breath caught.

Seriously. She was Going. To. *Die.*

She hovered there for just a second, soaking in the feeling of his body blanketing her, fluttering her eyes shut to bask in his closeness.

But as good as it felt—and as much as she never

wanted to move again, ever in her life—she couldn't stand there and take a crummy shot just because a hot guy was scrambling her brains.

Carefully, she stood up again. He moved with her. She glanced at him over her shoulder, and his face was inches from hers, his kissable mouth *right there*.

She stepped away. She got the bridge down from the rack. Her face flushed hot as she set up her original shot again. If she missed, she was going to feel like twice the idiot now, but she knew herself, dammit all. She knew her own mind, and she knew her body and her abilities.

No guy was going to waltz in out of nowhere and try to tell her differently before he'd even seen her play.

She ignored the pressure of his gaze. Then, with a breath and a prayer, she pulled the cue stick back.

The ball careened forward, banking off the far rail before heading straight for the nine. Everything in her tightened as the nine rolled toward the side pocket, slower than she would have liked. It hovered on the edge for an agonizing instant.

And then it tipped right on in.

She wanted to shout and scream—maybe jump and dance. As it was, she restricted herself to a single pump of her fist before locking her gaze with Devin's.

"Watch out," she told him, breathless—and not just from the score. "I've been practicing, too."

Chapter Six

Okay, for real, though, where did you learn to play like that?"

Zoe laughed as she braced her elbow against the bar. Devin settled onto the stool beside hers. His knee rested against hers, and she shivered.

They'd been getting closer and closer all evening. She wasn't complaining, but there was a tension inside her chest. This didn't seem like it could last. A half dozen games of pool and almost as many drinks between the two of them had them both loose-limbed and happy. After their last match, when someone else had asked them for the table, she'd kind of expected him to call it a night. It was late, after all. But when she'd started making her way over to the bar, figuring she'd check in with Clay before heading out herself, Devin had come on over, too.

Now here they were. Sitting together, fresh drinks in hand.

Zoe shrugged and took a sip of her cosmo. "There was a pool table in the basement of my dorm my first year of college."

"And a shark there to teach you all?"

"Don't underestimate bored teenage girls trying to avoid writing term papers."

He chuckled. "Fair enough."

She stirred her drink, probably a little too forcefully. "Turns out, hustling pool is one of the most useful things I learned at school."

"Oh?"

"I mean..." Releasing the tiny straw, she gestured around. She couldn't quite keep the sour note out of her tone. "See how far that degree has gotten me?"

"I don't know. Doesn't seem so bad."

She shook her head. "Try telling that to everyone else."

"You mean your mom?"

"Among other people. Han and Lian don't seem super impressed, either." Sighing, she looked away, to the bottles of liquor on the shelf, the taps, the specials she'd written on the big black board the day before. "I mean, I had a great time at college—don't get me wrong. But the whole grand compromise of it all—me going so far away, to a school that cost so much..." Even with aid and a bunch of money from her mom, she was going to be paying off loans forever. "Mom let me follow my dream, but she hammered home that if I didn't pick something practical, I'd end up penniless in a gutter somewhere."

"And that's how you ended up going into accounting?" Devin asked, leaning his elbow on the bar.

"Pretty much." She pinched the little straw from her drink again and stabbed at an ice cube. "I'm good at math, and after the first year, none of the courses were before noon. Seemed like a good deal at the time."

"What if you could do it all over again? Without your mom hanging over your shoulder. Would you pick something different?"

The question barely computed. Zoe's parents had always had strong opinions about her life. After her dad had died, her mom had become even more aggressive in trying to control Zoe's future. She'd clearly been grieving. Zoe had been, too. She'd fought back about some things, but on others, she got worn down and just got used to going along.

"I don't know," she said quietly. "Maybe? There wasn't anything I was super passionate about at school."

"Was there anything you were passionate about outside of it?"

"Not really." Usually, when people asked her questions like this, it made her uncomfortable, but Devin's expression was so open as he gazed at her. He'd known her practically their entire lives, but it felt like he actually wanted to know more. So she dug deeper. "I liked normal stuff—hanging out with my friends, watching TV."

"Making friendship bracelets."

"Shut up." She flapped a hand in his general direction as if to swat at him. Her cheeks flushed warmer.

One corner of his mouth lifted. "I still have mine."

"You do not." Oh wow. She'd made them for everybody one summer. She'd found a ton of old embroidery floss from some kit her mother had never finished. Bored, she'd gone to town.

She'd picked the colors for the one she'd given to Devin so carefully. Blue for his eyes, orange and brown for the Blue Cedar Falls team colors. Red for the hearts she secretly drew around his name in the back of her diary. Because she was super, super cool and not a dork at all.

"I do," he promised, and for some reason, she actually believed him.

Her throat tight, she looked down at her drink again.

Silence held for a second. Then she continued. "But yeah. Just normal teenager stuff, mostly. I mean, I liked volunteering at Harvest Home, too, but if I'd told my mom I wanted to work at a nonprofit or go into social services or something, I think she would have flipped her lid."

"Did you ever try?"

"What? No." The idea had never occurred to her.

But maybe it should have.

That was too much food for thought for this late into the night, though.

"How about you?" she asked. "You said construction was sort of something you fell into. Did you ever think about doing anything else? Going to school?"

The question seemed to take him off guard. Furrows appeared between his brows. She wanted to reach over and smooth them out, but even with the soft intimacy that somehow surrounded them now, it felt like too big of a line to cross.

"You mean college?"

She nodded, sipping at her drink.

"Sort of?" He lifted one shoulder before setting it back down. "Mrs. Jeffries in the guidance department thought I should, but it was never in the cards for me."

"How come?"

"Money." He said it without any bitterness to his tone. "There's a reason I started going to Harvest Home, you know."

Right. Crap. "Sorry—"

"It's fine. I could have maybe gotten financial aid or something, but I needed to be out on my own."

"I can drink to that." She lifted her drink, and he clinked his glass against hers before taking a deep pull at it and setting it down.

He still seemed calm, but a familiar stiffness settled into his shoulders. A far-off look came into his gaze. "My mom died when I was young, you know. Really, really young. I don't even remember her. But my dad—he was…"

As he searched for words, Zoe sat up straighter. A girl couldn't hang around her big brother and his best friend all the time without overhearing some stuff. She knew Devin's home life wasn't great, but he'd never talked about it in front of her directly.

"Yeah?" She held her breath and reached out, brushing her hand against his. His skin was warm and rough, and she wasn't oblivious to all the other, different ways she wanted to touch him. But she dropped her hand away after one quick, encouraging squeeze.

The point of his jaw flexed. His bright eyes met hers for a second, shadows forming behind his irises. Then he looked away. "He wasn't a good guy—let's just leave it at that."

He picked up his glass again. Zoe bit her lip. She should probably leave well enough alone.

But the book he'd started to crack open didn't feel shut quite yet. She couldn't shake the sense that he *wanted* to talk about this. How many times had she caught him holding himself back? Was this just more restraint?

What would it be like if he let go?

And honestly. Poking the bear had gotten her this far.

"You don't have to."

He lowered his drink and stared at her in question.

She took a deep breath. "You don't have to leave it at that. If you don't want to." Her face warmed, but she wasn't backing down. "I'm happy to listen."

He regarded her for a long, silent moment. The sounds of the bar around them filtered in. It had felt like they'd been in their own little world this whole time, but there were other people here. Not many. It really was late. But a few. Clay was still kicking around here somewhere.

No one else mattered, though.

As the moment stretched on, she held her ground, waiting patiently.

Finally, he grabbed his beer and tossed the rest of it back. He gestured at her drink. She was tempted to finish it, too, especially when he put on his jacket. The taste of it soured in her mouth. She'd pushed too far, huh? Sometimes she did that. She set her half-full glass on the bar.

But then he tipped his head toward the door.

"Come on. Let me walk you home."

The offer took her by surprise. Neither of them had had so much to drink that they couldn't drive. She probably *should* drive. Getting her car in the morning would be a hassle.

But walking home . . . walking home was good.

Letting *Devin* walk her home. Well, that was downright great.

When he extended his hand to help her up? No way that was an invitation she could refuse.

His calloused fingers were warm against hers. He gripped her tightly as she popped down from the stool. Was she imagining it when he held on for a second even after her feet hit the floor?

He let go, and she dropped her gaze. She untied her flannel from around her waist and shrugged it on.

Then she followed him out into the night.

It was chillier than she was prepared for, but between the Asian flush from the little alcohol she'd had and the heat Devin radiated at her side, she didn't mind. She crossed her arms over her chest.

Devin didn't have to ask where she lived, of course.

He'd been hanging out at the Leung house for a decade or two. They were both quiet as they headed north on Main Street.

The crisp air smelled like fall, the last few leaves of the season just clinging to the trees. She hugged herself more tightly. The dark sky above shone with stars and a half-full moon. Twinkling lights draped over the white fences all along Main Street gave everything a cozy feel.

She sighed. When she'd first realized she'd have to move home, she'd spent most of her time thinking about how annoying it would be to have to camp out in her mom's basement. She'd been right about that. Her mother's constant, snide comments about her prospects had only added to the ambience.

She hadn't been thinking about this, though. Blue Cedar Falls was beautiful by day, with the bright blue sky above and the mountains all around them. At night it was quiet and still, and it just felt like…

Home.

A tiny shiver racked her, followed by a pang. Getting a real job would be great, but the more time she spent here in Blue Cedar Falls—and with Devin—the less eager she was to leave.

Misunderstanding her shiver, Devin glanced down at her. "Cold?"

"I'm fine."

Stupid, chivalrous boy. He whipped off his jacket anyway, leaving his arms bare. Really hot, sexy, muscular arms, but it still seemed unpleasant for him.

"I'm fine," she protested again, but he was having none of it.

He draped the jacket over her shoulders. Instantly, heat blanketed her. Oh wow. His delicious scent wrapped around her even more thoroughly, making her whole body come into another, deeper level of awareness.

"Looks good on you," he said, his voice rough. He snapped his mouth closed as if he hadn't meant to say that, but it was out there now.

There was clearly no point arguing anymore, and anyway, now that she had his jacket, it wasn't as if she wanted to give it up. "Thanks."

"No problem."

They hit the end of the downtown strip and turned right together. As the businesses faded away into little houses, the quiet grew. She glanced up at him.

She met the soft blue gaze staring back down at her, and warmth fluttered inside her chest.

"Thanks," he murmured. He pointed with his thumb in the direction of the Junebug. "For what you said back there."

Right. Talking about his not-a-good-guy father.

She got her head out of the clouds of teenage crush land and mustered a smile. "I meant it."

"I know." He directed his gaze forward, ducking to avoid a couple of low-hanging branches on an old oak. "Sorry it took me by surprise. I work with too many guys. Some women, too, but they act even tougher than the men. Nobody gets touchy-feely on the job site."

"What about friends?"

"You mean your brother?"

"Okay, yeah, never mind."

Han was a cool guy, deep down. To hear Clay talk about it, he'd offered all kinds of great relationship advice back when he and June were getting their act together. But Han had never gotten over their father. He'd died suddenly, almost ten years ago. All Han's plans for his life had gone up in smoke when he'd rushed home, eighteen years old and determined to take up the mantle and become the man of the house.

The loss still hurt in Zoe's heart, too, of course. She missed her dad. Losing him had changed the entire family. It had harshened her mom and aged her brother. Fortunately, she'd had Lian and Uncle Arthur to lean on, both during that first tough year and after.

But Han hadn't seemed interested in leaning on anyone. He was too busy taking over the business and the house. Deep down, though, she knew her brother too well. He'd been devastated.

Talking about someone else's issues with their father? He couldn't have handled it. He probably still couldn't.

Devin's gaze focused on something far off in the distance. His jaw hardened before going soft—like he was building walls around himself only to have to consciously decide to let them down.

"He was a bully," he said quietly. "A mean old drunk who told me I'd never amount to anything in my life."

Zoe's heart squeezed. "Devin...That's awful."

"When high school graduation came around, I still half believed him." His smile was pained. "I told myself I didn't, but asking for people to give me money so I could go fail out of college just the way he always told me I would? Nah."

She shook her head, but he kept talking. As they turned onto her street, his pace slowed.

"It was all stupid head games, I know. In the end, it didn't matter. The best route to getting out of his house was getting a job." The sharpness in his gaze finally eased. "Arthur hooked me up, actually."

"Sounds like him."

"Yeah, it does." Unguarded affection colored his tone—with maybe a little hero worship mixed in there, too. "I was always handy. He got me an interview at Meyer, and the rest is history. I got a good-paying job and an apartment." His jaw flexed. "And I never looked back."

A different kind of darkness shadowed his eyes now. He clenched and unclenched his hands at his sides.

"Devin..."

"It's for the best. I'm saving up for a house of my own, too. In another year, it'll be just me and some mutt out on the edge of town, and no one will ever be able to bother me like that again." He looked down at her and blew out a breath. "I'm glad. Honestly."

"Okay." There was more to the story than he was telling, but even she knew when a bear had been poked too much. "Well, I'm glad you're glad, too." With a soft smile of her own, she bumped her elbow against his arm. "For what it's worth, I think you turned out pretty great."

His lips curled upward. "You didn't turn out so bad yourself, Itch."

"Hey!" She swatted at him. That's what he and Han and their friends had called her when she was really bugging them.

"Sorry, sorry!" He put his hands in front of his face as she swung at him again.

And she was just goofing around—really, she was. He was, too. But she rose onto her toes and reached up, aiming for a good smack upside his head. "Take it back."

"I take it back. I take it back." He grabbed her wrists in his big, strong hands. He held on to her, stopping her from taking another shot at him.

He was breathing hard. She was, too.

Suddenly, it dawned on her exactly how close they were

standing. Her chest was practically brushing his. Heat radiated off his body, soaking into hers, and out of nowhere, she couldn't get enough air.

She darted her gaze to his. Surprise colored his eyes, like he'd just realized the position they were in, too.

But he didn't let go.

Forget fluttering. Her whole chest was on fire. She was dizzy with the unexpected rush of contact.

Of his gaze darting down to her lips.

A pang of wanting hit her so hard it took her breath away. She looked to his mouth, too, red and soft. She'd been dreaming about this since she was twelve, but this was real. Devin James was really standing here with her, looking at her.

"Zoe..."

Before he could move, a bright light suddenly blinded them. Devin jerked away, shielding his eyes. Zoe cursed.

Right. Without her even really noticing, they'd arrived at her house.

And the floodlights outside had just turned on.

Humiliated anger swept across her cheeks. She looked at Devin, but he was backing up—fast.

"Sorry. Good grief, Zo."

"What—"

"You should go in." His throat bobbed as he gestured at the house.

And it was hard to make out, given the glare of the lights. But yeah. That was her mom standing just inside the door.

She cursed beneath her breath. "Look—"

"You should go," he said again, firmer.

She wanted to laugh. Almost as much as she wanted to cry.

Five seconds ago, he'd been looking at her like she was anything but the little girl she used to be. His gaze had been hot as fire, his hands grasping at her wrists like he had no intention of letting go. He'd been about to kiss her.

Her. A grown woman, fully capable of making her own decisions.

"Devin." She hated the shakiness in her voice.

"Keep the jacket," he told her, backing away. "I can grab it from Han. Later."

"Devin," she called again.

Regret flashed in his eyes.

And that was what did it.

She couldn't decide which was worse—him regretting getting caught or him regretting almost letting it happen in the first place. Either way, if he regretted it already?

It didn't matter how much she liked him—how much she had liked him since she was twelve freaking years old.

She deserved better than that.

He turned and walked away. She watched him go for a long minute.

Fuming, she turned and stormed toward the house. The door swung open before she could get to it, which only pissed her off more. With her mom holding the thing, she couldn't even slam it behind her.

"Late night," her mom observed.

"I've been home later." She worked at a bar, for Pete's sake.

"Zhaohui…"

She rounded on her mom. "Save it."

Her mom regarded her. Zoe was vibrating with anger. At her mom for interrupting. At Devin for walking away.

At every freaking person in her life who treated her like a kid, who didn't trust her to know her own mind.

Her mother made a soft *tutt*ing sound in the back of her throat. She let the door swing closed. Lifting one brow, she leveled Zoe with her most skeptical gaze. "I hope you know what you're doing."

"Believe it or not, Mom," she gritted out, "I usually do." Only in this case, even she wasn't sure that was true.

Chapter Seven

"You want to talk about it?"

Devin looked up to find Arthur gazing at him across the worktable in the back of Harvest Home. He fought not to snap at him. Arthur didn't deserve any of his crap.

The only one who deserved that was himself.

"About what?"

Arthur just raised his brows, shifting his gaze pointedly to the mangled box Devin had been destroying in a vain effort to rip it open with his bare hands.

Okay, yeah, fine, so he was acting a little off.

Scrubbing his hand across his face, he grabbed the box cutter from the other side of the table and got back to work.

But Arthur wasn't going to leave this one alone. "Let me guess. Girl trouble."

Devin narrowly avoided slicing his finger off. Stupid. More carefully, he started again. "No."

"Boy trouble, then?"

Devin scrunched up his face in confusion. "What?"

"Never hurts to ask," Arthur said, waving away Devin's reaction. "Zoe yelled at me the other day, saying I'm too"—

he snapped his fingers a couple of times before finding the word—" 'heteronormative.' "

"Believe me, I still like the ladies." There was nothing wrong with being gay, obviously, but Devin had known from day one that he was into women.

And what he was into right now, apparently, was a girl who was too young for him, a girl who got under his skin like nobody else. A girl who made it easy to talk about things he never talked about. His dad, his life, everything.

A girl with dark, sparkling eyes, silky hair, and the softest hands. A girl he'd come so close to ruining everything with on Sunday night.

He swallowed hard, putting down the knife and clenching his hands around the edges of the box. Ever since he'd been a kid, this place had been a second home to him. The Leung house had become a third. Arthur, Han, and everyone else in their family trusted him. How would they look at him if they found out he was having wildly inappropriate thoughts about the youngest member of their family?

What would happen if he got with Zoe for real? Even if everyone accepted it…if it didn't work out, if their relationship hit the rocks or went down in flames…

Arthur and Han cared about him. Deeply. But at the end of the day, faced with the decision, they'd choose their flesh and blood over some stray they'd taken in.

Acting on his attraction to Zoe was a nonstarter. It couldn't happen.

So why couldn't he stop thinking about it?

Even a couple of days later, he could feel her skin, smell the sweet scent of her wrapping around him and turning him inside out. In the driveway of the Leung house—right where he and Han used to hang out when they were kids, when Zoe was *literally* a kid—he'd been inches from kissing her. The moment they'd shared kept playing in his head on repeat, and all he could think was, what if those lights hadn't gone on? What if Zoe and Han's mom hadn't caught him ready to claim those soft, rose-colored lips?

When would he have stopped?

How much would he have risked?

He shook his head. Fury burned in his chest, almost as hot as his arousal whenever he let his mind drift back to that almost-kiss. He was an idiot to be even thinking about it, much less actively imagining it.

So why was he torturing himself like this?

And why was Arthur just sitting there instead of trying to get him to talk?

"Okay, fine," he exploded. He glared at Arthur. Patient bastard had always been good at waiting him out until he finally told on himself. "Let's say there is a particular lady in question."

Arthur set aside the inventory sheet he'd been working on and gave Devin his full attention. "Okay."

"But it's a terrible idea."

"Most love usually is," Arthur said with a sly smile.

Devin shook his head, gesturing wildly with his hands. "Like, natural disaster kind of terrible."

Arthur just raised his brows.

"Okay, fine, maybe not that bad, but bad. It would cause big problems."

"What sort of problems are we talking about? Legal trouble?"

"No." Though a half dozen years ago, it would have.

"Work trouble?"

"No."

"Then...?"

Devin cast about for a second before landing on "Her family."

Of which Arthur was a member. This was so messed up.

"I can't believe they wouldn't approve of you."

"It's more complicated than that." Devin raked a hand through his hair. "But they'd have good reason to think it's a bad idea."

The Leungs had welcomed Devin with open arms. Here at Harvest Home, Arthur had taken Devin under his wing. As Han's best friend, Devin had free run of the Leung house. Sleepovers, afternoon hangouts. They trusted him.

Han trusted him. Han, who was so obsessed with keeping his family safe and secure. He'd always been protective of his baby sister. How many times had he confided in Devin about wanting to basically go check Zoe into a convent?

Devin hadn't been lusting after Zoe that entire time, but his attraction to her had grown and grown, from the spark he first felt at her high school graduation to this inferno now. The other night, first at Harvest Home and then later at the bar, he'd kept losing sight of who she was. She stopped being his best friend's sister or Arthur's niece. She'd become just...Zoe. Gorgeous, easy-to-talk-to, smart, funny, empathetic Zoe.

While Devin's thoughts spun out, Arthur kept regarding him with that steady, patient gaze of his. Finally, he sat back and exhaled long and low.

"Have I ever told you the story of how I ended up here?"

Only about a million times.

Devin managed not to thunk his head against the table. "Yeah."

"All of it?"

"I don't know," Devin said carefully.

"My family, when we came over, we started in San Francisco."

"Right."

"Moved to New York from there. It was crowded. Dirty. We worked hard, lived in a tiny apartment. Huilang and David and me with our parents." Huilang being Han, Lian, and Zoe's mom, and David their distant uncle.

"Okay…"

"I was the one who decided to set out and go somewhere else. Not an easy decision."

"I'm sure." There was no stopping Arthur now, so Devin strapped in for the ride.

"My father. He told me it would be big trouble if I left."

Devin perked up. This was a part of the story he hadn't heard before. "Really?"

Arthur nodded. "He had so many reasons it wouldn't work. He thought I was betraying the family by leaving them behind." He smiled, knowing and maybe just a little smug. "But I knew. There were more reasons to go. And you know what?"

"What?"

"I was right." He waved a hand around. "Look what I've been able to accomplish. I had a great career." He had, starting the Jade Garden restaurant. Socking away cash and making a whole series of unlikely investments that had enabled him to open this place and grow it year after year. "Brought my sister and her husband down here with me, and they've had happy lives. We all have."

"Okay…"

Arthur fixed him with a gaze like he could see right through Devin. Could he? Did he know more than he was letting on?

If he did, he kept it to himself. "You can't let fear push

you around. Worrying about what other people will think, what other people will do. It leaves you miserable. This girl—if she means enough to you, you go to her. You find a way to make it work. No matter what anybody else says, you hear me?"

For a split second, Devin considered it. He let go of all his concerns about Han and Arthur and Zoe's mom.

He let himself imagine going for it. Being with Zoe. Having her in his arms, talking to her the way he had the other night. Celebrating a great game of pool with a kiss.

Taking her to his bed.

A jolt of electricity zipped down his spine.

Yeah. He wanted that. All of it.

But before he could really talk himself into believing he could have it, a deep voice broke in.

"Wait—Devin's got a girl?"

All the hope that had started to rise in Devin's chest came crashing down. He turned to find Han in the doorway.

Right. Crap. It was Tuesday. Han or his mom or both— they always came by in the late afternoon.

Stupid. How could he have forgotten? How could he have asked Arthur of all people about Zoe—even in the most veiled of terms?

How could he have imagined this could work?

He forced out a laugh, but it was hollow to his own ears. "Nah, man. Me and Arthur—we were just talking."

Devin stood up, anxious, restless energy making it impossible to sit.

"Really?" Han asked, setting down a crate of leftover produce from the restaurant before wiping his brow. "Because it sounded like—"

Mercifully, Arthur stepped in to save him. "Your friend. He was talking in"—he cleared his throat—"hypotheticals."

Devin directed an appreciative glance his way. Leave it to Arthur to make Devin sound innocent without telling a single untruth.

But Han wasn't going to be deterred. "I don't know, man." He sized Devin up. "You have been a little weird lately."

"Work stuff." That wasn't an untruth, either. Taking over as shift leader had been great, but it had come with all the headaches he'd assumed it would.

Namely managing Bryce Horton.

But he wasn't here to complain about Bryce. Especially when Han was still regarding Devin with suspicion, and Devin was trying not to sweat.

Finally, Han gave him a playful shove on his shoulder. "Well, whoever the *hypothetical* girl is, I hope you win her over. Your dry spell has been going on for *way* too long."

"Like you're one to talk."

Han's gaze darkened. The fact he hadn't had a serious long-term relationship since he and May broke up after high school was a sore spot, and Devin had aimed right for it. "Whatever. Keep your secrets."

"No secrets to tell." And he was going to make sure it stayed that way. Needing some air after that close call, he grabbed a stack of inventory forms they'd already gotten through. "Gotta hit the head. I'll swing these by the front office."

"Thanks," Arthur said.

Han got to work. Relieved there wasn't going to be any more third degree, Devin headed out.

He had an ulterior motive for swinging past the office anyway.

The second Zoe came into view, his heart did something funny in his chest. She looked as beautiful as ever. She had when he'd first arrived, too.

She'd avoided his gaze in a way that was new, though. There'd been no flirty banter. She hadn't gotten in his space. She definitely hadn't come close enough for him to slip up and almost kiss her, and that was a good thing.

So why did it feel so awful?

Arthur hadn't known all the facts, so his advice hadn't been right, but there was one area where he'd been on the nose. Zoe did mean something to Devin. That meant he had to make this work between them. Not the kissing part, but the rest of it. He'd really started to think they were becoming friends. He wanted her, sure, but he also just plain liked her.

If almost kissing her meant losing her smiles and the way she looked at him and talked to him, then he'd screwed up worse than he'd realized. He had to make it right. Fast, before he messed this up for good.

He walked right up to the desk and put the inventory sheets in the bin. She glanced up at him. Her eyes sparkled for a second before darkening. Glowering, she looked away.

No smile. No "hello," even.

Guilt churned in his gut. She really was mad, and she had every right to be.

"You have a minute?" he asked. He couldn't keep the urgency out of his tone.

"Nope."

"Come on, Zo." He reached for her hand, only for her to snap it away.

"Uh-uh. No way." She darted her gaze around, but they were definitely alone out here. She still lowered her voice. "You of all people do not get to do what you almost did on Sunday night and then 'Zo' me."

Anger flashed in her gaze, only it was more than that.

She was trying to hide it, but she was hurt.

Was it possible to feel even worse?

"Just hear me out," he begged.

She narrowed her eyes. "Fine."

Crossing her arms over her chest, she stared up at him, fire and defiance in her gaze, and that really shouldn't get him feeling hot under the collar, but it did.

He didn't care that she'd just verified that they were alone. He did the same thing she had, glancing around, but he couldn't talk to her like this, one eye constantly looking over his shoulder.

"Come on."

He tipped his head toward the spare office behind the desk. Keeping her feet planted, she cocked a brow at him, and he shot a glance skyward before holding out a hand. "Please?"

With a gruff sigh, she rolled her eyes but then consented to follow him. Once they were both inside, he closed the door and flipped the lock.

He turned to look at her. Her posture was still closed and defensive, and he hated that. But what could he do? How could he get them back to the place they'd been the other night—all smiles and quiet confidences—without going too far?

"Look, Zoe." He was making this up as he went along, barreling ahead without a plan. "I'm sorry. Really."

"For what?" She tipped her chin up, the stubborn set to her jaw driving him to distraction. She started counting things off on her fingers. "For almost kissing me? Because if so, screw you. Or for jumping away from me like I'm a leper? Because if so, also screw you." She started advancing on him, her voice rising. "Or for treating me like a freaking child, the way everybody in my life does?" She was right in his space again, her eyes on fire. "Because if so"—she reached out and jabbed him in the chest—"screw"—she did it again—"you."

He grabbed her by the hand, and oh no. This was too much like the other night. She'd been swatting at him for his teasing then. She was righteously angry now. Guilt churned in his stomach, but his skin was prickling, her hand warm in his. He stroked his thumb over her palm, holding on even though he should let her go.

He should walk right out of this office. Out of this building and maybe off a short pier, but her cheeks were flushed, her eyes bright, and her soft red lips so wet and kissable, he was losing his mind.

"I can't," he said. "Your brother—"

"Isn't my keeper." She went softer against him, some of the anger fading out of her.

And it was like he couldn't stop himself.

He drifted closer to her, erasing the gap between them, licks of flame darting across his skin. "I don't want to be a bad guy."

He didn't want to take advantage. He didn't want to mess things up between them and lose the fragile friendship they'd been building—the one that had already come to mean so much to him.

What could they even have together besides friendship? Her time here in Blue Cedar Falls was clearly a stopgap. She was on her way to bigger and better things. His biggest goal in life was a house in the woods alone. If they crossed this line, it would change things forever. With her. With her family.

Keeper or not, he didn't want to violate Han's trust.

She gazed up into his eyes. The liquid brown of her irises melted something inside him. Reaching up, she grazed her fingertips across his cheek.

"You're not a bad guy, Devin." Her hand settled tentatively on the side of his neck, and the intimacy of it was almost too much. "I've been back home for months, and I swear you're the first person who's made me feel like you're actually listening to me. You care. A lot." She shook her head gently. "Bad guys don't do that."

He swallowed, scarcely able to think with her so close. Without his permission, his arm moved to wrap around her, and that felt so good. She was practically flush against him, warm and soft and smelling like heaven.

All his resolutions went up in smoke.

"This is a terrible idea," he rasped.

"Probably."

Then she rose onto her toes.

He was going to hell, because he met her halfway. Their mouths crashed together, and that was it. Something snapped inside him. Hauling her in against him, he let himself really feel her. Light exploded behind his eyes. Forget all his worries about the fact that she used to be a kid to him—Zoe Leung was all woman now. Her soft curves fit to his body like they were made to press together. She kissed like the spitfire she was, opening to him, nipping at his lips with her teeth, sucking on his tongue.

Groaning, he picked her up and sat her on the edge of the desk. This whole place was a disaster—the place they put stuff when they didn't know where it should go. Something clattered to the floor, but he didn't care. With a hand at the back of his neck, she reeled him in, and he went so happily. He lost his mind to the heat of her mouth, the warmth of her hips in his hands. Scooting backward on the desk, she folded her legs around him.

Alarm bells went off in his head.

What was he doing?

He tore himself away, only for her to drag him back in.

"Zoe," he gasped, kissing her again, but he had to stop.

She raked her nails through his scalp. "If you say one word about my stupid brother, I swear—"

"No." He laughed. "Just no."

But as he drew away, the kiss-bitten redness of her lips, her tousled hair, and her flushed cheeks told him the truth. They'd crossed a line. He knew how she tasted now, how perfectly she fit in his arms.

There was no going back.

But he wasn't a complete idiot.

"My place," he panted. "Not here."

She hooked her ankles behind his rear and pulled him in, and he saw stars.

He pulled away again and fixed her with a gaze that brooked no argument. "Not here."

She pouted, breathing hard, but she released him. He stepped away, and she hopped down off the table.

"Fine," she relented. She narrowed her eyes at him, but her voice shook. "No take-backs, though, okay?" She reached up to tap him on the head. "Don't overthink this."

Yeah. Like that was going to happen.

He grabbed her hand again. But instead of brushing her away, he held her gaze and brought the back of her palm to his mouth.

"No take-backs." He kissed the soft skin of her knuckles.

And seriously. He was going to hell.

But if the smoldering look in her eyes was any indication? It was going to be worth the ride.

Chapter Eight

Nervous anticipation and wary disbelief warred in Zoe's gut as she pulled up to Devin's building an hour later. Staying at Harvest Home and finishing the tasks she usually enjoyed had been pure torture—especially when Devin had slipped out. The dark look he'd given her on his way to the door had made her clench down deep inside.

But he'd been hot and cold over the past few days, to say nothing of the past few years. She had no idea what she was walking into here.

Still half expecting him to have changed his mind again, she got out of the car and headed up the walk. Bubbles formed and popped inside her chest. She was trying to keep her expectations in check, but his kiss had set her on fire. An hour of waiting had only stoked the flame. By the time she hit the top of the stairs, she was a riot of desire and nerves—if he turned her away after all that, she really was going to deck him. She reached the apartment number he'd given her, lifted her hand, and curled it into a fist. She took a deep breath, then steeled up her nerve and knocked.

The door swung open instantly.

Behind it stood Devin, and Zoe's stomach did a loop-the-loop.

Good grief, he was gorgeous. His sandy-brown hair was all mussed, exactly the way she wanted it to be after she'd been raking her hands through it all night. If it was possible, his jaw was sharper, the scruff there even more masculine. He stood there in a T-shirt and jeans, his feet bare on the hardwood.

His eyes shone midnight black with want, and just like that, all the doubt disappeared from her mind.

"Devin—"

"C'mere."

He reached into the space between them to drag her in.

She crashed into him with the same passionate, desperate need that had overcome them in the back office of Harvest Home. The kisses were just that bright and stinging, and she couldn't get enough. The door slammed closed behind her. With all his bulk, Devin pressed her into it, and oh *God*.

She'd known he was ripped, but feeling all that hard muscle awakened a need inside her. Wrapping her arms around his neck, she used what leverage she had to climb his body, and he helped her, lifting her up. She curled her legs around him.

The hot bulge of him against her center sent fireworks off inside her. He let out a noise that was pure sex as they ground together. She'd never gone from zero to sixty so fast. She was dizzy with it, barely able to think.

He moved them away from the door, holding on to her as he turned to carry her through his apartment.

She got only the most glancing impression of the place. It was neat but spare, no pictures on the wall. A plain beige couch, a glass coffee table, and a sage-green rug.

And then she didn't have time to even think about his

interior decorating, because that was his bedroom door he was hauling her through.

She pulsed deep inside as he practically tossed her down onto the big bed. He stood over her for a long moment, breath coming hard. Her entire body flushed. She liked being seen like this, liked the dark glint in his piercing eyes as he ran his broad hands along the tops of her thighs.

But the moment stretched and stretched. That same nervous flutter from earlier returned. "No take-backs?" she reminded him. She hated how it came out like a question.

He inhaled deeply. Then he nodded. "No take-backs."

Resolved, he climbed on top of her. As he kissed her again, slower this time, she wanted to pinch herself. There was no hesitation in him, and when she put her hands on his skin, under the hem of his shirt, he pushed into her touch. This wasn't some frantic, impulsive rush.

This was real.

Savoring every moment, she opened to him, curling her legs around his hips. The hot weight of his body settled over her. Every lick of his tongue and scrape of his teeth across her lips set her ablaze. Molten desire bubbled up inside her, and she wanted to take her time, but she couldn't wait.

She pushed his shirt up. Rising onto his knees, he grabbed the fabric by the back of the neck and tore it off, and holy crap. His muscles had muscles, all of him golden tan and smooth. A trail of hair led down to the button of his jeans, and she had to stop herself from ripping those open right away, too.

When he kissed her again, it was with a new intensity. A flash of burning arousal shot through her when his rough hands dipped beneath her top. She helped him take it off. Her bra followed, and he groaned.

"I've been trying not to think about these for so long." He buried his face in her breasts, and she laughed.

It didn't stay funny for long. Not when his hot mouth sealed over that tender flesh. Aching for more, she arched into him, running her fingers through his hair. Everything he did felt so good. Triumph had her flying high.

Until he started kissing lower down her abdomen.

"Devin," she moaned when he got to the waistband of her leggings.

Staring her straight in the eyes, he pressed one firm kiss to the very center of her through the fabric, and she practically came right then and there.

She reached for him.

He raced back up her body, sucking and biting at her all the way. As soon as he was close enough, she kissed him hot and deep, scrambling at his fly. She finally ripped it open and pushed his jeans and underwear down. The hot, hard length of him sprang free, and they groaned as one. He was huge in her hands, and she still couldn't believe this was happening.

As she stroked him, he tore at her clothes, too. She kicked off her boots, and it was all a mad dash until they were both naked. He paused just long enough to get a condom on. When he lined himself up, she had no doubts.

Still, he paused. "Zo…"

She sucked in a breath. Cupping his face in her hands, she brought his lips to hers for another, softer kiss.

"I want this," she promised him, and it was too true. With emotion she couldn't name, she told him, "I want you."

He closed his eyes.

His body sinking into hers turned her inside out. He felt so perfect as he ground against her, sending sparks surging through her.

"Zo," he repeated.

"I'm here." She was babbling. What was she saying? "I'm here, I'm here, I want you. I want this."

He pulled back, and she pushed into him until they fell into a rhythm. Pleasure started at the apex of her thighs, spreading outward until all she could see and feel and touch and taste was him. Over and over he drove into her, faster. She scrabbled at him, running her hands all up and down his back and shoulders.

"Zoe, Zo, I can't—you feel so good—"

"Devin, come on, please, I want—"

He slammed into her another half dozen times.

Her climax tore through her out of nowhere. Her vision flashed to black, and she squeezed every part of herself around him. Driving in deep, he called her name a final time. He pulsed inside her, and her entire world shattered.

Because this was *real*. She'd had sex with Devin James.

What had started as a challenge to see if she could get him to break had turned into a breaking down of her conception of the natural order of the universe.

She still had no real delusions that this could be more than a fling, but the impossible had already happened the instant he'd touched his lips to hers.

As she stared up at his ceiling in wonder, she pressed a hand to the center of his back.

Who knew? Maybe all her notions of what she could and couldn't have in this world were wrong.

Chapter Nine

"Watch out!"

At the sound of Terrell's shout, Devin jerked his gaze up from his clipboard.

Half his people were raising a section of the house's frame, Terrell and Gene up on ladders while the rest supported and spotted from below, only something wasn't right. Devin shot to his feet, gaze swinging wildly, the entire site going into slow motion. There—crap.

Off to the side, Bryce had let go prematurely, and Devin lurched forward, calling his name, but it was too late. Terrell's grip slipped without anyone to back him up.

The whole thing came crashing down.

Devin raced over. "Is everybody okay?"

"Yeah." Terrell scrubbed a hand over his face.

Devin checked in with everybody else, and no one had gotten hurt, thank goodness. He appraised the rest of the scene. The damage to the section that had fallen wasn't that bad, either, but it was still going to set them back a couple of hours—and that was before the headache of writing this up.

"I swore I had it," Terrell said, climbing down. His eyes narrowed as he glared silently off to the left.

Following his gaze, Devin flexed his jaw. He patted Terrell on the back. "It's just about lunch time anyway. Take a break, and then we'll get this cleaned up afterward."

He and the rest of the crew nodded.

Reassured that they were all okay, Devin stalked to the other side of the building, grinding his teeth together hard enough to crack.

A week had passed since he'd moved up to shift leader, and for the most part it had been going great. The team listened to him, and he'd handled the couple of issues that had arisen without much trouble.

Except Bryce.

Mostly it was little things like unauthorized breaks or screwing around on his phone when he was supposed to be working. Some of it was more serious, like using inappropriate language when talking to the women on the crew. Devin had documented it all, slowly building a case that even the folks who protected him couldn't ignore.

But this?

"Horton," he growled.

Bryce looked up from his phone. "What?"

"Don't 'what' me." Devin wanted to grab the guy's phone and chuck it in the cement mixer, only that would make a defect in the next house's foundation. Workers on the site weren't forbidden from being on them or anything; this wasn't high school. But when your eyes and hands needed to be on the job, they needed to be on the job. "Where were you?"

"Right there." He gestured toward where the crash had happened. "Weren't you watching?"

Old anxiety rose in Devin. His dad used to do that, too— reframing everything to make it out like Devin was the one to blame. He had to remind himself that wasn't true today.

Devin had been doing his job, keeping an eye on his team while also seeing to the rest of his duties. "You weren't paying attention, and somebody could've gotten hurt."

Bryce rolled his eyes. "Terrell's butterfingers aren't my fault."

Forget a headache; the incident report was going to be a full-on migraine. Enough other people would back Devin and Terrell up that Bryce had been the one to let go, but the fact of the matter was that this never should have happened in the first place.

"You not doing your job is your fault." Devin kept his voice restrained but barely. "I'm not going to turn a blind eye to this BS."

"Sure you won't." Bryce's smile was mocking as he patted Devin on the shoulder.

Devin shoved him off automatically. He clenched and unclenched his jaw.

He walked away, hating the hot feeling in his chest and the hotter one in his face. The sense of helplessness ate at him, making him feel like he was twelve years old all over again.

Sure, he'd document this entire thing, but there was no satisfaction in that.

How did he protect his people? Stop giving Bryce any jobs where he could put the other members of his crew at risk? Stop giving him jobs at all? Bryce would love that.

The unfairness made him want to punch something.

Instead, he drew in a few deep breaths, trying to calm himself down before getting back to it.

On impulse, he popped his phone out of his pocket for the first time all morning. A handful of alerts greeted him, and he scrolled through them. When he got to the couple of texts from Zoe, the remaining tension bled out of his body, and he couldn't hold back the warm smile that curled his lips.

Ugh, remind me why I'm shacking up with a morning person again? I need coffee and it's all the way over theeeeerre

A photo came with the message, showing her in his bed, her hair a mess where it lay splayed out across his sheets, and he had to suck in a breath. There wasn't a single inappropriate thing about the shot, but it didn't matter. The sight of her, all rumpled and gorgeous and soft from sleep...It did things to him.

He just wished he could be there to take advantage of it. To roll her over and kiss that red mouth until they were both breathless.

Or maybe—if it was a day when he wasn't working...to go make her coffee. Pancakes. Breakfast in bed.

He mentally shook his head at himself. What a sap.

A week now they'd been doing...whatever it was they were doing together. Giving in to the overwhelming force of attraction between them had been the easiest thing in the world. When she was around, it was like all his worries disappeared.

He'd thought it would be weird, going from her brother's best friend to her friend to maybe something more, but it hadn't been. At all.

They'd never had to have any intense conversations about what was going on between them, either. Even that first time, when he'd been nervous about risking everything for a night of fun, it was like she'd been able to see right through him. Proving just how well she knew him, she'd just climbed right back on top of him and kissed him senseless, then wandered naked into his kitchen to fix herself a sandwich. She'd called out to ask if he wanted anything, too. Casual—like it was the most normal thing. And you know, he had been kind of hungry after working up an appetite like that.

So she'd just slipped into his life. When they weren't having mind-blowing sex, they were sharing takeout pizza or introducing each other to their favorite shows. He still wasn't quite sold on *The Bachelor*, but watching her yelling at the TV made him grin, and she was surprisingly receptive to reruns of *This Old House* playing in the background the rest of the time.

His crummy, boring apartment felt warm when she was in it. So warm that he almost forgot for hours at a time that his entire goal in life was to build his house in the woods and get out of here.

His only regret was the same one she had. She worked nights and he worked days, and so there she was waking up at—he checked the time stamp on the message—ten in the morning, while he was up at six.

Shaking his head at himself, he tapped out a quick reply. *Wish I could've gone and grabbed you one.*

Her answer came seconds later. *It's ok, I managed.*

The picture that followed was of her at Bobbi's bakery on Main Street. She was seated at one of the little tables inside, a latte and an empty plate set next to her open laptop.

His smile faded slightly. She'd kicked it up a notch on the job search of late. That or, now that he got regular updates about her life, he was just more aware of it.

Every time she talked about it, a little pit formed in his stomach. Which was stupid. He'd known from the minute she moved back home that it was temporary. She was only here until the right opportunity came along, and he could be a big enough man to hope it showed up for her soon.

Even if, deep down, he never wanted her to leave.

"Hey, James." Bryce's voice had Devin jerking his gaze up. "Your girlfriend's here."

For a second, Devin's heart lurched into his throat.

No way. Zoe had just texted him from the bakery, and even if she hadn't—they hadn't exactly talked about it, but the one time he'd tried to bring up how he'd prefer to keep whatever they were doing together quiet, at least for the time being, she'd just rolled her eyes.

"Don't worry. Your secret is safe with me," she'd said before kissing his cheek. "My brother murdering you would be a real bummer."

And then she'd started kissing *other* parts of him, and well, that'd been the end of that.

Long story short, she wouldn't just show up at his work unannounced, and Bryce wouldn't know to call her his girlfriend.

Before he could work himself up any further worrying, he spotted Han's car in the lot—not Zoe's. Relief swept over him, even as a new kind of nervousness started to intrude.

Flipping Bryce off for being a homophobic prick, he started crossing the site toward the lot. As he approached, Han got out of his car and held up one of the same chopped-up liquor boxes he used for Jade Garden deliveries, and Devin managed a smile.

"Hey, buddy," Han said as he hauled the food over to the picnic table by the trailer, where they usually ate.

"Hey."

He and Han did this once a week or so. Their schedules didn't match up much better than Devin's and Zoe's. Lunch on the job site was one of the easier ways to get together most weeks.

As Han started unpacking the containers he'd brought,

Devin pulled apart a couple of paper plates. His stomach growled as the mouthwatering scents of whatever Han had cooked up today hit him.

"The mango pork's new," Han said. "And I tweaked the ginger on the veggies."

"Yeah?"

Han might've had to drop out of culinary school when his dad died, but you'd never know it. He cooked all day, and then he cooked some more on his days off. He tried out new recipes—fancy "fusion" stuff that he and his mom had agreed didn't fit with the Jade Garden's brand, though he did manage to sneak a few of the tamer test recipes into the Chef's Specials "secret menu" now and then.

As Han plated up the food, he tipped his head toward the guys eating sandwiches and leftovers at the other tables. "So, how's it going?"

Devin rolled his eyes. "Same as usual."

"AKA, Bryce is being a jerk?"

Devin glared, but he knew there had been no one close enough to hear Han. "Yeah, pretty much."

Han scooped meat and vegetables onto a bed of noodles, then went ahead and sprinkled sesame seeds and scallions and drizzled some sort of orange sauce over it all, because the parking lot of a construction site was a five-star restaurant in his eyes. He passed the plate over, and Devin smacked his lips.

"I'm telling you." Han opened a set of wooden chopsticks and pointed them at Devin. "You gotta stand up to guys like him."

The same old discomfort churned in Devin's gut, but he pushed it down. "Sure, just like you did with all the mean kids back in high school."

"Shut up, man."

Neither of them had gotten picked on too badly when they were kids. Han stuck out, one of maybe four Asian kids in the school at the time, but he'd been as charming then as he was now—the bastard. Devin had held his own. He never started any fights, but when any came his way, he finished them. The two of them and the rest of the gang they ran with—they were fine.

But Han's girlfriend, May, had gotten savaged by the mean girl squad. She acted like it was no big deal, but whatever had happened, it had been bad enough that May had taken off after graduation. She'd come back for Han's dad's funeral and a visit or two here and there, and that was it.

Han scowled and nodded at Devin's food. "So? You gonna eat or just give me crap about things that happened a decade ago?"

"Like I can't do both." He tore open his own chopsticks. He'd never be as good with them as Han was, but he managed okay. He eyed the food. "Nice presentation."

"Obviously."

He tried the pork first, because how could he not.

"Get some mango with it," Han urged him.

Devin raised a brow. He didn't ignore the advice, though. He scooped up a noodle for good measure and shoveled the whole thing into his mouth.

His eyes slipped closed and he thumped his fist onto the table.

"Uh..."

"Shh." Devin put a finger to his sealed lips as he chewed. Once he swallowed, he opened his eyes.

"Well?"

"Man, that's good." Salty and sweet, rich but not heavy. "The mango really makes it, huh?"

"Yup."

"You getting the garlic?"

"Uh-huh."

"But not too much."

"Close—I wouldn't do any more. But seriously. It's a keeper."

"Try the veg."

Devin forced himself to stop cramming delicious, delicious pork in his face. The vegetable was some weird green thing Han had been messing around with. It'd been a little bitter for his taste last time, but it'd probably go pretty well with the pork. He gave it a shot and nodded. "Yup. Cutting the ginger helped a lot."

"Thought so." Han flashed a smug, ever-so-slightly-secretive smile as he dug into his own plate.

"What're you up to?"

"Nothing."

"Yeah, I don't buy it."

Han had always had fun messing around with new recipes, but he'd been more intense about it of late. There was definitely something going on.

"You don't have to." Then his smirk deepened. "But maybe someday someone will."

Devin put down his chopsticks. "You aren't finally doing it."

Han had always idly talked about opening his own restaurant. It never came to anything, though. He was too busy at the family business.

"No." Han shook his head. "Not yet. But let's just say I'm working on something that might be a first step."

"Okay, you keep your secrets. As long as you keep the awesome grub coming, too."

Chuckling, Han nodded. "That I can do." He took a bite

of his own lunch and seemed pleased. "Speaking of which, I've got a few other things I'm ready to guinea pig. Dinner at my place tomorrow?"

Normally, Devin would jump at the chance, but heading to the Leung house made all the hairs stand up on the back of his neck. He cleared his throat. "Who all's going to be there?"

"Does it matter? Free grub, remember."

"I know. I'm just asking."

Han shrugged. "Bobbi and Caitlin probably. Clay if I can pry him away from the Junebug for a minute, and you know he'll want to bring June." He listed the names of a couple of other guys they hung out with regularly. Then he grimaced. "I think Zoe has the night off, so she'll probably invite herself."

"Oh?" Devin's voice came out strangled to his own ears.

"Maybe. Who knows."

Not good enough. But he couldn't probe any deeper without sounding suspicious. He rummaged around in his brain, trying to think of excuses why he couldn't go, but he came up with squat.

Zoe was a firecracker. She said their secret was safe with her, but she loved to push him, and he had to admit it—he kind of loved it when she did. But interacting with her at their family home, with Han right there? What lines would get blurred?

It wasn't just her he didn't trust. His fingers twitched. He was getting too comfortable hanging out at his apartment with her. They spent half their time naked or snuggled up or both. Reaching out and putting his hand over hers and pulling her into him was becoming second nature.

Would he be the one to slip up and give them away?

Oblivious to Devin twisting himself into knots, Han

pursed his lips. "Then again, she's been going out a lot recently."

"Yeah?" Devin's throat threatened to close again.

"It's super weird. She bummed around the house all the time when she first moved back in, but now it's like she's never there. I think she's sneaking out at night, too."

Devin tried not to choke on a piece of mango and pork. He coughed into a napkin.

"You okay?" Han asked.

No.

"Yeah, yeah." Fighting both to breathe and to come off as casual, Devin asked, "Is it really sneaking, though? She's in her twenties, right?"

"Fine, fine, whatever. It's still weird. I didn't think she had a lot of friends around here." He narrowed his eyes. "I'm pretty sure she's not dating anybody."

"Maybe she's just working late? The Junebug is a bar."

"Maybe." Han frowned. "You're right—it's none of my business. I just hope she's not doing anything stupid."

Devin's stomach flopped around inside his abdomen.

She was doing something stupid all right.

Namely him.

"I'm sure it's nothing," he lied.

Only he wasn't so sure of that.

He wasn't so sure at all.

———

"So...do you want me to stay away?" Zoe had her back turned to Devin as she brushed her hair, but her gaze flicked to his in the bathroom mirror.

He was a little groggy, still splayed out on the mattress, naked and boneless. She hadn't had to close the bar tonight, so she'd come over after her shift, which was great—he loved seeing her. But it was past his bedtime, and that last round had been particularly athletic.

There was something in her voice that told him he needed to pay attention, though.

He rose onto his elbows and rummaged around in his skull for enough brain cells to rub together. "What do you mean? It's your house."

Their pillow talk had inevitably turned to a discussion of the dinner party Han was holding at the Leung house. She'd seemed surprised to hear he was trying to find a way out of it.

"Yeah," she allowed. She set down her brush—one of a couple of her things that had somehow found a home for themselves in his bathroom this week—and came back over to the bed. As if she could tell that he wasn't at his best when she wasn't wearing any clothes, she pulled the covers up over her chest. "But Han is your best friend. I don't want to get in the way of that."

He wasn't quite tired or stupid enough to laugh. He'd only resisted her as long as he had because he hadn't been willing to risk Han's friendship or Arthur's welcome. Of course his being with her now was going to affect his relationship with her family.

He reached for her hand and held it in his, running his thumb along the lines of her palm. He should be stressing out right now, but it was hard to be anything but relaxed when it was just the two of them. She made talking about his feelings easy in a way no one ever had. "You aren't in the way. I'm just nervous he'll catch on to something being weird between us."

"Yeah..."

He closed his fingers around hers more firmly. "You know I don't like keeping this secret, right?"

"I know." She wasn't looking at him, though.

"It's just…"

"I get it. I'm probably not going to be here for long." She huffed out a breath and pitched her voice higher, putting on the fake-happy smile she always used when talking about her job search. "Fifteen more applications submitted today." She deflated back to a more natural tone. "No point rocking the boat for something temporary, right?"

Sourness coated the back of his tongue. This was good, them being clear with each other like this. It was smart and mature.

So why did he hate it so much?

He couldn't bring himself to agree with her, so he barreled on. "Look, I don't want you to feel like you have to stay away."

"And I don't want you to feel like you do."

"So we won't," he decided. "We'll both go—if that's what you want to do. And we'll just try to be normal. It'll probably be fine."

Her expression finally brightened. "Sure. We can do this."

"Of course we can."

"So, what do you think?" She scooted closer to him, and he breathed a little easier. "Does Han just keep living with our mom out of sheer martyrdom? Or is it because he's using her for her kitchen?"

Devin tipped his head back and laughed. Leave it to Zoe not to mince words. "He'd probably say it's to take care of your mom and save money."

"Martyrdom." She poked his arm with her index finger.

He took her hand in his and kissed her knuckles. "But you might be onto something with the kitchen." Devin had helped them redo it back a few years ago. "He'd never find an apartment with one as nice."

Gazing down at their joined hands, Zoe asked, "What about at your loner house in the woods? Any plans to build a giant kitchen there that he can use?"

"It'd be worth it just for the free food," he mused. But he shook his head. "I don't know. It's going to be a small place. Just me kicking around it."

"You don't think there'd ever be anybody else?" she asked quietly.

The question settled on him heavily. She was still studiously looking down. He brushed her hair back from her face, but it didn't let him see her eyes any better.

The answer should be simple. His whole life, he'd been dreaming of the day he could have a home of his own.

He glanced over at the bathroom, though. At the hairbrush and the toothbrush and the little bottles of lotion and soap.

He shrugged, noncommittal. "How about you? Gorgeous kitchen a must-have for your Realtor when you land your dream job?"

He kept his voice light, but forget heavy. This question sank inside him like a stone.

"Nah." She put her head on his shoulder. "It's not like Han would ever leave to come visit me."

I would, Devin didn't say. But her kitchen wouldn't have a thing to do with it.

Silence hung between them for a minute. He twisted his neck to press a kiss to her temple, but before he could come up with anything smart to say, a yawn snuck out of him.

She laughed and kissed him back before ruffling his hair. "Come on. Let's get you to bed. You have incident reports to write in the morning."

"Don't remind me," he groaned, flopping backward into his pillow.

She got up and turned off the lights, and wow, she was so great. As she slipped back into the bed beside him, he curled his arms around her. Even the prospect of dealing with more paperwork and more people letting Bryce off the hook couldn't bring him down.

Nope. Apparently, the only thing that could do that was the reminder that his time with her was temporary.

Which sucked. Because he was pretty sure he was going to get even more of those when he was pretending not to be sleeping with her at Han's party tomorrow night.

Chapter Ten

Y'all—don't even get me started on weird customers."
June held a hand in front of herself, palm out.

Zoe raised a brow and took another sip of her wine.

Ten minutes into Han's dinner party, she, June, and June's
friend Bobbi were standing around the island in the center
of the kitchen, trading work stories. Over by the stove, Han
prepped ingredients while trying to keep Ling-Ling from
stealing any of them—with mixed success. Between fond
rebukes to the dog, he kept a light conversation going with
Clay, Bobbi's girlfriend, Caitlin, and a couple of guy friends.

"Ooh." Bobbi rubbed her hands together. "This is going
to be good."

June smiled. "Let's just say there's a reason the Sweetbriar Inn now has an official policy prohibiting birds."

Zoe snickered, but before June could dive any deeper
into whatever guest at her family's B&B had prompted that
new rule, the doorbell rang, setting Ling-Ling off.

Zoe's pulse raced, and she put her glass down with a
thunk. "I'll get it!"

"Seriously," Han called after her, "nobody's fighting you
for it except the dog."

And okay, yeah, she was a little eager, racing to get the

door each time a new person arrived. But this time, she had extra reason to run. Devin was the only person they were still waiting for. This had to be him.

She skidded to a stop in the entryway, making sure her body was blocking Ling-Ling from getting out before flinging open the door.

And there Devin was. All six-foot-something glorious inches of him, his cheeks flushed from the chill outside, his blue eyes sparkling, and what was it about the way he lit up when his gaze fell on her? Her heart pounded, her ribs squeezing around it.

Her over-the-top reaction made no sense. He was just a guy, and she was in a weird, temporary place in her life. They'd basically agreed that whatever they were doing together was just for fun. The very sight of him shouldn't turn her to goo.

But she liked him so much.

She cast one backward glance over her shoulder before closing the door and launching herself at him. He caught her in his arms. Pausing only to set down the six-pack he'd brought, he pressed her into the freezing-cold siding of the house, and she didn't care about the temperature or the fact that he was so worried about getting caught.

His mouth was hot as it covered hers, his tongue commanding. She kissed him back with a hunger that had nothing to do with the promise of the upcoming meal. Running her hands through his hair, she soaked up every second of contact with him.

It wasn't enough. He jerked away, his breath coming fast, the darkness in his gaze pure torture considering what was coming next. "We should—"

"Go make out some more in your truck?" she suggested helpfully.

He buried his face in her shoulder, and she wrapped her arms around him as tightly as she could. "Don't tempt me, woman."

"Why not?" She gazed up at the stars and breathed him in. "It's so much fun."

"For you, maybe," he said, but there was a hint of darkness in his tone.

The corners of her mouth turned down. "I was just messing around."

"I know." Did he, though?

The mood broken, he gave her one last quick peck before letting go.

Stepping away, he gestured at his face. "Do I have any . . . ?"

"Just—" She reached up on her toes to swipe at the little smudge of lipstick at the corner of his mouth. Considering how they'd just been sticking their tongues down each other's throats, it wasn't bad. This long-wearing stuff was the best.

"Thanks."

"No problem."

He picked up the beer he'd set down and they headed inside. She stole another glance at him under the entry-way light as he stopped to give Ling-Ling a quick scratch behind the ear. There was no sign that anything was amiss. The way she'd run her fingers through his hair could have easily been the wind. No one would know.

She tried to remind herself that that was a good thing.

"I'll, uh, show you where to put your coat." She started to lead him down the hall.

"Please," her brother scoffed, appearing at the top of the half flight of stairs. "It's just Devin. He knows." Han smiled at Devin. "What's up, man?"

"Nothing," Devin replied.

"Was starting to think you'd gotten lost out there."

"Nah." Devin brushed past her. Out of her brother's sight line, he gave her fingers a reassuring squeeze before continuing on. He held up the six-pack. "Almost forgot these in the truck and had to run back for them."

"Nice." Han accepted the beers.

But as Zoe followed Han and Devin into the kitchen, she caught June gazing at her appraisingly. Crap—she'd checked Devin for lipstick smudges but she hadn't checked herself. She casually glanced at her reflection in the hallway mirror. Nope—she was basically okay.

Well, whatever. June could give her weird looks if she wanted to. Zoe wasn't going to act like she had anything to hide.

To prove it, she snagged a fried wonton strip off one of the appetizer plates. She dragged it through the plum sauce dip and popped it in her mouth. She really didn't know what that was supposed to prove, but it was freaking delicious, so it didn't matter.

Around her, all signs showed this to be a successful dinner party. Han was doing his thing, cooking and putting on a show. If it weren't so clichéd—and if they were Japanese instead of Chinese—he could've had a heck of a career at one of those hibachi places.

Zoe shook her head, trying not to stare at Devin, who had joined the loose cluster hanging out over by her brother. Han's parties were never formal or anything, but people usually put in a little effort. Devin had traded in his work clothes for a sharp blue button-down that made his eyes look even brighter.

She wanted to peel it off him.

"So, you wanna talk about it?"

Zoe tried not to jump when June spoke from right beside her. "Talk about what?"

June's friend Bobbi snickered.

Zoe's face went warm. Crap. She was really bad at this secretly banging her brother's friend thing, huh?

"There's nothing to talk about," she said, more firmly this time.

June didn't seem convinced. "Uh-huh."

"He's one of Han's friends." Zoe swallowed past the lump in her throat. "Gross."

"Gross? I mean—" Bobbi gestured with her wineglass at the guys. Her girlfriend, Caitlin, stood over beside them. "I don't even like dudes, and I can admit he's hot."

"They're all hot," June said.

Zoe recoiled. "Ew. My brother is not hot."

Shrugging, June took a sip of her wine. "May would kill me for saying it, but it's true."

"Seriously, though," Bobbi said, leaning in. "Devin's been sneaking looks at you almost as much as you've been sneaking looks at him."

"Really?" Her voice came out too high. She retreated to the side a bit to reclaim her wineglass and took a gulp.

"Really," June confirmed.

Zoe had to stop herself from glancing over at him to verify. "It doesn't matter. Even if he weren't gross." He was so, so not gross. "It's like I said—he's my brother's best friend, and you know how Han is." Her mouth felt dry despite the wine. "If either of us made a move, he'd flip his lid."

"I don't know..." June mused.

"Well, believe me, I do."

Devin and Han had both been plenty clear. A bitter taste formed at the back of her mouth.

At first, the whole off-limits thing had been kind of fun. But the more time they spent together, the more it twisted her up inside.

Being someone's dirty little secret wasn't great for the ego.

Not that that was stopping her from developing—ugh— *feelings* for the guy.

Yeah, she might be in denial about a lot of things, but that was a tough one to get away from. She wasn't an idiot. The way his touch made her feel all warm and squishy inside, the way her thoughts kept drifting to him throughout the day…It was like her teenage crush, only times a million, because now she knew he liked her, too.

Maybe not as much as she liked him, but more than enough to keep throwing gasoline on the fire in her chest.

She was saved from having to downplay things to June and Bobbi any further by Han flicking off the burners with a flourish. "Okay, y'all, grub's up."

Zoe downed another gulp of her wine before excusing herself. This was old hat. Positioning herself at her brother's side, she passed him plates, and he portioned out the food.

Her mouth watered. Han had been refining his stable of experimental dishes for ages, and they just kept getting better. Tonight's menu included a rice dish with pickled ginger and edamame, plus seared scallops in a basil sauce she never would have thought would work, but it did. Baby bok choy that he'd cooked over a little electric grill, and some mystery egg tarts he'd done in the oven. He scattered the lot with a drizzle of vibrant green and white sauces, chopped nori, and sesame.

Devin stepped in to pass the completed dishes out.

"Wow," Caitlin said as she received the first plate.

"Let me know what you think."

Zoe frowned at her brother. His voice had a different pitch to it. He was always proud of his cooking, but the nerves jangling around in there were new.

She didn't have much time to think about it. Before she knew it, everyone had a plate in hand. As they found places to sit or stand, appreciative moans and compliments sounded out around the room. Han shone a sly smile as he started eating, too, Ling-Ling parked hopefully at his feet. He made a running commentary—he always did. What worked and what hadn't, though as far as Zoe was concerned, it was all a hit.

The regulars in Han's guinea pig squad were easy to spot as they echoed Han's comments. Devin was a down-to-earth guy, but he'd been hanging out with Han long enough to mention something about the butter-to-shortening ratio in the crust of the savory egg tart. Zoe shook her head and just kept shoveling it in.

One of Han and Devin's buddies, Terrell, snapped his fingers. "I know what this reminds me of. That thing you made for my sister's wedding."

Han tipped his head to the side. "Did I do shrimp for that?"

"No, but the sauce."

"That was totally different," Han said.

Devin scrunched up his nose. "It was kind of the same."

"You know what it reminds me of?" June interjected.

"What?" Han asked. "And please tell me you have a better memory than these guys."

"She usually does." Clay chuckled, and Devin elbowed him in the ribs.

"Graduation," June said, sure of herself. "Your year. That meal you did at our place."

"Oh." A shadow crept across Han's gaze.

Right. Any meal he would have made at the Wu-Miller house would have been because of May.

Devin looked at Han with the same concern Zoe felt.

As if realizing her mistake in bringing that up, June continued. "Though this is way better. I mean, the graduation meal was amazing, but these egg tarts are next level. What's in them again?"

Han rattled off some of the ingredients.

Devin cleared his throat. "I think it's more like that Thanksgiving you cooked—what was it? Twenty seventeen?"

Han pulled a face. "That menu was totally different."

"Yeah, but the basil—"

"Oh man," Terrell said, elbowing his buddy. "New Year's Eve, like, five years ago."

"Yeah!" The dude's eyes lit up. He waved a hand at Han. "The one you did at the park."

"Fried turkey," Han agreed. "Seriously, guys, that was nothing like this."

"Didn't you have little pastries? I swear there was, like, basil in them like this."

"The basil is in the sauce." Han was smiling again now, which was something.

"Oh! Oh!" Terrell held up a finger. "Wasn't that the year we were picking gravel out of the cupcakes?"

"Man, who baked those?"

"Pretty sure it was me." Bobbi grinned.

"They were so good, it was totally worth it, even when—"

Devin slammed his plate down on the counter. His fork clattered against the china. Ling-Ling whined.

Suddenly, everyone got quiet.

Zoe sucked in a breath. Devin's face had turned a shade of purple. Thunderheads colored his eyes.

"What?" she asked.

Devin's gaze connected with hers for a fraction of a second, and it was like an iron band closed around her heart.

Devin glanced away. "Excuse me."

He stalked off. Zoe put her plate down. The band around her heart released, but it was replaced by a freaking jackrabbit, jumping up and down on the insides of her chest so fast, she could hardly breathe. She gripped the edge of the counter she'd been leaning against until her knuckles turned white.

Everything in her told her to follow him. His gaze was seared into her. His eyes had looked so *angry*.

But more than that, he'd looked so...

Lost.

A door slammed in the distance, and Zoe squeezed the counter even tighter. Han smacked himself in the forehead, then reached over to cuff Terrell on the back of his head, too.

"Ow—"

"Devin's dad," Han hissed. "Remember?"

"Wait." Zoe should shut up, but she couldn't. "What—"

Han shook his head.

Wincing, Terrell scrubbed at his face. "Oh, right. Crap."

Quietly, Bobbi turned to Zoe. "Devin's dad showed up drunk. He knocked over the cupcakes."

"Said some really awful stuff, too," Han added.

Zoe stared toward the corner Devin had disappeared around. It was like she was being yanked in that direction. He'd told her the other night that his dad wasn't a good guy, but seeing his reaction to someone bringing up that memory now...

She bit the inside of her lip.

Was he okay? No, of course not. How could he be?

She wanted so badly to chase after him. If she were really his girlfriend, she would do just that. She'd put her arms around him and hold him tight, and maybe—maybe he'd even let her.

Her stomach plummeted to the floor.

The only problem was that she wasn't. If she gave them away, he'd be even more furious—furious at her.

But she couldn't ignore this *pull*.

"Shouldn't someone go after him?" she asked.

Han shook his head. "Just makes it worse."

Everyone seemed to take that as definitive.

Slowly, people started eating and talking again, but Zoe couldn't hear any of it. She was listening so carefully for any sort of sound from the hallway. When she heard the bathroom door open, her heart leaped.

Speaking to no one in particular, she said, "I have to..."

She pulled out her phone as if that would explain her needing to step away.

June gave her a knowing glance that bordered on encouragement. Accepting that unexpected morsel of support, she took off down the hall at a measured pace, but as soon as she was out of sight, she couldn't help it. She broke into an all-out sprint.

Only to almost crash into Devin. His jaw was set, storms still brewing in his eyes, and she'd just come out here to check on him.

But she couldn't stand this.

She grabbed him by the wrist and hauled him down the hall.

"Zo—"

He resisted, but he finally let himself be dragged into

the next available room with a door. It was Lian's old room—now her mother's sewing room, but it would do. Her mom was working at the restaurant tonight, so she wouldn't notice.

As soon as the door was closed behind them, she launched herself at him. She wrapped her arms around his chest, but he was stone.

"You don't have to—" he gritted out.

"Shh."

He shook his head, but she wasn't having any of it.

She shushed him again. He stayed as stiff as a board for a long moment. Crap. Maybe she'd misread this entire thing. Maybe he didn't need comfort.

Maybe he didn't want any from her.

Well, too bad. She was giving it to him anyway.

She'd give him anything.

She clenched her eyes tight. That was probably so stupid of her. He wasn't in this with her for real. Even if he were—what kind of future could they have? He'd never be willing to face Han's wrath or risk Arthur's judgment. There wasn't any place for her in his lonely loner's house in the woods. Who knew how long she'd be staying in Blue Cedar Falls anyway? Getting invested was a waste, but she couldn't seem to fight it anymore.

Finally, Devin let out a sigh. He curled his arms around her, too. His posture softened as he pressed a kiss to the top of her head. "I'm fine," he told her.

"I know." People banging dishes on counters and leaving in a huff—that was always a sign that they were fine.

"I just..."

She leaned back so she could look him in the eye. The anger had faded from his gaze, replaced by something that made him look tired and older than he was. She sucked in a breath. "Han said it was something to do with your father?"

Devin nodded grimly. He pulled her back into a hug, her face pressed to his chest. Normally, she wouldn't mind being snuggled up with his firm pecs, but it was clearly a way for him to avoid her gaze. She allowed it for now.

Exhaling, he said, "Yeah. Told you he wasn't a good guy."

"You didn't tell me he was the 'shows up drunk to parties and knocks over cupcakes' kind of bad guy."

He shrugged, but she could practically feel his wince. "They told you that, huh?"

"Yup."

"They tell you the part about him smacking me around?"

She drew back. "No."

His grimace deepened. "Can we forget I just admitted it, then?"

"Seriously?"

"He was a jerk," he said, as if that were some kind of explanation.

"But he hit you?" More rumors and hushed conversations floated into her memory. She hadn't understood them then. But Devin telling her this . . . It slotted an awful lot of things into place.

Devin rubbed his hands up and down her arms, and she didn't need him to comfort her. Not when he was telling her about his pain. "It's okay. I'm fine now."

"How?"

His throat bobbed. "I got out."

"How?" An intense need to understand this man clawed at her. She shouldn't pry, but she wanted to know everything. "I mean—if you don't want to talk about it—"

"Your family, for one." His gaze connected with hers, a little light coming back to his eyes. "There's a reason

I was always at your place or hanging out in Arthur's basement."

"Right."

"And then, as soon as I was out of high school, I packed my bag. Started working. Got an apartment. The rest is history."

Was it, though? The pain of it still seemed to live inside him.

She put her hands over Devin's chest, trying to take in the breadth of him. This strong, incredible man, who'd dealt with so much and who still stayed open and kind.

It occurred to her again, just like that night he'd walked her home after they'd hung out at the bar. Did he ever talk about what had happened to him? How did the pressure of keeping it all inside not make him explode?

Gazing up at him, she took a deep breath. "What happened to him?"

"I have no idea," he said quietly, ghosts in his eyes. "I assume he rotted in that house for a while. I never went back. He never came looking for me except a couple of times when he was trashed." He shrugged. "When he did, I just called Officer Dwight to take him home. Otherwise, I had nothing to do with him. Year or so after I left, I got a drunk dial from him. Said he was set up in a trailer park in Florida."

"You think he'll stay there?"

"Honestly, I don't care."

He meant it, too. The pain in his voice was like a hand reaching into her chest and squeezing.

Zoe's family was her bedrock. She defied them and fought with them, but deep down she loved them fiercely. She never in a million years could doubt they loved her, too.

Devin... he didn't have that.

Slowly, she skated her hands up his chest. She took his face between her palms. His scruff was rough against her skin. She stroked her thumbs just beneath his eyes. "I'm so sorry," she told him quietly.

"It's nothing. Old history."

She repeated it. More firmly this time. "I'm sorry." She reached up onto her tiptoes, pulling him down to meet her. She kissed his lips. "I'm sorry."

"Zo..."

"I'm sorry." She kissed him again, soft and slow.

He melted into it, wrapping his arms around her. Holding on to him, she tried to pour everything she was feeling into the motion of their lips. He didn't want her to comfort him or to let her tell him how her heart ached for him, and that was fine. She'd make him understand like this.

Because any of her ideas about not getting invested? Not growing *feelings* for this man?

They were out the window. She'd tossed her sense of self-preservation right along with them.

All she could do was hang on.

And wait for the crash when they all hit the ground.

Chapter Eleven

A couple of weeks later, Zoe sat on the kitchen counter, texting with June about grabbing coffee, Clay about whether or not she could open the bar tomorrow, Lian about how she wanted to bang her head against the wall over her job search, and a group of high school friends about a time to meet up for drinks later that week—all without accidentally sending any messages to the wrong person. She snickered to herself as she sent a reaction gif to Lian. Take that, accounting firm looking for "attention to detail."

No sooner had the thought occurred to her than her screen went blank, a call from an unknown number appearing over her fifteen messaging threads.

Her first impulse was to ignore it—she'd talked to quite enough people excited to offer her a free time-share or help her with a problem at the social security agency. But one of the worst things about being on a job hunt was having to answer every call.

Bracing for the worst, she tucked her hair out of the way and brought the phone to her ear. "Hello?"

A male voice replied, "Good morning. Is this Zoe Leung?"

She sat up straighter. "It is."

"Hi, I'm Brad Sullivan from Pinnacle Accounting, following up on a résumé we received."

"Oh, hi!" She scrambled down off the counter and over to her makeshift office set up on the end of the dining room table. Pinnacle, Pinnacle—oh, right. It was a firm in Atlanta she'd applied to last week.

"I was hoping to talk to you about your interest in the position. Do you have a few minutes?"

She blinked about fifty-seven times. "Of course."

"Great." With that, he launched into a quick overview of the job she'd applied for as well as a series of questions about her experience and training, which she somehow or other managed to string together coherent answers to.

Slipping back into the accounting persona she'd honed during her coursework and internship was harder than it used to be. Once upon a time, it had felt like a second skin. Now it felt like a wet suit that was three sizes too small.

"All right," Brad said, "sounds to me like you're an excellent candidate. Let me just talk to a few people and we'll get you set up for an interview with the rest of the team."

It was a good thing the chair she was sitting on had a back, because otherwise she might have tipped right out of it. "Oh wow, okay, great."

"Just one last question—this job does require you to be on-site in our Buckhead office. Looks like you're in North Carolina right now, but I'm assuming you're prepared to relocate?"

"Yes," she said, but as she did, a stone lodged in her throat.

"Perfect." He rattled off a few more details, and they said their goodbyes.

The whole while, the tightness in her windpipe grew and grew.

Atlanta was a four-hour drive from here. A few months ago, she might not have cared. She'd lived away from home when she'd gone to college. She'd always assumed she'd have to leave again to get a decent job that was in her field.

But her time back here in Blue Cedar Falls had changed her perspective.

She liked being home. She liked seeing Han all the time and being able to meet up with Lian now and then. She liked Clay and June and working at the bar. She loved getting to spend time with Arthur and helping out at Harvest Home.

She loved…

She clenched her phone so tightly she worried the screen would break.

She and Devin had told each other that their time together was limited. He wasn't interested in anything serious; all he wanted in this world was a house of his own outside of town, and he never imagined sharing it with anyone, least of all her. He definitely wasn't interested in upsetting the balance of his relationship with her family.

Ever since Han's dinner party, when he'd opened up to her about his dad, she'd known that eventually he'd break her heart.

She just hadn't been prepared for it to happen so soon.

Maybe it didn't have to. A bubble of hope filled her chest. Maybe she wouldn't get the job. Maybe she could just stay here forever, working at the bar and helping Arthur run the food kitchen and sleeping with Devin and it would all be okay.

Right.

The bubble popped almost instantaneously. She needed this job. If it was offered to her, she'd have no choice but to take it and go. This was the moment she'd been waiting for, working toward, training for.

So why did everything about it make her feel so terrible?

Before she could even begin to get it all sorted out, the front door opened.

"Crap."

Instinctively, she scrambled to look busy, but sitting at her laptop with her spreadsheet open was about as busy-looking as she could get.

"Oh, look, you're awake," her mom said, deadpan.

Zoe drew in a breath and forced herself to smile. She hadn't gotten home until two a.m. yesterday after closing up the Junebug. The fact that she was up before ten was a miracle.

Try telling her early-bird mother that, though.

"Han went to the restaurant already?" her mom asked.

Zoe shook her head. "Took the dog for a hike first."

"Good. Ling-Ling needs more exercise."

"Ling-Ling needs you to stop slipping her extra treats."

"Me?" Her mother put her hand to her chest dramatically. "Never."

Right. "How was brunch?"

Zoe's mother ate with May and June's mom and a few other old ladies almost every morning down at the Sweetbriar Inn on Main Street.

Her mom waved a hand dismissively. "Same as ever." She headed into the kitchen to start a pot of tea. Managing to sound both casual and pointed, she mentioned, "Mrs. Smith's son got a big promotion. Branch manager."

"That's great." Zoe dug her nails into the meat of her palm.

The competitive instinct in her told her to brag about the interview she'd just landed, but she knew better. Her mom would get obsessed with it and have her cramming for it like the SATs. Better to keep mum.

But as her mother puttered around, getting everything together for her tea, Zoe kept running around in circles inside her head. She wanted to talk this out with someone. Devin, namely. He was so grounded, and he asked her questions that made her see things in a new light. Could she bring up her mixed feelings about moving without letting on that she was getting too attached to him? Probably not. He was working right now anyway. So were June and Lian and pretty much all of her other friends she might try to talk to about this.

Which left her with her mom.

With her teapot and little porcelain cup and saucer balanced on a tray, her mother returned to the table and took her usual seat at the head. She put on her reading glasses and opened up the newspaper.

Zoe fidgeted, glancing between her open laptop screen and her mom, but she couldn't quite figure out how to open up her mouth and say what was on her mind.

Talking—really talking—with her mother had never been easy. Her mom had this unique way of shutting Zoe down and making all her ideas seem foolish. Sometimes Zoe had enough force of will to barrel right through.

And sometimes she ended up picking a stupid major she didn't even like anyway.

She still couldn't decide who she was more upset with about that—her mother or herself. Clearly her mom wasn't entirely to blame. Yeah, Zoe had gotten a different version of her mom's weird guilt-trippy style of parenting, considering how much younger she'd been than her siblings when their father died. But Han and Lian—they were doing what they wanted to do. Or at least some variation on it. They were happy.

"Something on your mind?" her mother asked, not looking up from her paper.

So many things.

But the one she ended up blurting out was, "How come you always rode me so much harder than Han and Lian?"

Her mother's rapid blinking was the only sign that the question took her by surprise. With deliberate slowness, she set her teacup down and dabbed at the corner of her mouth with a napkin.

Stalling. Zoe was used to it.

That didn't make it any easier to wait her mother out. Chewing on the inside of her lip, she put her hands under her thighs, literally sitting on them to try to give herself patience.

Finally, her mom put the napkin down. She fixed Zoe with an appraising stare that lasted way too long for comfort. Inside, Zoe squirmed a little, but she remained firm.

Shaking her head, her mother let out a breath and looked away. "I ever tell you about the first day I picked you up from nursery school?"

Zoe deflated. She pulled her hands out from under her legs. "Probably."

"You were a mess. Glitter everywhere. Your teacher apologized, but I knew. It wasn't her fault."

Great, so Zoe had been a disaster since she was four. Good to know. "Look—"

Her mom talked right over her, slow and steady. Like a Zamboni. "Whole ride home, you never stopped talking. Told me all the friends you made, everything you did. You couldn't decide if you liked Joey best or Kim. Or costume party or building with blocks. Everything was your favorite."

"Right, right. I was a happy kid. I know."

Her mom's lips curled into a smile. "Ray of sunshine." She turned her gaze from the past and back to the woman in front of her. Her smile faded. "You remember what you told me you wanted to be when you grew up?"

Had she ever known? "No."

"I remember. Clear as yesterday. 'Princess astronaut veterinarian ballerina.'"

Zoe's face flushed warm. "I mean, I was, what? Four?"

"But you believed it. With all your heart."

"Mom..." She was beginning to lose her patience.

Her mother's voice rose by a fraction, her tone growing serious. "Your brother, Han. Only thing he cares about besides his family is cooking." Her mother jabbed her pointer finger into the table. "Han is easy."

Zoe frowned. She wasn't so sure about all that.

But her mom was on a roll now. She tapped the table hard again. "Lian wanted to be a teacher since she was six. Easy."

"But what about all the stuff you told me?" Zoe asked. Bitterness seeped into her tone. "Pick any career you want, just make sure it's comfortably middle class."

How many times had Zoe come home from school excited about some project in her communications elective or jazzed about a fundraiser Uncle Arthur was going to let her help out with at Harvest Home, only to be met with her mother's dismissive *tut-tut*ting?

"You." Her mother shoved that finger in Zoe's direction this time. "You were never easy."

"Great," Zoe grumbled.

"You weren't. Still aren't."

Zoe's cheeks warmed, and she squirmed inside. Clearly she'd been selling her mom's passive-aggressive streak short, because this direct insult approach was no peach. "Okay, okay, I get it."

Her mother shook her head. She was fluent in English, but she still muttered a few words to herself in Mandarin. It was one of her only tells that she was getting flustered.

"That's not a bad thing, Zhaohui. You always make it out like I'm attacking you."

"Uh, you kind of are." How else was she supposed to interpret her mom telling her to her face that she was, always had been, and always would be difficult?

"You were not easy, because you actually wanted to be princess astronaut veterinarian ballerina!"

"Who wouldn't?" That sounded awesome.

"You have your head in the clouds. Someone has to help keep you here. On earth where you belong." Fire burned in her mother's gaze.

And okay, Zoe knew her mom loved her and that she'd fight off an invading horde for her. But she occasionally forgot that the overbearing stuff was love, too.

Annoying, frustrating, occasionally infuriating love.

"You don't have to," she insisted.

"I do." Her mother reached across the table, and for the first time in what seemed like a long, long while, it felt like she was looking at Zoe. Not past her. No snide remarks, no judgment. She held out her hand. "I know it, because that's what your father did for me."

Zoe's eyes flew wide. Her mom almost never talked about her dad. "Wait—"

Her mother shook her head, her whole expression softening. "So like me, sometimes, my Zhaohui. I don't want you to learn lessons the hard way like I did." She extended her hand an inch farther, and Zoe slipped her fingers into her palm. "You have to be practical. You have to survive."

And Zoe would probably never fully understand her mother, but for one moment, she wondered if maybe she was right. If maybe they did have more in common than had ever been keeping them apart.

Her mother gave her hand a gentle, reassuring squeeze. "Look. I make you a deal."

"Okay..."

"You ever find job opening for princess astronaut veterinarian ballerina *with* pension and health insurance? I promise I stop riding you so hard."

Zoe laughed, and she swabbed at her eyes. This was making her way too emotional—especially considering her mom had basically just promised to never, ever give her a break.

She had about a bazillion other questions, but before she could figure out a way to give voice to them, the actual, honest-to-goodness phone on the wall started ringing.

Her mother patted Zoe's hand before letting go to stand and answer it.

"Hello—" She barely got through the word. A muffled voice came over the line.

Then all the color drained from her face.

———

"For crying out loud, James." Bryce looked up from the same set of joists he'd been supposedly assembling for the last hour now. "Your mommy calling you or something?"

"Mind your own business." Devin ignored his phone buzzing in his pocket again. This was the third time, and no, it wasn't his mommy. Dead women didn't call.

He was starting to get a little worried, though.

He drove the last nail home in his set and looked up, meeting Terrell's gaze. "You got this for a second?"

"Sure, man."

"You heard him," Bryce said, dropping his nail gun. "That's five, everybody."

"You already had your break, and you don't have time to take another." Devin gestured at the work still to be done.

Bryce pantomimed a yapping mouth, and Devin gritted his teeth.

The guy had been giving Devin a hard time since high school. Ever since Bryce had come on at Meyer Construction, it had been the same—like Bryce resented that a guy as powerful as the mayor's son had to stoop so low as to be working alongside schlubs like Devin. Devin's promotion had been salt in the wound. The backtalk had gotten worse and worse, and Devin had tried to turn a blind eye to it. He'd focused on the job and the work and let the personal stuff slide.

Goodness knew there was enough to focus on work-wise. Ever since the disaster the other week when Bryce had let half a wall collapse, the higher-ups had taken a personal interest in Devin's crew. Devin had shown Joe all the documentation he'd been gathering about Bryce's sloppy work, and Joe had been clear that Devin had his support. He just needed to keep collecting evidence to build a case that could hold up against whatever scrutiny they might get if and when the time came to finally give the boot to the mayor's son.

Ignoring Bryce, Devin made sure he was out of everybody's way before pulling out his phone.

Only to find three missed calls from Zoe.

His heart thunked around in his chest, thrown by a

whole warring set of reactions. Pleasure at hearing from her. Surprise, because she never called unless it was too late to come over and she still wanted to tell him something dirty.

Worry.

He tapped on her number and brought his phone to his ear. As it rang, he glanced around. The rest of his crew was still working. Bryce was continuing with his little tantrum, but he'd actually nailed two pieces of wood together, so who cared.

On the third ring, Zoe picked up.

"Hey—" he started.

"Devin."

He straightened, adrenaline rushing his system. Her voice was all breathy and watery and wrong. "What happened."

"Uncle Arthur. He had a heart attack."

A ten-ton weight fell right on Devin's chest. He changed direction midstride. "Where is he?"

"Pine Ridge."

"I'll be there in ten."

"You don't have to." She sniffled. "I just—I thought you should know. Arthur—"

Arthur was like a father to him. A better one than his own had ever been, but Devin couldn't focus on his own concern right now.

Zoe put on such a front. She acted carefree, like nothing could touch her, but under all that she was tender and soft, and he knew her well enough now. The raw emotion in her voice reached into his chest and squeezed.

"Who's there with you?"

"Just my mom. She's trying not to freak out, but it's not working. Han's on his way, but Lian's car broke down, so he had to drive out to Lincoln to get her."

Right. "I'll be there in ten."

"Devin..." The way her voice broke made him stop.

He exhaled out, deep and rough. He covered his eyes with his hand. "Do you not want me to come?"

Everything in him was itching to go. A crisis demanded action. This was Arthur they were talking about.

"I just...If you don't...You're working."

She'd called him three times. She'd reached out.

"Tell me not to come."

"I—"

"Tell me explicitly, specifically, that you do not want me there, or I am getting in my truck."

Silence held across the line. A sob broke it.

"I want you to come," she whispered.

He dropped his hand from his face. "Ten minutes." His voice was still too hard. With a deep breath, he forced himself to be soft for her. "Hang on, baby."

Then he hung up.

It was fifty yards to the trailer. He crossed it in big strides.

"Hey, James, you okay?" one of the guys called.

"Family emergency," he barked out. He tossed open the door to the trailer, but it was empty. He backed right out. "Where's Joe?"

The couple of guys gathered around shook their heads and shrugged. "Maybe down at corporate?" one of them offered.

Devin shucked his safety gear. "When he gets back, tell him I had to go."

"Okay..."

"Terrell? You're in charge."

And then a voice came from behind him. A stupid, teasing voice. "What did your mommy want, James? Need you to come home and have your bottle?"

Devin ignored Bryce. He didn't have time for this.

But as he headed for his truck, Bryce followed him. "Real nice, ignoring your employees while you're running out the door halfway through your shift. Super responsible. I can see why you got the promotion over me."

Real nice, ignoring your father. Worthless sack of—

Devin's father's words had no place in his head. Not now when he was on his way to help Zoe, to help her family, who had been better to him than his own flesh and blood had ever been.

"Maybe I'll fill out one of those write-up forms you keep doing for me—not that anybody reads them." Bryce leaned against the side of Devin's truck as Devin went to open the door. "You know that, right? That nobody listens to you?"

Just try to report me. Devin's dad had been stumbling, slurring. *Nobody's going to listen to you.*

"Get out of my way." Devin managed to keep from growling, but it was a narrow thing.

"Make me."

Devin hauled open the door of his truck and got in, but when he went to pull it closed behind him, Bryce was still there.

"Seriously, James. I want to see you do it." Bryce was in the way now, making it impossible to close the door. "Or are you too weak? Weak guy trying to boss everyone around." His voice dropped. "Not a great look. Think all of them will still respect you when they see me walk all over you?"

Devin looked past Bryce's shoulder before he could stop himself. Terrell and the rest of the team were back at work, but people were looking. Was that Bryce's angle? Trap him like this? Make him back down? Rub it in his face the next time Devin tried to call him out?

When would it end?

All Devin's life, he'd tried to keep his head down, work hard, stay out of trouble, and for the most part, it had panned out just fine. He had a great job, great friends. For the moment, at least, he had Zoe.

But what if it wasn't enough to keep quiet and do things the way they were supposed to be done?

What if he'd stood up to his dad a long, long time ago?

Righteousness surged through Devin's veins. "Move." When Bryce didn't budge, Devin turned. He got out of the truck, and that put him right in Bryce's face, and he didn't care. "Go back to work now or pack up your things."

"Whatever—"

And that was it. Devin was done. "You're fired."

For the first time, Bryce flinched. "Wait."

"Get off my site. Don't come back."

"You can't—"

"I can." Devin took a step forward, and as Bryce retreated, power filled Devin's chest. He didn't have to keep his head down. He didn't have to stay silent when people were treating him like crap. He was in charge. People trusted him to make the right calls.

And this was one of them.

"Terrell?" Devin shouted.

"Yeah?"

"Call security to escort Mr. Horton off the property."

"With pleasure."

"My father—" Bryce tried.

"Doesn't have any authority here. And if he shows up and tries to pretend he does, then I'll stand up to him just the same."

Devin had heard enough. This guy didn't deserve his time. He had to get to the hospital, had to find out if Arthur was okay. Zoe needed him.

He climbed back into his truck and slammed the door shut behind him. He put the key in the ignition, and the engine roared to life.

From the other side of the window, Bryce shouted, "My dad is going to destroy you. One word from me and you can kiss this job goodbye. That little piece of land you've been saving up for? You can forget it. My father—"

Terrell appeared behind Bryce, two security officers in tow. "Oh, shut up already, Bryce."

One corner of Devin's lips curled up. They'd all been tiptoeing around Bryce forever, but a dam had just broken.

He should have told Bryce off years ago. It hadn't even taken a punch or a shove. Just evidence and words and an unwillingness to be pushed around anymore.

But he didn't have any more energy to waste on that guy now.

Arthur was in trouble. Zoe was reeling. Han was on his way.

The most important people in his life were waiting for him.

And he'd do anything for them.

Anything.

Chapter Twelve

Ok, class is covered, Han's here, be there in 20

The text from Lian allowed Zoe to let out a sigh of relief.

Drive safe, she replied. She trusted her brother and all, but the look in his eyes as he'd taken off to go get their sister had shaken her.

It was the same look he'd had after their father died. Devastated. Determined. Hard.

She put her phone away, only to pull it back out again two seconds later. She couldn't focus on anything. The waiting room wasn't big enough for her to properly pace, and if she drank another cup of stale coffee, she'd shake right out of her skin.

The elevator at the other end of the room dinged, and she looked up. This was getting ridiculous. She'd been snapping her gaze to see who was arriving every time, but inevitably it was a group of doctors or nurses. Maybe another worried family with food from the cafeteria, a bouquet of flowers, or balloons.

Except this time, when the doors slid open, they finally revealed the face she'd been waiting for.

She leaped to her feet as Devin scanned the area. He

spotted her immediately. Their gazes connected, and something inside her broke down. He ate up the space with huge strides and pulled her right into his arms.

A sob erupted from her. She clung to him, which was stupid—everyone could see.

When she started to pull away, he only held her tighter, though, and she couldn't help herself.

She'd been trying to keep it together since the moment the phone had rung.

Uncle Arthur was in his sixties. He had high blood pressure. He was fit enough, but he never stopped, never took care of himself. Others always came first.

"Shh, I got you," Devin murmured.

Tears were leaking down her face. She breathed through them. "He's fine. He's going to be fine."

So why was she losing it like this?

Maybe it was because she finally had the option to.

On the way to the hospital, she'd had to be the one to drive. Her mother had been even more of a wreck than her, so Zoe had been strong. It made sense. Uncle Arthur was her mother's big brother, after all. They'd been through so much together.

Devin rocked her back and forth, whispering reassurances into her ear the entire time, and she melted into him.

It seemed like it took forever, but Devin's steady strength slowly seeped into her. The tears ebbed. She pulled away, reaching into her purse for yet more Kleenex. Dabbing at her eyes, she shook her head. "Sorry."

"Don't be."

She blew her nose, but her mouth started wobbling all over again. He was being so nice to her, when he must be all shaken up, too.

Sitting back down, she beckoned him to take the seat beside her.

"What happened?"

"Heart attack. Partial, they said?" She gestured at the door her mother had disappeared behind a few minutes before. "They let my mom go see him before he heads up to surgery. They're doing that—that balloon thing." Angioplasty? "And a stent. They think his prognosis is good." She waved her hands at herself. "I don't know why I'm freaking out."

"Hey, hey." He grabbed her hand out of the air and squeezed it. "It's okay."

"I just—" She forced herself to stop and take a few deep breaths. As she stared up into his eyes, an unshakable sense of safety wrapped around her. It made her mist up all over again, but it was better this time. Shaky, she buried her face in his shoulder. "I'm just really glad you're here."

Too glad. Good grief. She needed to pull herself together. Han would be back with Lian soon. Her mother would be coming out before she knew it. The moment any of them returned, Devin would pull away. The idea of having him so close but unwilling to actually touch her made a fresh wave of misery crash across her chest.

"Come on." He held her close, rubbing her back. "You said it yourself. He's going to be okay."

"I know," she said, but the reassurances rang hollow. The only thing that helped was him holding her, so she clung to him, trying to soak in his strength while she could.

Far too soon, the elevator let out another chime. When she looked toward the opening doors, a different sort of nerves stole over her.

There they were. Han and Lian. Ten minutes ago, she would have been trembling with relief.

Ha.

She dropped her face into Devin's neck for one last

breath. Then she tore herself away, and it actually hurt. She met his concerned gaze, and she hated having to do it, but she nodded toward her brother and sister.

Devin glanced in the direction of the elevator. He had to see them, but he didn't let go. Instead, he turned to Zoe. He stared deep into her eyes. A dozen emotions flashed across his face.

But the last one—the one that remained...

It was resolve.

———

Enough.

It was the same feeling that had come over Devin back at the construction site. When he'd been pushed too far, and he finally pushed back. He'd made himself heard.

And it had worked.

A strange, ringing silence eclipsed the riot of voices in his head.

He wasn't powerless. He wasn't unworthy of love or acceptance.

He wasn't going to hide what he wanted. How he felt. From anyone.

Least of all his best friend.

Least of all when it was going to hurt someone he cared about, someone he...

Well.

For a long moment, he gazed down into Zoe's deep brown eyes. She was shaking. Just minutes ago, she'd been crying. She'd gone soft in his arms, molding herself to him, leaning into him, and this wasn't about sex anymore. This wasn't some game to her. All his doubts about what she was doing with him finally melted away.

He held out his hand to her.

Without hesitation, she slipped her fingers into his palm, her eyes going wide as she sputtered, "But—"

He shook his head and raised his brows.

Her mouth snapped closed.

Like she understood him, she wordlessly rose to stand beside him. Their gazes held, and the rightness in his chest was so hot it burned. He curled an arm around her. Bending down, he pressed his lips first to her forehead. Then to her mouth.

He turned forward.

Lian spotted them first. Her eyes flew wide, and she started to divert Han, but Devin shook his head.

The second Han caught sight of them, he waved. A relieved grin crossed his face, only to fade in the next instant. His pace slowed, his brows furrowing.

A few feet away from them, Han came to a stop. "Devin." His mouth drew into a frown. "Zoe."

Zoe fidgeted the way she did when she was nervous, but Devin felt steady as a rock. He gave her fingers a reassuring squeeze.

"Hey there, Han."

Slowly, deliberately, Han darted his gaze between the two of them and their joined hands. "What's going on?"

Lian practically bounced up and down.

Maybe that shouldn't have given him confidence, but it did.

"Before you say anything," he started.

Han's complexion darkened. "Say anything like what?"

"We're in a hospital," Zoe interjected. "You try to murder us and they'll fix us up." She snapped her fingers. "Like that."

"Devin."

And Devin was standing his ground. He was refusing to let anyone push him around anymore. He wasn't going to live in fear of his best friend, and he wasn't going to hide the way he felt. He couldn't.

"I didn't mean for this to happen," he prefaced.

The vein in Han's temple started to bulge. "She's my *sister*, man. You were supposed to help me protect her."

"I am," Devin said helplessly. "I will." A lump formed in his throat.

Because he would. He'd protect her from anything that could possibly threaten her.

Even Han.

"I don't need protecting," Zoe insisted, because of course she'd never step back and let two men argue about her.

In the far reaches of Devin's brain, he registered the sound of Han laughing, but he couldn't focus on that right now.

This was Zoe he was talking about. The little girl he'd bickered with as a kid and the feisty, incredible, kind, wonderful woman he'd come to know since. She'd drawn him out of his shell over these past few weeks. She'd helped him let down his guard and see the world beyond the little piece of it he'd carved out for himself.

She made him happy. She made him want things he'd never even considered before.

He wanted them all with her.

"I love her," he blurted. The pressure behind his ribs popped, and he could breathe again.

Lian squealed, her hands over her mouth. Han looked like he might need heart surgery, too, but they were in a hospital. He'd be fine.

Zoe whipped her head around to gawk at him.

This wasn't how he'd wanted to tell her. He hadn't realized he wanted to tell her how he felt in the first place, but now that it was out there, he wouldn't take it back. Its truth radiated through him.

"I do," he confessed. "Sorry, but—"

"Oh my God, shut up, I love you, too, you idiot." Zoe flung herself at him, and if Han murdered them this second, it would be worth it.

Devin caught her in his arms and kissed her hard and deep. All this time, they'd been acting as if they were both okay with being casual, but apparently the only person he'd been fooling had been himself. Nobody made him laugh or turned him on or pulled him out of his head like she did.

For years now, he'd had dreams of building a house in the middle of nowhere, but those dreams had been about running away from the unhappy home he'd grown up in.

He wasn't running away from anything now.

At the sound of Lian clearing her throat, Devin tore himself away from Zoe. All around them, people cheered. Zoe hid her face in Devin's shoulder, blushing but happy.

He looked to Han.

The man had been Devin's best friend since they were in elementary school. They'd been through everything together.

But Devin had never seen Han's jaw come unhinged like this before.

"Wait—" Han held up a hand in front of himself. "Who said anything about love?"

"This guy." Zoe jabbed a finger into Devin's chest.

"Ow." He caught her hand and brought it to his lips.

He couldn't quite get a real lungful of air, though. Not while Han was looking at them like this.

"How long has this been going on?" he finally asked.

Devin looked to Zoe, who lifted a brow. "About a month?" he answered.

"Or maybe forever," Zoe said.

"Uh, but not like creepy forever, right?" Lian asked.

Devin scrunched up his face. "No."

"No." Zoe rolled her eyes. "Definitely not 'creepy forever.'"

He'd never laid a hand on her until this fall. But the truth of what she was saying smacked him upside the head all the same. He'd been looking at her differently since her high school graduation. Every time they'd hung out in the years since, he'd enjoyed her company more and more. The way they felt about each other now—yeah, it had been building for a lot longer than a month.

"I'm not even going to touch that one with a ten-foot pole." Han scrubbed a hand over his face. Then he let out a rough breath. "You're both happy."

"Yeah," Devin answered, automatic and sure. He glanced down at Zoe, and she nodded.

"Really, really happy," she promised.

"Well, that's good enough for me." Lian broke the tension by swooping in and hugging them both. She whispered something to Zoe that made her blush deeper. Pulling back, she smiled at Devin. "Welcome to the family."

Oh wow. That part hadn't even occurred to Devin. He'd been too busy worrying about how pissed Han would be.

His gaze shot to Han. It was too early to be thinking about this stuff, but if he and Zoe worked out...if they went the distance...

They'd be brothers. For real.

Han shook his head. As Lian backed away, he held out his arms. There was still a certain wariness to him, but any fury had left him. "Dude. You've always been family."

With that he came in and awkwardly hugged them, too, and it was like a ten-ton weight suddenly floating off Devin's chest.

Zoe squirmed away from her brother, leaving Devin and Han in a weird side-to-side bro-hug. Han took advantage of the opportunity to haul Devin down into what Devin was going to choose to assume was a joking headlock. He ruffled Devin's hair, and yeah. He was definitely playing at the edge between teasing and menacing.

"Seriously, though," Han muttered under his breath as he let Devin go. "You ever hurt her, and I will kill you."

Devin straightened up and cleared his throat. Han's smile was warm, even as he cocked a brow in genuine warning.

Devin looked at Zoe. It was so clichéd, but his heart swelled.

Beautiful, incredible Zoe. Whom he loved and who loved him. He couldn't help but smile.

Devin bumped his hand against Han's. "I'm going to hold you to that."

Something in Han's gaze shifted. His mouth curled at the corners. He bumped Devin's hand right back, and even more relief flooded Devin's chest.

They were going to be okay.

It wasn't going to be easy, but for the first time since Zoe had arrived back home…Devin was starting to think this all just might work out.

Chapter Thirteen

Read 'em and weep." Zoe laid her cards down on the table, showing her three of a kind.

"Ugh." Han tossed his cards aside.

Devin groaned and pushed the impressive pot of five sticks of gum and a half dozen of the wrapped hard candies her mom kept in her purse Zoe's way.

"Your deal." Her mom nudged the deck toward Lian. The two of them had been smart enough to fold as soon as Han and Devin started raising each other peppermints. Knowing exactly what she had in her hand, Zoe had stayed quiet and let them bid each other up.

Uncle Arthur had been in surgery for an hour or so now, and they'd had to dig deep into the well of ways to distract themselves—if for no other reason than that their mom was going to get herself kicked out if she bothered the nurses station anymore.

As Lian started shuffling, Zoe's phone buzzed in her pocket. She pulled it out.

Oh crap. "Sorry, gotta take this."

"Sure, sure," Han said. "Wipe us out and then walk away."

"I'll be right back."

Devin tilted his head in question, but she shook her head, telling him that everything was okay.

Despite the thread of dread spinning in her gut, she was even pretty sure it was true.

Demonstrating exactly how distracted she was, her mom didn't even question her retreating toward the elevator bank. Zoe turned away from her family before accepting the call. "Hello?"

"Hi, Zoe. It's Brad from Pinnacle Accounting again. I just reviewed your file with the team, and we're excited to get you scheduled for that interview. How does Thursday morning work for you?"

Zoe opened her mouth. All the mumbo-jumbo accountant-drone speak she'd managed to summon to the tip of her tongue while talking to him earlier that morning was right there, ready to come spilling out again.

But she closed her mouth.

She turned, looking back across the waiting room at her mom eyeing the clock, her brother and sister fighting over a couple of Werther's.

Her Devin, who was holding his cards close to his chest, literally. But figuratively, he was staring right at her with all of them right there for the entire world to see.

Sudden certainty filled her chest.

"Zoe?" Brad asked. "You still there?"

"Yeah, Brad." She gripped the phone more tightly. "I'm right here."

Still holding eye contact with Devin across the space, she took a couple of deep breaths.

Every time she'd discussed her job search with him, he'd asked her questions she hadn't been ready to answer. Questions about what she wanted, what she loved, what had motivated her to go down the roads she'd chosen.

She'd answered the best she could, but deep down, she'd known that she'd been hiding the truth, both from him and from herself.

She didn't care about some big corporate accounting job. She didn't want to go to Atlanta or Charlotte or Savannah.

She wanted to be here. With him. Working with Arthur and Clay and just living her life. Not the one her mother had charted out for her the second she'd been born.

She may be a dreamer, just like her mom said, but her head wasn't in the clouds. Her feet were firmly planted on the ground, and she was ready to stand tall.

"I'm sorry, Brad," she said. "But I've decided not to pursue this opportunity after all."

As she said the words, the rightness of them sank into her bones. There'd be consequences to this decision, but she was prepared to face them.

If Devin could stand up to Han for her, then Zoe could stand up to her mom. She could fight for her own happiness—and for a chance at a future for the both of them, here in Blue Cedar Falls, where they belonged.

———

"How is he?" Zoe practically bounced to her feet as Han and Lian returned to the waiting room after getting to go in and see Uncle Arthur in person.

"He's good," Han assured her.

"If already getting annoyed at Mom." Lian rolled her eyes.

Zoe could only imagine. She'd spent enough sick days at home with her mom—and her delightful bedside manner—to empathize.

"Can we . . . ?" Devin asked, standing and gesturing toward the door. Zoe's mom had wrestled her way back to sit with Uncle Arthur the second he got out of recovery, but outside of her, they were only letting folks in one or two people at a time.

Han nodded. He reached for his jacket. "I should go check on the restaurant."

Thank goodness they had employees who could open the place.

"Call if you need anything," Devin told him.

"Will do." Han looked to Lian. "You want to stay or go?"

"I'll stay awhile." She tipped her head toward the door before sinking into one of the seats near where Zoe and Devin had been sitting. "Go on."

As he pulled out his keys, Han paused for a moment. "Hey, Zo?"

"Yeah?"

"Thanks." His gaze met hers, and it wasn't as if it was the first time he'd made eye contact with her since he'd found out about her and Devin, but there was something different about the way he regarded her. Like he was acknowledging her as an equal and not some kid sister he had to protect. "Mom told me how you held things together this afternoon, when I was off picking up Lian."

Zoe smiled. "No problem."

Han nodded, new respect in his eyes, and it was too much to hope that he'd start letting the rest of his family help carry some of the responsibility he was always lugging around with him. But a girl could dream, right?

As Han took a backward step toward the elevator, Devin held out his hand. Another little thrill ran through Zoe as she slipped her palm into his.

And hey, the vein in Han's temple bulged only a little, so that was progress, right?

A nurse was kind enough to show Zoe and Devin to Uncle Arthur's room, but they didn't really need the guide. Her mother's voice rang out as clear as day the moment they rounded the corner. "*Jeopardy!* gets you too worked up."

"*You* get me too worked up." Her uncle muttered a more colorful rebuke in Mandarin.

Zoe shook her head and sighed. Well, at least it was good to know he was feeling better.

She knocked on the door, eyebrows raised. "You two playing nice in here?"

Her mother and her uncle both looked up and smiled. Zoe didn't miss the way they were still silently wrestling over the remote, though.

"Zoe," Uncle Arthur said, swatting at his sister's hand. "Devin." Then he seemed to notice the fact that they were holding hands, and his head tilted in question.

"Uh…" Devin rubbed the back of his neck.

Her mother followed his gaze and did a double take, though she recovered quickly. Letting Uncle Arthur have the remote, she stepped back, one brow raised.

With Han finally in the know, Zoe and Devin hadn't held back on the casual PDA while they'd been hanging out in the waiting room, but they hadn't made an announcement or anything, either. Her mom was usually uncannily observant, but apparently she'd been too busy pacing a hole in the carpet to notice all the shared glances or the occasional moments when Devin would put a hand on her back or her knee.

Zoe's face warmed, but she held her head high, meeting her mother's gaze.

Her mom clicked her tongue behind her teeth and shook her head fondly. "Guess you did know what you were doing after all."

Zoe huffed out a breath. "Sure did."

"Good," her mom said, firm. A sly smile curled her lips, and Zoe's throat went tight.

It would scarcely count as approval from anybody else's parent, but for Zoe's mom? She might as well have thrown her a "Congratulations on Nailing the Hot Guy" party.

Uncle Arthur's reaction wasn't nearly as subdued, his pale face eclipsed by a bright grin. "About time."

"Hey," Devin protested.

"'Theoretical,'" Uncle Arthur scoffed, tucking the remote under his leg to make air quotes.

Zoe didn't know what they were talking about, but that was all right. Letting go of Devin's hand, she stepped forward to kiss her uncle on the cheek.

He squeezed her palm and winked. Quietly, he murmured, "Good choice."

"I know."

She moved aside, and Devin took his turn giving Arthur a careful hug.

Her mom slung her purse over her shoulder. "I'll give you two a minute."

"Really?"

She patted Zoe's hand. "Just a minute. I'm starving. Did you know vending machines here charge two dollars for a Kit Kat bar?"

Okay, yeah, her mom running to the car to grab a free snack from the stash she kept there made a lot more sense than her actually giving them privacy. "Outrageous."

Her mom made a disapproving sound in the back of her throat, calling out Zoe's sarcasm, but with a quick pat to Zoe's shoulder, she kept walking.

Zoe turned her attention back to Devin and Uncle Arthur, who were engaged in a little sidebar of their own.

She rolled her eyes. "You don't have to threaten Devin if he hurts me. Han's already got that covered."

"You?" Uncle Arthur huffed out a breath and waved a hand dismissively. "You can fend for yourself. I was telling Devin that if you hurt him, you'd have to deal with me."

Devin looked kind of embarrassed about it, if secretly pleased.

Good. He deserved someone looking out for him.

Zoe dropped into the chair her mother had set up on the other side of Arthur's bed. As she did, Arthur struggled to sit up. She shook her head at him. "Relax."

"Your mother wouldn't let me have my phone."

"Nor should she have."

"I have to call Sherry." He scrubbed a hand across his forehead. "Ten people had appointments at Harvest Home today. Supper service—"

Zoe grabbed his hand and held on tight. "Is handled."

"The key—"

"Sherry already came by to pick up mine."

"Deliveries—"

"Have been postponed until tomorrow. All today's pick-ups, too."

"But—"

"Uncle Arthur." She gripped his hand in both of hers. "I've got it."

She sucked in a deep breath. Instinctively, she glanced up at Devin, but he just stood there, silently supportive. Because he was the awesomest dude in the world, and she was so freaking glad to have him at her side.

"Zoe..." Uncle Arthur started.

"Trust me." That's what she'd been asking everyone in her life to do since she graduated.

She could make her own decisions about who she wanted to date.

And about what she wanted to do with her life.

"I've been doing a lot of thinking." She stopped her uncle before he could interrupt again. "Not just today, but for the past few months. About my future."

That finally got him to let her speak. His mouth drew down into a frown, but she had his attention.

"You've been doing too much."

He shook his head, but she looked pointedly at the hospital bed he was all but strapped into.

"You do too much," she insisted again, "because you care too much. You take care of everyone all the time. Well, it's time we all took care of you." She cleared her throat. "It's time I did."

"Zhaohui?"

"I'm taking over Harvest Home." She kept going, putting it all out there before he could try to contradict her. "You'll still be in charge, obviously. It's your baby. But from now on, the day-to-day operations are on me."

"But your job—"

"Will be fine." She'd already talked to Clay about adjusting her schedule. It wouldn't be a problem. And she had some other ideas she was going to run past him, too.

Arthur started again. "Your job *search*. You had all those leads in Atlanta, Charlotte—"

Zoe shook her head. "My job search is over."

"But—"

"I don't want to be an accountant. And I don't want to leave Blue Cedar Falls," she said firmly. She looked at Devin, asking him to hear the weight of her words.

She was done worrying about what everyone else expected her to do.

Devin's own actions, telling Han about them, had been an inspiration. He wasn't going to let other people's opinions hold him back anymore. So neither was she.

"I like it here." She squeezed Uncle Arthur's hands. "I'm happy here. I have friends, family." Leaning in conspiratorially, she murmured, "And a really nice boyfriend."

Devin smiled, and her heart glowed. He wasn't going to fight her on this. Good.

Because she would fight. For her family and for her future and for her vision of how she wanted to spend her life, now that she'd finally figured it out.

"You don't have to..." Uncle Arthur put his other hand on top of hers.

"I want to. So you just focus on getting better. Leave all the worrying about Harvest Home to me."

Uncle Arthur finally smiled. "I wouldn't trust it to anyone else."

The warmth in her heart only grew.

"There are some grants we can apply for," he said, that gleam appearing in his eyes, exhausted as they were. "So we can get you a salary. If you go to my desk in the back office—"

"After you get out of the hospital," she assured him, reaching in to fluff his pillows. "Until then, you just rest." She nodded, both to him and to herself. "I've got everything under control."

Chapter Fourteen

Epilogue

*O*ne month later...

"So, as you can see in Figure C in your handout." Zoe clicked a button on the remote for the LCD projector she'd borrowed from Lian. She arched a brow toward her audience as the spreadsheet she'd meticulously compiled came into view. "Taking into account average rent for a one-bedroom apartment, food, gas, personal expenses, and an acceptable rate of savings for a person in my age bracket..."

At the back of the room, June silently wiggled her hand, reminding Zoe about the laser pointer in her other hand. Right. Thank goodness the two of them had practiced this together last night.

She aimed the little red dot at the total at the bottom of the column. "Projected monthly expenses can be satisfactorily accounted for with projected earnings."

"Hold on a second." Clay held up his hand.

"I know exactly what you're going to say, Mr. Hawthorne." Zoe flipped to the next slide. "Income is broken out in Figure D." As the assembled crowd all turned the pages in their handout, she moved the laser pointer to highlight each number as she explained it. "Earnings fall into two major categories. The first is the modest salary I'll be able to begin drawing from Harvest Home once our grant applications to expand our staff are accepted."

Uncle Arthur nodded, leaning forward to agree. "The grant proposals are very good."

"Thank you, Mr. Chao." Zoe shifted the pointer. "The second category is income from my part-time position in the hospitality industry."

"You mean waitressing," Clay said.

"Waitressing, hostessing"—she set down the pointer and remote to begin counting on her fingers—"bartending—"

"Okay, okay," Clay interrupted. "You're good, but—"

"And bookkeeping."

His mouth snapped closed. "Wait."

"Admit you need the help," June said from the back.

"Hey—"

"With these additional responsibilities, I've determined that I'll be earning a twenty percent raise."

"Twenty percent!" Clay balked.

Zoe's pulse ticked up, but she had full confidence in her value to him. She arched a brow. "You think you can find a new server who's as good as me *and* who can start doing your books for you?"

"She's got a point, man," Han agreed.

"This is a setup." Clay looked around at everyone with suspicion in his gaze. There wasn't any malice, though. The guy had been to war and ended up with a knee full of shrapnel and so many trust issues he might as well have gotten a subscription, but he knew he was among friends here.

"Of course it's a setup," Zoe's mom agreed. She gazed at Zoe with a knowing curl to her lips. "But you're not the one she's setting up."

Zoe's heart pounded harder as she met her mother's gaze.

Oblivious, Clay continued, gesturing at the screen. "She just gave herself a twenty percent raise."

"That I'm going to earn," she promised, still looking at her mom.

"You sure about this, Zhaohui?" her mother asked.

Clay sat back in his chair, arms crossed. "I'm not sure about it."

"Yes, you are," Zoe and her mom both said as one.

"I guess that settles that," Clay said.

June stepped forward to put her hands on his shoulders. She pressed her lips to his temple. "Accept when you're beaten, dear."

"Fine, fine."

As they spoke, Zoe and her mom continued their silent staring contest. Zoe could hear all her mother's doubts, and she expressed her confidence back to her, even as neither of them said anything at all.

This plan was going to work. She'd draw a low but respectable salary managing the day-to-day operations of Harvest Home. She'd augment it by continuing to work at the Junebug and taking over Clay's accounting. She liked both jobs. Her work at Harvest Home fulfilled her, while waitressing at the bar was both lucrative and fun. Doing a little bookkeeping would maintain her skills and her résumé in case she ever changed her mind. Uncle Arthur would be less stressed, and if he ever decided to retire, she'd be ready to step up and slide right into his place. It was a win-win-win-win.

Finally, Zoe's mother raised a brow. "Princess astronaut veterinarian ballerina?"

"Princess astronaut veterinarian ballerina." Zoe let out a rough breath as lightness filled her chest.

"Well, then." Her mother smiled. "I suppose I can't argue with that."

———

"Hey—James!"

At the sound of his last name, Devin looked up. Joe stood outside the trailer, waving him over.

"Got a sec before you head out?"

"Sure." He finished the last couple of joins he'd been working on before nodding to the crew. It was a few minutes early, but they'd made good progress today.

He helped with cleanup, but once it was all in hand, he patted his buddy Terrell on the back and gestured at Joe's office.

Terrell nodded. "See you in the morning, boss."

Devin took off, a spring in his step.

It still amazed him how peaceful the entire site felt now that Bryce was gone. The guy had talked a big game about getting his father to retaliate, but it had been precisely that: talk. Sure, the mayor's office had made a few overtures, hoping to get management to reverse his dismissal, but Joe had stood behind Devin's decision. In the end, Bryce had been more of a liability than he'd been worth. Last Devin had heard, the guy was heading back to community college. Devin hoped he learned some things while he was there, but as long as he didn't show up on Devin's job site again, he honestly didn't care.

Inside the trailer, Joe was perched behind his computer, same as always. He smiled when Devin knocked and let himself in, gesturing for him to have a seat.

Joe folded his big hands on top of the desk. "Just wanted to ask how things are going."

"Good." Devin pointed his thumb toward the door behind him. "We're on schedule out there, maybe even a little ahead."

"I know that. I meant with you."

"Me?" Uh… "I'm good."

Great, actually. He couldn't stop the little smile that curled his lips.

Work was less stressful. The bump in his pay from the promotion had finally started showing up in his bank account. Arthur's recovery was going well.

And then there was the conversation he and Arthur had had the other night.

His leg bobbed up and down in anticipation.

He couldn't wait to tell Zoe about it. He was leaving after his shift to go pick her up, and he was going to do just that.

It had only been a month since he and Zoe had gone public, but it had been the best month of his entire life. It was like the thing with Bryce; Devin hadn't grasped how much strain all the secrecy and sneaking around was putting on them both.

But that was behind them now. They were happy and in love. Han was still his best friend—even if he did look at him kind of funny now and then.

Well, he'd get used to it. Devin was in this for the long haul.

And after what he planned to show Zoe this evening, hopefully by the end of the night he'd know she was in it for the long haul, too.

"All right, all right." Joe shook his head. "I get it— you're a private guy. Well, I just wanted to let you know that we're real pleased with how you've taken over as shift leader. Your crew's doing good work. Word on the street is you've really turned things around."

"Oh. Thanks."

Joe's raised brows were pointed. "Wasn't an easy situation you inherited with Horton on your crew. But you handled it like a pro." With that, Joe pulled open the top drawer of his desk and fished out an envelope. He passed it over. Nodding at it, he said, "Little token of our appreciation."

Devin blinked in surprise. He glanced at Joe, who motioned for him to go ahead and open it. The check inside stared back at him, and his jaw dropped. "I—I mean—"

People got bonuses pretty regularly around here when things were going well, but this was generous, to say the least. He sputtered for another few seconds before Joe took mercy.

"'Thank you' is the phrase you're looking for, I think."

Right. "Thank you."

"You earned it." Joe closed the drawer and gestured toward the door. "Now get on out of here."

"Will do." Devin tucked the check in his pocket. He rose, turned to leave, then stopped and twisted back around. More fervently, he repeated, "Really, Joe. Thank you."

Devin didn't think he'd ever fully get rid of his old man's voice in his head, telling him he'd never amount to anything. But he had a lot of evidence to say otherwise of late. This bonus...the pride in Joe's eyes...They were the icing on what was already a pretty flipping amazing cake.

By the time he got back outside, the cleanup job was basically done, and folks were getting ready to head out. Devin gave everything one last check over before making his way to his truck. He drove the familiar route to Harvest Home, where Zoe stood outside waiting for him.

She hopped in the cab of the truck and leaned over the gearshift. He threaded his fingers through her silky hair, closed his eyes, and kissed her, and he was really never going to get over that, was he? How good she felt, how sweet she tasted.

How much he loved her.

"Hey," he managed when she pulled away.

"Hey, yourself."

The flush to her cheeks and the glazed darkness in her eyes almost derailed him, but he managed to keep his focus. "How'd it go?" he asked. "Your presentation?"

"Good. Really good." She rolled her eyes. "Clay's on board with the promotion, and Uncle Arthur was super supportive."

"And your mom?" That was the part she'd been worried about.

"I'm going to go with 'begrudgingly accepting.'"

"Hey!" Devin grinned. "So basically wild enthusiasm?"

"Next best thing."

"Good." He leaned in and pressed another firm kiss to her lips. "Knew you could do it."

Curling a hand in the collar of his shirt, she kept him close for a second. "Thank you," she said quietly. "For believing in me."

They kissed again. He tucked a bit of hair behind her ear. "Always."

She let him go and settled back into her seat. "So, what's the plan?"

The nerves he'd felt earlier while thinking about this moment melted away. "You mind going for a drive?"

She scrunched up her brows at him. "Uh...okay?"

Once she was buckled in, he put the truck back into first and steered toward the road. While he drove, he asked her about her day, and he told her about his. They commiserated over how tough it was to get Arthur to delegate and rest. She spoke with pride about her juggling act taking over for him.

But she had good people with her. Sherry and Tania had been only too happy to start managing the supper service by themselves most nights. Volunteers had come out of the woodwork to lend a hand, because that was what people in Blue Cedar Falls did. They took care of one another.

As he glanced over at her, warmth grew in his chest.

He was so glad to call this place home.

He was so glad she was going to stay. Here. With him.

Clearing his throat, he forced himself to focus on the road. Before long, he turned off onto the country route leading out of town.

Zoe shifted beside him. "You're not taking me out into the middle of nowhere to act out some weird serial killer fantasy, are you?"

Devin laughed. "Is that really the first thing to pop into your mind?"

"I mean..." In his periphery, she waved a hand at their surroundings.

"Not much farther," he promised.

Five minutes outside town, he put on the blinker.

"Wait—isn't this...?"

Zoe held her tongue as they took the gravel road he'd been imagining driving down for the last three years. He came to a stop where the road ended.

It wasn't much. Just a small clearing in the wooded lot. He pulled the keys from the ignition and reached behind his seat for the camping lantern he stowed there. He turned it on and flicked his headlights off. Twilight settled over them, quiet and peaceful. Exactly the way he liked it.

He opened the door on his side. For a second, Zoe sat there, gazing out the front windshield.

"You coming?" he asked.

She looked at him. "This is Arthur's place, right? The old lot he snatched up in his real estate phase."

"None other."

"What are we doing here?"

"Just come on."

She followed him out, wary but smiling. Maybe she had a clue. They went to the center of the clearing. He breathed in the woodsy scent of the air. Tipped his head up at the stars just beginning to come out.

"I know you've been doing a lot of soul-searching lately," he told her. "I did some of that myself a while back."

"Yeah?"

"You know about my dad. I was…kind of directionless for a long time after I got out of his house. Just so glad to be on my own, I wasn't thinking about what I really wanted, you know?"

"Sure," she said slowly. "I can see that."

He held out his arm, and she came into his embrace. The warmth of her against his side heated him all the way to his core. "Your uncle Arthur—he was a big part of helping me figure it out. I decided my goal was a place of my own. Not just a roof to live under that wasn't my old man's. A home."

His pulse sped up a tick, his mouth going dry. Getting nervous talking about this didn't make sense, but he couldn't seem to help it.

"Arthur promised me then and there that as soon as I could save up the money, he'd sell me this lot—at cost."

Zoe scrunched up her brow. "But he bought it twenty years ago. He must've paid, like, nothing for it."

Devin let out a quiet laugh. "It was a little more than nothing." A lot less than it was worth now, but on Devin's income, it was still a chunk of change.

A chunk of change that had taken him three whole years to save.

He was still a little shy, even with his promotion and his bonus. But that didn't matter.

"The other night, when I was keeping him company, he changed the deal."

"Yeah?"

Devin shrugged. "Apparently a heart attack gave him some new perspective. He doesn't want to make me wait anymore. He trusts me. Knows I'm good for it."

And he was. With the new promotion and the bonus he'd earned this afternoon, he'd be paying Arthur everything he owed in six months.

Pulling Zoe closer in against his side, he looked around. "He's signing it over to me next week."

"Devin. That's amazing."

It was. A kid like him who'd grown up with nothing, living off what he could get at the local food bank. Cowering in a dark house with a dad who made him feel like dirt.

And now he was here.

He had the Leungs for his family. He had Zoe tucked beneath his arm.

He had this land.

His voice went hoarse. "This weekend, I was wondering if maybe you'd want to look at some building plans with me."

"Sure, I mean—"

"For when you move in here with me." He didn't want her mistaking him. He wanted to be clear. Looking down at her, he swallowed back his last remaining doubts. "I know it's soon, but I know what I want."

Her bright, beautiful gaze met his through the dimness. Her lips curled into a smile, and her eyes shone. "Devin…"

"Building a house. It'll take time. This isn't right now, but—"

"Yes," she said. She rose onto her toes and kissed him. "Of course, absolutely, yes."

He clutched her in his arms as tightly as he dared, returning the kiss with all the wonder in his heart. "I love you," he managed to get out.

"I love you, too." She pressed her mouth to his once more before pulling back. "There's just one tiny thing you're wrong about."

"What's that?" He was having a hard time concentrating. She felt so good pressed against him.

But then she grinned. "The soul-searching. The figuring out what I want with my life."

"Oh?"

"I'm done with that." Her smile widened, and he felt it in the center of his chest. "I'm exactly where I want to be."

And just like that, so was he.

Here. In this home that they would build.

Together.

About the Author

Jeannie Chin writes contemporary small-town romances. She draws on her experiences as a biracial Asian and white American to craft heartfelt stories that speak to a uniquely American experience. She is a former high school science teacher, wife to a geeky engineer, and mom to an extremely talkative kindergartener. Her hobbies include crafting, reading, and hiking.

You can learn more at:
Website: JeannieChin.com
Twitter @JeannieCWrites
Facebook.com/JeannieCWrites
Instagram @JeannieCWrites

For more from Jeannie Chin,
check out the rest of the
Blue Cedar Falls series!

The Inn on Sweetbriar Lane
Return to Cherry Blossom Way
The House on Mulberry Street

Looking for more second chances and small towns? Check out Forever's heartwarming contemporary romances!

THE TRUE LOVE BOOKSHOP
by Annie Rains

For Tess Lane, owning Lakeside Books is a dream come true, but it's the weekly book club she hosts for the women in town that Tess enjoys the most. The gatherings have been her lifeline over the past three years, since she became a widow. But when secrets surrounding her husband's death are revealed, can Tess find it in her heart to forgive the mistakes of the past...and maybe even open herself up to love again?

THE MAGNOLIA SISTERS
by Alys Murray

Harper Anderson has one priority: caring for her family's farm. So when an arrogant tech mogul insists the farm host his sister's wedding, she turns him and his money down flat—an event like that would wreck their crops! But then Luke makes an offer she can't refuse: He'll work *for free* if Harper just considers his deal. Neither is prepared for chemistry to bloom between them as they labor side by side...but can Harper trust this city boy to put down country roots?

HER AMISH PATCHWORK FAMILY
by Winnie Griggs

Martha Eicher, formerly a school-teacher in Hope's Haven, has always put her family first. But now everyone's happily married, and Martha isn't sure where she fits in...until she hears that Asher Lantz needs a nanny. As a single father to his niece and nephews, Asher struggles to be enough for his new family. Although a misunderstanding ended their childhood friendship, he's grateful for Martha's help. Slowly both begin to realize Martha is exactly what his family needs. Could together be where they belong?

FALLING IN LOVE ON SWEETWATER LANE
by Belle Calhoune

Nick Keegan knows all about unexpected, life-altering detours. He lost his wife in the blink of an eye, and he's spent the years since being the best single dad he can be. He's also learned to not take anything for granted, so when sparks start to fly with Harlow, the new veterinarian, Nick is all in. He senses Harlow feels it too, but she insists romance isn't on her agenda. He'll have to pull out all the stops to show her that love is worth changing the best-laid plans.

RETURN TO HUMMINGBIRD WAY
by Reese Ryan

Ambitious real estate agent Sinclair Buchanan is thrilled her childhood best friend is marrying her first love. But the former beauty queen and party planner extraordinaire hadn't anticipated being asked to work with her high-school hate crush, Garrett Davenport, to plan the wedding. Five years ago, they spent one *incredible* night together—a mistake she won't make again. But when her plans for partnership in her firm require her to work with Rett to renovate his grandmother's seaside cottage, it becomes much harder to ignore their complicated history.

THE HOUSE ON MULBERRY STREET
by Jeannie Chin

Between helping at her family's inn and teaching painting, Elizabeth Wu has put her dream of being an artist on the back burner. But her plan to launch an arts festival will boost the local Blue Cedar Falls arts scene and give her a showcase for her own work. If only she can get the town council on board. At least she can rely on her dependable best friend, Graham, to support her. Except lately, he hasn't been acting like his old self, and she has no idea why…

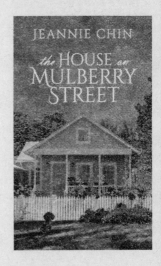

Discover bonus content and more on
read-forever.com

STARTING OVER ON SUNSHINE CORNER
by Phoebe Mills

Single mom Rebecca Hayes isn't getting her hopes up after she has one unforgettable night with Jackson, a very close—and very attractive—friend. She knows Jackson's unattached bachelor lifestyle too well. But in his heart, Jackson Lowe longs to build a family with Rebecca—his secret crush and the real reason he never settled down. So when Rebecca discovers she's pregnant with his baby, he knows he's got a lot of work to do before he can prove he's ready to be the man she needs.

A TABLE FOR TWO
(MM reissue) by Sheryl Lister

Serenity Wheeler's Supper Club is all about great friends, incredible food, and a whole lot of dishing—not hooking up. So when Serenity invites her friend's brother to one of her dinners, it's just good manners. But the ultra-fine, hazel-eyed Gabriel Cunningham has a gift for saying all the wrong things, causing heated exchanges and even hotter chemistry between them. But Serenity can't let herself fall for Gabriel. Cooking with love is one thing, but trusting it is quite another...

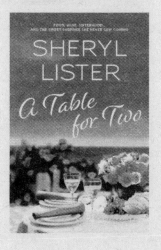